Calypso, Corpses, and Cooking

Also available by Raquel V. Reyes

The Caribbean Kitchen Mysteries
Mango, Mambo, and Murder

Calypso, Corpses, and Cooking

A CARIBBEAN KITCHEN MYSTERY

Raquel V. Reyes

CROOKED LANE

NEW YORK

Published in the United States by Crooked Lane Books, an imprint of The Quick Brown Fox & Company LLC.

Crooked Lane Books and its logo are trademarks of The Quick Brown Fox & Company LLC.

Library of Congress Catalog-in-Publication data available upon request.

ISBN (hardcover): 978-1-63910-106-1
ISBN (ebook): 978-1-63910-107-8

Cover illustration by Joe Burleson

Printed in the United States.

www.crookedlanebooks.com

Crooked Lane Books
34 West 27th St., 10th Floor
New York, NY 10001

First Edition: October 2022

10 9 8 7 6 5 4 3 2 1

To Tunisia, the best/worst
writing assistant-
All typos in the manuscript are hers.
She loves to rest her hind leg
on the keyboard.

Chapter One

Halloween was a week away, and we didn't have a single decoration up. The living room was littered with shopping bags, extension cords, four-foot-tall plastic jack-o'-lanterns, and one handsome Frankenstein.

"Babe, we're going to need a ladder and a staple gun," Frankenstein said.

"Can you borrow one from a neighbor?" I asked as I squeezed my foot into a shoe that had fit perfectly a few weeks ago but was now tight. My costume, like my husband's, was a modification of something I already had. I'd taken a white apron and smeared it with beet juice. In red marker, I'd written *Chef Vampira* on a paper toque, the tall hat fancy chefs wore. I was not a trained chef, but I had reached local stardom with my cooking shows, *Cocina Caribeña* and *Abuela Approved.*

"Do I look undead enough? Do I need more white makeup?" I asked.

"No, but I need more spirit gum. This bolt keeps falling off." Robert held the plastic hexagon out to me. For his costume, he'd taken one of his old, heavy New York suits and cut it to make him look like he was too tall and brawny for it. The cuffs were cut into a jagged hem, and the jacket's back seam was unstitched halfway. He'd used a hair product I'd found at the store called Moco de Gorila, gorilla snot, to slick his dark-brown hair into a hard shell. Gross name, but boy, did the stuff work. The green makeup and plastic bolts were from a kit. I knew he wouldn't need the wool suit in Miami, but it still pained me a little to see it in shreds.

We'd moved to a three-bedroom, two-bath house with a yard in Coral Shores, a village within Miami, from a tiny NYC apartment about three months ago. That was partially the reason there were no lawn decorations up. I'd had to buy them since we'd never had a yard or storage space for them before. The other reason was that it had been a whirlwind since I'd set foot back in my hometown of Miami. My best friend, Alma, had pushed me into an unexpected job that I now loved. It wasn't the food anthropology professorship I'd studied years for, but something slightly adjacent to it, at least. I did try to squeeze historical facts and tidbits about cultural crossroads into the show whenever possible. The show filmed once a week, and episode lucky thirteen was set to tape Monday. I planned to make joumou, Haiti's much-loved pumpkin soup, as a nod to the Halloween theme.

In addition to our new house and my new job, I'd gotten our son Manny settled into preschool. We'd bought real, grown-up, quality furniture and had a cement patio poured. Oh, and I'd helped solve a murder.

"Mami. ¿Dónde está Camo?" Manny asked.

"No sé, mi príncipe," I replied.

"Little man, I heard some rustling over there." Robert pointed to a pile of bags.

Manny, who had been in his police officer costume since he had sprung out of bed that morning, excited for the Fall Festival, called for his calico kitten. The festival put on by Agape

2

Montessori, his new school, was a much-loved village event open to the public. Or so I was told when the school's director talked me into having a booth. UnMundo, the Spanish language network that I worked for, had agreed to sponsor the booth and provide three hundred treat bags for the kids. Robert had also volunteered to staff a stall. His was sponsored by his environmental engineering consultant firm and was about the endangered Florida Atala butterfly. His educational non-candy giveaway goodies—a butterfly eraser and a pencil set plus butterfly temporary tattoos—were sitting on the dining room table neatly packaged in recycled paper bags, a project that had taken the two of us most of the night.

"Ponte las pilas," I said, looking at the time. Even though Robert didn't speak Spanish, he'd picked up a good bit of it being married to me and knew the phrase meant to get energized. "We need to get going, or we'll be late. I'm sure there's setup to do before the gates open at ten."

"Mami. ¿Puedo llevar a Camo con nosotros?" Manny asked. He was cradling the young kitten on its back, and the multicolored fluff ball had a paw on his cheek. I snapped a picture with my phone. Super sweet. The two were in love with each other. That was another surprise the whirlwind of the last three months had blown into our lives. We hadn't planned on having a pet, but Stormy Weatherman, the mother of the lady whose murder I'd solved, had shown up at our doorstep with the kitten last week. Manny had named the cat Camo, an odd name despite the cat's camouflage-like patterning. My son's favorite relative, Officer Gordon Smith, is to blame. The day Stormy came by, we were having a housewarming party to inaugurate our new patio, and Gordon happened to be wearing camo cargos. Gordon was also the reason for Manny's costume choice.

"No, mi amor," I answered. No, he could not take his pet to the fair. I encouraged him to put the kitten in his room and motioned for Robert to get the boxes of treat bags.

"Okay, got the first load." Robert walked toward the door. "Don't you have something on the stove?" he asked, glancing back to the kitchen.

"Huh?"

"That big pot of water. Did you start cooking something this morning?"

I didn't know what he was talking about, so I went to check. The cassava I'd peeled and left to soak in the large cast aluminum pot was on the eye. "Oh. No, that's not on. It's just soaking." I dumped the milky water into the sink and refilled it. I loved the root vegetable, but it took planning to prepare. It required a day—two was better—to leach the toxins from the tubers to make it safe to eat.

"Okay, let's go. Everybody ready?"

"What about my nuts?" The other bolt on the side of his neck was hanging loose.

"Fix it in the car," I replied, and handed him the tube of spirit gum.

Parking was already full at the Coral Shores Unitarian Universalist Congregation. Manny's school, housed on the church grounds, had gone full haunted-house vibe. Overnight the place had been decorated with bats, pumpkins, and a twelve-foot-tall blow-up black cat with an arched back. There was a photo-op pumpkin patch in the courtyard. It had hay bales with faux autumn leaves scattered on them. Because Florida. Can you imagine palm fronds turning all shades of red, orange, and yellow, then falling to the ground? No gracias. Miami already had frozen iguanas falling from trees whenever there was a cold snap.

The courtyard also had several painted plywood panels with ovals to stick a face in. There was a scarecrow family, a farmer with a pig wearing a witch's hat, and a dancing skeleton that looked like it had been copied from a vintage Grateful Dead T-shirt. The parents had gotten an email with images and details about what to expect. The festival didn't have an admission fee, but tickets had to be purchased for some activities. The tickets collected at each station would be converted to dollar donations to local charities. The pumpkin patch proceeds went to Urban Oasis Project, according to the email. I'd forgotten which other organizations would be benefiting.

"Go around back." The shout came from a woman with the stars and solar system on her dress.

"Mrs. Lucy!" Manny yelled from his booster seat. He waved and grinned with glee.

"What a perfect costume for the school's director. Love it!" I said as I turned the corner to drive to the back of the property. Agape Montessori was run independently from the church, but they had a symbiotic relationship.

"Ms. Frizzle is Mrs. Lucy? She looks so different," Robert remarked.

"Wigs and costumes have that effect. I wonder if her husband will be in drag. He is guapísima in drag," I said.

"What?" Robert gave me a quizzical look. He wasn't narrow-minded, just more middle of the road than me despite my conservative Catholic upbringing.

"Their Christmas card—sorry, their Yule card—was Sam Evans. You know Mrs. Lucy is married to CSUUC's choir director, right? Anyway, the card was Sam in a red dress and makeup. He was Holly Berry. Get it?" I laughed and then looked in the rearview mirror to back my Prius into the tight space between two other Priuses. Unitarian Universalists, I'd learned, were fans of the environment and social justice and LGBTQ rights. To say they were progressive and liberal was an understatement. The back field where the volunteers were to park had a double row of electric and hybrid cars. As we walked through them to find our stations, I noticed all the cars, except mine, had collages of stickers: *One Human Family*, *COEXIST* spelled with symbols, the walking fish, *My Other Car is a Broom*, *Love Your Mother* with an image of Earth.

"Miriam, I'm so glad to see you," Stormy Weatherman greeted me. She was dressed head to pointy toe in green with herbs and talismans hanging from her skirt's belt.

"Let me guess. You're an Irish kitchen witch," I said.

"You are correct." She bent at the waist to address Manny. "And how is our feline friend Camo doing?"

"I love her!" Manny replied. His ease with English had blossomed in the nine weeks he'd been in school. I'd been hesitant to put him in preschool but had to face the fact that he was no longer my little baby. The three-day-a-week program had been great for both of us. I had time to research and cook for the show, and he was making friends and learning to read.

"Excelente," Stormy said. She liked to practice the Spanish she'd acquired from her Argentinian husband, a second marriage, with us.

"Stormy, this tall green monster is my husband, Robert," I said, placing my hand on his bicep.

"Hello, Mrs. Weatherman. It's been a while. How are you doing? I was sorry to hear about Sunny. My deepest condolences." Robert took her hand in his, tilted his head, closed his eyes slowly, and nodded like he was saying a silent prayer.

"Thank you." Stormy sniffled and withdrew her hand. She shook away the emotion that was building.

I couldn't imagine the unbearable grief of losing both of her children in such tragic ways. Rayne, her firstborn, had taken her own life as a teenager. And this past August, Sunny had been killed by Juliet Pimpkin's maliciousness. Sunny was only thirty. She had been in recovery from a cocaine addiction and doing really well until Juliet came back into her life. *If you look up mean girl in the dictionary, you'll find a picture of Juliet Pimpkin.*

It was impressive that Stormy wasn't buried under a blanket crying all day. People dealt with grief in different ways, I guessed. She'd chosen to immerse herself in projects for the school, like a memorial garden in honor of Sunny, who had attended Agape for elementary school.

My arm was yanked board stiff. Manny had sprinted forward a few steps and strained my grip on his hand. His best friend and classmate, Sophia, was with her mom, Pepper, setting up a bean bag toss game.

"¿Puedo?" Manny pleaded.

"Sí, pero te tienes que quedar con ellos, okay?" I instructed my son.

"Okay, Mami," Manny said as he ran to his friend.

Pepper waved to me and gave me a thumbs-up. After the kids had hugged each other, Sophia twirled to show off her Disney princess costume. It was the yellow one. Belle.

"Give us our marching orders," I said to Stormy.

She consulted her clipboard. "You"—she pointed to me— "are toward the front on this side. Booth three. And you, Robert, are across the aisle in booth twelve."

"Perfect. Let me find my space, and then I'll get the stuff from the car," Robert said, looking at me. He then shifted his gaze to Stormy. "It was good to see. I hope we can mend some of our families' history."

"Yes. You must come to dinner. And stop by the house anytime to see how Camo is growing." I kissed Stormy on the cheek as we departed.

"I forget sometimes that you know everyone. Founding family and all," I said to Robert.

"It's a blessing and a curse, to be honest." Robert gave me a side hug. "I'm sorry you got dragged into it. But hopefully, that will all be over soon. Juliet's court date is coming up. Let's hope she gets the book thrown at her. I still can't wrap my head around it. Drug smuggling!"

"Shh! Lower your voice. There are children and parents all around."

Juliet had *accidentally* given Sunny a diet drink powder that was actually cocaine to hook Sunny back on the drug. The woman had manipulated and played with Sunny throughout her teens and early twenties. Thank goodness Juliet was sitting in jail, partly because of my sleuthing, and couldn't hurt anyone else.

Mean girl, smuggler, *accidental* murderess Juliet was also my husband's third cousin, whom he'd dated briefly in high school, and her father was a business associate of Robert's. It was messy, to say the least.

"Delvis!" I shouted at the blue-haired woman leaving booth three. "I need to catch her." I patted my husband on the back and left him at his booth.

Delvis's blue hair was not a Halloween costume, nor was she a senior citizen. Delvis was the producer and director of my YouTube cooking show, *Abuela Approved*.

"Ooo, Chef Vampira, I like it," Delvis said. "The bloody apron is a nice touch."

"I have fangs too." I took the teeth from my apron pocket and popped them into my mouth.

"Let me take a shot for our Instagram. Here"—she handed me one of the treat bags—"make sure the logo shows."

I bared my fangs as I held the sealed swag bag with UnMundo's globe logo. "What's in here?"

"Caramelos from Dulces Cubanos, a Hialeah candymaker Ileana likes." Delvis leaned in and whispered conspiratorially, "I think she's dating the owner."

I didn't need to know about our boss's love life, but I was happy to hear that the host of UnMundo's morning show supported a local business. The little swag bags were heavy.

"What else is in here?" I said, and gingerly loosened the sticker that held the bag shut. "Yum. I love ajonjolí. Ooo, and dulce de leche, de coco, de maní." The candies might be foreign to the majority of white American kids in the village, but I had grown up on them. Hialeah, a Spanish-speaking municipality, was a few miles from Coral Shores but a world apart. Both were part of metropolitan Miami. The hard sesame candy was my favorite, with the peanut brittle coming in a strong second. "Did you make a few bags nut-free?"

"Yeah. The ones with the *Abuela Approved* sticker are caramel only. I added some Chupa Chups and a mini UnMundo fútbol to make up for there being less candies." Delvis pointed to a box of bags under the table.

I opened one and inspected it—three caramels, two lollipops, and a foam soccer ball. "Cool. I don't know how many trick-or-treaters will have nut allergies, but we don't want to leave them out of the fun."

"I know, that's the worst. When I was a kid, un viejo in our neighborhood would give out boxes of raisins and pennies." Delvis made a face. "No kid likes pasas over chocolate."

"Note to self: raisins are a no-no. How about chocolate-covered raisins? Chica, I'm so behind in my Halloween prep the stores will be out of candy by the time I get around to buying ours." I slid into the booth and set my purse on the folding chair.

Delvis laughed. "Doubtful, but you might have to pay a premium. Okay, I've got to go. You good?"

"I'm good. Hey, thanks for bringing this stuff. I'll return the tablecloth and banner on Monday."

"Cool. See you at taping." Delvis waved her tattooed arm at me and left.

"From the network?" Robert asked as he approached my booth.

I nodded and began lining the goody bags into rows.

"Babe, can you help me? I have a screw loose." He pointed to his neck and passed me the glue. "It keeps coming off."

"Come around." I motioned for him to come into the booth and sit.

He held my purse in his lap, knowing I, like most Cuban women, had a superstition about putting my purse on the floor. Setting it on the floor was a sign of disrespect to your money. It would walk away, and you'd be poor.

"Stay still." I peeled the old glue off and painted on a new layer. Holding the plastic bolt to my husband's neck until the glue dried, I scanned the promenade. There was a pumpkin-decorating booth with a pyramid of baby pumpkins. Next to that was a prize wheel with stuffed narwhals, sparkly puzzles, and coloring books stacked around it. Then there was Robert's butterfly booth. "Who's that lady? I think she's looking for you."

Robert swiveled his head to see what I was talking about. "Oh no. Hide me."

I moved to block the line of sight. "Who is it? You never hide from people."

"That's Lois Pimpkin, Juliet's mother." Robert sighed.

"What is she doing here? And why is she looking for you? Do you think she wants to stir up trouble? You had nothing to do with Juliet being caught."

"It doesn't matter. Lois thinks her daughter can do no wrong and that she couldn't possibly be the mastermind of a multimillion-dollar smuggling operation. She swears it's a case of mistaken identity." Robert made air quotes and shook his head.

"Stop moving your head." I added glue to the other prosthetic for good measure. "Well, what does Paul Pimpkin say about it? I mean, you kind of work for him. That's got to be awkward."

"Paul is embarrassed. He's actually thinking about changing Pimpkin Development to something without the family's name in it to distance himself from her and Pimpkin Global. But you know, Samford *is* paying for his granddaughter's lawyers. I mean, he kind of has to, since Pimpkin Global doesn't look good in all of it. Juliet used PG's shipping containers. Best-case scenario is she gets a light sentence."

"Stay still. This stuff needs to dry." I stole a glance at Lois. She was still pacing in front of Robert's empty booth like a madwoman.

"Paul knows she's guilty. But his wife is next-level delusional about their daughter's criminal tendencies. Lois blames everyone but her precious Juliet. Paul and Samford are barely talking, from what I've heard. And Lois isn't making the family dynamic any better with her conspiracy theories about Colombian cartels.

Samford has always disliked his daughter-in-law and wishes she'd just shut up. He's hired some serious guns."

I looked across the promenade. "Well, the coast is clear for now. She's gone, and you no longer have a screw loose." I smiled and tried to kiss him, but my vampire teeth got in the way. I took them out, narrowed my eyes, and grinned. "You can't get away from me that easily."

"Trust me, I don't want to get away. I'm a willing victim to your vampire charm."

Robert pulled me to his lap, and we kissed. Just as his hand slid onto my rear, someone in our proximity cleared their throat.

"This is a G-rated event."

We broke our embrace and turned toward the voice.

"Hi, Pepper. Everything okay? Where are the kids?" I asked.

"That's what I came to tell you. The gates are about to open, and I have to run the cornhole game. So Gabriela has the kids. I hope that's okay," said Pepper, referring to her live-in nanny. She was dressed as a farmer in overalls, a checkered shirt, and a ratty straw hat.

"Of course. Thanks for telling us."

"I'll find them and give her some money for tickets," Robert said.

"Don't worry, Frankie sweetie. I gave her forty dollars." Pepper's Oklahoma accent was coming on strong, which happened when she drank. I hoped her tumbler had coffee in it and not Kahlúa. Maybe it was for effect, to add authenticity to her costume. Pepper's best friend, Elliot, had died suddenly, and instead of going to grief therapy, she was self-medicating on bad days. For a little while, Elliot's death had been thought suspicious and maybe linked to Sunny's, but it turned out she had died from a rare liver disorder exacerbated by bad herbal medicine from that quack doctor Fuentes. Sadly, I hadn't figured out she was taking too high a dose of rue until after the fact.

Pepper dug into her bib pocket and pulled out a red ticket. "Here's my ticket." She waved it at us. "Come on, on with the show. You two are like a Hallmark romance movie. Two starcrossed monsters, the undead and the once-dead, find love at the county fair."

Robert and I laughed. I popped my fangs back in and made like I was going to bite Robert's neck.

"Maybe this Hallmark romance is actually a murder mystery," Pepper said, rubbing her hands together.

"Don't jinx me," I batted back to her.

Chapter Two

"Happy Halloween!" I waved to the Spiderman and his adorable pirate little brother, who would only say "Shiver me timbers" in response to my questions. The next set of trick-or-treaters to come up to my booth got the same questions. *What are you dressed up as? Do you have a nut allergy?* The mom of the My Little Pony girl thanked me for having a nut-free option. Yes, her daughter would take one of them.

"Here you go, Pinkie Pie," I said.

"I'm not Pinkie Pie. I'm Princess Cadance. See, I have an alicorn horn and a tiara," the eight-year-old informed me.

"Forgive me, Your Royal Highness." I curtsied.

"Who's this?" she asked, and pointed to the sticker on the nut-free goody bag. "Is she a cartoon show?"

The logo for the YouTube Spanglish version of *Cocina Caribeña—Abuela Approved*—was a big-head, tiny-body caricature of me.

"That's me. I have a show, but it's not a cartoon. It's a cooking show."

The cooking tutorials were aimed at young millennial Latinx (as opposed to me, an old millennial) and Gen-Z Latinx who hadn't learned to cook.

"Mommy, I want to watch it. I like to cook."

The mom looked at me with an *Is it kid-safe?* expression. I told her it was one hundred percent kid-safe, then showed them the landing page for the show.

"Is it in Spanish?" the mom asked. "We don't speak Spanish."

"There are some Spanish words, but it's all in context. I don't think you will have any problem figuring out what I'm talking about." I bent a little to get at Princess Cadance's level. "Just remember to always have an adult with you in the kitchen for safety. Knives are sharp."

"I know. Mommy never lets me chop the vegetables." The girl rolled her eyes.

I grinned and kept my laughter to myself. It was humorous when it was someone else's kid. Would Manny have a similar attitude in a few years?

There was a lull in customers for the first time in two hours, so I sat down to rest my feet.

"Coño, my feet hurt." I reached down to take off my shoe that wasn't kicking off easily.

"Isn't that a cuss word, Ms. Quiñones?"

I covered my mouth and raised my head. It was my sister-in-law Sally. She was married to Robert's older brother, the middle brother. "Oops, did I say that out loud?"

"Yes, you did." She laughed. "You don't want to know what I let slip sometimes."

"Something tells me you cuss like a sailor."

"Just call me Sailor Sally."

"Where are the girls?"

Sally pointed across the aisle to Robert's booth. Sally's daughters, Reagan and Savanah—or as Manny called them, Rae and Vana—were getting goody bags from their uncle. The girls were dressed as Disney characters. The younger one was Mira, the royal detective from her favorite show. The older girl, Savanah, was Ariel, complete with red wig and mermaid tail. Their father was with them, and he sent them across the way to us so he could chat with his brother.

"Not in the Halloween spirit?" I asked.

"Us? Wait and see. We're saving our costumes for Halloween night. You'll die when you see them. They are so good." Sally embraced her daughters when they ran to her.

"Hello, Tía Miriam," Reagan said. She'd taken to calling me tía instead of aunt, and I liked it. Especially since I didn't have any siblings and I didn't think my cousin Yoli was going to have any offspring soon, if ever.

When my attempt to stuff my feet back into my shoes failed, I pushed them under the table and stood up. The cool grass felt nice on my bare feet. The girls ripped into their UnMundo sweets bag and had me tell them what each new-to-them candy would taste like. One chose the milk candy to try and the other the coconut one.

A commotion exploded at Robert's butterfly booth. Lois was back. Juliet's mother was pointing fingers at Robert and saying something. Andrew, Sally's husband, was doing his best to diffuse the situation.

"Why aren't you helping her?" the woman yelled.

Sally's face wrinkled with concern. "Where's Manny? I think I'll take the girls to find their cousin."

"Primo," Reagan corrected. I loved that she was fascinated with learning a second language.

I looked at my phone for the last message from Gabriela. She'd been updating me on their whereabouts all morning and sending pictures. "They were at the bounce house a few minutes ago."

Sally ushered the girls away from the hubbub, which was getting louder.

"You know my Juliet is innocent! It's the Colombians. She would never . . ." The woman turned from Robert and directed her ire at Andrew. "And you! A lawyer. Why aren't you helping? She's family, for goodness' sakes."

Andrew, in his good sense, didn't reply to her bullying. All eyes were watching, and parents were giving the booth a wide berth as they hurried their kids away from the disturbance.

"Mrs. Pimpkin, I'm going to have to ask you to leave." Officer Gordon, in his bicycle patrol uniform, put his hand on the woman's back. She jerked away like his hand was molten lava.

"Get your hands off me! Police brutality!" she shouted and scanned her surroundings for an ally.

I wished I had been quick enough to record the spectacle. She was out of her mind with indignation.

"You can't tell me what to do. My family built this town."

Gordon calmly instructed her to move along. "Mrs. Pimpkin, I'm respectfully asking you to leave the premises. This is a family-friendly event, and you are disturbing the children."

"Pfft." She jutted her chin out and smoothed her white short-sleeved sweater set.

Gordon tried to escort her by the elbow, but she shirked his grip. Her erratic movement sent something flying.

"My tennis bracelet! See what you've done. You broke it. I'll file a damage to personal property complaint with the chief of police. *And the mayor!*"

Gordon calmly retrieved the piece of jewelry from the grass and presented it to her. The way he was holding it made it look like a baby snake. It glinted and sparkled in the Florida sun. "Here you go, ma'am."

"Well, help me put it back on, since it was *your* fault it was torn from my wrist," she said, holding her arm out, palm up.

Gordon fastened the diamond strand to the woman's wrist. I could tell he'd had enough of her. His calm and cheery nature was being pushed to the limits.

The woman tutted and primped her blonde hair. "What's your name, Officer?"

"Officer Smith."

"You're one of them. I ought to—" She dug her hand into her purse, and panic rose in my chest. Was she reaching for a gun? She'd be just the type to have a pearl-handled gun *for protection*. I instinctively shied as her hand came out of the purse. Thankfully, it was only a key ring. She brandished the fob and jangly keys in my husband's direction.

"You'll pay for this treason, Robert Smith! All of the Smiths will pay." She marched away, nearly knocking into a Mario Brother. Gordon followed her out.

I looked at Robert and Andrew across the way. We all had our jaws open in shock. I mouthed, *What was that about?* to my husband. He shrugged, his eyes wide. Soon the promenade filled with children again. Robert went into his "Save the Rocklands to Save the Butterfly" speech, and Andrew left him to it.

I texted Sally and asked her if she could mind my booth. I was hungry and needed a bathroom break. Plus I wanted to know what Mrs. Lois Pimpkin had said to Robert before the screaming started.

Sally replied that she'd be there as soon as she handed the kids off to Andrew. While I waited for her, I sent my mom the photo I'd taken of Manny and Camo that morning. Mami y Papi managed a vacation property in the Dominican Republic. They'd gotten the offer and made the move a few months before Robert and I decided to move back to South Florida. De verdad, every day I wished they were here. Diamond bracelets and hostile matriarchs were out of my comfort zone. I knew Lois Pimpkin wasn't close family and was related to the Smiths via Marjory, Robert's mother. But still, the exchange had been tense. Most of Robert's family were fine, nice even. But wow, were they different from mine. We were working-class immigrants, and they were privileged old money. It was weird, and I didn't know if I'd ever get used to it.

"Thanks for helping me," I said, forcing my feet back into my shoes. "Hey, did Andrew say anything?" I switched places with Sally. "You know, about the scene Juliet's mother made."

Sally began restocking the rows of goody bags on the table. "No. Just that she appeared out of nowhere like a phantom."

"Hmm. Maybe they *are* supernatural," I said, trying to lighten the mood. "Robert has referred to Juliet as a ghoul once or twice."

Sally threw her head back and laughed. "Accurate. Oh my *gawd*, that woman. She's the reason I quit the Women's Club."

"Wait. You were a member? I thought you had to be seventy or older."

"Seems like it. But yeah, Marjory pressured me into it. She swore I wouldn't be the youngest person there. That there was a younger generation taking the reins. It was right after Savanah was born. I blame pregnancy brain fog."

"I remember the fog. I'd walk into a room and forget why I was there. I'd lose my sunglasses when they were right there on my head. Gracias a La Caridad that it eventually goes away."

We joked some more about things we didn't miss about being a new mom. Then I went to the church building to find the restroom. As I washed my hands in the ladies' room sink, something my tía Elba said to me crossed my mind. She'd been at our housewarming the other weekend and, in her usual cryptic woo-woo way, had suggested I was pregnant. I'd thought she might be psychic, as my period was late. But then, the following day, I'd had some spotting and known my period was on its way.

"That was a week ago," I said, looking at my slightly puffy face in the mirror.

"What was a week ago?" a voice asked from the accessible stall.

I knew the voice but hadn't realized the orange legs I'd seen belonged to my mejor amiga, Alma. I craned to look over the stall's door. "What are you wearing? Are you a stripeless tiger?"

"¿Que qué?" Alma struggled to get her arm into the orange bodysuit. "There is no such thing as a stripeless tiger. I'm a crab. The Coral Shores Little Cleats Crab, to be exact." She flushed the toilet with her neon-orange sneaker. "I'm judging the costume contest at one."

"Where's your shell?" I moved out of the way so she could get to the vanity.

"I left it in the school director's office con los premios." She dried her hands on a paper towel. "Can you help me get into it? Or do you have to go back to your booth, Ms. TV Star? You know you never did thank me for getting you that interview. Where are my roses? My champagne? My fancy macarons flown in from France?" Alma winked at me.

"Very chistoso." I knew she was joking, but I did owe her a big thank you. Maybe I'd dedicate an episode of the show to her favorite dish and mention our friendship—and her real estate company.

In Fellowship Hall, there was a six-foot foam crab shell on a table outside the director's office door and two claw mittens.

I helped Alma into her carapace, careful not to muss her hair, and looped a basket of candy into the crook of her arm. The mini chocolate bars in the basket were emblazoned with Alma's company logo. After her arrest a few months ago, she'd been working hard to rebuild the community's confidence in her. It didn't matter the arrest was due to a false and anonymous tip by the real guilty party, Juliet Pimpkin. I guessed the ridiculous costume was part of her plan to win Coral Shores over again and remind them she'd sponsored their kids' soccer league for the past four years. As a Cuban American, she hadn't lucked into being the top-selling Realtor in a rich white neighborhood. She'd worked very, very hard for it. If you were born with melanin, you had to work smarter, harder, and longer than your white counterparts and never make a misstep to get half the recognition you deserved. It was exhausting, and I marveled at Alma's perseverance.

I held the door so she could get through it sideways. The upside of her outfit was that it was lightweight. The downside of it was that it was wide, very wide. If she turned without looking, she might knock a gaggle of tweens over like bowling pins. A bevy of children rushed her as we approached the build-a-bat-house craft station. I doubted her basket of chocolate would last the length of the midway.

"We'll catch up after the contest. Besos." Alma sent air kisses in my direction.

"See you later, Crabcakes," I said.

As I walked away, my stomach grumbled. Why had I mentioned crab cakes? Now I was craving alcapurrias de jueyes. The yummy fritters made from plátanos and yautia and stuffed with crabmeat tasted best hot from the fryer. The school's email had promised food trucks, and I was on a mission to find them. I looked over my shoulder to check on my friend's status, and my stomach grumbled again.

"What is wrong with me? I ate three hours ago," I said, then began mentally listing all the crab recipes I knew. *Curry crab and dumplings from Trinidad and Tobago, coconut curry crab, crab with callaloo, matoutou de crabs from Martinique, cangrejos enchilada Dominican style, whole crab with garlic cilantro butter* . . .

Was it wrong that I was so hungry I wanted to eat my BFF with a little mojo de ajo y mantequilla?

Chapter Three

I stopped briefly at Robert's booth to tell him I'd bring him some lunch on my way back. Then I followed the hum of generators to the food court area. There were three food trucks in a semicircle with a grouping of picnic tables in front of them. I guessed the first served vegetarian fare, judging by the chibi mushrooms, carrots, and eggplants adorning the sides of the vehicle. Second was a grilled cheese truck called Grillz. Its logo was a gold-toothed grin with cheese dripping from the corners. And the third truck, the one that called my name, was Fritay All Day. It had a Haitian flag hanging from its awning, and I could smell the hot oil and spices from here.

The menu hung next to the open service window. Everything sounded so good. Checking out what the other patrons were eating, I saw that the sides were served in paper boats and the meats were on a stick, a little like Puerto Rican pinchos or kebabs. Easier for dining alfresco, I guessed. I decided on the griot, chunks of citrus-marinated pork shoulder, for Robert. My tastebuds were salivating for sides. The akra/fried malanga, bannann peze/fry-cut tostones, and of course pikliz/spicy slaw relish would satisfy my cravings nicely.

"Next," the window attendant called. "What would you like today?"

The man's deep voice was warm and round but didn't have a Haitian twinge. He sounded like he was from up north, Chicago maybe. I'd gotten my undergrad there. The city had a strong Black community, and I'd enjoyed learning about the history of places like Bronzeville and about the Great Migration. In terms of food anthropology, it was a great place to be. When Black southerners moved to Chicago in the early 1900s, they, of course, brought their food culture with them. That was why beyond jazz and blues, the city had tasty southern eats. *Mmmm, biscuits.*

I placed my order and tapped my debit card on the white payment pod.

"Ay, no. I forgot to order drinks. Sorry, can I add to my order?" I asked.

"Of course." The man passed the handwritten order to the counter behind him.

"Do you have Jupiña?" I asked. The pineapple soda, originally from Cuba, had a can that looked like the ripe fruit. It was bottled in Miami and hard to get outside of South Florida. I hadn't had one since I'd come back and suddenly wanted one desperately.

"No, I'm sorry, we don't," the man said.

"Try the Cola Couronne. It has a little pineapple flavor to it with a touch of orange and banana. Very fruity," the cook in the truck said.

"Sure, I'll try it. I love pineapple soda."

"In high school, this girl and I would argue about the flavor of Jupiña all the time. I still don't think it tastes like pineapple," the cook said.

"Marie? Is that you?" I asked.

"Q?" The woman turned around for the first time. "Oh my. *Girl*, where have you been? I haven't seen you in ages." Marie removed the basket from the fryer and told the man to plate the order. Then she went down the steps at the back of the truck, where I met her for a hug. "So good to see you. What have you been up to? I heard you were in New York or something. Are you here visiting your family?"

"I was, but I just moved back. Is this your business?" I pointed to the truck.

"Wi," she replied in Kreyòl. "I've had her for about a year. That's my husband, Jamal. We met at Johnson & Wales."

I waved to the man who had taken my order. Marie had been the only Haitian person in our very Cuban and Spanish-speaking Catholic school. But we had a nursing track, and Marie's mom really wanted her daughter to be a nurse. That obviously hadn't worked out as planned. Johnson & Wales was a culinary college. Marie told me she had a ten-year-old daughter who was running around the fair with a friend. We exchanged phone numbers and promised to get together soon.

"Here, two colas on the house. Any friend of my wife is a friend of mine," Jamal said, placing the chilled bottles on the counter.

"Mesi, Marie," I said, putting a bottle in each apron pocket. I didn't remember much of the Kreyòl she'd taught me other than yes, wi, and thank you, mesi.

I carried our lunch cautiously, fearing a spill from being bumped by a tiny monster. A stream of superheroes, princesses, witches, and supernatural spookies was moving rapidly away from the booth area and to the back of the property. A four-foot-tall grim reaper talked excitedly about goats and pigs. The petting zoo must have arrived. I wanted to visit it with Manny and hoped the bunnies and chicks wouldn't be too touched out by closing time when we'd be able to get to it.

"Lunch delivery," I said.

"Perfect timing. I've lost all my customers." Robert took two of the food boats from me and set them on the table.

"That's not all you've lost." I pointed to his neck. "One of your bolts is gone."

"Really? Argh!"

"That is the most Frankenstein you've sounded. Let me hear it again."

"Aarrrgguh! Frankie hungry. Frankie want food." Robert put his arms out straight as boards.

I handed him the fried pork griot on a stick. He stood, and I sat. "Do you want a fry?" I offered him one of the fried plantains. He accepted it and unscrewed the caps on our sodas.

"So, what was that with Mrs. Pimpkin?" I asked as I shoveled a forkful of the pikliz into my mouth. Marie hadn't gone wild with the heat. It was well balanced and delicious. I'd sometimes had some of the pickled slaw with so much Scotch bonnet pepper in it that it made my upper lip break out in a sweat on the first bite.

"Don't worry about it."

"When you say *don't worry*, I worry. So spill the beans, Frankie."

"I'm sure her threats are hot air and nothing more."

"Threats? Now you *have* to tell me. What did she say to you before the yelling started?"

Robert took a glug of the yellowish-orange soda. "It's nothing. I've already talked to Gordie about it."

"It's not nothing if you've bothered your police officer cousin about it. What did she say?"

"She threatened to call immigration, and she kept conflating Cuban and Colombian. She's gotten it into her head that you're a Cuban national and that you've pinned the drug trafficking on Juilet in order to free your comrade, Dr. Fuentes." Robert laughed.

"That's bananas. I'm glad she didn't come to my booth. I might not have been able to hold my tongue."

"Oh, she was looking for you. But she thinks you're Afro-Latina. She actually used the word *Negress*." Robert raised his eyebrows and opened his eyes wide.

"Love when the racism bubbles to the top so everyone can see it." I shook my head. Detective Frank Pullman had warned me that Coral Shores had a discriminatory past. In the 1950s it had been a sundowner town—meaning if you were darker than a sheet of paper, you weren't welcomed in the village after sunset. That was seventy years ago, but prejudice is passed down through the generations. The Pimpkins might have been the founding family to put the discriminatory rule into place, for all I knew.

"What are you thinking?" Robert asked. "You've got that faraway look in your eyes."

"Something Detective Pullman said to me during the investigation into Sunny's murder." I sighed. "Did you know that your hometown didn't allow Black people in it past dark?"

"No. I mean, I don't doubt it, but I never heard anything like that. I'll ask Senior." That's what Robert and his family called his father.

"Good enough to clean your house, cook your food, and keep your hedges trimmed, but not good enough to walk on your sidewalk."

"Huh?" Robert asked what I had mumbled.

"Nothing." I took a deep breath. It reminded me of Mami's stories about the English-language-only prejudice she and Papi had faced when they first came to Miami. The 1980 Mariel boatlift ignited a backlash against Spanish speakers that lasted over a decade. If you spoke Spanish at your place of work, your job was threatened. People minding their own business were harassed in the street. There were English-only signs in the windows of stores. Mami had told me about one time when the police were called on a beautician for speaking Spanish with another stylist. The lady having her hair done swore they were talking about her and demanded they be arrested. Miami in the eighties was hostile. That lady was probably rolling in her grave now. Miami was officially multilingual. The county government communicated in English, Spanish, and Kreyòl.

My phone binged. It was a text from Gabriela to Pepper and me. The costume contest was about to start. I knew the kids would be promenading past the booths, according to the email we'd gotten. I kissed Robert and hurried across the lane to my post.

"Thanks so much for watching the booth," I said to Sally.

"No problem. I mostly doom scrolled. Only a few kids came by for treats." Sally and I switched places. "Is that your friend Alma?"

I turned to where she was pointing. "Oh, I've got to film this." Alma was walking—okay, it was something similar to walking but more like scuttering side to side while moving forward in a zigzag—toward the church building with a headset mic on. And she was singing!

They're creepy and they're kooky. Mysterious and spooky. They're altogether ooky. We're at the Agape Family Fair.

I could barely hold in my laughter. Sure, my BFF loved the spotlight and had been the lead cheerleader of our high school's squad, but her crab strut was on another level. As she danced by, I gave her a thumbs-up. "You go, Crabcakes!"

"Work it," a familiar voice said.

I followed the direction of the broadcasted voice and saw that it was Jorge, our Mambo-cise instructor, with a microphone standing by a display of golden pumpkins. Jorge Trujillo was a member of the CSUUC and led the LGBTQ group. And he was the most fun exercise coach with the best taste in music. Gracias a La Caridad he didn't know he had been on my suspect list a few months ago. That's a hard thing for a budding friendship to come back from. I waved at him, and he waved back. Jorge had a frizzy wig on, vintage runner short shorts, a muscle T, white Reeboks, and scrunchy socks.

"Who is he supposed to be?" I asked Sally.

"Richard Simmons, maybe?"

"Who's that?"

"The exercise guy from the eighties." Sally waited a beat to see if I'd clued in to who it was. "*Sweatin' to the Oldies?*" She looked at me again.

"Nope. No idea."

"Come on. I bet your mom had one of his videotapes." Sally swatted my arm. "My mom had the whole frickin' collection. Richard Simmons is the reason the Peggy Sue song makes my ears bleed. My mom. In our living room. In her neon spandex and matching sweatbands. I was *sooo* embarrassed by it as a kid. I never invited any of my friends over after school because I was afraid she'd be dancing in front of the TV."

I chuckled at Sally's younger self. She was a strong woman who worked as an advocate in the court system—hardly the type to be embarrassed or care what others thought of her. We clapped as the age groups paraded by. The tweens were first. A homemade anime costume won top honors in that group. The seven-to-nine-year-olds were next. They consisted primarily of witches and superheroes. Sally and I smiled and waved as Savanah walked by us. Jorge announced the winner and prompted the last group to strut their stuff. I looked for my son amongst the kidlets. I expected him to be with Sophia, but he was holding hands with his cousin Reagan, to my surprise. The group of about twenty four-to-six-year-olds got to the end of the promenade and turned to face the crowd of parents and adults.

"We have a tie," Jorge said, after Ms. Lucy had whispered in his ear. "The best costume award goes to the detective and the police officer."

Applause rose as Jorge moved to Manny and Reagan. He held the microphone for them to answer his question. "Can you tell us about your costumes?"

"I'm Mira, the Royal Detective," Reagan said. "And this is my primo, Officer Manny."

When the mic was put in front of Manny, he shook his head no and looked downward, all of a sudden shy in front of a crowd. But Reagan had no such qualms about public speaking. She took the mic and proceeded to tell the assembled that detectives—she used the magnifying glass around her neck as a visual—found the bad guys, and then police officers arrested them.

"Teamwork," she said. She and Manny raised their clasped hands. Sally and I moved closer to the action to take pictures of the cuteness.

Delight filled the air. Alma had spray-painted pumpkins with a numerical first marked on them between her large foam claws, which she clumsily presented to each of them. As the other kids left the limelight to rejoin their parents, Jorge made a few announcements.

"CSUUC's"—Jorge's accent made the *U*s come out as *juju*—"LGBTQ group is looking for a truck and trailer to make a float for the Thanksgiving parade. If you can help, please let me know." He passed the mic to Alma.

"I have gifts for everyone that participated in the costume contest. Kids, bring your parents with you to collect your Dunkin' Donuts gift card." Cheers from little ones erupted. Alma waved an orange claw over her head.

"Wow, Alma is really going all out. That's like a hundred gift cards," I said to Sally. I did the math in my head; even at only five dollars a card, that was well over $500. I knew it was a business expense, but I felt so bad for her having to rebuild the community's trust and opinion of her. Juliet had damaged so many people's lives. "I hope she gets life."

"What?" Sally asked.

"Nothing. My brain forgets it is connected to my mouth sometimes." I laughed. "Let's go get the kids."

Manny, Reagan, and Savanah skipped toward us as we approached. I noticed that Gabriela, holding Sophia's hand, was keeping eyes on Manny. She was such a good childminder. She was going to make a fantastic teacher. After her Agape practicum finished, I hoped the school would hire her to stay on full-time. I let Gabriela know I was taking Manny with me and that she was off the hook.

"Yo gané, Mami." Manny showed me his gold pumpkin and beamed with pride.

"Sí, mi príncipe, sí."

"I want to show Papi." He was switching between Spanish and English more and more fluidly. He spoke Spanish to me but changed to English when talking to or about his father.

"Vamos a buscar a tu papá." It only took a quick look around to find a six-foot-tall green monster. "Allá." I pointed to his father and uncle conversing by a tree.

31

"I'll take Manny to his dad," Sally offered. "And then he can hang out with us for a while."

"Are you sure?"

She nodded, and I thanked her. I reminded Manny to listen to his aunt and kissed him on his head.

As I walked back to my post, a woman dressed in white entered my booth.

Mrs. Pimpkin? Is she back? Has she figured out who I am? Am I next in line for her rage?

Cautiously, I approached with my phone set to video. If she was going to make a scene, I was going to record it.

"Finally. I've been sitting here for ten minutes." Marjory Smith, my mother-in-law, was sitting in my booth with the foot of her crossed leg ticktocking in annoyance.

I could call her on her lie or let it go. *Let it go, Miriam.*

"Marjory, I wasn't expecting to see you here. The festival doesn't seem like your type of thing. Are you looking for Robert? He's across the way." I pointed and hoped she'd go away.

"No. I'm looking for you." She unfolded her arms and stood.

I smiled and waited. *What fresh hell does she have in store for me?* Her passive-aggressive cuts had dropped off dramatically after Juliet's arrest. But I knew the stalemate wouldn't last forever. Marjory had made it plain and clear that she liked Juliet over me. Juliet was Robert's second—or was it third?—cousin. She was slim, blonde, wealthy, and from the right lineage. She and Robert had dated for a few weeks in high school until their familial tie had grossed him out. But his mother still held out hope that her son would dump me and return to her. *Sorry, not sorry, Marjory; that is never going to happen.*

"I have good news. You're going to like it," she said.

Is this a trick or a treat? I had my reservations.

"I've put you in charge of the Women's Club gala and menu."

"Um, I'm sorry. What?" I asked.

"You are a cook. Aren't you?" Marjory's closed-mouth grin translated to *I've done you a favor, peasant.*

"Yes, but I'm not a member of the Women's Club, nor do I want to be."

"Don't be ungrateful." Marjory brushed past me. "With Juliet's unfortunate situation keeping her from her club duties and leadership, her committee members have dropped the ball. We all need to pitch in and help. It is for your people, after all. I thought you'd be delighted."

"My people?"

"Island people. That's your thing, isn't it? *Co-seen-ah Caribbean*—that's the name of your show." She was not being kind despite her attempt to say kitchen in Spanish. I knew it was her way of getting in a dig. She'd insulted the show to my face and behind my back plenty of times.

I looked at her, speechless.

"Good, that's settled. The event committee was scheduled to meet on Wednesday. The meeting room is already booked for ten AM at the club. Don't be late," she said, and left.

I was right. There was no way Marjory would do something genuine and nice. Nope. No. Definitely a trick and not a treat.

Chapter Four

The next morning, after a lazy Sunday sleep-in and a big breakfast of guava and cream cheese pancakes, the boys started decorating the house and yard. Manny "helped" his father wrap the trunk of our royal poinciana tree with orange lights. It looked like an old lady with a loose skirt circling her knees. As I parked the car from my drugstore run, I noticed they'd put ghost window clings in my study window. I entered the house, stepping over extension cords from the various jack-o'-lanterns and inflatables yet to be plugged in.

"¿Dónde están?" I asked when I didn't see them in the living room.

"In here," Robert replied from our bedroom. "Camo slipped out of the house twice already. So we're setting her up in the bathroom and locking her in."

"Mira, Mami." Manny held up his drawing for me to see. He'd drawn a red stop sign in crayon, more trapezoid than octagon in shape, on half the sheet. The other part of the page had a pretty good facsimile of his calico kitten, Camo. "No dejes que Camo salga." He looked at me with a very serious expression.

I tried not to crack a smile as I replied that I would obey his directive. "Mi amor, I'm going to take a few minutes, but then I'll be outside to help finish the decorations."

"No problem, babe," Robert said while taping his son's illustration to the door. "Just don't let the cat out. I doubt we'll be as lucky next time."

"Lucky?"

"Yeah, she stayed on the front step, thanks to a lizard. The lizard kept running around and into Manny's pumpkin. It was cute. But you know we might not be as lucky next time, and I'd hate for her to get lost. We should get her a collar with a name tag."

"Probably a good idea. We can go to PetSmart later today. They probably have them. Right?"

"Yeah. Let's do that." Robert nodded. He picked up Manny like a log and took our giggling son out of the room.

"I'll be out there to help in just a few."

"No problem, take your time," Robert said as he closed the front door to the house.

I took the box from my purse and slipped into the bathroom. It was time to find out the truth. *Is Tía Elba psychic?*

"Hola, Camo. I heard you were a naughty kitty." The kitten was in Manny's jack-o'-lantern candy bucket, which I guessed they had used to lure her back inside the house. It was a greeting-card-worthy image. *Meow.* "Meow to you too."

I read the instructions, opened the packet, and took out the stick.

"Here goes nothing. Or everything." I took a deep breath and took the test. Camo toppled the bucket as she leaped out of it to swat the plastic wrapper I'd let fall to the floor. I watched her as I waited the three minutes for the results. At two minutes, faint blue lines appeared. At two minutes thirty seconds, the lines were darker. By three minutes, there was no doubt.

I looked at myself in the mirror. "Okay. So, I guess we are actually and officially pregnant. Wow. Okay. This is good. It's good. It *is* good." I wasn't trying to convince myself. I mean, we *had* talked about growing our family. We wanted Manny to have a sibling. And at thirty-two, now was better than later, but . . . *But what, Miriam?* My job. What would I do about my job? I'd gotten the job because the original host was on maternity leave. Just last week, when she was supposed to return, she'd asked for another three months. Her baby had developed some health issues that called for doctor visits and tests. *Pobrecita.* I was happy to stay on as *Cocina Caribeña's* host now that Ileana Ruiz had me taping it. I'd nearly cut my thumb off the first time I'd hosted live. Blood was not a good look for morning TV.

Thinking about work reminded me I needed to practice my pumpkin soup recipe before tomorrow's studio session.

I scooped Camo into my arms. "Missy-pooh, we are going to have a baby in the house soon. What do you think about that?" She was smaller than a newborn, but not by much. In eight months, I'd be cradling our new daughter or son. An electric chill of anticipation ran through my body. A baby. I. We were going to have another baby. The kitten began to purr. She looked at me with loving eyes, then flicked her tail into her paws to play with it. "You are too cute." I kissed her on the head and put her down.

Closing the bathroom door, I began to worry about my job again. I loved my newfound career. I was using my food anthropology degree as I'd never imagined. In a way I'd never envisioned for myself. I didn't want to quit it or lose it.

Miriam, stop catastrophizing. You have options.

"I do have options. Maybe I could prerecord three months of shows." I stopped in the living room and picked up a comical tombstone for the front yard. "I'll ask Delvis about it. I'm sure it will be fine," I said. Feeling a little more secure, I went outside to break the news to my husband.

"Did you hear? Lois Pimpkin is missing," a woman with a British accent said.

"No, I hadn't. Missing?" Robert asked.

"Hola, mi amor. What's happening?" I asked.

"Oh, hey, babe. Let me introduce you to Mrs. Brown."

"Call me Gillian," she replied. "You aren't my student anymore."

Robert blushed. "Gillian was our school librarian and the reason I like British mysteries. Every week she'd give me a new one to read. Sometimes from her own collection."

"Ah, yes. I remember you especially liked P. D. James and Ian Rankin," she said.

"Inspector Rebus," Robert said.

They both nodded in happy reminiscence.

"Gillian, this is my wife, Miriam Quiñones."

"A pleasure to meet you." She extended her hand.

I shook it. She had a surprisingly firm grip for such a willowy frame. "So nice to meet you. Do you live around here?"

"Just around the corner. I was taking my daily walk when Robert spotted me."

I liked her already. She called my husband Robert and not Bobby. "What were you saying about Lois Pimpkin?"

"Oh, the poor dear is missing. She didn't come home last night. Carol Longworth rang me this morning with the news."

"I'm sure she'll turn up. She probably checked herself into the Biltmore or something." Robert put his hands into the pockets of his madras shorts. "So, about that ladder."

"Ah yes, come along. It's in my garage. You're welcome to borrow it." The woman stepped off our lawn and onto the sidewalk. "Miriam, please pop round for tea. I'm number three-two-five on Dolphin, the house with the roses."

"Thank you. I look forward to it."

"Be right back, babe." Robert kissed my cheek before strolling off with Gillian. The pair were in deep book talk within seconds.

Manny, who'd been playing with his police car toy, running it up and down our front walkway, came skipping over to me. "No suena Mami."

I tested the siren button. The batteries were dead. I was tempted to tell my son I couldn't fix it. The high-pitched *wow-wow-wow* had rattled my nerves ever since Cousin Gordon had given it to him. But my son's trembling lower lip tugged at my mom heart. Manny and I went into the house in search of double As.

As I searched in the kitchen for the mega pack of batteries I remembered buying just last week, I thought about Mrs. Pimpkin. Was she really missing? Was it official? *Doesn't a person have to be gone twenty-four hours before it becomes real?* Or was she, like Robert had suggested, taking a spa day at the Biltmore? I hoped it was nothing sinister. I wasn't a fan of the Pimpkin women, but I certainly didn't wish them ill. *Well, maybe Juliet a little, but not her mother.*

Chapter Five

"Ay, que susto," I said, jumping out of my skin as I emerged from the bedroom hallway and into the open living space of our house.

I wasn't accustomed to the gigantic furry spider that Robert had hung over our front window. It gave me a fright Monday morning as I padded to the kitchen. It had also spooked me the night before when I heard a scratching noise around three AM and had gone to investigate it. I'd had a restless night. The opportunity to tell Robert we were expecting hadn't presented itself. I wanted him to know before I told Alma. We'd wait a few more weeks before telling our parents. It wasn't being superstition as much as practical. A woman's body sometimes rejected the implantation. It was just biology. There was no need to get our families excited until the second trimester.

As the Cuban bread toasted, I reviewed my recipes and story notes for my recording session later in the morning. Then I checked the Around Town app. The police department that regularly posted reminders to always lock your car doors and cancel your newspaper subscription if you were going on vacation had a bulletin about Lois Pimpkin.

If you see this woman, please call the police department imme-diately. Her family is concerned that she may be disoriented or con-fused. She was last seen at seven PM Saturday.

"Morning, babe," Robert said. "What are you reading? You look worried."

"Lois Pimpkin is really missing. Look at this police notice they've just issued." I passed him my phone.

"Hmm. A little weird, but she will show up. She probably went away for a few days to blow off some steam or something."

"Is that like her?"

"I don't know her that well, but it is something my mother did and still does every once in a while. She'll pack a bag, leave Senior a note, and go to the Biltmore for a day or two. I remem-ber when we were teens and Dad would get the bill. He'd always joke, 'Boys, two days of peace and quiet cost a pretty penny.' Junior, Andrew, and I loved that we got to eat pizza and junk food while she was gone. No coffee?"

Caffeine was on the no list when you were pregnant or breast-feeding. I thought I might as well go cold turkey, but *maybe* I could start slow by cutting down to just one a day. I needed a little focus and energy after last night's interrupted sleep.

"Coffee, sí." I began packing the espresso grounds into the greca's filter basket. "Mi amor, did you hear any weird noises last night?"

"Hmm?" Robert looked up from a work report he was reviewing. "No. I remember you got up to go to the bathroom, I think. Why? Did you hear something?"

"Yeah, it sounded like something was scratching at the door. I looked out the living room window but didn't see anything."

"Could be a raccoon or a possum."

"In the city?"

"We might be in Miami, but Coral Shores is one of the most densely treed areas of Dade County, believe it or not. Perfect habitat for them."

I poured the café into two mugs of hot milk, making sure mine was on the whiter side. *I love you, coffee. I'm going to miss you so much.*

"We should get a wildlife camera. That would be cool. It would blow Manny's mind."

"What, Papi?" Manny was carrying Camo and rubbing the sleep from his eyes.

The moment to tell Robert the good news evaporated. I'd have to wait until little ears with a big mouth were not present.

"Hey, little man. Mami thinks she heard a raccoon last night knocking on our front door."

"Outside? I want to see." Manny changed directions and headed to the door.

"It's probably long gone by now, buddy." Robert left the table and went to his son.

"Open. Let's see."

"Okay." Robert unlocked the door, and they both looked out onto the front step. "Nothing there but lizards, little man."

Camo twisted free from Manny's embrace and pounced onto the welcome mat. Robert dove after the kitten.

"Mami, Mami, Mami. Camo se escapó."

"Gracias a La Caridad she has a name tag now," I said as I went to join them.

"I've got her. She ran behind the planter after a lizard again." Robert put the kitten in the large rectangular pocket of his robe. He shut the front door behind him. "She didn't get far, thank goodness." He used a movie trailer voice. "Camo, the Lizard

Hunter." He lifted her out of his pocket and put her on the otto-man in the living room.

"What's in her mouth? Did she bring a lizard in with her?" I was not happy about the idea of a crippled—or worse, gutted—reptile loose in our house. I'd stepped on one too many desiccated bodies with my bare feet growing up in Miami.

"Nah, I think it's a twisty tie from the decoration. Over-packaging. Such a waste of resources. It makes me mad."

"No mad, Papi," Manny said.

"It looks like it's silver," I said, seeing it glint in the morning sunlight beaming through our front window.

"Yep, the ties were silver foil. I thought I picked them all up, but I guess I missed one," Robert said.

Camo jumped from the ottoman to the floor and then darted under the gray sofa. I got on my stomach and looked underneath it to see what she had in her mouth. Whatever she was batting between her paws skidded on the terrazzo to the opposite end of the couch. I reached for it and got it before she reclaimed her toy.

"Honey? Does this look like a part of Mrs. Pimpkin's brace-let?" I held up a two-inch section of a tennis bracelet with a few of the diamonds missing.

"What? Let me see that." He took it from me and examined it. "Babe, this is probably from Manny's playmate, your friend's daughter." He gave the links back to me.

"Sophia?"

"Yeah. Remember, they were wild yesterday." Robert mim-icked a monkey, and Manny followed suit. "Wild monkey play-date." The pair's laughter got rowdier as they scratched under their arms and jumped about.

"Okay. Okay. Ya. Vete a vestir que tienes que ir al colegio," I said to my son. I then poked my lips out in a silent direction to Robert that he should help his son get ready for school.

I looked at the segment of bracelet. "These don't look like rhinestones. But maybe . . ." I put it on the counter to ask Pepper about it later. Sophia *had* been in full princess regalia for their playdate.

The next-door neighbor's Vizsla, Tom, barked. If the dog was in the backyard for his morning whiz and doodle, then I needed to get in gear. *Seven already.* I heard the neighbor yell at Tom to be quiet. The dog was being more vocal than normal. Maybe the raccoon was still roaming about.

As I passed the counter on the way to get dressed, I fiddled with the piece of jewelry. It didn't feel fake. It was definitely metal and *not* plastic.

Rich people probably have expensive play jewelry.

Miriam, stop with your suspicious mind. Why would Lois have come to your house?

"Because she was yelling at your husband two days ago."

"Babe?" Robert asked from our en suite bathroom.

"Nothing, mi amor, just talking to myself."

Robert walked out of the bathroom, drying his mouth from brushing his teeth. Now was as good a time as ever to tell him. I moved toward him.

"Roberto, I have something to tell you."

"Babe, are you okay? Is something wrong? Your voice is very serious." Robert drew closer.

"Everything is good—really good, actually. Um . . ." I took a deep breath and held it. I was never good at announcements or creative with surprises. *I should have put the test stick in an envelope or something. Yuck, no!* I exhaled. "I'm pregnant. We're pregnant."

"Babe! Really, babe?" His arms were spread-eagle in suspended motion.

"Yes."

Robert's arms swooped around me as he lifted me into a twirl. We nearly fell onto the bed in his exuberance. "How far along are you?"

My feet back on the ground, he kissed me before I could answer. I kissed him back and ran my hands down his biceps to quiet his energy. "I don't know, maybe eight or ten weeks. Please don't say anything to anyone until I've gone to the obstetrician. Please." I looked into his eyes. He nodded in agreement.

"I know. I know, but you don't think anything is wrong, do you?"

"No, but for Manny's sake and our families, I want to make sure it sticks. I don't want their anticipation to become disappointment. You and Alma are the only people I'm telling."

"Okay. I got it. Oh, babe. I'm so happy."

"Me too."

We broke our embrace when we heard Camo's tag and bell tinkling. I watched as she jumped onto the bed, nearly clearing it but having to use her claws to make it over the edge. Manny followed, giggling but dressed for school in blue shorts and a shark-print T-shirt. I put my finger over my mouth to remind Robert not to spill the news.

After we'd all gobbled down a little breakfast, Robert offered to take Manny to Agape, since I was a few minutes behind schedule and it was a studio day for me. As I got into my car, I saw our neighbor exit his house with Tom for their morning run.

The copper-colored dog strained his leash and moved toward the gate that hid our garbage can on the side of our house.

"Tom, stop it," Mr. Nelson said.

I lowered the passenger side window. When we'd first been introduced, he'd said, "I'm Tim, and this is Tom. Tim and Tom." I was in perpetual fear that I'd call him Tom and the dog Tim. So I stuck to calling our neighbor by his last name. Which, to be honest, was also a little confusing, because Nelson sounded like a first name to me. Papi had a primo named Nelson.

"Sorry. I don't know what's gotten into him today. He normally doesn't bark this much."

"Robert said there might be a raccoon in the neighborhood," I offered.

"That's got to be it. Come on, boy." He clicked his tongue and got the dog off the scent and into a jog. I waved at them as they passed behind my car.

I didn't have time to check if the garbage can was closed. Or if we had a mess of food waste along the side of the house. That little corridor of the yard wasn't visible from the kitchen window. *I need to get to UnMundo.*

"I'll deal with it later," I said to myself as I backed out of the drive.

Robert was probably right about the noise I'd heard last night. It must have been a raccoon.

"Please go back home, Mr. Raccoon. I don't need any problems." I turned up the radio and accelerated.

Chapter Six

After makeup, where I learned all about Viviana's failed Tinder date, I stowed my purse in my designated cubby and started to the set.

"Miriam, what are you cooking today?" Viviana, the makeup artist, asked.

"Soup joumou," I replied. She gave me a quizzical look, so I explained. "A beef and calabaza sopa from Haiti. It's very good and un poquito picante."

"Can you save me some? I want to try it."

"I'll try. I'll ask Delvis," I told her and waved adios.

"Ask me what?" Delvis queried.

"Vivi wants to try today's dish. Can you save her some?"

"Yeah. I'll make sure the crew puts some aside for her." Delvis moved her wavy blue locks off her forehead and gave a direction to whoever was talking into her ear.

Walking through the dim UnMundo studio and its maze of equipment and cords with Delvis, I thought about how and when to mention the pregnancy to her. It would have to be before the baby bump started to show.

The set lights were on when we got to the *Cocina Caribeña* kitchen on the *La Tacita* stage. The live morning show had finished filming at nine, and Ileana, the show's host, waved to me as she exited to her dressing room. A calabaza, the hard winter squash that grows in the islands, was at the end of the counter. It had a Haitian flag on a wooden dowel stuck into it and a plate and bowl beside it—the scene for the final shot. I checked and arranged the ingredients for the day's dish. The teleprompter blinked to life with the words I'd be saying. After the sound guy adjusted the overhead mic, the show's salsa-tinged intro music played. Showtime.

"Bienvenidos a *Cocina Caribeña*. Hoy nos vamos a Haití para una sopa deliciosa e histórica."

As I deseeded the pumpkin and chopped the other vegetables and herbs, I told the viewer that the soup was also called Independence Soup, as it was eaten on January 1 in honor of the country's liberation from France. It was a delicacy denied to the enslaved Africans and Free People of Color. Before the revolution, only French plantation owners were allowed to eat the rich soup. So eating it was sweet justice and celebration over oppression and colonialism.

Thanks to the magic of TV, I didn't have to wait for the pumpkin to cook. A puree was ready for me to use. And the beef had been marinated overnight. I mentioned the episode's sponsor as I dropped their product—bouillon cubes—into the stewpot. I was getting good at it and no longer stumbled over surprise lines on the teleprompter. The heat released the aroma from the shallots and the Scotch bonnet peppers. Normally a pleasant smell, it made me nauseous. *Not good. Not good.* While the overhead camera zoomed in on the bubbling dark-yellow liquid in the pot, I ducked below the counter to take a sip of water. Then I opened the refrigerated drawer and tore off a mint leaf from the leftover bunch that was an ingredient from last week's recipe. The mint smell and oils helped calm my morning sickness. I popped back up, kept cooking, and ended the segment by urging the viewers to give the delicious stew a try. "Perfecta para otoño." And it *was* perfect for fall with its spicy warmth. However, Miami was more likely to get a soak-you-to-the-bone tropical storm than a leaf-turning cold front.

I left the stew to finish cooking another thirty minutes. The PA—production assistant—would take care of plating it for the segment's final image. Then the crew and hopefully Viviana would enjoy it for lunch.

"See you Wednesday," Delvis said as I left the stage.

"Ay," I said, and hit my forehead with my palm.

"¿Qué? ¿Hay un problema?"

"No. Just my suegra committed me to a thing on that day—a fund raiser for hurricane relief. Don't worry, I'll cancel her."

"Espérate. Hurricane relief? For where?"

"Not sure, but I think it is a general fund for the Caribbean."

"Is this something we could tie into *Cocina Caribeña* or *Abuela Approved*?" Delvis had her hand over her mouth with her fingers drumming her cheek. I knew that look, and it meant she was inventing more brand exposure opportunities in her mind.

"No inventes. Let me find out about it first. Okay?"

"Let me know. I can push back our session if you need me to. The more your face is out in the community, the better for the show."

"Gotcha." *Great. Why did I have to open my big mouth?*

As I removed my stage makeup and changed into my street clothes, I reminded myself I wanted to keep Delvis and *La Tacita*'s host, Ileana, happy with me. The morning show was the reason I had the YouTube channel. And I truly loved my *Abuela Approved* show.

Pepper picked up Manny from school on Mondays to give me a little extra time at the studio if I needed it. He loved playing with his bestie, Sophia. The swing set at the Hallstead house was like a tot lot in the midst of a botanical garden. It was gorgeous and state-of-the-art. Although Pepper and I didn't have a long history like I did with Alma, she had become a true friend.

My stomach switched from nauseous to hungry as soon as I parked at the strip mall. My cousin's restaurant, which was nicknamed Tres Sillas but actually called Tres Palmas, was near UnMundo. I stopped by whenever time permitted. The little three-seat restaurant had been expanded since I'd worked there as a teen. Tía Elba y Tío José had given it over to Yoli a few years ago. But Tía still helped with the morning prep and cooked the day's special.

I hoped Tía had already left for the day. She'd known I was pregnant before I had. She'd probably demand I give a gratitude offering to Yemayá, the orisha of children and mothers. Tía was serious about La Regla de Ocha, her religion. *Actually, that's not a bad idea.* I stepped into the botánica a few doors down from the restaurant and bought a white candle and a bottle of agua florida. On the way out, I left the change from my purchase at the feet of the six-foot-tall Saint Lazarus outside the store. The coins would be collected and given to a charity for the poor and sick.

"Yolanda, tu prima está aquí." Bette, busy making espresso at la ventanita, announced my presence to her fiancée. A few seconds later, Yoli came out of the kitchen, tucking a dish towel into the string belt of her apron.

"Hey, cuz." Yoli kissed me on the cheek and motioned for me to join her at the lunch counter. "What did you make today? No, don't tell me. I'll find out Friday from Mami. She never misses *La Tacita*."

Bette's customer had left, and she joined us, bringing a little cup of coffee—my usual cortadito, the smaller version of a café con leche. *Oh, coffee, how I love you. But I love baby too.*

"Ay, gracias, pero I already had coffee at work," I lied.

Yoli took it and drank it in two gulps. I ordered a batida de fruta bomba and two croquetas. The three of us chatted until they had to attend to patrons. One of those patrons was Bette's sister Omarosa.

"Hola, chica. How are you?" I asked.

"Todo bien. Work's a little slow, but I know busy is just an emergency call away." Omarosa sat on the stool my cousin had vacated. "Someone will lock themselves out of their house." She laughed.

Her sister placed a shot of espresso and a glass of water in front of her and told her the specials. Omarosa chose the soup of the day, potaje de lentejas. I tried to drink my papaya milk shake, but it was too thick for the straw, so I opted for a spoon. The sweet fruit smoothie was just what my rolling stomach needed.

"How did your date go with Gordon?" I asked.

"It was nice. He's nice."

"Nice, like you want to see him again?" I hoped my match-making had been a success. I'd introduced them the day of our housewarming party.

"If he calls, I'll say yes." Omarosa smiled. Her bright white teeth contrasting with her dark Dominican complexion. She was slightly taller than her sister, but they shared the same strong female vivaciousness.

"He hasn't called you?"

"We casi casi"—she flipped her hand back and forth, symbolizing *almost*—"had a second date, but I was on call, and he was on call, and well, we only got as far as the parking lot of the restaurant before our phones beeped with emergencies. He had to go see about a missing person."

"Oh wow. Was that last weekend?"

She nodded. "Si. And I was really excited about the restaurant"—Omarosa ate a spoonful of the lentil stew—"the raw bar over by the Miami River."

I'd read about it and wanted to try it too. But raw shellfish was off the menu for me for at least nine months. Her mention of Gordon's missing-person call got me thinking about Lois Pimpkin, and then my brain jumped to the strange noises I'd heard and then Roberto wanting a wildlife camera.

"Do you install those door camera things?" I asked. Not the same as a wildlife camera, but it killed two birds with one stone. *Bad analogy.* We needed a new doorbell, and a door camera *would* capture wildlife like my sharp-toothed MIL.

"Yeah. I've got a few in my van, actually. You want one?"

"I don't know. Are they expensive?"

"Tu eres familia. I got you. I can even install it today."

"Dale," I said, doing my best impersonation of Pitbull, aka Mr. 305.

After we fought (and lost) with our respective relatives about paying the lunch bill, Omarosa followed me home. I sequestered Camo in the hall bathroom per Omarosa's suggestion, since she'd have the front door open most of the time to install the wiring and such.

"Can I leave you here?" I asked.

"Claro."

"Cool. I've just got to run pick up Manuelito, and I'll be back in five minutes."

"No te preocupes." Omarosa had a cordless keyhole saw in one hand and a screwdriver in the other. She was telling me not to worry, but I was worried. What was I going to come back to?

I alerted Pepper that I needed an easy extraction, and she promised to have Manny ready and at the curb. But when I pulled up to the Hallstead house, they weren't outside. The million-dollar abode looked onto the bay, had a rooftop pool, and was designed by a famous architect. I was still boggled as to how my life had gone from poor to posh. As I debated going in or waiting, Pepper and the kids appeared. Lowering the window, I thanked her.

"No problem," Pepper said as she passed Manny's mini backpack through the window. "There's a permission form in there that you have to sign. FYI." She helped my son into his booster, then we said a quick good-bye.

I was back on Manatee Drive in less than five minutes. The place where the original 1952 doorbell had been was a hole with wires protruding from it like a sci-fi alien octopus. Omarosa was on the step reading a manufacturer's diagram.

"We're back," I called to her.

Manny had unbuckled himself and jumped from the car as soon as I'd opened the car door. He stopped to hug Omarosa, then continued his energetic rush into the house.

"Some lady—she said she was your suegra—stopped by and left this." Omarosa handed me a flyer with a color picture of Lois Pimpkin and a police hotline number. "She also asked me for a spare key."

"Sinvergüenza. Ay, ay, ay. My mother-in-law is back to her old tricks. You didn't give her one. Did you?"

"*Nooo.*" She shook her head in slo-mo.

"Gracias," I replied.

A blur of fluff zoomed by us, followed quickly by the sound of rubber shoes on the living room floor.

"Mami, Camo se escapó." My son's voice was in full panic mode.

I should have warned him not to use his bathroom because of the cat. Manny skirted by us and over to the royal poinciana tree, where the kitten had stopped. Camo's tail flicked back and forth as she crouched and hunted a lizard on the tree's trunk. It was a game of chicken, and the lizard blinked first. The slim tan-and-brown reptile ran into the grass. Camo zipped after it. I was a step behind Manny as he tried but failed to grab his pet. She slipped under the side fence after her prey. *The raccoon and the garbage. Oh, no, Camo is going to be covered in stink.* I reached over the top of the gate and unlocked the latch.

"Camo. Camo. Ven acá," Manny cooed. His kitten was covered in wet coffee grounds with a banana peel on her back and a lizard in her mouth. The cat let him pick her up. "Help. Mami. Help."

"Sí, mi príncipe. Dame la gata." I reached out to take the cat.

"No, Mami. Help." Many motioned to the side of the house.

In brownish-red letters, the words HELP MURDER were smeared on the stucco wall of my house. The letters of the second word were separated like musical notes on a staff, all at different levels.

I knew raccoons were supposed to be smart, but when did they learn to write?

Was this a Halloween prank or something more sinister?

Chapter Seven

"Miriam, don't worry. It's probably the same pranksters that rearranged the skeletons at the Ormand house." Gordon blushed.

"What did they do with them?" Officer Gordon showed me a photo on his phone, and I understood his blush. It looked like a scene from an adult movie—three pairs of skeletons in very intimate acts. "Do you know who's doing it?"

"We have a good idea, but we need proof. It happens every year. Adolescent hijinks. Maybe your new door cam will catch them in the act." He smiled and looked in Omarosa's direction. "Excuse me." He sauntered to her van.

Watching their body language was like watching a rom-com movie meet-cute moment. They were clearly into each other, and I secretly loved the idea of Latinizing the Smith family. Omarosa flashed a thumbs-up at me when Gordon turned his back on her to answer Manny. My son's patience had run out, and he desperately wanted the attention of his favorite relative.

"Hey, little man." Gordon crouched to Manny's level. "I heard you were the one that found the scene of the crime. Good work."

"Scene of the crime." Manny repeated the words. "Like *Mira, Royal Detective*."

"You like that show, don't you? Reagan and Savanah like it too."

"We watch together." Manny beamed with pride.

His spoken English skills were expanding exponentially, as was his sight word recognition. But I had to ask myself, *Is "help" on his pre-K vocab list?* Probably. Thank goodness murder wasn't a word he could identify. I walked over to the tumbled trash can and examined the scrawled message.

"Tom!"

"Who's Tom?" Gordon asked as he joined me by the garbage pile, which had a squadron of flies buzzing over it.

I checked for Manny and saw that Omarosa had him engaged in cleaning up the installation debris. "The neighbor's dog, Tom. He wouldn't stop barking this morning. I thought it might have been the raccoon from last night, but it makes more sense that it was intruders. I bet Tom scared them away. Pretty ballsy to pull pranks in the daylight."

"What do you mean, last night? Did you hear a disturbance?"

"A noise woke me up around three-ish. Robert thinks it was a raccoon, but raccoons don't write, do they?" I chuckled.

"No. No, they don't."

"So can I clean this mess up?" I moved toward the torn garbage bag.

"Actually, wait a second. Don't touch anything. I'll be right back."

Gordon went to his patrol car and returned wearing gloves and holding a spray bottle. He sprayed the letter *H* and then shined a UV light onto it. "Too much light. Can you get me a garbage bag? A black one."

"Sure." I opened the side door of the garage to the area that served as our laundry room and storage. On the shelf next to the garden sheers, I took a bag from the box of heavy-duty yard debris bags. Handing it to Gordon, I watched as he put it over his head and held it to the wall, making a little tent. I heard the spray bottle squirt, and then Gordon said, "Huh." He gave me the bag to hold and went to his trunk for something else. As a teen, I'd watched *Murder She Wrote* reruns with my mom, translating the occasional phrase she didn't understand. And I'd watched British police procedurals with Robert. I knew what that spray and UV light meant.

"Are you taking a sample? Why? Isn't that ketchup or sofrito or something?"

Gordon took a sample from the *E* and put the swab into a tube and then an evidence bag. "Probably." His mood had changed from chillin' cousin to expressionless police face. "You're free to clean up. I'd help, but I need to get this to the station. Just in case."

"In case of what?" I asked. I knew, but I wanted to hear him say the words *in case it's blood.*

Gordon slammed the trunk shut and didn't answer me. "See you later, little man." He waved to my son, started his patrol car, and carefully backed out into the street.

Rounding the corner just in time to see the police car turn on its nonemergency but still *Get out of the way* lights was my BFF, Alma. She lowered the window and leaned across Anastasia, her assistant, in the passenger's seat.

"What's going?" Alma's face told me she was masking a little PTSD from her arrest.

"Nothing. No te agites. We got hit by the Halloween pranksters," I replied as I got close to her car.

"Oh, like the Ormand house." Ana laughed wholeheartedly. "I saw the pictures on Around Town. Someone blurred the private parts like it was pornography." The remnants of Ana's Russian accent came out when she dropped her professional persona.

"Where did they get you? Last Halloween, we had five houses hit with eggs and TP." Alma and Ana shared a *Been there, done that* look between them. "Is that Beatriz's sister? Osmari?" Alma asked uncertainly.

"Omarosa. She's just installed a door camera for us. "¿Quieres un café?" I asked them.

"Ay, sí. I'm dying for a coffee." Ana was half Cuban. Thanks to the exchange program between the two countries, her parents had met and fallen in love.

Alma parked, and the pair came inside. I asked Omarosa to join us, but she said she'd gotten a service call and needed to get back to Hialeah. She gave me an instruction sheet and told me I needed to download the app to my phone. We kissed good-bye, and I told her I hoped her next date with Gordon went uninterrupted. While the coffee percolated, I settled Manny into his room for a nap—or, as we were now calling it, since he was all of a sudden *a big kid*, quiet time. He sat on the love seat in his room with Camo on the cushion by his head and started to page through his library picture books. I seared the image into my memory as I carefully closed the door with a soft click.

"Ay, carajo. Too late for espumita." I'd miss the first spew of espresso that made the caramel-colored foam possible. "How about an ice latte?"

"Okay," my guests replied in unison.

I opened a can of leche condensada and poured about half of it into a carafe. I added ice cubes and the unsweetened coffee plus whole milk. The condensed milk had enough sweetness that there was no need to add sugar. Snapping the silicon cap onto the carafe, I shook it over the kitchen sink and served the frothy drink in a pair of tall glasses with green parrots on them. For my drink, I chose water.

Alma and Ana were looking at the missing-person flyer on the dining room table.

"Have you heard if she's been found?" I asked.

"No. We had two open houses this morning, so we were kind of busy," Alma said.

"There is nothing new on Around Town." Ana waved her phone at me to show the social network's feed. "Maybe she was kidnapped."

"¿Que qué?" Alma queried and took a sip of her drink. "Yum, this is good. Almost as good as the one from Vicky's Bakery."

"Thanks. But yeah, Ana, what do you mean?" I shifted on the bench to face her more directly.

"Okay, so I know this is random, and you did not hear it from me, but there is a rumor that Juliet owes some money to Kostas Borisova. So maybe they kidnapped her mother to ransom for the debt."

"That's farfetched. No? Who is Boriska, anyway?" I asked.

"Kostas Borisova. He owns most of Sunny Isles and Hallandale and Golden Beach," Alma said, listing several municipalities in north Miami-Dade and south Broward counties, "and a penthouse in Aventura."

"And he's Bratva. Not a guy to mess with." Ana tucked her chin in and shook her head.

"What does Bratva mean?" I asked.

"Like Mafia."

"*Mafia.*"

Alma and Ana nodded.

"Wow. Really? Is that a possibility?" I asked.

"It's gossip, so maybe not true. Forget I said anything." Ana took her glass to the kitchen and ran water in it. She then went to stand by the French doors and looked into the backyard. "Is that a mango tree in the backyard by the playhouse?"

"Yes. We planted it a few weeks ago." It was a gift from Roberto and would take a year or two to produce fruit.

"Changing the subject. What's on the menu for the gala?" Alma's eyes became devilish as she grinned.

"The meeting is the day after tomorrow. I *soooo* don't want to go," I said.

"You have to! This might be the first year it will actually be fun and have flavorful food. Por favor"—Alma made prayer hands— "please. I've had enough prosciutto melon balls for five lifetimes."

"I'm not even a member of the Women's Club. Why am I on the committee? Also, I might be the only committee member. Marjory gave me the impression the others have abandoned ship. You have to come with me so I'm not the only person under the age of seventy. You owe me." I wagged my finger at my friend.

"That's not fair. Muchas de las damas are in their late fifties and early sixties." Alma smirked.

"Like my mother-in-law! I can't face being stuck in a room with her for an hour. She's probably on the committee, right?"

"You need a squad." Ana returned to the conversation.

"Like Taylor Swift?" I questioned.

"No, like AOC, Rashida, and Ilhan. A fierce women squad." Ana crossed her long legs and pivoted toward the glass doors. She looked into the backyard and toward the mango tree again.

"She's right. If you're the new boss. You should choose who's on the committee." Alma tapped my forearm. "Ask your friend Pepper."

"Maybe I could get Sally to come too," I said.

"That would make your suegra happy."

I gave Alma the evil eyes. The last thing I wanted was to make that woman happy after all the slights and microaggressions she'd subjected me to.

"Okay, I take it back." Alma laughed. "It would make Marjory *jealous* that you got Sally to join the club when she couldn't."

I daydreamed about walking into the Coral Shores Country Club in a white pantsuit with my squad of fierce women— Alma, Pepper, Sally, me, and Marie. "Marie! I should ask Marie to join the committee." I gestured toward my BFF. "You remember Marie from school. No?"

"Nurse Marie?"

"Yes. Except she's not a nurse. She's a chef with a food truck."

"That was her truck at the festival? She'd be perfect. Ask her!" Alma beat a rhythm on the table like it was a conga drum.

"Ms. Diaz, we need to get back to the office. You have a showing at five, and we just got an offer on the Stone Crab property." Ana stood and smoothed her short skirt.

"Whenever she calls me Ms. Diaz, I know I'm in trouble," Alma joked. "Okay, let's go. Gracias por el café. Text me the details about the meeting."

We kissed at the door, and I waved good-bye, then I went to check on Manny. Turning the knob quietly to peek in on him, I found he'd dozed off. Camo was curled up beside him. The kitten opened one eye, stretched a leg, yawned, and then returned to her slumber. My son's naps were getting shorter and shorter. Manny was a month shy of four and a half, and he'd be five and some change when the baby was born. *The baby. We are having a baby!* I hoped the age gap wasn't too big and they'd be friends.

Taking the installation sheet with me, I went to the study, sat in my newly acquired reading chair, and propped my swollen feet up on the window seat. While the app downloaded, I replayed Ana's comment in my head. *Bratva. Is the Russian Mafia involved in Lois's disappearance?*

It took a minute, but I set up our doorbell video feed to notify me only if someone stood on the doorstep and rang. I didn't need a bing every time a person walked in front of the house via the sidewalk—like the two women I saw at the moment walking by the window. It was the British lady, Mrs. Brown, Roberto's school librarian. She stopped and said something to her companion. They looked toward the house, noticed me in the window, and held up a bag. Forced to acknowledge them, I went outside to greet them.

"Hello, Mrs. Brown," I said.

"Call me Gillian."

"Gillian. Thank you for lending us the ladder the other day."

"It was my pleasure. I'm glad we caught you at home. I have some books for Robert." She handed me a bag of paperback mystery novels. "I think you might enjoy one or two of them yourself. This series is about an archaeologist like you," she said, holding a book by Elly Griffiths book.

"Oh, I'm an anthropologist, not an archaeologist. I dig culture, not dirt." I smiled.

"I told you so," her companion said with a lilty Jamaican accent.

"Oh, my giddy aunt, where are my manners? This is my houseguest, Patricia Campbell," Gillian said.

"A pleasure to meet you, Ms. Campbell." I offered her my hand.

"Patricia will do, girl." The woman's hand was warm and her grip was firm, but not in an intimidating way—in a strong, caring woman way.

"Are you visiting for long?" I asked.

"The usual amount of time." She adjusted her blouse and fanned herself. Miami was warm throughout the winter, with only a week or two of sixty-degree weather.

"Patricia comes to visit her son and his wife," Gillian explained.

"How nice. I hope you enjoy your vacation." Tom and his owner passed by us at that moment. The dog barked in the direction of our garbage can. Alma's arrival had distracted me from the cleanup. The gate was open, and the mess was still there. "Excuse me, ladies, I'd invite you in, but I forgot I have a chore calling my name." I pointed to the scattered garbage.

"Let us help you," Gillian said.

I tried to talk them out of it, but they insisted on helping. Patricia held a fresh bag open for me as I transferred the spilled garbage into it. Gillian righted the refuse can.

"Teenagers. The same lot every year," Gillian said.

"You know who the pranksters are?" I asked.

"Hold on, hold on. What is that?" Gillian pointed to the writing on the wall. "They've graffitied your house. That's a step too far."

"*Murr-durr.* Out in the streets." Patricia said it like a popular song I'd heard plenty of time on WDNA's *The Reggae Ride* show. It was a catchy hook that I'd now forever associate with Patricia Campbell. That's how my brain worked sometimes.

"That's not paint. Is that a curry?" Patricia inspected the scrawl.

"Sofrito." *I hope.* "I'll have to get the hose and some soap," I said. "Don't worry, I'll get to it later."

"It will be hard to clean if you let the sun bake it," Patricia said.

Gillian, who'd taken the garbage bag from her friend, tied it and put it in the can. "Where do you keep the hose?"

"At the edge of the patio. Just turn the corner." I pointed.

"I see it." Gillian stepped out of view and onto the patio.

"Excuse me. I'll be right back with some soap." I left Patricia, went into the house, and came out the side door with a bottle of dish soap.

"Miriam, do you have a dog in the backyard?" Gillian asked.

"No, why?" I squirted a stream of blue soap at the wall.

"I thought I saw something moving in the Wendy house." Gillian squeezed the hose's spray nozzle.

"Windy what?" I questioned.

"Your son's play cottage." She pointed toward the corner of our lot.

"Oh!" I laughed. "It must be that darn raccoon."

"Best be careful. It could be rabid if it's out in daylight." Gillian stopped spraying.

I made a mental note to have Robert check the yard that evening before we let Manny play in it.

"It's not budging. I'll need a brush." Patricia snapped her fingers and gave me a stare that reminded me of Sister Romero, my third-grade teacher, when she meant business.

I got a stiff-bristle scrub brush from the garage and handed it to her. I asked her if she'd ever been a schoolteacher. She had.

Did stern looks come naturally to the profession, or was it an acquired talent? I wondered. When Patricia finished and Gillian was satisfied that the wall was thoroughly rinsed, they left to continue their walk. Patricia joked that it was more of a patrol than a leisurely stroll, and her British friend did not object. It seemed Ms. Gillian Brown was the unofficial neighborhood watch.

Chapter Eight

The following morning, I woke up early with an intense craving for fresh orange juice. *I guess baby wants vitamin C.* "I should probably get some prenatal vitamins," I whispered to myself as I closed our bedroom door to let Robert get his full sleep.

In the kitchen, I sliced three oranges and squeezed them on the vintage green glass juicer I'd gotten at a Hell's Kitchen open-air market. The shallow moat filled quickly, and I strained the juice over a glass of ice. As I repeated the step with each half orange, I made a mental to-do list. *First, call Marie and invite her to join the gala committee. Second, get the other squad members on board. Third, I should pull a few cookbooks from the study. Fourth—*

"Aaaaaaaah!" A scream pierced my quiet contemplation.

I went to the living room window to see what was going on. A morning walker was pointing at the Halloween tombstones in the front yard. The inscriptions on the molded plastic grave markers were supposed to be funny, not scary, but the woman's scream had definitely been in the horror film octave. I tightened the belt on my robe, made sure my *Anthropologists do it in the field* nightshirt was well covered, and went outside to see what was the matter.

"Good morning. Is everything okay?" I asked. Finally, seeing what the woman was seeing, I knew it was *not* all right. The body of Lois Pimpkin was lying faceup in front of the marker. "Is she breathing?"

"I don't know." The walker inched forward a bit. "It doesn't look like it." She kept her feet out of reach of Lois, like she expected the body to suddenly come alive, grab her ankle, and pull her into the depths of hell.

"Do you have your phone? Call 911," I said. I thought I saw Lois's mouth open slightly.

"I never take it with me. I like to listen to the birds," the woman said. Her eyes were saucers, and she was dancing from pink Nike to pink Nike.

"Okay, stay here. I'll run and get mine." I dashed inside, grabbed my phone, and closed the curtains while calling the police. "Hello, this is Miriam Quiñones." Remembering the Smith name meant something in Coral Shores, I added the hyphen. "-Smith. I live on Manatee. We need an ambulance. Lois Pimpkin is in my yard, and she's grave." I shut the front door behind me.

The crowd gathering in my yard looked like a pack of mourners at a funeral. The words I'd just spoken to the dispatcher felt like a bad joke. I hadn't meant them to be insensitive, but there she was, Lois Pimpkin, lying supine with a tombstone above her head.

"I hear the sirens," I said, and ended the call. I sent Robert a text. *Keep Manny away from the window. Don't go outside until I give the all clear. Lois Pimpkin is in our yard. There is blood.*

"Okay, everyone, please back up and give the EMTs some room." The lookie-loos did as I asked but like children playing Mother May I. *Take two baby steps back.* I noticed the man with the coiffed giant poodle had his phone trained on the scene. He was probably livestreaming the drama to Around Town. I purposely stood in front of him and blocked his view. Respect and kindness were in short supply in the digital age.

The controlled pace of the EMTs was always unnerving. *Shouldn't they have more prisa?* A stethoscope was placed on Lois's chest, numbers were called out, and an oxygen mask went on her face. Her body was lifted onto a carrying board and put onto a waiting stretcher. As she passed by me, I saw that the dried blood on her forehead was from a severe gash. The right side of her scalp was gunky. *Is that brain?* I sucked in my breath in horror. *No, that's the fideos from the soup I threw out.* Lois had noodles and onions in her hair. And blood. Lots of caked-on blood.

Lois hadn't reacted in any way to the medical team as they touched her and worked to revive her. Was she going to survive? The ambulance doors shut, and the vehicle drove off. Replacing it was a black SUV with tinted windows. I couldn't see the driver, but I knew who it was.

"Ms. Quiñones. I thought I recognized the address."

"Hello, Detective Pullman," I said.

Frank Pullman had been a guest at our housewarming party. We'd had an adversarial beginning to our friendship. He was the one that had falsely arrested my BFF. But then he'd called a truce and asked me to be his eyes and ears, and we'd bonded over oxtail stew.

"I should have known you'd be involved in this somehow."

"This has nothing to do with me," I said, swiping my arm from shoulder to shoulder like a metronome.

"Except it *is* your front yard," Pullman said. He gave me a squinty-eyed glare. The man was a Black Humphrey Bogart from the square chin down to the mannerisms. If it weren't for Miami's humidity and heat, he'd probably be wearing a trench coat instead of workout clothes.

"Yes, and I was obviously in my house minding my own business." I overlapped the lapels of my robe and cinched the belt tighter. "What's your excuse? You just *happened* to be driving by my house." Wow. The lack of coffee was making me cranky. *Take a chill pill, Miriam. Don't upset the police detective.*

"Yes, Veronica, I was on my way to the gym when I heard the dispatch. Tell me what you saw."

Pullman's nickname for me was Veronica Mars. The titular character was from a show I'd never watched, but I thought it had to do with a high school student, a long-lens camera, and a pit bull. None of those things were me. He also sometimes called me Jessica Fletcher, a reference I understood but resented. It wasn't my fault bodies seemed to drop in my vicinity.

Gordon arrived on the scene, and Pullman directed him to take names and statements and then disperse the crowd. I told Pullman everything I knew, which was next to nothing. I'd heard a scream, come outside, and seen a woman staring at the body of Lois Pimpkin, which had prompted me to call 911. The detective walked around the now-not-funny tombstones and to the east corner of the front yard, the bedrooms side of the house. For the first time, I was happy Manny's room didn't have a window. I didn't need my son waking up to Pullman's mug peering at him. He was already obsessed with law enforcement. The still-unfurnished guest bedroom was at the front of the house. It had a window facing the front yard. Robert's and my bedroom had a window that looked onto the backyard. But Manny's room and the hall bathroom squeezed between them didn't have windows. *When the baby comes, we should move Manny to the front room and make his room the nursery.* Ideas for themes filled my head. *I could do giant flowers on the wall. Or parrots. Maybe a rain forest motif.*

"Miriam. Miriam." Pullman snapped his fingers. "Miriam."

"Huh?" I came back to earth.

"Do you always leave your side gate open?" Frank asked.

"No. Both gates should be locked." I pointed to the garage side and the east side. Whereas the gate that hid the trash can was visible from the street, the east gate wasn't. It was at the back of the house.

"Did the yard service come yesterday?"

"No, they were here on Friday. Why?"

"Hmm." Pullman was the king of the nonanswer answer. "Mind if I have a look?"

"No, but my family is having breakfast right now. They'll see you from the dining room," I said.

"That's okay. They won't bother me."

He wasn't what I was worried about. I followed Detective Pullman down the side of the house, passed the air conditioner condenser, and through the unlatched gate. He walked with his hands clasped in the front pocket of his Alvin Ailey hoodie. One of his sons was a dancer. The other was studying to be an astronaut. Looking at the grass as he walked, he hummed but didn't share his thoughts. We were halfway to Manny's play-house when Gordon joined us.

"Detective, how would you like me to proceed?" Gordon asked.

"Get an officer to the hospital and give me a status update on Mrs. Pimpkin. Is she awake? Can she talk?" Pullman resumed his meandering inspection.

I heard the French doors open and saw my pajama-clad son running toward us. He took a flying hug toward Gordon that was met with equal admiration. Roberto mouthed, "I couldn't stop him. Sorry."

"Excuse me," I said, holding a hand over my mouth. Baby nausea had hit. I beelined into the house, rinsed my mouth with water in the kitchen sink, and wiped a cool, wet cloth over my face and neck. The wave of sick lessened. I opened a green tin of Export Sodas and took out a few to nibble on. The ice in the orange juice I'd abandoned had melted, making it watery. I drank it anyway. Dusting the cracker crumbs from my lips, I returned to the yard, where Gordon gave me a peculiar grin.

"Manny, do you mind if I take a look in your playhouse?" Pullman asked my son.

"Okay," Manny replied.

We watched as the detective peered into the plastic log cabin. Gordon moved us to the cement patio and kept Manny engaged in chatter about police dogs. Roberto put his arm around my waist and kissed the top of my head.

"So what's the story?" Robert whispered.

"Mrs. Pimpkin was rushed to the hospital. She had blood on her head. It didn't look good. She wasn't moving," I replied in a low voice.

"How did she get into our yard?"

"¿Qué sé yo?" I shrugged. "Do you think she was coming to yell at you some more?"

Gordon gently pushed Manny to return to us so he could talk to Pullman in private. Codes and words were relayed into Gordon's walkie-talkie.

"Ms. Quiñones, could I bother you for a cup of your delicious Cuban coffee?" Detective Pullman asked as he moved to sit at the patio table. Clearly, he was planning on staying a while.

I took my family back inside the house and tried to have a normal Tuesday morning breakfast. Before making Pullman's requested beverage, I changed into shorts and a top, brushed my teeth, and pulled my black shoulder-length hair into a low ponytail. My day's plan to research in the study and organize for tomorrow's committee meeting went out the window as soon as the K-9 unit showed up. Manny danced in front of the French windows begging me to let him go outside. I told him we could watch from the patio but we couldn't pet the sniffer dog because he was doing a job and needed to focus. *I wish I could focus on my job.*

We watched the German shepherd in the police vest sniff from Manny's playhouse to the side yard, where the *Help* message had been. Then it went back to the log cabin and down the other side of the house. Gordon joined us at the patio table to ask for a dish of water for the dog. I took Pullman's dirty *taza de café* with me and returned with a plastic container.

"Here. Use the tap to fill it up." I pointed to the sink by the built-in grill that was our new outdoor kitchen.

"Thanks. Merle will appreciate it," Gordon said.

"Merle. Is the dog name Merle?" Manny, who'd been very good about staying in his seat, was desperate to meet the dog.

"Gordon, is there any chance Manny can pet Merle?"

"I'll ask."

"Thanks. I'll get some drinks for the officers." I observed Gordon introducing Manny to Merle and his handler before I crouched in front of the minifridge and pulled out a six-pack of Coke, a Sprite, and a lone bottle of malta. *The K-9 handler looks Latino, so maybe he'll drink it.*

"Let me help you with that." Gordon tried to assist me as I stood, cradling the beverages against my chest. "A woman in your condition should be resting. I'm sorry for all this stress."

"My condition?" I asked. I set the drinks on the table.

"You're glowing, and then the morning sickn—"

I stopped him midword with a splayed hand. "Did Robert tell you? Roberto, voy a darte un—"

Gordon interrupted me before my anger got rolling. "No, no, no, no. I guessed, but I'm right, aren't I?" He grinned.

"Yes. But we haven't told anyone. I'm swearing you to secrecy! You cannot tell a soul. Promise?"

"What's this about secrets?" Pullman appeared beside us.

"Nothing," Gordon and I said in unison.

"Family stuff," I offered as an explanation.

Detective Pullman looked from one of us to the other, then gave one of his *hmm*s.

Tom barked from behind the hedge, and Merle's ears perked up. With water dripping from his mouth, he pulled his handler to the row of ficus that provided the privacy between our yards.

"Sorry," Mr. Nelson called from his yard. "I guess that raccoon is still around."

Tom kept barking.

"No. We've got a dog back here. Don't worry." I got closer to the shrub fence. There was a thin spot in the foliage where we could partially see into each other's properties. "They found Mrs. Pimpkin in our front yard this morning."

"Oh, is that what all the noise was? Is she okay?" Mr. Nelson asked.

"They've taken her to the hospital," I replied.

Tom, who was off leash, ran the length of the divide, Merle tracking him from our side. We then heard Tom jumping against the tree in his yard. Merle pulled his handler to the back corner of our yard, where the canine commotion was taking place.

"I think there's something in my tree," Mr. Nelson called from his side.

"Maybe there really is a raccoon," I said.

"No, I don't think so, unless they make a whirling noise," he said.

"Sir. Can you please put your dog up and let us into your yard?" The handler spoke for the first time. *He's definitely Cuban.* His voice was loud and round, and he sounded like he'd grown up in Hialeah or Westchester. Cubanaso to the core.

We followed Merle out the gate and into Mr. Nelson's yard. Told to stay at a distance, Gordon, Pullman, Manny, and I watched as Merle barked into the grapefruit tree. Tom reciprocated with whines and door scratching from inside the house.

The Cuban officer called Gordon over, and after a quick conversation, Gordon put on a pair of gloves, then deftly climbed into the tree. He jumped down a few seconds later, holding a mangled drone.

"Helicóptero," Manny screamed. "Ese es el helicóptero que ví el otro día."

It was the first I'd heard of it. I asked my son what he meant, and he told me that a toy helicopter had been flying over the yard the other day, actually a couple of days in a row. My son had never seen a drone, so naturally he picked the thing it most looked like. As Gordon walked by us, I noticed one of the blades had dried mud on it.

Not mud.

Blood!

Chapter Nine

I t took another hour, but eventually, the police frenzy in our yard ended. Roberto had offered to cancel his morning consultation, but I promised him I could handle them and Manny on my own. After all, it wasn't like it was my first police investigation rodeo. The patrol cars and K-9 unit left, but Pullman and Gordon stayed. After they'd interviewed Mr. Nelson, the two wore a path in the lawn, retracing the scent trail Merle had made.

Tap, tap.

I looked up from my recipe research, a cookbook from the Bahamas, to answer the knock on the French doors.

"Come in. Would you like another coffee?" I asked.

"Por favor," Pullman answered. He was conversant in Spanish thanks to his Colombian wife and twenty years on the force in Miami. "Can I ask Manny a few questions?"

"Sure. But please don't mention Lois. He doesn't know about the ambulance and all that," I cautioned, then called my son out of his room.

Manny, with Camo at his heels, frolicked into the dining room area. In Spanish, I told him the detective wanted to ask him some questions. Manny sat on the bench side of the table, lifting his kitten onto it after she failed to clear the height. The kid was grinning ear to ear. It was like his favorite show come to life. Gordon sat across from him, Pullman at the end. While I assembled a tray of cups and a plate of Maria cookies, the men chatted with my son about his cat and school. Listening in, I was impressed by Manny's improved English. Because we wanted our son to be bilingual, I spoke to him solely in Spanish and Robert in English. That's what the research said was best. But with the last year's job search and move, Robert hadn't been around as much, so Manny's acquisition of words had been stunted. Also, our NYC neighbor who had babysat him when I was prepping my dissertation was Dominican and had spoken to him in Spanish per my request. Montessori three days a week had introduced him to an English-speaking peer group, and he'd made up the lost ground in the blink of an eye.

I set the tray of drinks on the table and served Pullman and Gordon their espressos. I opted for mango-pineapple juice for me and my son, who hungrily grabbed one of the mildly sweet cookies to go with it. Now that I was seated, it seemed the real questions could start.

"Manny, can you tell me about the helicopter? You said you saw it before," Pullman asked. His voice was grandfatherly and not the sardonic tone I usually got.

"I saw it after we did Halloween decorations." Manny took a bite of the cracker-like cookie. "Sophia saw it too."

"Is Sophia a friend of yours?" Pullman asked.

"Sophia Hallstead. They go to school together. Her mom is Pepper," I said.

Gordon nodded and made a note on his pad.

"What was the drone—I mean, toy helicopter—doing?" Frank raised his eyebrows.

"Flying." Manny took a sip of juice and looked at the detective like he was an idiot.

Gordon chuckled.

"Did you see it any other time?" Pullman took the final sip of his coffee.

"Yes."

"May I?" I asked.

Pullman gave me the go-ahead, and I phrased the question differently and in Spanish. To which Manny replied with a disconnected story about his and Sophia's playdate on Sunday afternoon.

"Did you get that?" I looked at Pullman.

"Most of it, but I'd like the full translation," he said.

"The kids saw the drone flying over our house Sunday when they were drawing with chalk on the sidewalk. He also saw it last week flying in the yard behind ours." I put my hand on my stomach. Gordon noticed and smiled. I gave him a *Keep quiet* look.

"Manny, do you play in your cabin every day?" Frank asked.

"Yes. But not for two days." He held up two fingers in a V.

"Sunday night—well, really, Monday morning—I heard scratching. Robert thought it might be a raccoon, so we haven't let him go outside in case the animal was still around." After the words came out of my mouth, I began to doubt if there ever was a critter. *What if the noise I heard was the drone landing on the roof or hitting the side of the house? Could those things be flown at nighttime?*

"And then Monday you found the message written on the wall of your house." Pullman's tone had shifted into law enforcement mode.

"Yeah, but I thought you said that was a prank," I said, looking to Gordon.

"Maybe, but maybe not. Have the results come back from the lab?" Pullman directed the question to Gordon.

"No, not yet." Gordon turned to me. "Miriam, did you activate the door cam yet?"

"Oh yeah, I forgot about that. You think it recorded something?"

"Can you log in and let me review it?"

I passed my phone to him once I'd entered the app's password. Gordon and Pullman put their heads together and watched the small screen. Camo jumped on the table, and I scolded her to get down. Manny then asked permission to leave, and I gave it to him. It seemed the interrogation had moved into a different phase. Gordon and Pullman were intensely focused on my phone.

"Ms. Quiñones"—Pullman calling me by my last name was never chummy—"you didn't get a notification from the app?"

"No. I set it for doorbell only. What's on the video?"

"Lois Pimpkin is on the video." Gordon handed me my phone, and I watched the eerie video.

In the farthest periphery of the camera's field of vision, Lois crawled from the side yard to the Halloween headstone. The shadowy infrared video felt like a zombie movie from the VHS era. It was creepy and scary but also unreal.

Pullman got a call on his phone and stepped away from the table. He strolled into the living room and listened to the caller while peeking out the closed curtains.

"What do you think happened to her?" I asked Robert's cousin.

"Something or someone hit her on the head," Gordon replied.

"Yeah, but where? In our yard? Why? And when?"

"That's what we need to find out. And by *we*, I mean Detective Pullman and the police, *not* you. Stay out of this, okay? Especially now that . . ." He pointed to my stomach.

"You better not tell anyone." I gave him a steely glare.

"Tell anyone what?" Pullman had materialized beside me.

"About next week's recipe." It was a lame lie, but Pullman accepted it. Or perhaps he had more pressing matters on his mind. He whispered something into Gordon's ear that caused him to hurry away—followed shortly after by Pullman's own exit.

With quiet restored, I got back to my to-do list. *First priority: menu ideas.* As I left the study with an armful of cookbooks, my phone beeped a new sound. Dropping the books onto the ottoman in the living room, I checked the notification. It was the door camera. Marjory was on my front step. The impulse to hide and not answer was strong. I didn't need any of my mother-in-law's basura after the stressful morning I'd had. She rang the doorbell twice in quick succession, which got Manny's attention.

"Mami, alguien está en la puerta." Manny skipped into the sala and up to the door. He waited for me, since he knew never to open the door without an adult present.

"What took you so long? Were you asleep? I've been out here for five minutes." Marjory had her arms crossed.

Rise above, Miriam. Don't let her bait you into a tit-for-tat.

I took a deep breath before answering her. "No." *But I wish I were asleep.* "I had my head in a book. A cookbook, actually. Research for tomorrow's gala meeting."

Marjory seemed appeased by my answer to why she'd had to wait a millisecond. "I've come for Douglas." She patted Manny on the head. *He's not a dog! Show some emotion! Chill, Miriam.*

She's not a hugger. Let it go. "I'm taking my grandson to the science museum for a behind-the-scenes tour of the new jellyfish exhibit. Only generous donors are given that kind of access. Did Bobby not tell you?"

"No, *Roberto* must have forgotten." I hated that she called my husband Bobby and my son Douglas. Robert preferred his proper name, and she was the only one who used Manuelito's middle name instead of his first. "But we've had a hectic morning."

Marjory's blank face told me she hadn't heard the news about Lois. I debated whether to elaborate but decided against it. The sooner I got her out of my house, the better. I told Manny to get a jacket and put on his shoes. I hadn't been to the Frost yet. It had been built while I was away. But I remembered field trips to the old science museum and planetarium, where it was always cold inside. I wondered if they'd moved the giant prehistoric sloth sculpture from the old site to the new one. It was so weird and looked like a yeti crossed with a kangaroo.

"Don't cook anything spicy. Or common. People are expecting haute cuisine at two-fifty a ticket." Marjory sat on the blue sofa and eyed the pile of Caribbean cookbooks on the ottoman.

Does she expect me to do the actual cooking? Is that why she signed me up for it? Probably. I mean, she does think anyone with brown or black skin is the help. And common! Like that's a bad thing. What the actual . . . Deep breath, Miriam. Deep breath. Don't let her status snobbery get to you. And she can say haute cuisine *with a French pronunciation, but Spanish words are like caca in her mouth. Stop, Miriam. You are working yourself up.*

"Don't worry, Marjory. The menu will be elegant and exciting to the palate. It will be like you've taken a vacation to a five-star island resort."

"Humph."

We sat in icy silence, waiting for Manny. When he joined us to put on his shoes, Camo came too. The kitten jumped onto the sofa next to my mother-in-law. Marjory startled, then recoiled. I swore I heard her murmur, "Fleabag." Camo, not getting the desired response to her divine feline cuteness, hissed and leaped down.

"Well, that's a first. I've never heard her do that," I said, trying to hide my deep satisfaction.

"Ready!" Manny popped up from the floor.

I checked to make sure he'd put his slip-on sneakers on the correct feet. Then I scooped Camo the Lizard Hunter into my arms and opened the front door for them.

"Bye. Have a good time. When can I expect you back?" I asked.

Marjory replied, "Three PM."

I closed the door, dropped Camo into a chair, and gathered my cookbooks. Seated at the dining table, I flipped through them, trying to find one unique recipe from each island culture.

"Argh, this is going to be impossible. I need help." Anastasia's words came back to me. "I need a squad." I shot off text messages to Marie, Sally, Alma, and Pepper, inviting them to be part of a new era in Coral Shores, one that was younger, more inclusive, and socially conscious. I knew I was reaching, but big dreams started with grand optimism. All four responded that they could attend tomorrow's meeting.

With the gala planning on hold for the day, I lost myself in the foreword of a cookbook, reading about Britain's colonial influence on Jamaican food. I dozed off with the heavy book in my lap and my feet propped up on the chaise side of the sofa. When the doorbell chimed, I roused. I hoped it was the excitement from the day that had knocked me out and not the baby. I could not afford to be napping this early in the pregnancy.

Checking the door cam app, I saw that my invitation to stop by anytime had been taken literally. Gillian Brown and Patricia Campbell were at the door.

"I hope we aren't disturbing your lunch. We were just passing by and . . ." Gillian said, letting the unsaid hang in the air.

"No, no. Come in." I stepped aside so that they could enter, then opened the living room curtains, and the room brightened immediately. I stacked the cookbooks on the windowsill. "Have a seat. Would you like a glass of water? I'd offer you tea, but I'm afraid we aren't tea drinkers. Sorry, I've only got tilo." The medicinal nerve-calming linden leaf tea was a staple in most Cuban American houses, and mine was no different.

"Water will be fine. No ice in mine, if you don't mind," Gillian said.

"Do you take yours room temperature too?" I asked her Jamaican friend.

"The colder, the better," Patricia said. I could see the beads of sweat on her forehead.

I kept up small talk, mostly about the weather—an expected ninety-degree high—while I poured our drinks. Setting the trio of waters on the round glass-and-metal coffee table, I sat and waited for it. I knew they weren't here for a social visit. They were here for chisme. They wanted the gossip from the horse's mouth, and I was the horse.

"Is it true Lois was found in your yard?" Gillian asked.

I nodded.

"Alive?" Patricia asked, and leaned into the conversation.

I blinked while I processed Patricia's question. *Is that disappointment or curiosity?*

"They've taken her to the hospital. I don't know anything more than that," I replied.

"Poor Paul. First his daughter and now his wife." Gillian took a sip of water.

"What do you mean, *poor* Paul? That man is as rich as King Solomon. His money will solve his problems." Patricia tutted.

"Money doesn't fix a broken heart." Gillian smoothed a wrinkle in her skirt. "And that is all that man has had. He lost his mother when he was young, then his college sweetheart was killed in a car crash, now his daughter is in jail, and his wife is in a coma from a blow to the head. See what I mean? Tragedy has beset him at every turn."

"Gillian, girl, you still burning that candle?" Patricia turned from her friend and shook her head. Under her breath, she said, "Trouble deh deh."

I hadn't said anything about a coma or a blow to the head. *How does she know those details?* I should be the one asking her for the latest chisme.

"Pfft," Gillian replied, and diverted her eyes from her mate. She gazed out the window toward the tombstones. "It must have been quite a fright to find her in your garden."

"It was, but I didn't find her exactly. A woman on her morning walk. I'm sorry I don't know everyone yet. I think she said she was a bird watcher." I shrugged.

"Susan," they said in unison.

"Wouldn't hurt a fly," Gillian said. "A vegan." Her British pronunciation of the word was new to my ears. *Vea-gen.*

"Who do you think done it?" Patricia pivoted on the sofa to face her friend. "I suspect it have something to do with her drug-dealing daughter. All them riffraff is violent."

"Oh, my giddy aunt, I hadn't thought about that. They kidnapped her. And as she struggled to escape, they hit her with a pistol. That must be how she got hit on the head. Struggling to escape, see what I mean?"

"And then they threw her out da car as they came round the corner." Patricia slapped her leg and bounced in her seat.

"Yes! She rolled onto the swale. The poor dear tried to crawl to safety, but she didn't make it to the front door."

"No, Gilly. The woman play dead. Hoped they wouldn't come back for her."

I watched the exchange between the two. It was like when a film plot gets outrageous and you can't believe it's gone there. *Drug gangs. Kidnapping. Pistol whipped.* The next thing they'd say was that there was a car chase with Will Smith and Martin Lawrence at the wheel like a scene from one of the Bad Boys movies.

I knew, or at least I had a pretty good guess, that Lois had been hit on the head by a drone. The very drone that had gotten stuck in Mr. Nelson's tree. Manny had said he'd seen it flying about a few days before. I wondered why. Probably some teenager's expensive toy. Maybe the pranksters?

"Excuse me, sorry to change the subject, but have either of you ladies heard about teenagers flying drones in the neighborhood?" I asked.

"Drones?" Gillian tucked in her chin. "The remote-control things?"

I nodded.

"I know the council uses them for code enforcement. They're very strict about permits too. You can't put a shed in your back garden without a permit. And they'll fine you if your roof hasn't been pressure cleaned. No matter that you're a pensioner on a fixed budget." Gillian spoke as if she'd had personal experience with the code officer.

"Them drug dealers use 'em too. Just like Amazon." Patricia wagged her finger in the air. "See what I tell you, it's the drug gangs. Oooooo." Her face lit up like she had the answer to a *Jeopardy!* Daily Double. "What dat graffiti say again? *Mur-dur*? Could be the Red Rum Posse? *Mur-dur* spelled backward. They're bad trouble. Did that Juliet girl get messed up with dem?"

"No, Patricia. Juliet wasn't smuggling with the Jamaicans. She was working with the Chinese. You know they have a long history with opium. And then there was that Cuban fellow—no offense." Gillian looked at me. "He was bad business. Might be him getting his revenge."

Jamaican posses. Chinese opium smugglers. I need to get these two out of my house before they jump to alien abduction as a theory. They were just as bad as Ana with her Russian kidnapping rumors.

I gathered the partially drunk glasses from the coffee table, and they got the hint. Patricia, Gillian, and their outlandish theories departed.

Chapter Ten

"**C**oño," I cursed. My finger dripped blood. The water I was using to wash the tin of octopus before chucking it into the recycle bin turned pink. I wrapped my injured finger in a paper towel and applied pressure, but the blood soaked through. "Ouchie! Ouchie! Ouchie!" Holding my finger tight, I ran to the bathroom and exchanged the bloodied wrap for some ointment that slowed the flow, and then I put on a wide Band-Aid. Camo came scampering out of Manny's room to see what I was doing. I gave her a pet, and she sniffed my hand and wrist. Were all felines fond of seafood? *Or maybe she is just a Miami cat with the ocean in her veins.*

Thankfully, the ensalada de pulpo I'd just started to make wasn't contaminated. I spritzed the sink and counter with cleaner just to be safe before resuming. After I'd chopped the onion and bell pepper, I added a teaspoon of minced garlic, a few shakes of oregano, olive oil, and vinegar.

My stomach audibly grumbled. "Bebé, are you hungry for octopus? Are you a mermaid? Oh, Sirena is a good name. Tengo que ponerlo en la lista," I said as I peeled the smooth, bark-like skin from the half avocado I'd taken from the fridge. Florida avocados grew to almost football size. They were less buttery than the Haas variety but just as nutritious and delicious. I sliced a Roma tomato, grabbed a bag of Gilda crackers, and took my two-salad lunch to the patio.

Halfway through my lunch, I realized that maybe sitting on the patio wasn't such a good idea. Manny's play cottage was in my direct line of sight, and if I pivoted to the right, then I was looking at Mr. Nelson's tree. Lois Pimpkin and the events of the day were inescapable. I took my phone out, clicked the Pandora icon, and selected the Jarabe de Palo radio station I'd made. It had lots of rock en español that I could sing along to. I knew Spotify was the music aggregate most people my age used, but I liked that Pandora learned my likes and made suggestions that were usually spot-on. Like the first song, a fave by Los Fabulosos Cadillacs. I closed my eyes to the marching samba band drum and whistle intro. I sang the first line, a warning called out to someone on the run, at the top of my lungs. The political lyrics, an anthem to those who protested and resisted a dictator who had disappeared thousands of people, were clever and full of double entendre. *They're looking for you, matador.* After the grita, I tapped my fork on the edge of the table to the fast staccato beat. When I opened my eyes, the police were standing in my backyard.

"¡Coño!" I screamed as I clapped my hand to my chest. "You scared me." I lowered the volume, then stopped the song. "What are you doing back? And how did you get in?"

"I wanted to test a theory," Detective Pullman said.

"Your side gate doesn't lock," Officer Gordon Smith added.

"No, but it closes with a hidden latch. Do I need to buy a padlock? Gordon, you told me Coral Shores was safe," I said. I took a final bite of salad, wiped my mouth, and pushed my lunch plate to the middle of the table. "Have you heard anything about Mrs. Pimpkin? Is she going to be all right?"

The two exchanged looks before Pullman spoke. "She is still unconscious. But they are hopeful for a recovery."

"Gracias a Dios," I said.

The detective pulled the chair out and sat. He'd changed from his workout clothes to a suit. His tie, dark blue with tiny gold stars, was knotted loosely at his neck. From inside his jacket, he removed an evidence bag. "Does this look familiar?" Pullman slid the plastic bag to me.

"It looks like one of Robert's Frankenstein screws. Where did you find it?" I asked.

There's that look between them again. What is going on?

"It was in Mrs. Pimpkin's pocket," Pullman replied.

"She must have taken it from the Fall Festival when she was at his booth. You were there, Gordon. You remember. She was yelling at him like a banshee."

Gordon nodded, then asked to use the bathroom.

"Tell me about the altercation," Detective Pullman said.

"It wasn't an altercation." I used air quotes. "It was all her. She yelled something about . . ." I took a beat to remember the scene. "Okay, sí, it was something like Robert should be helping Juliet. She was guilting him and also complaining that I was somehow involved because Fuentes is Cuban."

"It is my understanding that she was also looking for you. Is that true?"

"That's what Robert said."

"Did she find you?"

"No. I don't think she knows what I look like."

"Is your husband very protective?"

Pullman's face was as expressionless as a freshly painted wall. But I knew what the question implied. He wanted to know if my Roberto had hurt Lois Pimpkin to protect me from her. I needed to manage my reaction wisely. *Don't explode, Miriam.* This was the theory he was testing. After all, Lois had been found in our yard and had probably been in Manny's cottage. *Ay mi madre, she was probably there overnight.* I opened my mouth to reply with a calm *I know what you're thinking, and no way,* but Gordon came out through the French doors, holding a bag.

"Whose blood is this?" Gordon held the bag out to us.

"Mine," I said, and showed them my bandaged finger.

"You look disappointed." I tilted my head at Gordon. He sighed deeply. I could see he was uncomfortable. "What are you not telling me?" Gordon cast his eyes to the ground. "Gordon! What is going on?" I turned to Pullman. "Out with it. Say whatever it is you need to say."

"Where is your husband right now?" Pullman asked.

"At work."

"He left the scene this morning before we could question him." Pullman looked me in the eye and didn't blink.

"Call him." I waved my cell phone in the air. "Go to his office." My voice was getting louder. *Cálmate, Miriam.*

"That won't be necessary. We can come back later. What time does he get home from work?"

"Around five thirty," I said.

"We are going to need a DNA sample from him," Pullman said, scraping the chair on the cement patio as he stood. "And we will take that"—he pointed to the bloody paper towel in Gordon's possession—"to rule you out."

Gordon looked at me with pain on his face. He mouthed an *I'm sorry* and grimaced.

As soon as they'd left, a panic attack hit me.

"¿Qué carajo está pasando?" I ran my fingers through my hair. What was happening? Did they really think Robert had hurt Lois? Did they think I was in on it too? Pullman always played his cards close to his chest, but maybe I could get some information from Gordon. He *was* Robert's cousin. *I'm sure I can twist his arm and get some info from him.*

My panic was still vibrating in my chest, but a few deep breaths calmed it. I texted my BFF and asked her to come by as soon as possible.

Like now! I need you.

Okay. Voy. Dame cinco.

I took my dishes inside and washed them. The doorbell rang, and the app on my phone beeped. I didn't bother to look at it because I knew it was Alma.

"Why didn't you tell me about Lois?"

"Hola, Mami."

I was hit by love and hate the second I opened the door.

Manny hugged my legs, then ran to his room with a newly acquired giant shark plushie. It was nearly as long as he was tall. I heard him telling Camo about all the fish he'd seen at the museum's aquarium.

"Well? What do you have to say for yourself?" Marjory asked. She stepped over the threshold and closed the door behind her.

I wasn't going to put up with yet another interrogation, especially not one from my mother-in-law. "Thank you for taking Manny today. It looks like he had a great adventure. Did you enjoy the jellyfish exhibit?"

"Answer me. Why didn't you tell me about Lois this morning when I came to get Douglas? She *is* one of my dearest friends." Marjory crossed her arms and shifted her weight to one leg.

"I assumed you already knew and were being sensitive to your grandson." I patted the air with my hand to ask her to keep her voice low. "We don't want to scare him."

"Hmph." Marjory tapped her heel and shifted her weight again. Her lips pursed, and I could almost hear the enamel on her molars cracking. Words of venom were about to spew forth.

Ding-dong.

Gracias a La Caridad, Alma had arrived. Reinforcements.

"I thought that was your car, Marjory. So nice to see you. Terrible news about Lois. But I'm so glad she's been found." Alma air-kissed Marjory and plunked herself into one of the living room chairs.

Marjory narrowed her eyes, gave us both a steely look, and left in a huff.

"Was it something I said?" Alma asked as soon as the door clicked shut.

We both laughed.

"So tell me. Why did I need to drop everything and rush over?"

I snuck into the hall and shut the door to Manny's room. Then I sat down and told my bestie all about the bloody drone, the Frankenstein screw, and what Pullman insinuated.

"And I'm pregnant."

"¿Que qué? You're pregnant?" Alma covered her mouth with both hands.

"Yes. I wanted to tell you like more happy, but like, I'm so stressed out."

"Mi'ja, this is such good news! Shh, shhh, shh. Forget about all that other stuff right now." Alma moved to the sofa to sit beside me. She stroked my arm and calmed me down from the ledge. "It is all going to be okay. Don't let that old white woman steal your joy."

"Who do you mean? Lois? Or Marjory?" I asked.

"Both of them. Don't even waste a second on them. You're having a baby!"

"Shh! We haven't told Manny yet. We want to wait a few more weeks. Just to be sure, you know."

"I know a great ob-gyn. I sold—"

I interrupted and finished Alma's sentence for her. "—her a house."

Alma gave me a *You think you are funny* look. "Sit still. I'm going to make a tilo to calm you down."

"Tilo might solve the immediate problem of my nerves, but what about the Lois problem? The police think Roberto had something to do with it. I mean, Alma, they did find her in our yard!"

"Cálmate. Tilo first, then we solve your other problem. Come on, you figured out Juliet's drug-smuggling scheme and her plot against Sunny Weatherman. You cleared my name. You got this. Don't jump to doom and boom." Alma went to the kitchen and began making tea.

"It's doom and gloom, not boom," I corrected my friend.

"Gloom, boom, doom, whatever. You know what I'm saying."

"Pero you know"—I sat on the stool by the counter—"figuring out that Fuentes-Pimpkin connection was luck."

"Luck and smarts. Plus she's alive. Right? It's not like last time. No one is dead." Alma put the tea bags into the mugs.

"That's true."

"Chica, it is going to all blow over," Alma said as the kettle whistled.

Or blow up. Maybe boom was the right word after all.

Chapter Eleven

A not-his-cousin police officer was waiting in the driveway when Robert got home. They took a cheek swab and zipped away with it. After I'd filled my husband in on my roller coaster day, he insisted we dine out so I could catch a break. I suggested Chef Creole's, since our baby seemed to be a mermaid and was demanding seafood. We took our shrimp and conch fritters to the bay and ate on the benches with the twinkle of the Miami Beach skyline playing on the water. Manny played with a pair of siblings whose parents had had the same idea as us, dinner alfresco. On the way home, we took a tour through the village to see the Halloween decorations. The end of the day was super nice and just what I needed to destress. I went to bed relaxed and in the arms of the man I loved.

"Buenos días mi amor."

In the fog of being half-awake, half-asleep, I thought I was in a badly dubbed Brazilian telenovela. But when I opened my eyes, I saw it was actually Robert and his slightly off accent. I loved that he tried to speak Spanish for me.

"Don't get out of bed. Manny and I made you breakfast."

"Wow. Did I oversleep? What time is it?" I checked the clock. "Manny is going to be late for school."

"Stay there. Manny has two parents. I've got this handled." Robert kissed me.

"Is he dressed?"

"Of course. Did you think I'd take him in his pj's? Now, rest. I'll bring you your breakfast."

He returned with a tray and our son.

"Mami. Mami. Yo cociné." Manny proceeded to explain the deconstructed fruit salad, powdered sugar, Maria cookies, and Os masterpiece in my lap.

"I stopped him before the chocolate syrup." Robert grinned.

"Thank you," I mouthed.

"Okay, little man, kiss your mom and grab your backpack."

Manny did as his father said, but not before bringing Camo to my bed so I wouldn't be "sola." The kitten was content to play with her tail while I ate the least sugarcoated bits of pineapple. But when I moved my foot, she pounced on it.

"That's my cue to get out of bed." I scooped Camo into my arms and deposited her onto the floor. "Good thing your little claws can't pierce through the covers. But I know that day is coming soon." I laughed. "And you better not do that to the baby."

After I'd showered and dressed, I made an edible breakfast, some buttered toast, and a mug of hot milk with just a splash of café. *I don't want to give you up. I love you.* I savored the smell of the strong espresso coffee before I poured the extra down the sink. A few minutes to ten, I tucked a notebook and pen into my bag and headed to the Coral Shores Country Club.

Alma was waiting for me in the club's lobby when I arrived. The club screamed old money and old Florida, from the white columns across the front of the two-story building to the curved twin staircase.

93

"Hola, chica," I said, kissing her. "Do you know where we are supposed to meet?"

"In the upstairs conference room, according to your suegra."

"Where is she?" I looked around in a panic.

"Chill, bruh. She left you this." Alma handed me a three-ring binder.

"So you saw Marjory?"

"She's out there somewhere." Alma pointed to the glass that made up the back wall of the club's lobby. A giant oak with beards of Spanish moss dangling over an artificial pond was framed in the vista. Bunkers and sand traps dotted the manicured golf course.

"Is there an alligator in that pond?" I asked.

A voice came from behind me. "I wish! I'd have pushed Marjory in it a long time ago."

"Sally!" I wrapped my arms around my sister-in-law. "You are so bad."

"Please. You were thinking the same thing," Sally said.

"You aren't wrong," I said.

We all laughed and passed pleasantries until the others arrived.

"Ana?" I called to the svelte blonde who'd exited a door down the hall. "Anastasia?" The woman didn't turn toward her name. "Alma, did your assistant come with you? She's welcome to join us."

"No, she's at the office," Alma replied. "She's doing the MLS input. Business is back up. I've gotten four listings this week!"

"Candela." I applauded the return of my friend's top-seller status as I kept looking in the direction of the mystery lady. "What's down that way?" I pointed to my right.

"The bar, the Pro Shop, and the kitchen," Sally said.

"Oh, I'd like to see the kitchen," Marie said as she joined us. "Will we get a tour? This is my first time at the country club." Marie took in the grand staircase's marble steps and white wrought iron railing with palm fronds and egrets designed into it.

Alma and I gave Marie hugs, then I introduced her to Sally. Pepper walked in at that moment, and my squad was complete.

"Actually, Sally, can we have a tour? I've only seen part of the club myself," I said. The last time I'd been there, I'd seen only the lobby, the bathroom, and the event room where Sunny Weatherman had dropped dead beside me. I certainly wanted to exchange that memory for something more pleasant.

"Sure, why not? I guess I'm the longest Coral Shores resident among us." Sally pointed to the glass wall behind the grand stairs. "That's the golf course, designed by some champion golf master. Follow me." She strolled to the right, and we followed. "That's the Pro Shop."

We all looked in as we passed. Clubs and rackets adorned the walls. A chisel-jawed sandy-haired guy with the beginnings of a dad paunch was showing a putter to a fit older visor-wearing woman in plaid Bermuda shorts.

"The bar is through there. Stiff drinks, and honestly—The. Best. I. Mean. Perfect. Lychee martini." Sally motioned to the left half of the hallway.

There were "yums" all around. I didn't know I was going to have FOMO for alcohol. But yep, I was feeling the aching longing. At least with coffee, I could have a splash, but definitely no wine or liquor for me for the next eight months plus breastfeeding.

"What's through this door?" I asked, and pointed to a wooden door to the left of the Pro Shop. It was the door I'd seen the blonde come out of.

"Stairs to the offices? I think it is for staff only. There's an elevator in the bar that most people use. But they take the brides up the double stairs for the wow factor. *Imagine the perfect photograph of you and your husband standing here with the sunset behind you.*" Sally used a mocking sugary tone.

"I have a feeling you own one of those?" Marie asked.

"Yes," Sally replied. "So cheesy."

"Me too," Pepper said. "I gave it to my mother. She loves it. Oklahoma weddings usually happen in barns. So my country club wedding in trendy Miami was quite *the thing*. Every time some celeb gets photographed on a yacht or caught at a South Beach club, Ma's quilt guild buddies ask if I was there. I mean, my life is *very* different than it was in Oklahoma, but I've yet to meet a celebrity."

"You're from Oklahoma?" Marie asked Pepper. "What brought you to Miami?"

"My husband's from here." Pepper's country twang was slipping out again. "Where are you from?"

I cringed slightly for my friend Marie. That innocent question was so laden with racism when it came from a white person. I'd been asked it plenty of times during my academic pursuits, and it was always code for *Why are you here? You don't belong.* But Marie handled it in her usual head-on way.

"From Haiti. My family came on a boat when I was a kid. There were sixty-five of us crammed onto a little fishing boat. It capsized during a storm three miles from shore. We could see the lights of Miami Beach as we clung to the boat's debris. But then sharks swarmed. They picked us off one by one. I watched my little brother, Jean Luc, get eaten by a tiger shark," Marie said.

Pepper and Sally gasped. Alma and I just looked at each other and tried not to giggle.

"Naaah. I'm joking. I'm from North Miami, but my parents are from Haiti." Marie winked at me.

"Nice add, the Jean Luc bit. Does he know you're telling people Jaws got him?" I asked.

"Pfft! In his version, I get torn apart by three sharks." Marie held up three fingers.

As we got closer to the kitchen, we could hear the banging of pots and pans, the hiss of steam from the industrial dishwashing, and a cacophony of voices. The words were distorted, but the volume was getting louder. An employee hurried out through the aluminum swinging doors and smack into our squad.

"Sorry," the man said. He gracefully spun and changed course to avoid our cluster. His kitchen whites were covered in orange-brown smears, like a souffle had exploded on him. We watched as he hurried to the bar. A moment later, he ran by us like a quarterback avoiding a linebacker, but instead of a football, he held a bottle.

"Amaretto?" I pondered.

"Cointreau," Pepper corrected.

"Hmm, yum. I love a sidecar," Sally said.

"I'm more of a margarita girl myself," Marie said.

"Margaritas don't have Cointreau in them, do they?" Alma asked.

"The original recipe does," Marie replied. "I took a mixology course at Johnson & Wales."

"Good to know. So I'm putting you in charge of making a signature drink for the gala," I said with a big grin at Marie.

"What?"

I nodded and patted her on the back.

"I guess that's what I get for opening my big mouth." Marie chuckled.

The cacophony of noises from the kitchen distilled into one baritone grumble, then something hit the bottom of the metal door. A cracked pumpkin rolled through the middle of the split doors and wobbled to a stop, propping one side open. A staff person with fear in his eyes looked out the porthole window. Through the gap the pumpkin had created, we could hear the rantings of the baritone voice.

Marie moved closer to the gap. She put a finger over her mouth to hush us. The voice was speaking in French. Suddenly, Marie backed away and, with arms wide, ushered us from the doors in time to avoid being hit by the explosive exit of the French chef. He gave our group a moment's scrutiny while straightening his tall white hat, then flourished a bottle of supermarket salad dressing at us and marched away. We all watched him open the stairwell door and vanish in a huff of what I was pretty sure was some grade A cussing. *Merde* sounded like *mierda*, so I knew that one, but I couldn't figure out *je m'en fous*. Marie translated it for us. The chef was mad as hell because carving jack-o'-lanterns was beneath him, as were the packaged condiments. He'd trained at the finest restaurants in Europe—fresh, seasonal, artisanal, and all that.

I poked my head in and looked at the kitchen. A row of pumpkins in varying degrees of dissection sat on the metal prep table in the center of the room. Half a dozen bedraggled staff were there. A tall, thin woman—named Beverly, if the large cursive embroidery on her chef's whites was to be believed—raked pumpkin guts from the metal prep table onto a tray. The others were frozen, like they'd just gotten a call from Ghostface.

Sally, Pepper, Alma, and Marie each looked at the kitchen from a safe distance before Sally led us through the bar to the elevator.

"I'm worried the chef is going to hate cooking a Caribbean menu for the gala," I said as the small elevator opened and we squeezed into it shoulder to shoulder. "He seems difficult."

There was a chorus of *uh-huh*s.

"Nah. All chefs are hotheads. Don't worry. Anyway, I think one of the staff is Haitian. He had a flag bandanna tied around his neck. Your menu will be safe with him," Marie said.

Bing.

The doors slid open, and we filed out. To the right was a terrace with outdoor dining tables and a small bar. A club employee was mopping the painted cement floor. The view of the greens was impressive. The golf carts on the paths reminded me of my son and his toy car track. Sally led us across the atrium into a carpeted suite of offices. A circular reception desk was ahead, and there was a gentle hum of activity despite there being no visible staff.

"If I remember correctly, the conference room is past the executive offices," Sally said.

"Can I help you?" a woman holding a mug of tea asked.

"We're with the Women's Club. We're looking for the conference room," Alma said.

"Oh, sure. Are you Marjory's daughter-in-law?" the ginger-headed lady asked.

"*Nooo.* Not me."

"Hi." I offered my hand. "I'm Miriam Quiñones-Smith. Marjory is my mother-in-law."

The forty-something woman set her tea at the front desk and shook my hand. "She told me you were Spanish." She smiled a receptionist smile, the kind where you don't quite know if it's genuine or fake. "Right this way."

She led us by several closed doors, one of which had a brass plaque that said GENERAL MANAGER on it, where the chef's bellowing baritone was seeping through the wooden door. Our guide sped up to move us away from what was clearly a heated argument happening in the office.

"Here we go." She showed us into a baby-blue boardroom with a long oval table. On it were silver pitchers of ice water sweating into black honeycomb coasters. There was a pad and pen at each place, along with a faceted drinking glass on a paper coaster. An arrangement of fresh flowers stood on the credenza next to a black phone. "Let me know if you need anything." She closed the door behind her.

"Okay. Let's get started, I guess." I placed Marjory's binder on the table and got my notebook from my purse. I flipped through the binder quickly. "Okay, this is a lot of information I don't need right now. Alma and Sally, you've been to the gala. What's it like?"

They each told me their impressions. Pepper added that she'd attended one a few years back and that the only thing good was the open bar.

"The band was worse than awful," Pepper said.

We brainstormed ideas on how to bring the event into the modern age. Pepper wanted a reggae band. *Too much. Too soon.* Sally suggested a band she'd heard at an Equality Dade fund raiser with a repertoire of Latin tunes and American pop. *Better.* Alma had already volunteered to take on the silent auction and the advertising tasks, so that was in the works. The ideas kept flying, and I wrote down each one, no matter how outlandish. *A photo station with parrots from Jungle Island. Pepper's idea.* But Marie's suggestion was brilliant, and it solved the issue of the chef, who I was positive would not like frying hundreds of tostones. She suggested we get food trucks to represent each island's cuisine. She knew of a Puerto Rican–themed truck, a

Jamaican one, a Cuban one, and of course, her Fritay All Day would handle the Haitian food.

"We can do samples, small plates like appetizers so that everyone gets to try everything," Marie said. "I bet I can find a few other trucks. I know someone that knows someone with a truck called The Flying Fish."

"Bajan cuisine?" I asked.

"Yes, from Barbados." Marie was about to continue talking but was stopped by the deafening clap of a door being slammed. A stream of French expletives followed.

The chef was on the move. Alma got up and cracked our door.

"Don't be nosy," I chastised her.

"Shh!" She gave me a *Shut up* look.

A figure lumbered by. As it crossed from view, Alma turned back to the squad. "I didn't know a person could turn that shade of red. He is *ma-a-ad*."

Through the crack in the door, we heard a woman's voice say, "Give me that." And then we all heard what could only be described as a bone-chilling thud. Alma rushed into the hall, the rest of us following like ducklings behind her. On the lobby floor, between the curved twin staircases, was the chef. It looked like he had fallen over the railing. A halo of blood pooled around his hatless head. Staff from the Pro Shop ran to the scene. They looked from the body to the group of us at the railing.

"Oh no, oh no. I can't get caught up in this. The police are going to come, and they will want to question everyone. I've got to be at the studio soon. I can't do this again," I said, and ran back to the conference room to gather my things.

I observed the ginger-haired receptionist leave the general manager's office, followed shortly afterward by my next-door neighbor.

"Mr. Nelson?" I asked.

He glanced at me as he walked by. His pace was controlled panic, and he looked haggard—nothing like the chill take-the-dog-for-a-jog man I was used to seeing.

"I'll get you out the back way. Come on." Sally grabbed my hand.

She took me down the elevator, through the bar, out the door the golfers used, past several parked carts, and onto a hedge-lined path that got me to the parking lot. Luckily, I'd self-parked and didn't have to retrieve my keys from the valet. I thanked Sally and apologized for deserting the squad.

"Don't worry. Go. It's like you were never here. I'll fill you in later." Sally blew me a kiss.

"This place is cursed! Every time I come here, someone dies." I started my Prius and clicked my safety belt. "Or maybe it's me that's cursed."

As I drove out of the club's parking lot, two police cars and a black SUV drove in. The driver of the SUV, Detective Pullman, looked directly at me as I went by.

"Oh no, it's me. *Definitely me.* I'm the one that's cursed."

Chapter Twelve

"Delvis, if I tell you what the last two days have been like, you would not believe me," I said. We were in a recording booth at the UnMundo network. I leaned back against the egg-crate foam on the wall and let out a breath.

"Chica, I told you we could do this tomorrow," Delvis replied.

"No! This is the only sanity in my life right now. I need this. Where's my script?"

Delvis handed me a pair of stapled pages. The voice-over I was there to record was basically an English translation of the Spanish but with some funny lines added by Delvis. She always encouraged me to improvise with any food history or cultural bits I wanted to add. The postproduction team could insert visuals to stretch the video to meet the audio time. They also liked to animate my avatar in the *Abuela Approved* logo. They'd have her sitting on the edge of the cooking pot or on whatever vegetable I was about to chop.

"How did the hurricane relief thing go?" Delvis sat on a stool with one foot on the floor and the other swinging. "Is it something we can tie into the show? I can ask the network to sponsor it. I'm pretty sure I can get it sin problema."

"I don't know. I don't know if I'm ever setting foot in that club again. Like I said, I've had a really bad couple of days."

"¿Qué pasó?"

"I'll tell you after we get this done." I pushed off the wall and got behind the microphone. Delvis went into the booth with the mixing board and monitors. By the third reading, I was in character and even threw in a few lines of food anthropology ad lib about the vegetables enslaved Africans had introduced into the Caribbean diet.

I told Delvis about the body count I was accumulating. She couldn't believe my bad luck any more than I could. She suggested I go to the botánica and get a despojo from the santero, which wasn't a bad idea. *Not a bad idea at all.* The shocked state of flight I'd been in was being replaced with the emotional reality of having seen another recently dead—*Dare I say fresh?*—human. Some spiritual counsel and an energy cleanse were an appropriate response. Baby Sirena needed a calm environment to grow in, not a fearful and anxious one. I left the recording room with every intention to go by the botánica, but the advertisement playing on the wall-mounted screen in the UnMundo lobby stopped me in my tracks.

¿Quieres una sonrisa brillante como diamante?

No pierdas un instante; llama al Doctor Blanco. ¡Hoy!

I couldn't believe my eyes. *Do you want a smile as bright as a diamond? I'll tell you what I want. I want to know why you aren't behind bars!* Dr. Blanco was Dr. Mario Fuentes. *How is he out of jail?* Like really! He'd been part of Juliet's cocaine smuggling enterprise. And he'd accelerated Elliot's death with his irresponsible herbal tea. I knew he wouldn't get prosecuted for murder, but I'd thought at least manslaughter and impersonating a medical doctor. And drug trafficking! *Come on!* There were boxes and boxes of cocaine in his office!

The address running across the bottom of the ad was not the same as his herbal apothecary's had been. I took a blurry screenshot and marched to my car. After I shot off a quick message to Pepper about picking Manny up a little later than planned, I backed out of my parking space and set off to find Dr. Blanco.

* * *

At the address, I found a freestanding cinder-block building with a chain link fence around the property's perimeter. It felt like one of those small used car lots minus the overpriced lemons and bunting. When I entered the address in the map app, it gave the business name Benny's Barrio Barato. That certainly sounded like a cheap car sales pitch. No other businesses around meant I had no excuses or subterfuge. I couldn't say I was in the area for something else.

Miriam, if you are going to do this, then just do it. Put on your big girl pants, mi'ja. I turned the Prius off and clicked the lock. As I walked through the open gate, a car pulled in and parked. A middle-aged woman and her twentysomething daughter got out. The younger woman dressed in a striped shorts-romper assured the older one that the procedure didn't hurt. I slowed my pace so they could enter before me. *Okay, this is good. I'm not alone.* I rummaged in my bag for a comb and pulled my wavy black hair out of its ponytail. Combing my hair into a center part gave me a different look. Not that it was the best disguise ever, but with the sunglasses, maybe it might take Dr. Fuentes a few minutes to remember my face. *Fuentes. Blanco. Whatever he was calling himself lately.* "I should just call him Dr. Con Man."

The interior was a light gray with a white laminated reception counter. I sank into one of the black faux-leather chairs and began reading the trifold brochure from the holder on the wall. It was the normal boasts and promises of pearly whites. There was an image of Dr. Blanco in protective eyewear holding an apparatus that looked like a checkout scanner but with a purple glow radiating from it instead of a red one. *It's him, no doubt. How is he out of jail?* He'd dyed his hair white, shaved the mustache, and fixed his teeth, but it was definitely the man I'd help catch.

The real Mario Fuentes was an actual dentist from Cuba. *At least he's not lying this time.* And gracias a La Caridad he'd straightened his crooked teeth. *Who would go to a dentist with snaggled teeth?* From what I'd learned of Fuentes's history from Jorge, his Cuban dentistry diploma didn't transfer to a license to practice in the States. Miami being the home for fraud, get-rich-quick schemes, and high beauty standards, he had easily reinvented himself as a plastic surgeon. That version of Fuentes had killed Jorge's friend Miz Fiyah in a butt lift procedure gone wrong. *He used caulking! What decent person injects bathroom caulk into a living being?* Fuentes had wiggled out of being prosecuted for that death. He'd then started his second bogus career as a medical doctor turned herbalist, which got Elliot and, in a roundabout way, Sunny killed. Now here he was in his third makeover. *I bet this is a scam. Two hundred ninety-nine for two treatments? He probably uses $17 drugstore whitening strips. No, he probably uses clear tape and bleach. I hope no one gets injured or dies.*

The receptionist called the pair of women into the procedure room. She took their cash payment first, of course. I'd learned all I could for the moment. It was crazy for me to be here. *Like what am I going to do, make a citizen's arrest? March him to the station and demand Detective Pullman lock him up? Again?*

"I'll ask Sally. If she doesn't know, then Drew will," I said as I slammed my car door. She knew most of the criminal lawyers and district attorneys in South Florida because of her legal advocacy work. I selected her number and hit the speaker icon.

"Hey, I was about to call you. They're just letting us leave," Sally said.

"You're still at the club? But we didn't see anything."

"I know, but Alma mentioned we'd looked into the kitchen and heard an argument."

"Ay, ay, ay, Alma."

"I'm afraid your name *was* mentioned. It couldn't be avoided. Sorry. So expect a visit from our friendly Coral Shores police. Are you still at the studio? Maybe stay there a little longer. I can get Manny if you need."

"I'm still in Hialeah, but I've finished recording. Don't worry about Manny. I'm sure Gabriela is watching him and Sophia. Anyway, that's not why I called. Have you heard anything about charges being dropped for Mario Fuentes?"

"What?" Sally's voice spiked.

"I was just at his *new* place of business. He's out of jail." I stopped at a red light.

"How is that possible? The evidence against him in the drug trafficking case is solid, according to the DA."

"I don't know, but he has a new con—teeth whitening. And a new name, Dr. Blanco."

"That's not right. Let me make a few calls and see what I can find out."

"That would be great. Thank you."

We said good-bye, and I called Alma.

"Dímelo cantando."

"I'm stopping at Vicky's Bakery. What do you want?" Vicky's was a Hialeah institute and the caterer for every backyard baby shower and birthday party. There was always a line of folks waiting to pick up their trays of croquetas, bocaditos, and pastelitos. But my favorite get when we visited the bakery was a señorita, also known as a Napoleon. I loved the contrasting textures of the thin mille-feuille puffed pastry sheets and the creamy custard layers. It was late in the day, and they were usually sold out by then, but my baby mermaid was hungry again, and this time it wasn't for seafood.

"Hmmm. Could you get me a flan? Whatever flavor looks good."

"Little one or big one?"

"Dos chiquitos, porfa," Alma said. "One for me and one for Ana."

"Okay, I'll see you pronto." I planned to drop the single-serve flans at her office on my way to Pepper's so I could find out what exactly Alma had said to Pullman before I had to face the music.

In the bakery, I took a number and amused myself looking at the brightly colored display cakes made of Styrofoam and dried meringue. Disney was well represented. But my all-time faves were the doll cakes. The ones made to look like a big quinceañera hooped skirt.

"Ciento tres," the attendant called.

I waved my ticket and handed it to her. She wrote my order on a green receipt, then repeated it to me.

"Dos flanes, una señorita, seis torticas de Morón, un jugo de naranja. ¿Algo más? Tenemos flan de calabaza."

She had me sold. I added two large pumpkin flans to my order—one for Robert and one for the Hallsteads. My husband loved the caramel-topped custard, and I wasn't going to have the time to bake this week. The buttery sugar cookies were for Manny and Sophia. Everyone was taken care of, including baby. I got the last señorita in the case.

I scarfed down the pastry before backing out of the space but slowly sipped the fresh orange juice as I drove the ten miles back to Coral Shores. Entering Alma's office with their treats in hand, I called out my BFF's name. She greeted me with a kiss and showed me to the signing room.

"Signing room?" I asked,

"Sí, where you sign the paperwork. Duh." Alma gave me a look to match. "You have something here." She pointed to her chin.

I touched my chin and found a smear of the icing that had decorated the top of my señorita. I licked my finger and smiled. "Mmm."

"Gross!"

"Not gross, yummy," I replied.

"What's yummy?" Ana entered the room.

"Flan. Here." I offered her the white bag. "There are spoons inside."

Ana's face lit up. The three of us sat at the glass-topped table. I waited until they'd each had a bite of flan, Cuba's take on crème brûlée, before I asked for details about the chef's death.

"Bien feo," Alma stated. "The EMT were there in seconds, but he'd lost too much blood. It was como un lago."

I imagined a lake of blood with a body on a blow-up float and shook my head to clear the gory image from it.

"And then the questions. So many questions. It wasn't like last time with Elliot. The detective had un montón de questions. Why were we there? What was our business with Sebi Malkov?"

"Who is Sebi Malkov?" I asked.

"The chef," Alma replied.

"But I thought he was French."

"Turns out he's Russian."

"Who's Russian?" Ana, who'd been focused on her phone, asked. She placed it screen down on the table. The Swarovski crystal–studded case caught the light and twinkled.

"The guy that died at the club," Alma said.

"I thought you said a guy from the kitchen died." There was an emotion in Ana's voice that wasn't quite worry but something akin to it. She took a bite of her flan, leaning over cautiously so that none of the caramel syrup would fall on her pastel outfit.

I remembered that I'd thought I'd seen Ana at the club. I hadn't seen the woman's face, only her blonde hair and tall, thin frame from the back. *Was the figure in the hall wearing a pink skirt? I don't remember.*

"*Yeah*, chefs work in kitchens," Alma said in her signature *duh* tone.

"Do you know him?" I asked.

"Miriam, no seas boba. Just because Ana is part Russian doesn't mean she knows every ruso in Miami." Alma wiped her mouth and folded the napkin into a tiny square.

"I dated a Sebi Malkov," Ana said.

Alma did a double take. "Ay Dios, do you think it is the same guy?"

Anastasia had picked up her phone again and was scrolling. She found what she was looking for and turned the screen toward us. "Is this him?"

The couple in the photograph looked like they were at a party and had just been told a joke. They had champagne flutes in their hands. The woman had her head thrown back laughing. She had black hair, but the angle obscured the details of her face. The man in the photo was looking directly at the camera. There was no doubt about his identity.

"Sí, that's him. Lo siento." Alma squeezed her assistant's forearm.

"I'm sorry too. Did you date a long time?" I asked.

"It took me a few dates to realize he was un comemierda." Ana used the Cuban catchall phrase for a crappy person. "Such a spoiled brat. His family buys him everything he wants. They have a house account with Versace. They are stupid rich."

I couldn't identify Ana's mood. She wasn't sad, but she wasn't gleeful. It was something in between, like maybe he'd gotten his just desserts.

Chapter Thirteen

After Alma's, I went to get Manny. Pepper was thankful for the flan. She told me her version of the police story. It was the same as Alma's, except she had photos.

"Pepper, I don't want to see a dead body," I said, pushing her phone away from me.

"Don't be gross. I would never do that! No, I took pictures of the crowd so you can catch the killer." Pepper put her hands on her hips. "Like on those true crime shows when they look at the crowd because the bad guy always returns to the scene of the crime to see his handiwork."

"What?"

"You are going to investigate like last time. Right?"

"Noooo." I shook my head in an exaggerated wag. "The chef is none of my business. The only reason I got involved last time was because they arrested Alma. I'm not going to stick my nose into this. No way."

"Okay, I hear you . . . um, but you were pretty good at it, sweetheart."

"Pepper, I was terrible at it. I got caught breaking and entering. I didn't put the pieces together until it was almost too late.

And now it looks like my meddling might have mucked up the whole case because Fuentes is out!"

"What?" Pepper's voice rose, as did her perfectly plucked eyebrows. "The man who killed my best friend is out of jail. Scot-free?"

"I don't know if he is out for good or just out on bail, but he is out, and he has another con going. Teeth whitening."

Pepper looked around the yard, then back to me. "Did you ask your brother-in-law about it? He'd know. Right?"

"I've asked Sally already, but she hasn't had time to get back to me. She has a lot of connections at the courthouse because of her advocacy job. She'll get an answer faster than Drew."

"Okay. But you're going to find out, right? I mean, he caused Elliot's death. I know she had liver disease, but that could have been treated. She didn't have to die at thirty-three." Tears swelled up in Pepper's eyes.

Sophia, with Manny two steps behind her, came up to us. "What's wrong, Mommy? Are you crying about *Nell-e-ot* again?" The almost five-year-old had great concern in her voice.

"No, honey." Pepper wiped her eye with a manicured finger. "Dust flew into my eye, that's all."

Her daughter looked at her with disbelief but proceeded with her mission anyway. "Can Manny stay for dinner?" the little girl asked with all the hope of a kid asking Santa for a real live unicorn.

Pepper and I exchanged microexpressions.

"No, sweetie, another time. Ms. *Key-known-es* and Manny have to go home to their house now. Don't worry. You'll see each other at school on Friday and then for Halloween too."

Our two preschoolers' moods lifted at the mention of the candy-laden holiday. I gave Manny a five-minute warning, then told Pepper I'd have them over for a family dinner next week.

"Back to the investigation," Pepper said. "You are going to look into it. I mean, it happened before our eyes."

"No. No, it didn't. What did we see? Nothing. We saw an angry man dash by a crack in the door, and then we heard a horrible noise. We didn't see him fall. He probably slipped on the marble." I put the strap of my purse back onto my shoulder.

"Come on, Miriam. You think he slipped on salad dressing? Someone had to have pushed him."

"None of my business." I shook my head at her. "Vamos, Manny." I motioned to him that it was time to go.

"I think it was someone from the kitchen. He *was* yelling at them."

"Gordon Ramsey yells at his kitchen staff all the time and he's still alive. Like Marie said, chefs run hot. Also, it's *none* of our business. And, like you said, salad dressing. He *did have* a bottle of vinaigrette." I gave her a peck on the check and thanked her for taking care of Manny so I could work.

On the short ride home, Manny told me about his and Sophia's plan to keep some of their Halloween candy for the Easter Bunny—so that the bunny would have enough candy for all the kids. I loved the way little kids thought.

Detective Pullman was in front of our house when we arrived. He got out of his car, greeted Manny with a high five, and gave me the *You thought you could avoid me* look.

"I didn't see anything," I said as I unlocked the front door.

"But you *were* there, *and* you left in a hurry. Not a good look, Ms. Mars." Pullman closed the door behind him.

Manny scampered off to his room. We heard Camo meow at him. She sounded happy to have her person returned.

"Have a seat." I motioned to the stools at the counter. "I have to prep dinner. So you'll have to interrogate me while I work."

"This is not an interrogation." He took a sip of the water I'd placed in front of him.

"Okay, if you say so." I dumped the cassava water, refilled the pot, set the burner to medium, and added three pinches of salt. "When a detective is waiting for me at my house, it sure feels like an interrogation."

"Veronica, I thought we were friends." Frank Pullman put his hand over his heart.

I sliced the onions for the mojito sauce. I poured a few tablespoons of olive oil into a bowl, added a heaping spoon of minced garlic, and threw in the onions. "Pass me two oranges, please." I pointed to the fruit basket on the dining table behind him.

"This one?" Pullman held up a smooth-skinned juice orange. "Or the sour ones?"

"Sour." I took the bumpy oranges and rolled them on the counter to make the squeezing easier. "So what do you want to know? For the record, I didn't see anything. Nada." I waved the knife in a ticktock. "I saw a figure run past our conference room door, and that is all I saw." I cut the oranges in half. With a fork to twist and loosen the juice, I squeezed the sour orange into the mixture.

"I'm more interested in what you *heard* in the kitchen." Pullman rested his arm on the counter.

"We heard yelling. Part of it was in French. The chef was not happy about carving pumpkins. The staff was quiet, and I got the feeling they were trying to lay low. Like he had these outbursts often."

"Was he threatening anyone in particular?"

"How should I know? My French is limited to food names and a few Kreyòl words. You know he's not even French. He's Russian. Such a poser," I said with a surprising amount of anger. Where was my mad mood coming from? Pregnancy hormones, maybe. I made a predinner appetizer of Gilda crackers, guava paste, and farmer's cheese. My mermaid was hangry.

"How do you know he's Russian?" Pullman assembled a cracker for himself. He hovered it in front of his mouth and waited for my answer.

"Anastasia told me. She dated him for a hot second." At that moment, Pullman took the first crunch. It was like a light bulb over my head popped on and then shorted out in a crackle. I'd just unintentionally put Ana into this mess. *How is he so good at making people say things they don't want to say? Carajo.* I took a play from his book and redirected the conversation. "How is Lois Pimpkin doing?"

He stared at me for a beat, then dusted his chin for crumbs. "She's in and out of consciousness. Still disoriented. They're running some blood tests. She might have ingested something. But she will be okay."

"Did she say why she was in our yard?" I cut a second onion.

"No." Pullman's no was quick and final. Which told me he was in cop mode and not sharing information. This also meant that he probably knew why she was in our yard, but he wouldn't share it with me. "Tell me about your neighbor, Mr. Nelson."

"I know more about his dog than I do about him." I took the rotisserie chicken from the fridge and began pulling the meat from it. "He moved in last month. The couple that sold the house were part of Marjory's set. I was happy to see them go. I swear they were spying on me and reporting my every move to my mother-in-law." The chicken carcass was all bones. I'd picked most of the meat from it. I rewrapped it and put it in the trash. "I only just found out he works at the country club today. He's like the manager or something."

"Hmmm."

He'd done it again. Pullman had given me no info, and I'd given him tons. But he'd probably already known about Mr. Nelson. *Right? Should I mention that the chef was probably yelling at Mr. Nelson right before his death? Nope. I'm not getting involved.*

"Babe, I'm home," Robert called as he entered the house.

"I'm in the kitchen with Detective Pullman," I called back to him.

"Detective." Roberto extended his hand to Pullman.

"Mr. Smith."

Robert put his work satchel on the dining room bench before coming into the kitchen to kiss me.

"Any word on Lois?" Robert asked.

"As I was telling your wife, Mrs. Pimpkin is still in the hospital, but it looks like she will recover."

"That's good to know. I ran into Paul today. He looked like he'd slept at the hospital. Poor guy." Robert pulled a stool out and sat.

"Did you see him at the Everglades site?" I asked.

"No. It was at a Chamber of Commerce lunch. The mayor and council were in attendance. I think Pimpkin Development is the lead bid for the country club redevelopment." Robert loosened his tie.

"Are they tearing the club down? I haven't heard anything about it." I noticed Detective Pullman paying close attention to our conversation. In the pot I was going to use for my chicken dish, pollo a la vaca frita, I started the onions caramelizing.

"Nah. They're building some cabanas by the pool, but the major build is a boutique hotel with views of the golf course. The club wants to be a new stop on the PGA circuit, and they have a silent investor with deep pockets helping it happen." Robert rocked his stool back on two legs, leaning his back against the wall for support. "I think that's why they hired Tim Nelson." He used his thumb to motion toward our neighbor while popping a broken cracker into his mouth.

"He doesn't seem like a golfer," I said. I put the shredded chicken in with the onion.

"I don't know about that, but I do know he's flipped some big resorts in the islands." Robert got up and went to the fridge. He held up a bottle of Heineken to Pullman with a *Will you join me?* expression.

The detective shook his head. "What else do you know about Mr. Tim Nelson?"

"Hmm. He's from Miami, but not a Coral Shores boy. He went to Ransom or Gulliver, I forget which, but I know he was the star of the tennis team. I think he even turned pro for a few years."

"Mami, tengo hambre," Manny cried. He had Camo in his arms and was walking through the living room toward us. "¡Papi!' He handed his kitten to Frank and gave his father a big hug.

Pullman petted the calico cat before depositing her onto the floor. "I'll let you all get on with your dinner. Thanks for your time. Sorry to intrude."

"You're not staying for dinner? You know my wife is an amazing cook, right?" Robert said with a smile.

"Oh, yes. I know all about *Abuela Approved.*" Pullman winked. "But my wife is also an excellent cook. And she is making my favorite tonight."

"What is it?" I asked.

"Ajiaco. Claudia will have my head if I miss her dinner." Pullman smoothed his tie.

"Smart man. Never tick off the chef," Roberto said, blowing a kiss in my direction.

"Especially if you live with them." Pullman chuckled as he headed to the door.

Chapter Fourteen

M anny skipped into the recreation center's day care. He was the oldest of the group at age four and a half. The young women that ran it loved him and were happy to see him.

"It's been a while," the young woman with the pixie cut said.

"I know. I know. But I'm back now."

"Good. Because we missed our best helper." She smiled at Manny, and he beamed it back to her. "Your son is so patient and sweet with the littler ones."

Well, he is going to need that skill before long. I rubbed a circle over my belly and then caught myself. I didn't know how much longer I could keep the pregnancy a secret. *Make that appointment, chica.* "Thank you. That is so nice to hear. Besos, mi amor." I blew a kiss to my son before walking down the hall to Jorge's Yoga with Showtunes. I loved his Mambo-cise class, both for the high-octane dance moves and for the excellent playlist. Jorge had the best taste in music. *Too bad his DJ career was thwarted by Juliet Pimpkin.*

But the idea of gyrating to salsa, reggaeton, and merengue made me think of my baby mermaid in a stormy ocean. That was why I'd thought I'd try Jorge's gentler exercise class. He'd billed it as stretching and gentle yoga but to Broadway tunes. *Yo no sé. Suena un poquito loco.* Also, I wanted to ask him about the company that managed the country club. If Pimpkin Development got the contract to build the boutique hotel, that meant Robert's environmental consulting firm might get hired, since Robert often worked with them. Jorge had worked for the same management company in Colombia. It was how he had finagled his work visa to come back to Miami after Juliet got him deported.

"Juliet," I steamed.

"Boca sucia. Don't say that name around me." Jorge's sweatpants were rolled to the hips. He wore a green *Wicked* T-shirt that had been altered into a racing T.

"Sorry. I was talking to myself." I put my bag in a cubby. "Pero actually, I kind of need to ask you about what happened to you after she—"

"Chica, the only thing that I want to talk about is that that *beach* is rotting in jail. Con ese fake doctor Fuentes." Jorge pressed play on a track from *Cats*, the one about being alone in the moonlight.

The chisme gene in me was strong, and I had to fight the urge to tell him the gossip that Fuentes was free and scamming again. *Miriam, stay on task. Find out about Nelson and the resort management company.* "I know. I don't like her either. Pero listen, I need to ask you about the resort you worked at in Colombia."

"You mean Chancletas?" Jorge touched his toes.

"It was called Chancletas, like Sandals? No me digas." I shook my head in bewilderment. "I'm amazed they haven't been sued."

"Ay, mi'ja, they were. Un montón de veces. But not because they stole and translated a name." Jorge swooped his arms in the air in a ballet move.

"Tell me!" I stepped closer.

"Well, there was the Canadian couple that got sick from bad booze. And then the guy that got left by the dive boat. Like in the water, with sharks y todo, for hours. Oh, and then the woman that walked in on the maid, she was actually a *you know*, using the room to *you know*."

"Wow. Really? I thought it was like a five-star hotel."

"It turned into one. Y gracias a Dios, they changed the name. Now it's called Solimar, and Shakira takes her kids there for vacation. Ay, no, not this song." Jorge skipped over the *Man of La Mancha* "Impossible Dream" song. He choose "Breathe" from *In the Heights*.

"So what happened? Did it change owners?"

"Sí y no. They got a new investor with a lot of money that needed to be washed. You know what I mean, right?"

I looked at him blankly.

"Hi, Maggie. Hi, Fred." Jorge waved his students into the room. "Pick a spot. We are starting on the floor today."

I grabbed a loaner yoga mat from the drying rack where they'd been disinfected with spray, placed it on the floor in the front row, and went back to my fact-finding mission. "Is the new investor Mr. Nelson?"

"Mister who?"

"Mr. Nelson. He's an executive at the club." I sat on the purple mat that smelled like Lysol.

"Maybe. Why?" Jorge asked me while acknowledging the folks entering the room.

"He's my neighbor."

"Después de clase," Jorge said. He gracefully stepped onto the raised platform in the front of the studio with an arabesque that got applause. "Everyone ready? Good. Feet together. Make a butterfly if you can. Good. Now bend to the side." The answer would definitely have to wait until after class. "On My Own" from *Les Misérables* was playing, and people were singing along, a practice that Jorge encouraged. "Singing is exercise for your lung muscles."

I didn't know half of the songs, but that was okay, because I enjoyed the movements, and the final meditation in dead man's pose was like a power nap. I felt great afterward. Gracias a La Caridad that the final song was an instrumental. The lady behind me was the opposite of pitch-perfect. As I waited for the class to disperse and for another chance to talk to Jorge in private, I checked my phone.

"Four voice mails." I went to the corner of the room, held the phone to one ear, and put a finger in the other. Three of them were short.

"Where are you?"

"Pick up!"

"Call me when you get this."

The last message was longer and more frantic.

"They arrested Ana! They arrested Ana! I can't believe this is happening again! Where are you? I need you. Por favor." Alma's voice was cracking. I knew she was near tears. I shot off a text to her.

@ rec center be home in five meet me there

I wrestled my bag from its cubby and signed Manny out of childcare. Alma arrived just as I was putting the key into the front door lock.

"I can't believe this is happening again." Alma's eyes were puffy. She kissed my son on his head and followed us into the house.

Manny ran to his room to find Camo.

"¿Mi'ja, qué pasó?" I asked.

Alma plopped onto the sofa. "We'd just gotten to the office. Ana was checking emails, and I was preparing an offer on the Sailfish and Palm Drive property. It's a lovely midcentury in need of a little TLC."

"Alma. I don't care about the house. Tell me about Ana."

"Sorry. Perdóname. Okay, mm, so I was on the computer when someone knocked on the door. Which you know was weird because, like, the door was open. Ana went to answer it. And I hear Robert's cousin say, 'Anastasia de Palma, please come with us.'"

"So, wait. Did they cuff her?"

Alma thought for a second. "No."

"So maybe she isn't under arrest. Maybe they just want to ask her a few questions about her ex-boyfriend."

"But she's not answering her phone!" Alma combed her hand through her hair and made a fist of dark locks.

"That doesn't mean she's been arrested," I said, trying to comfort her.

"Can you find out? Call Gordon."

I took a deep breath. I didn't want to abuse my family ties, but at the same time, my BFF was in emotional distress. "Okay."

Gordon replied to my *Is Ana under arrest?* text message instantly with good news but not the best news. *Not at this moment* left the window open for *But now she is*. Before Alma could read my screen, I blackened it.

"Let's have a tilo," I said.

We went into the kitchen, where I prepared two mugs of tea. Late October in Miami sometimes surprised its residents with a cool breeze, and since Manny wanted to play in his cottage, we took our drinks to the patio. I inspected the cottage to ensure Lois and the police hadn't left any surprises, then joined Alma. She looked exhausted and wired all at the same time.

"Don't worry. I'm sure it will all be okay," I said.

"But what if she's in jail?"

"She wasn't at the club. Right?

Alma nodded in agreement.

"So there's no way they can arrest her."

Alma gave me the *¿Tú eres estúpida?* look. She'd been arrested on false and planted evidence, so of course she was no longer naïve about *innocent until proven guilty.*

"Okay. Okay. Okay. I know. Pero cógelo suave. Until we hear otherwise, we have to assume it is only for questions."

We sipped our tea and watched Manny run around the backyard, collecting leaves. He informed us he was making a bed for el mapache. I didn't have the heart to tell him that our mysterious raccoon visitor was actually a drone.

"Oh, I forgot to tell you. I made you an appointment with my ob friend. Tomorrow at ten," Alma said.

"I could have done that."

"She's not taking new clients. She's doing it as a favor to me. There," she said, sending me the contact information.

I felt the phone buzz in my pocket but didn't look at it. A few seconds later, it vibrated again.

"Thanks. I need to go and probably would have dragged my feet another week or more."

"Yo sé. Chica, how long have I known you?" It was a rhetorical question. "I know you need a little push."

"Don't make me think about pushing!" I laughed.

"Chica, you did natural already. Maybe go with the epidural this time." She raised her eyebrows and chuckled.

My phone alerted again, and again I ignored it. There was no point getting my BFF in a tizzy when we'd just changed the subject.

"What color do you think I should paint the room?" I asked, hoping to keep her distracted.

"You can't decide that until you know if it is a girl or a boy."

"Porfa. Babies don't care." The phone buzzed in my pocket. I resisted the urge to check it. "I remember putting Manny in a super cute pink onesie that had red hearts and pandas." I moved my hand in a dismissive wave and clucked my tongue. "Come on, you visit all these ritzy houses. What's trending in nursery styles?"

"Muted gray and yellow."

We both made yuck faces. But mine stuck when I saw who was coming around the side of the house.

"Marjory." I forced a smile.

"I've been at the front door for fifteen minutes! I thought you got a new doorbell. Clearly, it's broken and needs to be fixed." My mother-in-law sat at the teak table with all the indignation of a slighted queen.

The only thing I needed to get fixed was the side gate lock. I should have looked at my phone the last time it vibrated. Then maybe I could have held the gate closed and avoided seeing my mother-in-law. Sigh.

"I'll check into it. So why are you here?"

"The gala, of course! It's less than two weeks away! I knew I shouldn't have trusted you with something this important," Marjory said.

Alma tensed, and I could tell she was about to come to my defense. I patted her arm to let her know I had it. If the last few months of living in the same town as my MIL had taught me anything, it was that I needed to stand up for myself more—especially when it came to Robert's judgmental, snobbish, and closet-racist mother. Truth be told, I'd glossed over the fact that we'd have barely two weeks to pull it together, but I wasn't going to let her know that.

"Don't worry, Marjory. We had an extremely productive meeting. All the details are ironed out. Even down to a signature drink and the band," I said.

"Did you not read my notes?" Marjory cocked her head and narrowed her eyes. "We've already hired the band."

"Yes, exactly." I smiled to cover my lie. Alma kicked me under the table to let me know she was taking over.

"And I have some incredible donations for the silent auction. A wine club subscription, a fishing charter to Bimini on a ninety-foot yacht, a private jet to NYC with a hotel room overlooking the Macy's Thanksgiving parade, matching Rolex watches, pet grooming for a year, a ski trip, VIP passes to Art Basel including the preparties, and a chef's table at the Bazaar."

"Oooo, I'd like to win that. That's José Andrés's restaurant on South Beach, right?" I asked.

"What about a Britto? We always have a Britto. His work is very popular with our ladies." Marjory wagged her finger.

"I'll follow up with him. I don't know if we will get a sculpture again this year, but I'm sure he will donate something." Alma smiled.

"I expect daily updates," Marjory said as she stood up from the teak chair. "Now where is my grandson, Douglas?"

I cringed. It was apparent she was using Manny's middle name just to annoy me. So I reciprocated. "Manuel," I called. "Manuelito. Manny." Manny stuck his head out his cottage window and then skipped over to hug his grandmother.

"Can you not keep his clothes clean?" Marjory hissed in my direction. The knees of Manny's pants were soiled.

"He's a child. Playing. In his own backyard," I said.

I love my husband. I love my husband. I am not going to kill his mother.

Manny scampered back to his imaginary play. And Marjory made her exit. I followed her through the house and disingenuously thanked her for her visit. On my way back to Alma, I checked my phone. Yes, one of the buzzes I'd ignored was for the doorbell camera, and one was the ob-gyn contact share. But there was also a reply from Gordon.

Does she have a lawyer?

My jaw dropped. I stepped out of the house, and Alma looked at me.

"¿Qué? What's wrong?" Alma asked.

"Um. Maybe we should call Drew."

"What do you mean? What do you know?" Alma shook me by the shoulders. I showed her the text exchange. "Ay Dios. No, no, no, no, no. Miriam, promise me you will help."

"Of course I'll help," I replied.

"You know, like last time. You have to find out the truth." Alma clamped her arms around me.

I felt like a clueless fluffy bunny trapped by a boa constrictor.

Chapter Fifteen

Luckily, Alma had houses to show. And to be honest, she needed the distraction. Her worrying wasn't going to get Ana freed. Besides, it seemed Ana already had a lawyer. We'd called my brother-in-law on Ana's behalf. Drew made a few inquiries and texted me that Anastasia de Palma already had representation.

After a breakdown of panic and waterworks, Alma finally left. I promised I'd look into *it*, but I didn't know what *it* was until I had more information. Had Ana been at the club that day? *Maybe.* Had she pushed the chef to his death? *Doesn't seem like her.* What if the whole thing was an accident? A lovers'— okay, ex-lovers'—argument that had gotten physical. *Maybe.*

Until I could talk to Ana face-to-face—and if she was in jail, that might not happen—I needed to concentrate on the things I had control of or rather needed to get control of, like the gala! I found the three-ring binder my MIL had given me and flipped through it while I made lunch. Skipping over the many pages of single-spaced Women's Club history filled with founding family names, I went to the event contract with the club.

"It's right there in bold print. How did I miss it?" I underlined the band name with my finger. A piece of pulp from the grapefruit I was cutting landed on the plastic report cover. As I wiped it off with a dishrag, I noticed the name Luxe & Leisure. "That has to be the country club's management company."

"What's a country club?" Manny asked.

"En español," I chided.

Manny repeated his question in Spanish. My reply was wacky but accurate. A country club was a day care for adults, but instead of Legos, story time, and snacks, they had golf, a bar, and a fancy restaurant. When he asked for clarification about what a bar was, I sat him at the table and told him to eat his fruit salad. I heated a plate of leftovers in the microwave, then divided the steaming malanga and pollo onto plates.

Before joining my son in the dining room, I shot off a text to Marie—*I need to talk to you about the food trucks*—and left my phone in the kitchen so I wouldn't be tempted to look at it. Meals together were a time to be *together*. I wanted to model good behavior for Manny. He didn't have any electronic devices at the moment, but Marjory had already promised him an iPad for his fifth birthday. I clenched my jaw as I remembered her words.

"It will improve his English."

Pick your battles, Miriam. And set the language to Spanish.

Manny ate the shredded chicken with his fingers, and we talked about plans for the afternoon. He wanted to play with Rae and Vana, but his cousins, who were one and two years older than him, had full-time school and after-school care. I suggested we go to the park later instead. After putting the dirty dishes in the dishwasher, I picked up my phone to see if Marie had responded. She had.

Come by. I'm at Pétion Park until 4 pm.

I figured the park was in North Miami or Little Haiti since it bore the name of Haiti's first president. I hoped it had a play set. There'd be a better chance of running into kids if we waited until after two PM, so I read Manny a story. To my surprise, he dozed off with Camo beside him. I wasn't going to look a nap-horse in the mouth. I gingerly closed the door to his room and took advantage of my gifted time. Flipping my notebook to a blank page, I made a priority list—ten days and counting. Looking through Marjory's event bible, I saw that the event was mostly boilerplate, thanks to it being an annual occurrence. The contract specified that the Women's Club had use of the entire bottom floor of the club: the bar and restaurant, the ballroom, and the Flamingo Room.

"Nope, that's not going to work. Too many ghosts."

Images of Sunny Weatherman getting defibrillated in the Flamingo Room flashed in my mind—followed by Chef Sebi Malkov bleeding on the lobby floor.

"Anyway, we need to be outside for the food trucks."

That would be the first thing on my to-do list: confirm with the club that we could hold the event outside. The area where I'd seen the golf carts parked would be perfect. It had the view of the tree and pond, and if it rained, the party could escape into the bar with its panoramic windows. "It will work great. We can put the silent auction in the bar." I scribbled a few more notes:

Confirm food trucks—Marie
Make the menu—me & Marie
Create signature drink—Marie
Check band—Pepper (with guidance)
Invitations and tickets—Sally
Contact the nonprofit—me

It dawned on me that I didn't know anything about Karib Kids, the charity that would be getting the funds raised by the gala. It sounded more like a preschool than a relief organization. *Why do people think it's cute to make the C a K? Stop confusing the children with bad spelling.* I found a pamphlet and what looked to be pages printed from a website in the event bible.

Karib Kids (complete with crayon-scribble font) was a non-profit based in Miami that provided direct funds and materials to grassroots groups in the Caribbean that focused on improving the lives of infants, mothers, and children. There was a picture of a woman in earthquake-rocked Haiti receiving a carton of Pedialyte. Another image showed boxes of books being delivered to a school with a blue tarp roof. The italics under it said it was a school in Puerto Rico. There was another photo of mothers in Carriacou receiving a bag of diapers and clothing. I flipped the brochure over and read the names of their board of directors. It was an impressive list of Miami CEOs and personalities.

"Ileana Ruiz!"

My boss was on the board. That sealed it. I needed to take Delvis up on her offer to ask UnMundo for sponsorship. I put that on my to-do list too. Scrutinizing the roster of names and companies supporting Karib Kids, I saw Luxe & Leisure. My curiosity was sparked. A quick internet search provided me with the resorts the company managed. Solimar, formerly known as Chancletas, was on the list as a well as Coral Shores Golf Club.

"Hmm, I guess the club is getting a name change."

I felt something brush my ankle, and then I heard the purring.

"Hola, Camo." I picked up the warm fluff ball and asked her if nap time was over. My answer came from her human. Manny barreled out of the bedroom hall and proclaimed it was time to go to the park.

Calypso, Corpses, and Cooking

A few minutes after I shoveled the event binder and my notebook into a canvas satchel, we left the house. Pétion Mini-Park was in Little Haiti in an area branding itself the Little River Cultural District. The gentrification of the area had gotten a lot of pushback, from what I'd heard. One of the *Miami Herald* articles I'd read had reported that all new businesses seeking permits had to hire thirty-five percent of their staff from the local neighborhood. *It should be one hundred.*

The park was small, as the name suggested, and egg shaped. At the point of the egg was a gated play area. On the wider part, a statue of the Haitian president stood on a coral block in the middle of a concrete circle with benches around it. Marie's food truck was on the park's edge, equidistant between the two. I heard a faint school dismissal bell from the K–5 a few blocks away. I hoped that meant a few kindergarteners would appear and Manny would have some playmates.

"What can I get for you? Oh, hi. You're Marie's friend." Jamal snapped his fingers, fumbling for my name.

"Miriam," I said.

"Q!" Marie turned toward the order window.

"Nice place to park the food truck," I said.

"It's decent. We get a lunch crowd if the weather is nice, and the kids come by after school to buy popsicles," Jamal said.

"Yo quiero," Manny peeped.

"What flavors do you have?" I asked.

"I make them myself—all fresh fruit and just a touch of sugar. Today, we have soursop, tamarind, and sorrel/coconut milk," Marie replied.

My stomach grumbled. It seemed my mermaid wanted a frozen treat too. "One tamarindo and one guanábana. I mean soursop," I said.

"I got you. I knew what you meant." Marie handed me a white conical on a wooden stick.

Manny bit into his, and his face lit up. When I tasted my tangy pop, I let out a *yum* too. While Manny and I indulged in the tropical flavors of Marie's craft-cicles, a line of kids in wacky outfits snaked into the park, each clutching or waving their two dollars. It was spirit week at Miami-Dade schools, and each day had a different theme. Today was crazy socks day.

An eight-year-old in blue Cookie Monster knee-highs ordered the half-red, half-white popsicle. It looked delicious and seemed popular with the kids. The deep burgundy red against the creamy coconut looked appropriately gory and fitting for Halloween. Sorrel, the sepal of the roselle hibiscus, was popular in Jamaica as a tea and a Christmas punch, but I'd never seen it used in a popsicle. I made a mental note that I should do an *Abuela Approved* episode on the dried pod in December.

"Hi, Dad. Hi, Mama," a girl in braids said.

Marie exited the truck to hug her daughter. Marie introduced me, and I asked Zora if she'd like to earn ten dollars babysitting Manny so I could talk to her mom. Marie gave me a *That's too much money* look.

"She's only ten," Marie whispered.

"It's fine. And I need to talk to you. Can you take a break?"

"Yeah. Jamal can handle the school crush." She winked at her husband.

I watched Zora and Manny enter the gated area and mount the swings. With my son in good hands, Marie and I sat on a bench to talk shop.

"So, good news/bad news. The gala is the Saturday after Halloween," I said.

"I know. I looked at the event bible." Marie crossed her legs and pushed her red sunglasses up her nose.

I scrunched my face. "I mean, it doesn't give us—well, you—a lot of time to get the food trucks, but on the good side, most everything else about the gala is already planned." I took the notebook from my canvas tote and opened it to a blank page. "So, who do we have? Fritay All Day making tostones—I mean bannann peze—with your fabulous pikliz. Good with you?"

"Wi," Maria replied, then took the pad and pen from me. "I talked to . . ." She wrote down the names of two other trucks. "I'll confirm the menu with them and their rates. Some ingredients are going to be more expensive than others. But the food truck business is all about adaptability and versatility, so I know my people will make it work. I'm guessing you want to do a lechon for the Cuban element? The caja china will be a nice spectacle. The guy I'm thinking of puts on a nice show of removing the pig from the cooking box and chopping it into servings with a cleaver."

I nodded that it was perfect. Ten minutes later we had the menu set. Marie made a few quick calls, and five of the seven trucks were locked in.

"Should we use the club kitchen for anything?" I asked. "Dessert?"

"With a dead chef, the kitchen might be out of order. I don't know." Marie grimaced.

"You said one of the staff was Haitian. No? Maybe we could work with him. And the contract states we have the entire club for the evening, including the waitstaff. This is a ritzy group. They will expect some passed hors d'oeuvres or something."

"Okay. Okay. What if the bannann peze is passed. The whole white-glove-and-silver-tray thing."

"Silver trays. Really?" I made a face.

"Q, you said ritzy."

"I know, but I was thinking more like service. These people like to be served. And I want them to be in a good mood so they bid high on the auction, you know. It is for a good cause."

"So trays with a plantain leaf on them and free-flowing rum. Oh, that reminds me. I know of a craft rum distiller. That will add some prestige."

"Cool." I watched as she jotted down the name and lamented that I would not get to taste the alcoholic concoction.

"What if we get the kitchen to do mini flans and espresso shots? They have the ovens and cooler space to handle that volume." Marie tapped the pen on her knee.

"That sounds good. We need to talk to the kitchen as soon as possible. Something had to have been planned or at least discussed before Juliet and her committee fizzled. No?"

"I agree. Let's go over there now. Jamal can close without me. And Zora can watch Manny a little longer." We went to talk to Marie's daughter. I doubled my kid-watching offer. And Marie cut her eyes at me and hissed, "Too much. You will spoil her."

"No. She needs to know that caregiving is a valuable service and is not free," I said.

We jumped in my car and got to the club in no time. As I entered the lobby, a chill ran up my spine, and my arms broke out in piel de gallina. The floor was glistening like it had just been waxed and buffed. There was no evidence that a man had died there yesterday.

"Shouldn't we have an appointment?" I asked Marie. I wanted to backtrack and do this another day. My stomach was queasy. And I didn't think it was the morning sickness that usually hit me in the afternoon. It was the reality of having had another brush with death. Someone had lost their life on that floor.

"Q, you okay?" Marie patted my back. "You look pale."

I walked along the edge of the room to avoid the spot where the chef had landed. "Yeah, I'm okay—just, you know, super weird to be here. Let's take the elevator."

We turned to the right and traced the path that Sally had taken us on yesterday. As we passed the staff stairwell where I thought I'd seen Ana, I looked at the ceiling to see if I spotted any security cameras. There were none. Marie stole a look into the kitchen via the porthole window.

"Quiet. It's probably staff meal break," she reported.

We walked through the bar, where a few middle-aged men were drinking beer and talking about birdies and bogeys. A white-haired man with a martini stared at us with menace. I knew the look meant *You don't belong here.* I threw my shoulders back and stood a little taller.

"Q, don't give him the satisfaction." Marie had, of course, felt it too.

The elevator opened, and we passed by the picture window.

"That's where I thought we could have a few of the food trucks." I pointed down at the line of parked golf carts.

"Might be a little tight for all seven trucks, but the rest can be in the parking lot. It will flow if we do it right."

"May I help you?" The receptionist looked like a J.Crew model in a green shirtdress.

"Oh, hello again. We were here the other day," I began. The receptionist nodded that she indeed knew who we were. "Who do we talk to about our event?"

"Valerie Thomas. She is the head of catering and events. Follow me, and I'll see if she is available."

We followed her to her circular desk and passed the general manager's office. The door was partially open, and curiosity got the better of me.

"Hi, neighbor," I said.

Mr. Nelson looked around his computer screen, recognized me, and stood. "Ms. Quiñones, what a pleasant surprise. What are you doing here?"

"I'm helping with the Women's Club gala. I didn't know you worked here." I did, but it served me to act airheaded. "Were you here the other day when that poor man slipped and fell? Awful. We were in the boardroom when it happened."

Mr. Nelson, who'd been about to come around his desk to greet me, sat suddenly instead. "Yes. I'm sorry about that. He was a troubled man. I hope it will not affect your opinion of the club."

"Troubled? Do you think he jumped?" I asked. The height was only fifteen or twenty feet. *If someone was going to kill themselves in a dramatic swan dive, wouldn't it be from a greater height?* "We did hear yelling right before it happened."

Mr. Nelson shifted in his ergonomic chair and resumed working on his computer.

"Oh, really? I'm sorry for the unpleasantness." He tilted his head to the side. "I trust the police to do their job. I wish I could chat longer, but"—he pointed to his screen—"I have a deadline."

"Of course. I apologize for the intrusion. We can catch up later, neighbor." I heard a nervous laugh as I turned from his doorway. Marie and the receptionist were waiting for me.

"Miss Thomas will see you now."

We were shown to the events and catering office. A dark-haired woman in her late thirties greeted us. The walls of her office were hung with photos of the club decorated for wedding receptions. Behind her desk was a shelved hutch with more framed photos. In one of them, I thought I saw Gordon.

"Is that Gordon Smith?" I pointed to the silver frame.

"Yes. Gordie's my cousin."

"Oh wow, so does that mean we're related?" I asked, then explained that Gordon was my husband's cousin as well.

"I'm from the poor side of the family." Valerie leaned in like it was a dirty secret. "My mother divorced and remarried. I grew up in Tampa but spent summers in Coral Shores."

"Speaking of family. We need to get back to ours." Marie raised her eyebrows at me.

I took the hint and got down to business. Valerie loved the food truck idea and assured us it wouldn't be a problem. She and Marie talked number of servers and plates and utensils. CSCC was going green. She gave us the option of using the club's white porcelain, or they could order biodegradable bamboo plates and bowls. Since people were walking around, I thought the bamboo would be lighter. Marie and Valerie agreed.

"Do you think the club kitchen could handle the dessert and coffee?" I asked. "We were thinking bite-size flan and Cuban espresso."

"That shouldn't be a problem. Let's go talk to Beverly right now," Valerie said, and motioned for us to come with her. She walked toward the grand staircase.

"Is there another route?" I asked. "We were here the other day when the guy—" I drew a swan dive in the air.

"Sure." Valarie led us to the staff stairwell.

"Actually, wasn't he the club's chef?" Marie asked. "Does that impact our event?"

"No, no. Chef Malkov had only been with us a few weeks. Beverly, the person we will speak to, has been the sous chef at the club for several years. She's great." Valerie looked over her shoulder at us as she reached the bottom of the stairs. "She was supposed to be the head chef, but the board of directors voted for Malkov." She opened the door to the hall.

"Voted?" I asked.

Valarie again leaned in conspiratorially. "A little nepotism, but his credentials were great. French trained. It would have been nepotism either way with both of them on the board. And Sebi was very talented." She pressed a knuckle to her lower eyelid.

Marie and I looked at each other with raised eyebrows.

"Here we are. Chef Beverly, do you have a minute?" Valarie brought us into the belly of the kitchen.

"Absolutely." A blonde woman in chef's whites emerged from a hole-in-the-wall office. "Is this for a wedding?"

Valarie introduced us and explained what we wanted. Chef Beverly hid her disappointment when she heard about the food trucks. She said she'd be happy to handle the desserts and suggested we have more than one offering.

"Do you know how to make dous makos? It's a Haitian fudge," Marie explained.

Beverly called for someone named Pierre, and the Haitian man Maire had identified last time appeared. He was carrying a bin of vegetables. After introductions, Marie took the reins and spoke to Pierre in Kreyòl. They had an animated conversation between themselves as Beverly and I discussed coffee. She told me the quality and temperature of the espresso would suffer due to the volume we needed. We compromised, and she agreed to order Café Yaucono, a Puerto Rican brand. It was a mellow, low-acid coffee with sweet, nutty tones. In reality, it was probably more in line with the palates of the gala attendees anyway.

"Pierre can handle the dous makos, no problem, and he suggested a few other bite-size desserts," Marie said. She told us they'd discussed gizzada (a spiced coconut pie from Jamaica), rum balls or rum cake, pone (a gooey baked cassava, pumpkin, coconut, and spice bar from Trinidad), and of course, the flan.

On our way back to the park, Marie filled me in on her conversation with Pierre. He'd said Chef Malkov had made the place a pressure cooker. The kitchen operated in English, but Malkov had insisted on giving orders in French. That wasn't a problem for Pierre, but the rest of the staff had been confused. Plates went out wrong. The produce and meat bill had tripled. Beverly and Malkov were constantly arguing.

"The kitchen calls her Beverly Hills," Marie said with a laugh.

"Why?" I pulled up to the curb behind Fritay All Day.

"You didn't notice the nails and perfect hair? Also the lipstick?" I had noticed the nails and a sparkling blue rock on her finger. "Working in a kitchen is hot and dirty, but she always looks like a movie star," Marie said, getting out of my car.

"Like Marilyn Manson," I said.

Marie laughed big. "I think you mean Marilyn *Monroe*."

"Oh yeah. Not the same. At least I didn't confuse the film star with the murderer, Charles Manson."

Chapter Sixteen

Fridays were my prep and practice day for *Abuela Approved*. But my schedule got derailed due to the doctor's appointment. After dropping Manny at Agape Montessori, I went to the obstetrician's office. The doctor, an Indian woman from Grand Cayman, was lovely. Dr. Singh did a sonogram and told me my mermaid was eleven or twelve weeks old. It would be another May birth for the Quiñones-Smith family. As soon as I got to my Prius, I blasted the AC and burst into happy tears. I held the grainy black-and-white sonogram photo; it was real. Sitting in my car on Coral Shores Boulevard with jitneys, bicyclists, and pedestrians passing by, I video called my mother.

"¿Niña, qué te pasa?" Mami asked. She was on the patio of the Punta Cana property that she and Papi managed.

"Nada, Mami. Todo está muy muy bien." I assured her everything was okay, and then I held up the sonogram picture.

My dad heard her screams and came running. For about five minutes, my parents and I rejoiced like we were physically together and not nine hundred miles apart. I sorely wished they hadn't moved away from Hialeah, but I was thankful we at least had technology that kept us connected. I told Mami to keep the secret a little while, as I wanted to be the one to tell Tía

Elba and Yoli. Plus I didn't want it out in the world yet because of my job.

I tucked the sonogram shot into the visor and headed home. When I got there, Alma was waiting for me.

"So how did it go? What did Dr. Singh say? Is it hembra o macho?"

"Too soon, but we can find out next visit. But honestly, it doesn't matter as long as the baby is healthy," I answered.

"Can we have a gender reveal party? Please, please, please, por favor." Alma made prayer hands.

"No, chica. No way. Those things are out of control. No gracias." I put the key into the front door lock.

"Okay, fine, be like that. Can I at least throw you a baby shower? I promise I'll make it gender neutral. Everything yellow like a rubber duck. Ooooo, that's a cute party theme." Alma was already on her phone searching for bathtub ducks. "Mira." She shoved the screen in my face. "¿Qué cute, no?" The floaty had a shell tiara and fish scales.

"A mermaid duck?" I chuckled and then remembered the photo was in the visor. "Carajo, I left it in the car."

"Super cute, no? And they have cowboy ones and princess ones and pirates and devils. Okay, no devils, but zebra and—"

Alma kept listing the varieties while I retrieved the sonogram picture. As I slammed the car door, Detective Pullman rolled to a stop in front of Mr. Nelson's house. A flutter of dread landed in my chest, but it was quickly displaced by an odd feeling of disappointment when Pullman ignored me and went directly to Mr. Nelson's house, not even looking my way. I slowed my pace and watched my neighbor answer the door. He had wet hair, and his pressed shirt was untucked. His dog Tom nosed Pullman for affection. While the dog's body language was relaxed and friendly, the two humans weren't as loose. Pullman was in cop mode, with a ramrod spine and an expressionless face. Nelson had fidgety hands that played with buttoning and unbuttoning his shirt collar.

"Good morning," I called to them loudly. The two turned to my voice. "Detective Pullman, you are welcome to drop by for café after you finish." He jutted his chin at me in acknowledgment. "You too, Mr. Nelson."

"Thank you, but I have to get to the office," Mr. Nelson said.

I watched as Nelson reluctantly gave Pullman entrance into his home.

Hmmm.

When I got inside my house, Alma was still rattling off the variety of rubber ducks available.

"What do you think about dinosaur ducks? That could be cute, no?" Alma moved to the edge of the chair and held her phone out for me to see.

"I know Manny would love it." I smiled. "I'm hungry. Do you want a smoothie?"

My BFF followed me to the kitchen and watched as I scooped the dark fire-orange meat from a mamey. I set the large single seed aside. If Mami were with me, she would tell me to plant it. I decided to put it on the windowsill by the sink until I found a pot.

"What's going on with Ana?' I asked. "You said she got a lawyer."

"Ay Dios, that is a crazy story. So, listen, she's there at the police station, and this guy shows up saying he is her lawyer."

"So, like, she didn't call him?" I plopped the fruit into the blender and got the can of condensed milk from the fridge. I added two glops from it and shook in some spices.

"No. She didn't even know him." Alma slammed her palm on the quartz counter. "He's the lawyer for this tycoon we've sold a few properties to. I told you about that, right? Ana has been helping me expand to the Sunny Isles and Aventura areas. Ella es candela. I wish she would get her real estate license already. For real."

I held my pointer finger up in a warning, then started the blender. When it finished whirling, I asked, "So what happened?"

"She played along. Whatever the lawyer said to them did the trick, because she was released."

"Pero, like, was she even under arrest?" I poured the thick shake into the glasses.

"No, they just wanted to ask her some question. Pero you know how that goes. First the questions, and then all of a sudden you are locked in your house with a cop guarding the door and your business is ruined."

"Cálmate." I waved my hand in the air. "You know that was all Juliet's doing. She's the one that made the anonymous call that got you arrested. Back to Ana. ¿Qué pasó?"

"They asked her some questions about her ex-boyfriend. You know, things like, *When was the last time you saw him? Did you argue? Where were you that morning?* And then"—Alma snapped her fingers—"like that, she was let go."

"What else did she tell you? Do they think she was involved?" I took another sip of the rich, ice cream–like drink. The vanilla extract, cloves, and cinnamon gave it a mild pumpkin pie flavor.

"I don't know. She went home and crashed. I gave her the day off today. Pobrecita. Being questioned by the policía is super scary." Alma made a *Been there, done that* face.

The door cam sounded. I didn't need to look at the notification to know who it was. "That's the detective. I invited him for coffee. He was at my neighbor's."

"Whyyy?"

"Don't be like that. He's not that bad. Also, he was probably coming over here after he finished there anyway. I mean, Lois Pimpkin was found in my yard with her head a mess." I started walking toward the front door. "Ay Caridad, I hope he's not here to tell me she died."

"I don't want to wish anybody dead, pero, like, she *is* the mother of that bruja that got me arrested. So, like, that evil had to come from somewhere." Alma got her bag and shadowed me.

"I hear you. But supposedly Juliet is exactly like Samford, her grandfather," I said with my hand on the door handle.

"Whatevs." Alma kissed my cheek, smiled politely at Frank, and skirted by him. She made the *Call me* sign behind his back and hurried to her car.

"Bienvenidos," I said, and welcomed him in. "Espresso or café con leche?"

"Con leche, please. You know this isn't a social call."

"I guessed. But I hope it's an update and not bad news." I packed the fine grains of the black coffee into the filter.

"Um. How is Ms. Diaz's assistant doing after the death of her friend?" He sat on the stool that Alma had just vacated. *Spooky. Was he picking up vibrations from our convo?*

"Detective Frank Pullman, I know your tricks. Out with it. Your update first."

"I can tell you we've recovered the images from the drone."

"Do they show who hit Lois Pimpkin over the head?" I poured a few drops of coffee into the sugar and made the paste that sweetened Cuban coffee.

"Yes and no." Pullman crossed his arms and leaned back a microfraction.

"You're having fun with this, aren't you?"

Frank laughed.

"Come on, out with it." I microwaved a mug of milk and glared at him until the oven beeped. "Come on. I thought I was your eyes and ears in the community. *And* it happened in my yard, so I think I have the right to know if there is a machete-wielding lunatic in my neighborhood."

"Machete-wielding lunatic. What led you to that, Jessica Fletcher?" Pullman narrowed his eyes.

I grumbled and narrowed my eyes at him in return.

"It was not a machete, but it was a blade. It appears the drone attacked Mrs. Pimpkin. Mmm, this is just what I needed."

I looked on with envy as he drank his Cuban cappuccino.

"That little helicopter toy knocked her out?" I poured myself a glass of water.

"Let's just say it didn't help matters. She was already suffering some confusion from toxicity. That might be why she attacked the drone with your water hose."

"What kind of toxicity? And what was a drone doing flying through my backyard in the middle of the night?"

"All good questions, Veronica." Pullman licked the milk foam from his lips.

"You are not going to tell me anything, are you?"

"Excellent deduction, Watson."

I grumbled and bit my tongue to hold back the string of Spanish cusses that wanted to fly at him.

"Thanks for the coffee and conversation. We should do this again soon." Pullman stood, pushed the tall chair under the counter, and began walking for the door.

I followed him all the way to his car with him refusing to say another word. He grinned at me as he drove away. I put my hands on my hips and growled. Tom, the Vizsla, barked.

Turning around, I saw the dog at his front door as Mr. Nelson was attempting to leave.

"Hi, neighbor," I said. He waved and shut the door. "Wild about the drone, right? I guess the mystery is solved."

Nelson looked at me like a startled animal. "Are you accusing me of something? I had nothing to do with what happened to Sebi."

¿Que qué? Where did that come from? Before I could find out what he meant, he'd started his car and backed out of his driveway.

Chapter Seventeen

I woke up when a cookbook slid off my chest and landed on the rug with a thud.

"Candy! Baby, don't eat all the candy," I shouted as I swam up from my dream. "Ay Caridad, what in the world was that?" Sirena, with a mermaid tail and all, was scarfing down caramelos that her older brother was dropping like bread crumbs. Manny was wearing my Chef Vampira costume, and he constantly had to push the too-big hat from his eyes.

"Candy! We don't have candy for Halloween." I looked at the time and realized I was late to pick up Manny from preschool. I texted Pepper. She replied that we'd already made those plans.

Duh. It's Friday. You are supposed to be prepping for the show, Miriam.

I removed Camo, my nap companion, from the orange pillow and straightened the sofa cushions. All evidence of my sloth erased, I freshened up and headed to the store. I texted Sally when I got to the store.

How many kids should we expect for Halloween?

200–300. We get kids from the neighboring villages sometimes.

I looked at my phone in shock. Sally's estimate was mind-boggling and wallet-emptying. Adding five more large variety bags of candy to the five already in my cart, I continued shopping for the caldo Gallego stew I was going to make for dinner. It would do double duty as practice and supper. The hearty stew contained cannellini beans, chorizo, smoked country bacon, potatoes, and a leafy green. Many recipes used spinach, but I preferred callaloo, the Caribbean spinach. Adding two bunches of the locally grown veg to my buggy, I went to the meat section and got the cured sausage and bacon. The cashier recognized me from *La Tacita* and asked for a selfie. I sometimes forgot I was celebrity adjacent and regretted not taking a little more care with my appearance. But I smiled and agreed. The clerk tagged the *Abuela Approved* social media handle, and before I had loaded the groceries in the car, Delvis messaged me with a starry-eyed emoji. She loved when fans found me in the wild.

At the house, there was a surprise waiting. Roberto's Tesla had just pulled up to our house.

"Mi amor, you're home early," I said. "Is everything okay?"

"Can't a guy take a half day off to spend with his wife? Here, give me those." Robert took the grocery bags from me.

"You have a golf date, don't you?" I looked at him with one eyebrow raise.

"*Babe.*" He smiled his wickedly handsome grin.

"Roberto." I matched his incredulous tone.

"Yes, but not for another hour." He set the shopping bags on the counter and embraced me. We kissed, and he gave my bum a little squeeze. "So tell me, what did the doctor say? Do you like him?"

"Her. And yes, I like her a lot. Oh, I have a picture!" I unwrapped Robert's arms from my waist and went to get the sonogram image. "I got a little emotional and called my mom right after the appointment. So she knows. Sorry, I know I said we'd wait until after twelve weeks and tell everyone at the same time, but I'm almost there. Probably eleven weeks." My voice was getting high and fast.

"Babe, she's your mom; of course you were excited. No worries." He kissed me on the forehead and stroked my back. "When are we going to tell my family?"

"Mami is the only one that knows—well, Mami y Papi. Let's get through this weekend, and then maybe we can plan a barbecue and let everyone know at the same time." I opened the fridge to put away the cold groceries. "I need to tell Tía and Yoli too. And figure out how to tell work. Can you go to the car and get the last bags?"

I took the biggest stockpot I had and dumped two candy bags into it. It would be cute to give out the treats, especially since my Chef Vampira costume would make a repeat appearance.

"Look who I found outside."

Robert's voice had a fake happiness to it. I peeked my head into the living room.

"Marjory," I said, and stopped myself from saying *Speak of the devil.* "To what do we owe the honor?"

Marjory pushed her sunglasses up and onto the top of her head. She crossed her arms and tapped her monogram-bedazzled toe like a musician counting time. "When were you going to tell me your little surprise?"

My stomach flip-flopped. Robert looked at me from behind his mother and mouthed, *I didn't say anything.*

"Food trucks!" she shouted.

I let out a sigh of relief. She was only there to berate me about the gala.

"Tacky, tacky, tacky. How dare you? I warned you. I knew." Marjory's toe-tapping became foot-stomping. She was practically foaming at the mouth. "I shouldn't have trusted you to handle the gala. What was I thinking, expecting taste and class from someone with your background?"

"Mother!" Robert said.

"It's all right, Roberto," I said. It wasn't, and I was glad my husband had finally come to my defense. He rarely heard or saw how Marjory treated me. But the *all right* was because I had it handled. I was tired of taking her insults. "Marjory, I'm very good at what I do. I've studied food and culture for years. I have a PhD. My *background* is exactly what the gala needs. Or did you mean my Cuban background? Or is it that my parents have to mop and clean for their money? It wasn't handed to them in an inheritance?" I unpacked the dry goods and used whatever was in my hand to punctuate my sentences with sound. "I am doing you and the Women's Club a favor. You want a younger crowd. The food trucks will bring them. You want a Caribbean menu. Each food truck will represent a different island. And if you haven't heard, the country club doesn't have a chef. So it is actually a stroke of genius to have the food trucks. Thank goodness my friend Marie had the brilliant idea."

"The hoity-toity Haitian woman that calls herself a chef. Yes, Beverly told me about her," Marjory said.

"You are calling my friend, whom you've never met, hoity-toity because she's a Black woman. And yes, she is a chef, a trained chef with a degree!"

Robert was speechless. He'd never seen me talk to his mother like that. I always held my tongue and played nice for the sake of peace and family tranquility.

"Marjory, I think it's time for you to leave." I shooed her toward the exit. "I will make this gala the highest-earning gala in Women's Club history. Karib Kids will get a big fat check. Like you said, it is for *my people*, after all." I slammed the door with her staring mean-eyed at me from the front step.

"Oh my god, that was the sexiest thing I've ever seen," Robert said. He put his hands on my cheeks and kissed me hard.

"Estás loco." I laughed. "Your mother is—"

"Difficult," he interrupted.

"I was going to say something else. Um, racist, classist."

"Classist, I'll give you. But racist? No." Robert shook his head. "She has a Black friend. The British ambassador to the Virgin Islands."

"Roberto, you are kidding me. I know she's your mom and you love her, but come on—" I was about to school him when the door cam sounded. I hoped it wasn't Marjory back for round two. "Gordon?" I kissed him on the cheek and invited him inside. "Is this social or work?"

He was in his bike uniform. "Both." He held up his water bottle. "I was hoping I could get a little ice."

"Of course." I took it, and we all went to the kitchen.

"Where's my buddy?" he asked.

"Over at Pepper's," I replied. I put several cubes in the American flag–decorated bottle and filled it with cold water.

"Ooo, what are you cooking?" He looked at the array of groceries and opened the lid of the stockpot. "Mmm, Crunch bars." He took one of the fun-sized treats.

"I'm making a bean and chorizo stew. You want to come back for dinner? Manny would love it."

"Yeah, cuz, come to dinner," Robert said, then went to change for his golf game.

"Okay. What time?" he asked.

"Seven. And bring Omarosa," I replied.

Gordon was straining to look out my kitchen window. "Can you see into your neighbor's property?"

I put a can of garbanzo beans on the shelf. "No, not from that window. You can see a little of his yard from the patio through the hedge. Why?"

"Do you ever hear any music or loud parties? How often does he have guests over? Do you see the same people coming and going?" Gordon was now at the French doors and looking out to the patio.

"What's this about? I'm not a nosy neighbor. I don't keep tabs on him. Is this about the drone and Lois? Should I be worried?" I smelled the head of garlic before putting it in the terracotta keeper. "Is Tim Nelson dangerous? He seems nice and kind of boring. His dog is the most interesting thing about him. Gordon, what are you not telling me?" Now curious, I looked out the kitchen window.

"Miriam, you know I can't share the details. Detective Pullman will have my badge."

"He came by for a coffee this morning right after he talked to Nelson."

"So you know the techs got some photos from the drone's memory card."

Is it a lie of omission to play along like I do? I mean, now I know. "Uh-huh, but I don't know the details."

"Let's just say they're *very* interesting. What's that saying? *Beware the quiet ones.*" Gordon came to the counter to get his water bottle.

I grabbed it first and held it behind my back. "Gordon, you can't say something like that and then walk away. I have a child in the house. Think about Manny. You want him to be safe."

"I'll be keeping my eye on Nelson. Don't worry. Look, I'm not supposed to tell you, but you're right. You have a small kid and another on the way. I guess it is a good thing you can't see into his house." *I never thought I'd be happy we don't have windows on the side of the house.* Gordon leaned closer and hushed his voice to a whisper. "You neighbor seems to have an alternative lifestyle. The drone images are X-rated."

Gordon didn't strike me as homophobic. I'd guessed Nelson was probably gay when I'd heard him call his dog Tom of Finland once. I hadn't known who the artist was until I was in college and a roommate took me to a gay nightclub. Since I'd been raised Catholic and pretty traditional, bare-chested men in leather weren't the prints on *my* bathroom walls, but to each their own. The posters made me laugh, but I didn't care who was gay or not gay.

"What do you mean? Gay is completely normal," I said.

"Not gay." Gordon's voice returned to a whisper. "Kinky. Like leather and studs and stuff."

"Really?" I couldn't picture mild-mannered Mr. Nelson acting out his Tom of Finland fantasies, and I didn't want to either. Our neighbor's private life was his business. I didn't care what went on between consenting adults behind closed doors.

"Yep." Gordon took the bottle from me. "And it seems the chef was into it too."

"Sebi Malkov?"

Gordon nodded. He held up three fingers. "It was a me-nod-gie."

His French was off, but I got what he meant. And it put a whole new spin on Chef Sebi's death. Maybe Ana was involved after all.

Is Ana into that stuff?
Did he have photos of her?
Was he blackmailing her?
Did she push him?

Chapter Eighteen

Roberto had arrived to dinner late, begging forgiveness. He swore it couldn't have been avoided. "I had to save the poor guy." According to my husband, Paul Pimpkin had had three too many whiskeys and had started making a scene at the club bar. Paul accused his father, Samford, of dirty dealings, stealing his daughter from him, and hating his wife. "Babe, it got ugly. Samford was almost taunting him. Saying stuff like 'You're better off without her' and 'She's a gold digger.' What kind of parent says that about their daughter-in-law?" I wanted to point out the irony, but Omarosa and Gordon were there, and my stew was ready to be served.

We had a nice dinner on the patio under the stars. I caught Gordon looking in my neighbor's direction more than once. Omarosa told us about their plans to bike the fifteen-mile Shark Valley Trail in the Everglades soon. My caldo Gallego was a hit. I'd used canned cannellini beans instead of soaked beans like I normally would, but it made the recipe easier for the busy home cook. Manny had a blast, and getting him wound down from the excitement took some patience. By the time Robert and I got the table cleaned up and our kid in bed, it was late.

I fell asleep as soon as my head hit the pillow. My body was making a whole other human, which took a lot of energy. It also seemed to be giving me *very* vivid dreams.

I woke up Halloween morning with images of Samford Pimpkin holding a whip, my neighbor on a dog leash, and Cyrillic letters spray-painted on the wall. It was like a bad fan art version of a Tom of Finland poster, and I wanted it scrubbed from my brain.

"Mami, levántate. Hoy es *trico tri,*" Manny squealed in my ear as he hugged me in bed.

According to Pepper, her daughter and my son had talked about nothing else yesterday. I blinked my eyes open and looked to my husband for rescue.

"My Spidey senses tell me it is going to be a *long* day," I said.

"All right, little man, let's give your mom some space. Come help me make breakfast," Robert said, pulling a pair of basketball shorts over his Star Wars boxers.

I motioned for Robert to come close. "Nothing sugary, please. Eggs and toast would be great." My stomach tossed and turned like a hurricane sea. "Maybe just toast for me." The morning sickness needed to end, and pronto.

After breakfast, I went to my study to work on recipes for upcoming shows while Roberto and Manny went to Target. Robert's Frankenstein costume didn't work without the neck bolts and green makeup. The outing was more about entertaining Manny for an hour than anything else. We both knew finding a costume on Halloween was a fool's errand.

I emailed Delvis the list of ingredients for Monday's taping and checked a few food anthropology sites and journals. A new book about Black foodways in the South piqued my interest, and I hit order before I could stop myself.

"We're back!" Robert called from the living room. "Babe, you will not believe the costume I scored. It is *perrrfecto*."

"Aww, look at you rolling your *r*'s like it's your first language." I stepped out of the study and kissed him. "Okay, so what is it?"

"Nope. Not until tonight. I want to surprise you." He held two bags busting at the seams with candy. By the door, there were several other bags of Halloween things on the floor.

"Okay, as long as it's nothing scary or gross," I said, eyeing a skeleton sculpture and a fuzzy tarantula leg escaping from the white-and-red bags.

"Cross my heart and hope to die." Robert made an X on his chest.

"Ay, ay, ay. Don't say that!" A chill ran through me.

"It's just an expression." He kissed my forehead. "Are you turning superstitious like your Tía Elba?"

"Ha. Ha. Ha." I looked at the time and realized it was earlier than I thought. "Mi amor, I think I'm going to go to the fitness center and catch a class. Too much candy temptation."

"No problema, babe. Manny and I have plenty to do."

I swapped sandals for sneakers and left. Jorge had classes back-to-back on Saturdays. If I didn't catch Yoga with Showtunes, I'd catch his Mambo-cise. The doctor had assured me salsa dancing wouldn't hurt the baby. Plus Gordon's revelation about Mr. Nelson and his kinky lifestyle was bugging me. Jorge had worked for the resort management company. Maybe he'd heard some gossip.

All the staff at the center were dressed for the holiday. A black cat was at the registration desk, a Thor and a Loki were in the weight room, and the kids' room attendants were all Disney princesses. To my surprise, Jorge was not in costume. Well, at least I thought so until he turned around and I saw he had on drag makeup.

"Chica, I'm so glad to see you. Espérate." He held his hand in a *stop* gesture. "You have to see the full effect. Close your eyes."

I did as he asked, and when I opened them, I saw Carmen Miranda. Jorge had tied a striped sarong over his shorts and put on a fruity turban. "Wow!"

"I know. Right? I call her Candy Miranda." He pointed to the taffy and Smarties glued amongst the bananas and grapes. "I had chocolate bars, pero they fell off."

"You know you are perpetuating a stereotype." The words were out of my mouth before I could stop them. I'd read a paper on the Brazilian actress who inspired the Chiquita banana mascot during my dissertation research. Her samba outfit and coquettish mannerisms cemented the stereotype of Latinas as spicy, exotic seductresses. A stereotype we are still fighting to this day.

"Mi'ja, drag is all about stereotypes to the extreme. We make fun of them. We flip them. We own them. We make them entertainment. You need to have a *RuPaul's Drag Race* marathon."

"Okay, I see your point. But you will admit that only works because you're Latino and gay. No? Like, I could *not* get away with it. If I wore that, I'd just look like a *hot mamacita* and get catcalls." I tilted my head and made duck lips.

"Tienes razón. So, what's your costume for tonight?" Jorge asked as he greeted a pair of women entering the room with a wave.

"Chef Vampira again. I know I'm not very creative, pero I don't have your makeup skills, mi'jo."

"You want me to do your makeup? I can come by before the party. I think it's on your block." Jorge clapped in excitement. "Y puedo ayudar con el tric-o-tri."

"¿Donde?" Sally had mentioned she and Drew were going to a big costume party, and I wondered if it was the same one. Jorge and Sally didn't exactly run in the same social circles.

"I'll text you," Jorge said, before calling the class to order.

We danced and sweated to Halloween-themed music. Most of it was in English, since Halloween isn't really a thing in Latin America and the Spanish-speaking Caribbean. A couple of the Spanish language songs were about witchcraft and love enchantments. My favorite was El Gran Combo's "Tú Me Hiciste Brujería." It never failed to get my shoulders and hips moving. It was a great workout, but I didn't accomplish my objective. *Does Jorge know anything about Tim Nelson and his proclivities?* Jorge was too busy to chat with me after class.

I was still singing and dancing when I walked into my house—*Bruja, bruja, brujita.*

"You're happy," Robert said. "Bruja—that's witch, right?"

"Yep. Ay Caridad, what have you done to Camo? Pobrecita." Poor little Camo was on the rug, trying to scratch off a pumpkin stem hat.

"Manny saw it at the store and begged me to buy it. I couldn't get the pumpkin part of it on her. I think it's a two-person job." Robert laughed. "She was not a happy cat."

"I bet. So when do the kids start ringing the doorbell?"

"Little kids start showing up about an hour before sunset. We should be done before eight or whenever the candy runs out," Robert said as he unwrapped a Hershey's Special Dark.

"At the rate you're going . . ." I let my words trail off.

"I'm eating for two," he said, putting his hand on his belly.

"Very funny. And that's my excuse, not yours." I snatched a Mr. Goodbar from the pot and savored the salty peanuts and sweet milk chocolate.

Robert did parent duty while I got a bit more research work done in the study, some of which wasn't food related. I spent almost an hour scrounging the internet for information about my neighbor. There were plenty of write-ups about him turning aging properties into five-star resorts. I found newspaper photos of him shaking hands with a government official at a resort in Cancún. The caption said the hotel had created a nature preserve on its property. There were more like that one. Nelson with a Jamaican fashion model in front of a backdrop for Appleton Estate, the rum brand that had sponsored the party. That was at a resort in Montego Bay, Jamaica. The worst thing to come up in the search was an unflattering shot of him in a Facebook post. He had red, dilated eyes and was being fed a forkful of lobster. Butter dripped from the morsel. The other images in the post were of food, cocktails, and what I guessed to be a chef's table dinner party.

So the guy likes good food.

I like good food.

Who doesn't like good food?

Was Chef Sebi's food bad?

Was Nelson punishing him for bad food?

What? Miriam, why did you go there?

I need to see the drone pictures for myself.

Chapter Nineteen

J orge arrived at four that afternoon with a rolling suitcase makeup studio.

"Didn't you say you had a costume party tonight?" I asked my clean-faced friend.

"Sí, pero I have time. I'll do my makeup after yours. Let's go, chica. You're a vampire. No?" Jorge opened his trunk of tricks.

While Manny and Robert kicked a neon-checkered fútbol in the backyard, Jorge made my golden-brown skin look sallow and gray. He did lowlights and highlights on my cheekbones and used a liquid liner to give me winged eyes.

"Okay. Go brush your teeth," Jorge said.

"¿Qué? Do I have bad breath?" I put my hand over my mouth and tried the smell test.

"Vete." He shooed me away.

When I came back, he was arranging a tube of dental glue and what looked like pointy acrylic nails on a tea towel.

"Are those fangs? And you are going to glue them to my teeth? Are they safe?"

Jorge rolled his eyes and told me to chill. He dried my canines and tried a few sizes. Once he had the right ones, he glued them on. After they dried, he applied a matte-purple, almost-black lipstick. He then held up a mirror for me to see his creature feature masterpiece.

"Wow. Jorge, this is *so good*. Like, increíble de verdad," I said.

Robert and Manny came in from outside.

"Babe, you look amazing."

"Scary!" Manny said. I gave him the *Speak in Spanish* look. "Espooky!"

I laughed and corrected him. "Aterrador. Muy aterrador."

While the boys changed into their top-secret costumes, I made mamey batidos for all of us. Between whirls of the blender, I asked Jorge about Nelson.

"Mira, there were always rumors about him. But I never saw anything with my own eyes. Y también, he was only at Chancletas a few weeks before I left. Everybody says he's tough pero nice. I mean, like, if you are not doing your job to his five-star standards, claro, you are going to get fired. Pero, like, he gave people chances to improve. You know?"

I took a slurp of the shake. Thanks to not being able to close my mouth entirely because of the fangs, half of it fell out of my mouth. I found a wide silicone straw so I could finish my fruity dinner.

"So you never heard anything about whips and leather?" I asked. I mean, it wasn't like that stuff was illegal, but it was, *you know*, kind of weird.

"Chica, leather es una subcultura gay. No es un big deal."

"What do you mean?"

"It's like biker," Jorge explained. "It's an aesthetic, you know. Like what you like. Like what you are attracted to. Like I bet you like David Chocarro y William Levy." He named two telenovela stars. "Y tambien Wilmer Valderrama y maybe un joven Benjamin Bratt como en *Miss Congeniality*. Am I right?"

"How did you know?" It was true. Bratt from the Sandra Bullock movies was cute.

"Because your husband has the same classic look. You like that macho-guapo look. It is what it is," Jorge said.

"Okay, so what aesthetic do you like?" I asked with sincere curiosity.

"Same." He smiled a wicked grin. "Your husband is yummy."

"I know! Right?" I tapped Jorge's arm.

"Are you ready for the big reveal?" Roberto called from the hallway. "Cover your eyes."

I heard two pairs of feet.

"Okay, now," Roberto said.

Jorge and I looked at each other and burst into laughter. My husband was a strip of bacon, and my son was a fried egg.

"Tell me this isn't the perfect match to your chef costume."

Jorge and I were still laughing, and Manny had caught the giggle bug too.

"You're a chef. We are breakfast. *Come on*, it's perfect," Robert looked like his feelings were hurt.

"Sí, mi amor. It's perfect," I soothed him.

"Yummy, bacon," Jorge said under his breath to me.

After Robert and Manny had their shakes, we took a few family photos, which I sent to Mami y Papi. About thirty minutes later, the doorbell began to ring. Jorge helped give out candy but then excused himself to start his transformation. He had been hired as entertainment for a cocktail party, and after his gig was over, he was going to South Beach for the real party.

I refilled the stockpot with candy six times. Up until that point, it had been families with little kids. Many of them were in coordinated costumes. I'd seen the Incredibles, a farmer with a family of cows, Galileo with twin stars, Marvel superheroes in varying configurations, Minions, *The Wizard of Oz*, and last but not least Sally, Drew, Rae, and Vana dressed as Toy Story characters. Sally was Little Bo Peep in a hoopskirt. Drew was Woody. Rae and Savanah were sheep.

"You look amazing!" I shouted as Sally and her family came up the walk. I'd brought a chair onto the front step so I didn't have to worry about Camo escaping every time I opened the door for a trick-or-treater.

"Thanks. So we'll pick up the girls by midnight. Okay?" Sally said.

"No problem. Robert set up a sheet in the backyard to watch a movie. Sophia is here too. I think Pepper and her husband are going to the same party as you all. So don't worry. The kids will have fun," I said.

"Slow down!" Andrew yelled at a car driving faster than a snail's crawl past my house. "There are kids in the street!"

The car pulled into Nelson's driveway. I couldn't see who got out of the car because the royal poinciana tree blocked my view. Robert, who'd taken Manny out to trick-or-treat earlier, had mentioned that Nelson's house had an honor bowl of candy—well, not a bowl but a storage tub. I'd assumed Nelson wasn't home.

"Where's Gordie when you need him?" Andrew looked around for his cousin. "Are those his lights down there?" He pointed to a police car with its flashers on parked in the crossroads. "I'm going to get him. That driver needs a ticket."

"Calm down, Drew. No harm done," Sally said. She took Rae and Vana through the house and came out the side gate.

I waved good-bye to my sister-in-law and brother-in-law. A draft of air conditioning hit me, and I turned to make sure Camo wasn't sneaking out the door.

"So, you like?" Jorge asked. His face was orangy-pink with lines of white. He had a bra with one green cup and one pink and a green plastic fringe skirt. "I call her Sue-She Sashay-mi."

My light bulb finally went on. "So, that's wasabi, and that's ginger?" I pointed to the Magic Sand and papier-mâché on his bra. His skirt also made sense. It was like the fake grass plate garnish. "Super, super creative. Wow."

We were interrupted by a tall grim reaper sans parents. I guessed the tweens and teens wave was starting. I asked Jorge to pass out candy while I ran into the house to use the bathroom and check on my brood. Camo was safely asleep and locked in the bathroom. Her pumpkin outfit was on the tile floor, where she'd scratched and wiggled out of it. Looking out the French doors, I saw that Robert was handling ringmaster duties by making shadow puppets on the white sheet he'd strung up.

Before I brought out the croquetas and fruit cups I'd prepared, I took a second to send Delvis the images Jorge had taken of me as Chef Vampira cutting a bloody steak. He'd insisted on props. The mermaid in my belly grumbled, and I ate one of the ham croquetas as I carried the tray to the backyard. Setting the food on the teak table, I noticed the lights were on at Nelson's house. Like always, the shrubbery and drawn curtains didn't let me see anything other than a glow. *How did the drone see into his house?*

Chapter Twenty

We were down to a handful of chocolates, but the trick-or-treating had pretty much stopped, except for an occasional teen. I didn't mind that their costumes were bad and hardly costumes at all. One girl dressed in cutoffs and a band T-shirt told me, "I'm a psychopath. They look just like everyone else." I laughed and threw a few bars into her plastic Publix bag. Teens were still kids and deserved some fun and free candy.

I left the stockpot on the front step for the stragglers and called it a night. Jorge was at my kitchen table repairing a press-on nail.

"Okay, chica, me tengo que ir. I'm supposed to be there at seven forty-five. Which house is this?" Jorge asked, holding his phone for me to read the DragStar message.

"That's next door. That's Nelson's house. Nelson hired you, and you didn't know?"

"Mi'ja, it's gig work. They send an address and a phone number, and I show up. This one asked for a food-themed personality. Any special requests cost two hundred fifty extra." He put on his green pumps and stood. "Can I leave my suitcase here?"

"Claro. Come on, I'll walk you over," I said.

Some witchy tweens were across the street with a cautious parent following behind at a distance. A few cars cruised by, stopping every few houses to let their kids out. The neighborhood was not deserted, but the main event had definitely passed. I noticed the car was no longer in Nelson's driveway. The tub of candy was empty except for a lone Tootsie Roll. I pushed the transparent container to the side and rang the doorbell. Tom barked, but no one came to answer the door.

"Do you hear that?" I put my ear to the blue-tinted hurricane glass door. "It sounds like someone is throwing up." A sound I had become too familiar with of late.

"Abre la puerta," Jorge said, pointing to the knob.

Tom, at the door, began whining. The Vizsla scratched at the metal doorframe.

"You think there's something wrong?" I asked.

"Open the door!" Jorge pushed my hesitant hand away and turned the handle.

Tom looked at me with his copper eyes and barked a loud and direct command. He then turned as if motioning for us to follow him. The house smelled of fresh herbs and baked fish. The dining room table was set with crystal goblets, black chargers, and purple blown-glass pumpkins. Mr. Nelson was prone on the terrazzo floor with foam at his mouth.

"¡Ay Dios! Jorge, call an ambulance. Go get the police," I said, pointing to the open front door. "Down the block. Go!"

Jorge's heels *tick-tick-tick*ed across the marble, and his green skirt flapped as he ran outside. Tom, the Vizsla, paced beside his owner.

"Mr. Nelson, stay with me. We are getting help." I wanted to turn him over or pat his back, but I stopped myself. In my mind, there was a neon sign flashing *Crime Scene*—complete with a flickering letter *C*.

"Che-ff," Nelson moaned.

"Yes, I'm here. What did you eat?"

"Che-ff."

"Help is on its way. Are you allergic to anything?" I asked but got another mumbled *che-ff* reply. Did he have a shellfish allergy? I'd smelled fish. Maybe the menu was seafood themed. But if you were allergic to crab, or mussels, or conch, why would you serve it? *It doesn't make sense.* "Do you have an EpiPen?"

"The ambulance is coming," Jorge said. He was at the door and fanning himself from his mission. "And the police too."

I heard a big engine and saw the red rescue vehicle through the open door. I stood from kneeling to give the first responders space. Gordon was the caboose. He looked in, saw me, and audibly sighed. I shrugged back at him. *I didn't ask for this.* The next person through the door would be Detective Pullman. Gordon turned, went down the steps, and took his post at the end of the walkway. Curious onlookers stopped to see what was going on.

I smelled burning. Nelson's house had an open design. The dining room was on the right, the living room on the left, and the kitchen was at the back of the space. A long island housed the stovetop, a prep area, and refrigerated drawers. It was a lot like the set of *Cocina Caribeña*, except where the stage had a backdrop, Nelson had cabinetry. I bent to see the oven's display and pressed off. Then I put on the silicon oven mitts and removed the smoking snapper.

"He warned me you were involved."

Straightening myself from stooping, I heard the voice before seeing the man. I kneed the oven door closed and placed the hot pan on the range. Pullman scratched the stubble on his square chin.

"I'm not involved!" I countered.

"Says the woman in the kitchen baking a fish." Pullman looked over at the medical team, then back to me. "Stay there. Don't touch anything."

The detective took out his phone and began recording the scene. He focused on Nelson, who was still moaning *Che-ff,* but with less ánimo. That meant he was fading. While Pullman videoed, I looked around the kitchen for any clue I could find as to what Nelson had eaten. The counter was spotless. The sink was dry. I'd been ordered not to touch anything, but tapping something with my shoe didn't count. The door to the trash silently slid open. On the surface were squeezed citrus hulls, white butcher paper—*probably from the fish*—and green-yellow peels that I couldn't identify. *Bell pepper, maybe. Is that a mussel shell?* I saw a smidgen of a shiny black convex surface. I looked for a wooden spoon or something I could use to move the refuse around. *Technically that wouldn't be touching.*

"What are you doing?" Pullman asked, walking toward me.

"Nothing." I looked at him across the counter. Behind him, the responders were taking a motionless Nelson out the door. Tom followed his owner. One of the rescuers told the dog it was going to be okay and to stay. Tom whined. "Come here, boy," I called to the dog. He looked from me to the stretcher and then back again like he was deciding what to do. Then he trotted over to me and sat by my feet with his body weight against my leg. "It's going to be okay, boy."

"Miriam, we'll need to fingerprint you." Pullman jutted his chin to me.

"Ay, ay, ay. Que enredo," Jorge said from the couch.

"And you too, hula girl."

"I'm not hula. I'm Sue-She Sashay-mi." Jorge pointed to his bra. "Wasabi and ginger."

"Clever." Pullman was being sincere, but it was hard to tell, since his cop-mode voice was monotone. "What's your legal name?"

"Jorge Trujillo."

"And why are you here with Ms. Quinoñes?"

"I was at her house. I did her makeup. It's good, no?"

Pullman appraised me with scrutiny. "Yes. But why are you here at this house?"

"He hired me."

"To do makeup?"

"No, to do a show."

"Mr. Nelson hired you to *entertain*."

I didn't like the innuendo. We were both going to get arrested for something if he kept talking.

"Detective, I think the dog needs to go out," I said. Tom hadn't moved from my side, and he'd given no indication that he needed to pee, but his tail thumped the floor at the word *out*. "Can I let him into the backyard?"

Pullman huffed. "No. You stay there. Come on, boy, show me out." The dog trotted down the hall to the back door. Pullman knew the way as well as the dog, and I remembered he'd been in the house the day Lois and the drone were found.

What's in those drone photos?

Focus, Miriam. He'll be back in a second.

With the silicone mitt still on my hand, I gently dug in the garbage. There was a paper napkin with the country club's crest on it. *Not unusual, since he works for the club.* There were cheese wrappers—goat and some other type. I tapped the refrigerated drawer with my knee, and it slid open. Inside were six stemless martini glasses filled with ceviche and a white pastry box with *Key Lime* written on it in green marker. I saw the cheese tray with grapes and a little jar of honey on the counter behind me. There were also six plates garnished with a tomato medley salad. *Did Nelson hire a caterer? Is that whose car was in the driveway?*

I heard voices and spun toward them. Three men and two women were on the front path, asking Gordon what was happening. Five plus Nelson was six. *The dinner party guests.* I didn't recognize any of them as Coral Shores faces, but that didn't mean they weren't. They were dressed nicely, and if the volume of their voices was any indication, they'd already had a few drinks.

"Where's Tim? Is this the right house?"

"He invited us to dinner."

"I'm hungry."

"Did the Uber leave? Call it back."

"Let's go to South Beach."

All of them talked at once and tried to get past Gordon and into the house. Gordon used his radio, and another officer quickly appeared. The officer shut the front door. The house got eerily quiet.

"Can I go now?" Jorge asked, after he'd examined his reflection in a wall-mounted mirror.

"No," Pullman replied from the hallway. Tom had been let out into the backyard. The detective came into the kitchen, observed the open drawers, and gave me a disapproving look. "What part of do not touch anything did you not understand?"

"I hit them with my knee by accident. These fancy kitchens are like that," I said.

"Humph." Pullman closed his eyes and pinched the bridge of his nose. "Miriam, tell me where I'm going to find your fingerprints."

I thought a second. "I turned off the oven. So definitely on the touch pad and in the silicone mitts."

"What about the front door? Was it open when you arrived?"

"I opened it, but it wasn't locked," Jorge said.

"I rang the doorbell. And then we heard gagging and the dog barking," I said.

"Tell me again why you two are here?" Pullman pointed his finger from Jorge to me.

Jorge explained that he'd been hired via the DragStar site. "I didn't know it was him. I get an address y nada mas."

"I walked him over. His stuff is at my house. You can come see. Actually, can I go home? I've got a backyard full of kids."

"Yes, I heard," Pullman said.

The crime scene techs arrived. They removed my silicone mitts and bagged them.

"Both of you, come with me," Pullman said.

We followed him out of Nelson's house and into my house. Gordon had been occupied with the dinner guests, but according to what he reported to Pullman as we passed him, names, addresses, numbers, and photos had been taken and an Uber was on its way.

"Stay here. Do not leave your property," Pullman said in my living room.

"It might be an allergic reaction. A lot of people don't know they are allergic to shellfish until they have severe reactions. I thought I saw mussel shells in the garbage. And there was a cold seafood salad. I thought it was ceviche, but it could have been conch. Conch is shellfish." *I'm rambling. Stop talking, Miriam.*

"For someone who doesn't know anything, you seem to know a lot, *Veronica*," Pullman said. "I'll be back to ask you some questions."

"Should we call a lawyer?" I asked.

"Are you guilty of anything?" Pullman raised one eyebrow.

"No, but I know how these things go," I replied.

Guilty until proven innocent.

Chapter Twenty-One

Pullman made good on his threat to return. He questioned us. Gordon questioned us. Wash.

Repeat.

Drew put an end to their questioning when he showed up to collect his girls. I mean, yes, he did his lawyer thing—*Gracias a La Caridad that I married into a family of legal eagles*—but better than that, he reminded us about the speed demon. I got my laptop, and all parties gathered around like it was the final episode of *Friends*.

"See, I was at my house giving out candy the whole time," I said.

"Okay. Fine. Stop there. Rewind. Rewind," Pullman said.

I chuckled. The late night and nerves had me *cuckoo for Cocoa Puffs*. I mumbled, "Be kind. Rewind."

Pullman threw me shade and replaced me with Gordon. The two stared at the frozen frame.

"I wish this was in color," Gordon lamented. "At least then I could narrow my search with the exact color of the car."

"Omarosa had it in her van, and it was a deal. Sorry. But at least we have video. Right?' I said.

"The car was silver," Drew said. "I remember it."

174

"I thought it was white," Sally said with a bit of a good-time-had-been-had slur.

"No, it was definitely silver," Drew said. "Driving like *The Fast and the Furious* with kids around."

"She was going a *little fast* but not reckless," Sally said from the couch. It had been her evening to let loose. She was a droopy-eyed drunk Little Bo Peep with a larger-than-life piece of sushi beside her. Jorge was on the couch scrolling through social media and whimpering every so often at the pictures of the party he was missing.

"She? The driver was a woman?" Pullman asked.

"She. He. I don't know, but it wasn't Vin Diesel." Sally laughed at her joke.

The door camera was blurry past the end of our pathway, and there was a sidewalk full of trick-or-treaters. It very well could have been a person in a clown costume for all that could be made out from the video.

"Does Mr. Nelson have one of these things?" Pullman asked.

Gordon shook his head no.

"No. He has Tom," I said. *What is wrong with you, Miriam? Not a time to be funny.* "Actually, what about Tom? Who's going to take care of Nelson's dog?"

Pullman looked into our backyard, where Robert and the kids were crashed out on pillows and blankets. A Pixar movie was projected onto the sheet. The face of a boy in a Cub Scout uniform wrinkled with an evening breeze.

"Thanks for volunteering," Pullman said.

"What?" I replied.

"Gordon, go get the dog for Ms. Quiñones."

"But we have a cat. And I don't know the first thing about dogs," I protested.

"Walk them twice a day and feed them twice a day," Pullman advised.

"For how long?"

"A dog that size needs a thirty-minute run, probably." He continued to scrutinize the image on my laptop.

"No. How long will we have to keep the dog? Is Nelson going to be okay?" I asked.

"Forty-eight hours, maybe. They've pumped his stomach, and they're flushing his system with IVs."

"So he's going to be okay. It was an allergic reaction. Right?"

Jorge, Sally, and Drew perked up and waited for Pullman's response.

Watch. All this drama and the questions will be for nothing. Just Pullman overreacting because—I didn't have a good explanation for why he'd overreact other than the fact that I had coincidentally been in the vicinity of another dead or near-dead body. Lois. Okay, there was that. Lois had been found comatose in my yard. And then there was the drone. That connected the two of them. *Is this connected? No, I'm sure it's shellfish.*

"It appears he has no known allergies." Pullman's statement filled the air in the room like the sound waves of a gong.

I rattled my head. "So he's talking?"

"Sir, I went ahead and brought the dog's bed. I hope that's okay," Gordon said, entering the house with a large faux-fur rectangular pillow. "Where do you want him, Miriam?"

I shrugged and pointed to the spot between the door to the study and the entryway table. Gordon undid the dog's leash. Tom accommodated himself on the bed with his head on his paws. He looked sadder than sad. *El pobrecito. Do dogs get depression?*

"Officer Smith, get a copy of this video. Let's see if we can ID the driver," Pullman said, pointing to my laptop. He moved to the living room, where he asked Sally and Drew to repeat what they remembered of the fast car.

Gordon sat at the table and inserted a thumb drive into the USB port of my laptop. I looked over his shoulder. A window popped up, and I noticed a file titled "Drone" was saved on the thumb drive.

"This is going to take a few minutes to download," Gordon said and excused himself to use the bathroom.

I slipped into his seat, stealthily made a copy of the drone file, and hid it in the desktop folder named Research. *Ay mi madre, Miriam, you just stole evidence.* I promised myself that I'd go to confession. *I am heartily sorry for having offended thee, but all of this is happening in my backyard! And I need to know what it is about for the safety of my family.*

It was almost one AM before all the invited—and uninvited— guests had left. Roberto took Tom out for a walk while I got Manny to bed. He was super excited to have a dog spending the night with us and begged for him to sleep in his room. Roberto and I postponed that discussion with a *Maybe tomorrow*. Camo, finally released from her locked room, zoomed around the house like she'd had twenty Red Bulls. Manny giggled at her acrobatics and speed. The calico fluff stopped midzoom to sniff Tom's bed. I had no idea if the two animals were going to get along. I hadn't been raised with house pets. Papi had had a pair of finches once. He'd kept them in a cage on the patio until one day we'd come outside to find only feathers and fur. So I knew birds and cats didn't go together. My worries were put aside when Roberto returned, and Tom patiently let Camo sniff and paw at him. I set up a bowl of water for our canine guest and prayed the lion and the wolf would be as peaceable as the Book of Isaiah promised.

"I hope Tim is okay," Robert said.

"He looks like he's settling in fine." I pointed to the dog being licked by the cat.

"Not Tom. Tim, our neighbor."

"It's late, sorry. Yes, I hope our neighbor, Tim, is okay."

Robert put his arms around my waist and kissed my neck. "Babe, you have got to be tired. Come on, let's go to bed already. The cleanup can wait until tomorrow."

I let him walk us—still in a hug—to the bedroom. When I went into the bathroom, my reflection scared me. I'd completely forgotten I still had vampire makeup on. It took half a pack of makeup remover wipes and a good bit of scrubbing to get back to my normal coloration. Roberto was snoring by the time I got into my nightshirt. *No, that's not him. It's me.* Baby was craving orange juice and chicharrones.

I sat at the dining room table with my glass of jugo de naranja and a bag of fried pork skin. My laptop was in the middle of the table, just out of reach. *Now's as good a time as any to look at that drone file, Miriam.* My inner voice wouldn't be quiet until I'd opened the computer and clicked on the folder. I recognized my backyard and roof, although I'd never seen it from twenty feet in the air. Next was an image of Lois pointing the garden hose at the drone. Then several close-ups of her forehead. *Ew, I guess that's when it attacked her.* I shifted in my chair to put my feet up on the side bench, and Tom raised his head in concern.

"Shh. It's okay, boy, go back to sleep," I said softly.

Tom let out a breath, and Camo woke. She stretched and then moseyed toward Manny's room. The dog then came to my side and put his head on my thigh. He looked at me with his greenish-brown eyes, and my heart broke a little.

"Your person will be back soon, don't worry."

I played the scene in my head again. We'd walked in and found Nelson on the floor. There had been gagging sounds, and there had been some vomit but not tons. *Was it an allergy, or did the driver of the car poison him with something? And why? Who would want to hurt him? Does it have anything to do with flipping the country club, or was it about something else?*

"What was your person into, Tom?" I asked the dog as I petted his flat head.

Going back to the file folder, I opened the numerically labeled images until I found the ones with Nelson in them. The shots were taken through the living room window. *Those curtains are never left open.* Nelson had moved in a month or so ago. I had been glad to get rid of the previous owners. They'd always been looking out their window whenever I came in or out the side door. I could have sworn they were spies for my MIL. When Nelson moved in, he'd replaced the blinds with curtains that stayed drawn. I'd noticed the change. *Did he leave them open for the drone?*

The images were not full frame because the curtain was only open at the window's top corner. I could see Sebi, the chef, Nelson, and a woman. All three were shirtless. *Are they dancing?* I selected the next image. The trio were laughing. The woman had a bottle of champagne that she was pouring into Sebi's mouth. The next images showed Sebi laid out on the dining room table in nothing but black latex boxers. His hands were under his head. *Does he have on oven mitts?* The woman was spraying whipped cream into his mouth. The final image in the folder was the oddest. Sebi had whipped-cream peaks all over his body, and the woman was devilishly wielding a whisk over the vulnerable chef. Nelson was in the shadows but looking directly at the camera.

It's like he expected the drone to be there.
It's like the scene was staged for the camera.
But why? Blackmail?
Is whipped cream that risqué?

Chapter
Twenty-Two

S unday morning, Robert made us a late breakfast. I loved our
outside kitchen and was thankful the weather was mild so
we could enjoy it. Manny and Tom played fetch in the yard. As
I crunched into a slice of crispy bacon, I remembered my vow
to go to church and confess my transgressions. I knew the priest
would tell me to say the rosary five times or something as my
penance. *I don't want to deal with Catholic guilt today.* What had
I done wrong? Nothing. *Miriam, taking something without asking is wrong.*

"Mi amor, I'm going to the church at Montessori today. Do
you want to come with us?"

"Babe, I've got a tee time. But next Sunday, I promise," Robert
said. He kissed my head and then cleared the dirty dishes.

On the way to Coral Shores Unitarian Universalist Congregation, Manny kept asking if he would see his classmates.

"No, mi príncipe, Gabriela y Sophia no van a estar."

He didn't quite get that the school and church were separate
things that shared the same grounds. I expected some of the
school families might be members of the church, but many of
them weren't. Pepper had been so bombed last night from the
grown-up party that she hadn't even gotten out of the car when

181

they came to get Sophia. It was eleven AM now; she probably wasn't even awake yet.

"Welcome to CSUUC," said a woman in a cotton dress with embroidered marigolds on it. "If you have a photograph for the Dia de los Muertos altar, you are welcome to put it there now. But there will also be a call to come up during the service."

She handed me an order of service that had José Posada's *La Calavera Catrina* and an apple with a Celtic knot on it. I'd learned that Unitarian Universalism was different than most churches I'd grown up with, but that was a bizarre cultural mash-up even for them, I thought. "The children go to their Religious Exploration class after the Story for All Ages."

Manny and I took our seats. Ms. Lucy was in the front of the sanctuary with her husband, the choir director. Manny wanted to go see her, but I told him he'd have to wait. He saw a few kids from the K–1 class and waved to them. A teen came down the aisle with a basket of crayons and offered Manny a coloring sheet of sugar skulls. I selected a variety of crayons from the basket and thanked the young person. The pianist began playing, and I opened the order of service to see what hymn we'd be singing. Apparently #51, "The Lady of the Seasons' Laughter."

"Sophia!" Manny squealed.

I turned and saw Pepper and her daughter in our row. Pepper had on dark glasses and was holding a framed picture.

"Hi. I didn't know you went to this church," I whispered to my friend.

"Every once in a while. I like that it's spiritual, not preachy," she said.

I noticed that it was Elliot in the picture frame and gave my friend a side hug. She was still in mourning over the sudden death of her BFF. Elliot had been in her first trimester when she died. A double loss, especially since she'd tried IVF so many times. A shiver went through me, and I asked La Caridad to protect the little sirena growing in me.

The song ended, and the reverend said some words, then lit an oil lamp that she called a chalice.

"It's time for the Story for All Ages. The young people are invited to come to the front," the reverend said.

My son squirmed in his seat and looked at me for permission to go.

"Sí, pero te tienes que quedar con Sophia," I told him. The two of them scurried to the front.

The lights dimmed, and Stormy Weatherman emerged from the shadows. The projection screen above the dais morphed from song lyrics to a bonfire. She was dressed like she had been at the Fall Festival, as a green witch. She sat on the top tier of the platform and asked the kids to sit in a circle before her.

"Tonight, when the sun sets, a very special holiday begins. It is called *Sow-win*. It is a time to honor our loved ones that have died," Stormy said.

I looked in the order of service and saw that the story was about Samhain, a pagan holiday. I'd seen the word but never heard the proper Gaelic pronunciation. Stormy talked about the symbolism of the bonfire and about the Irish tradition of burying an apple, a food offering for the departed.

I loved discovering food traditions that mirrored similar ones in other cultures. The Celtic pagan tradition of feeding the dead was not unlike the Mexican Dia de los Muertos practice of taking your relative's favorite meal to their grave site. The Japanese did something similar during the Buddhist Obon festival, where the ancestor altars were cleaned, then adorned with special foods. I'd grown up with Tía Elba symbolically feeding the orishas, so none of it was weird to me, but it certainly wasn't what I'd expected to witness at a church in conservative Coral Shores.

After Stormy's story, a children's procession song was sung a cappella. It was a single verse repeated. With the kids on their way to RE, which I guessed was the equivalent to Christian Sunday school, a more contemplative atmosphere settled on us. There was another song, but this time performed solely by the choir. I flipped to the back of the program and read the Unitarian Universalist principles. There were seven, and unlike the Ten Commandments, there was no *thou shalt not*. It was more *here are some goals and truths to make the world better for everyone*. The first one and the seventh resonated with me. *Respect the inherent worth and dignity of every human*. It made me think of Sebi Malkov. According to Ana, he had not been a nice or honest guy. But did that mean he'd deserved to die in such a violent way? *Did he slip on salad dressing? Or was he pushed? Who would push someone over a rail? And why?*

The seventh principle was about the interdependent web of existence. I immediately thought of a spiderweb: touch one string and all the others moved too. It was like the ripple effect of a stone thrown into calm water. No matter how bad a boyfriend Sebi had been, he was still someone's son, and his death would undoubtedly cause a hole in a parent's heart. His absence would cause other holes, too, like at the club. He'd been the head chef. That left a void that needed to be filled. Every team needed a leader. *Who will be their new chef? Maybe the sous chef that was promised the position in the first place.*

The dead-and-departed vibe of the service had me going down dark alleys in my mind. Pepper wiping a tear from her cheek pulled me back into the present. A short woman with sleek black hair and a rainbow kitten tattoo on her forearm spoke. She looked familiar. It took me a second, but I placed her eventually. She was a member of Jorge's LGBTQ group that met at CSUUC.

"Hello, everyone. Most of you know me as Letty, but my full name is Leticia Octavia de Salazar Guzman, and my grandparents are from Aguascalientes, the birthplace of José Guadalupe Posada. He is famous for *La Catrina*, the skeleton in the feathers-and-flowers hat on the cover of today's program. I visit them every year, but last year was the first time I'd been there for Dia de los Muertos."

Leticia talked us through a slide show from her visit. There were larger-than-life papier-mâché skeletons in a parade, an image of her family's graveside vigil, and a close-up of a plate of chicken in a red sauce.

"That's pollo San Marco. My abuelita makes hers with peaches, pears, and dried apricots. It also has a lot of cinnamon. It was my tío's favorite dish. That's why we made it. That's him."

The slide advanced to a picture of a happy guy sitting on the edge of a fountain in a plaza.

"He died in a motorcycle accident earlier that year. We all miss him. He was the fun uncle. I remember trying my first guava soda with him. That was his favorite drink después de la cerveza. I didn't think beer would be appropriate at church, so I brought a soda today to add to the altar."

She held up a bottle of pink Jarritos soda and placed it and a framed photograph on the altar. She pointed to the sugar skull she'd placed on the table earlier and held up a large round loaf of bread called pan de muerto.

"Thank you, Leticia," the reverend said. "We appreciate you sharing your culture with us and allowing us to celebrate our dead in such a beautiful way. And now, if you have a photograph or memory of a loved one you'd like to honor, please come up to the altar, light a candle, and say a few words if you feel so moved."

A line formed at the microphone. Some people spoke; others, like Pepper, just said the deceased's name and their relationship to them. I was surprised to see Valerie Thomas from the country club. She was Gordon's cousin. I remembered Valerie wasn't close with the Smith family—something about a divorce. *Whose photo did she put there?* The altar was crowded with picture frames, trinkets, and remembrances like a six-inch Eiffel Tower—"We honeymooned in Paris in 1973"—and lots of colorful but thorny bougainvillea stems. They were still in bloom, thanks to our hot South Florida climate. I couldn't make out who Valerie was honoring, and she hadn't gone to the mic.

After everyone had had their chance to speak, the pianist played an instrumental version of "Cielito Lindo." It was all I could do not to sing along. *Ay, ay, ay, ay, canta y no llores.* I wondered if all of CSUUC's services were as thoughtfully multicultural.

Pepper had removed her sunglasses, and although her eyes were red-rimmed from crying, she seemed to be lighter of spirit. I reached out and squeezed her hand.

The reverend made a few announcements, and then she asked Stormy to give the departure blessing. The first stanza was in Gaelic, which I didn't understand, but I guessed the second stanza was the translation. It was about the year's wheel turning from sun to shadow.

"The altar will be tended all week. You are welcome to retrieve the photographs of your loved ones now or next Sunday," the reverend said. "Today's vegetarian lunch is prepared by the social justice committee with proceeds going towards the restoration fund for Lincoln Memorial Park, the historic Black cemetery."

"Lunch? Are you staying for it?" I asked Pepper.

"Probably. I'm sure Sophia will be hungry."

"The kids. Where do we pick them up?"

"I can get them. They're usually playing outside or finishing up a craft. You get in line for lunch, and I'll meet you there." Pepper smiled and left the sanctuary.

The Dia de los Muertos table had a few people around it. I was curious to see the sugar skull up close and the photographs, especially Valerie's. *Am I being morbid? Un poquitito, a little.* The frame Valerie had held was silver. The altar had only two metal frames. One was of a man in his sixties on a boat showing off a large fish. The other was of Sebi Malkov. *That must be hers. But the other one could be her dad?* I thought back to our brief meeting the other day. She'd said Malkov was a nepotism hire. I'd gotten the vibe that she'd known him only a few weeks. Why would someone make the effort to memorialize someone they barely knew? People left flowers and teddy bears in spontaneous public memorials all the time—the kindness of strangers. Maybe Valerie was just a caring soul, a nice boss.

I got in line for lunch. Leticia was in front of me, and I struck up a conversation with her about pan de muerto. She'd baked individual buns to be served with hot chocolate as the lunch's dessert. The bread was a sweet dough flavored with orange-blossom water and decorated with bones formed from the bread. The tradition went back to the 1500s, and some said it was a Catholicization of a Mesoamerican amaranth-and-honey bread.

"Some people add sesame seeds on top or sprinkle it with sugar. But my abuela taught me to make it with anise," Leticia said.

"I can't wait to try it," I said.

"Dip it in the hot chocolate." Leticia made an expression that let me know it was more delicious that way.

Pepper and the children joined me just as our lunch was dished up. With plates in hand, we found a table and sat. The meal was colorful. I appreciated the fresh greens and yellow teardrop tomatoes. Manny and Sophia loved the honey-teriyaki tofu sticks.

"May I join you?" Stormy Weatherman asked.

"Of course," Pepper replied. She scooted over to make room.

"Your story was fascinating, especially the part about the apples," I said.

"Aw, yes. Well, you are a food historian." Stormy chuckled.

"Is that a pentagram?" Pepper asked about the star pendant around Stormy's neck.

"Uh-huh. After Sunny died, I decided to stop giving a da—" She glanced at the children. "I stopped pretending I cared what *good society* thought about me. I've embraced my pagan roots. I've even joined a coven." Still in green attire, she cackled.

Pepper's eyes widened, and she choked on a forkful of salad.

"Don't worry, darling. We aren't old hags with warts turning people into toads." Stormy took a sip of apple juice.

"What's a toad?" Manny asked.

"A big frog," Stormy answered.

"I want to be a frog," Sophia said. "Can you turn me into a frog?"

"Me too," Manny added.

"Ribbit, ribbit," the two said in unison.

"I seem to have misplaced my wand. But I can make dessert appear. Who wants dessert?"

There was another round of ribbits.

"I'll help you," I volunteered.

Stormy and I walked back to the lunch line. The main course had been cleared, and baskets of golden buns were in its place. The social justice folks were busy ladling hot cocoa into coffee cups. Hand-lettered labels denoted which grouping was cow's milk and which was almond milk. I used a plate as a tray for four cups and carried another in my hand. Stormy stacked the sweet buns into a pyramid on her plate. I noticed a new helper in the kitchen loading the washing machine. It was Valerie Thomas.

"Do you know Valerie?" I asked.

"I knew her when she was small. She and Sunny had a few playdates. After the divorce, we didn't see much of her," Stormy said.

"Did you know she works at the country club?"

"I'd heard." Stormy set the plate of bone-decorated rolls on the table. "She's a bright girl. In the short time she's been here"—Stormy fanned her fingers to illustrate that she meant CSUUC—"she's streamlined the hospitality program. They could never find enough volunteers to manage a full lunch, and now they have the next six months covered. She has a way with people. But I think she's searching for love in all the wrong places, know what I mean? It breaks my heart to see a young woman with such potential get turned around by a man."

"Who are you talking about?" Pepper asked.

"Valerie Thomas," I replied, before I parceled out the buns on napkins and gave everyone their hot cocoa. The bread was delicious, with just a hint of orange essence. It was hard to tell that the ridge on the crust was meant to be a femur. "Try dipping the bread in the hot chocolate like it's a churro."

"What's a churro?" Sophia asked.

"It's like a long doughnut originally from Spain," I told Manny's bestie.

"Valerie Thomas? That name sounds familiar," Pepper said. Her voice was far off, like she was talking to herself.

"Do you know her? She's the head of catering at the club. And another Smith cousin," I informed her.

"No. That's not how I know her." Pepper took a bite of bread and chewed. Her eyes looked to the heavens as she searched her brain for the information. "It will come to me. Do they have any coffee?"

"Always," Stormy told her. "Ask one of the lunch people. It will be shade-grown and fair-trade." She laughed.

"Ms. Weatherman, can I get you a cup?" Pepper asked. The green witch shook her head no. "Miriam?" Pepper put her hand on my shoulder.

"No, thank you. I'm enjoying the hot chocolate," I replied.

"I thought Cubans never said no to coffee," Pepper teased, and left us.

"Staying away from caffeine? Hmm." Stormy gave me a once-over. "I thought I felt two energies. When are you due?"

My eyes got big, and I puckered my lips into a *shh*. "Don't tell anyone. We aren't ready to announce it yet."

"Mum's the word. But you'd better hurry up. You'll start to show soon."

If Stormy had *felt* the baby's vibrations, then I knew Tía would too. *I need to see her today and get it over with.*

Pepper returned with a steaming mug of coffee. "I know where I know her from."

"Where?" I asked.

"I've met her twice. Once on a yacht and once at a meeting."
"And?"

"Nothing. She was nice. I got the feeling she was lonely. Her date had abandoned her, and she didn't know anyone at the party. Neither did I, actually. The host was one of Mike's business connections. Some Russian billionaire. Nice boat. *Awful people.*"

Chapter
Twenty-Three

S unday afternoon, I'd had the best intention to visit Tía Elba and spill the beans about baby, but my body had a different plan. Rest. I fell asleep reading about how dried codfish had become a staple in Caribbean cuisine. The preserved protein, called bacalao on Spanish-speaking islands and salt fish on the islands colonized by Britain, was a boon in the hot climate, where food spoiled quickly. The salt-cured white fish from the cold North Atlantic waters was a part of the slave trade. Ships from New England would cross to Cape Verde, purchase captured and enslaved human beings, sell them to plantations in the Caribbean, return north laden with spices, and then load their hulls with salted cod to sell to the sugar plantation owners to feed their enslaved African workforce. Sugar, spice, rum, cotton, and cod were all tainted with the blood, sweat, and tears of harsh labor and violence. I woke from my nap thinking about interconnectedness. Africa and its people were connected to the wealth of North America and to the foods we still ate.

Can I put that on the gala's menu?

The gala was only a week away, and there was so much left to nail down. *A walk will help me focus.* I put on my sneakers and grabbed Tom's leash.

"Mi amor, I'm going to take the dog for a walk," I said to Roberto as I looked into Manny's room. My two men were building with Duplo blocks. In bright primary colors, the construction site had a bulldozer, a crane, and a dump truck. Camo was in on it too. She was the demolition team.

"No problem, babe. When you come back, I have to tell you about my golf game," Robert said. "It was productive. I'm a shoo-in."

I distractedly said something affirming to my husband and started making a mental checklist of gala loose ends. Tom was easy to walk. He didn't pull or stop to smell every palm tree trunk, although he did whimper as we passed his house. *How is Nelson?* My mind began to wander back to the scene Jorge and I had walked in on. Nelson's fancy dinner party had nearly killed him. We'd probably gotten there in the nick of time. A few more minutes and he might have died. Scary. *Shake it off, Miriam, and focus on the gala.*

"Okay, I need to check in with Alma about the auction. Sally's doing ticket sales. Marie has got a handle on the food trucks. And I'll talk to Ileana tomorrow at UnMundo about the charity. What am I missing?" I looked at the Vizsla as if he'd answer me. "Pepper! Pepper is in charge of the music. I hope the calypso band is good."

"My son plays the drum. What you need a calypso band for?" a voice asked from behind a tree.

"Sorry. I talk to myself sometimes." I stopped, and Tom sat at my side.

Patricia Campbell stepped out from the tree's shadow. The Jamaican woman sucked air through her teeth and side-eyed the canine. "He bite?"

"I don't think so."

"Tall girl, see that red fruit up there. Can you reach it down for me?" She pointed to a single ripe ackee pod. "The last of the season. Let me hold him."

I passed the leash to her and stepped onto the lawn. On my tiptoes, I was able to pull the branch down enough to grab the fruit. "Here you go." She took the split-open fruit and dropped it into the bag she was carrying. "Are you going to use it with salt fish?" I thought about the article I'd just read.

"You like ackee and salt fish?"

"I've only had it once, and it was made with canned fruit." Patricia's expression told me she felt sorry for me. "But I liked it. I'd love to have a recipe for it. Would you show me how to make it?"

We made a plan for her to come to my house the next day. I had some cod that I could start rehydrating in the morning. It would be my contribution to the cooking date. She said she'd bring everything else.

"Likkle muore," Patricia said, waving and walking away.

"Where are you going? Isn't this Gillian's house?" I motioned to the two-story stucco house with barrel tiles.

"No."

I caught up with her. "That's not Gillian's tree?"

"You can't let good fruit go to rot." Patricia kept walking.

The unwritten rule for neighborhood fruit was that if it hung over the sidewalk or fence, it was fair game, but stepping onto someone's property was a no-no. I'd seen plenty of angry posts about it on the Around Town app. *Oh, great. That's all I need is a photo of me stealing fruit. I'd never hear the end of it from Marjory.* I chuckled at Patricia's nonchalant thievery. She was right. It was criminal to let good fruit go to waste. I bet the property owner didn't even know what they had. Ackee was not sold next to the apples and pears at Publix. Although it was sometimes called an apple.

Tom and I turned and went in the opposite direction. The late afternoon was turning to dusk. A good number of people were outside dismantling their Halloween decorations. I passed pleasantries with a few parents I recognized from Agape. When I got home to our still fully ghoulish house, Robert and Manny were on the patio. Manny saw me through the French doors and came running into the living room.

"Cierra tus ojos, Mami," Manny shouted. "Es una sopressa."

Tom barked at the excitement level. I undid his leash and closed my eyes as instructed. *I hope the surprise is supervised.*

"Hey, babe. Why do you have your eyes shut?"

I could feel the heat of Robert's body near me. "Manny says you have a surprise for me."

He laughed. "Open your eyes. The surprise isn't here yet." Robert put a finger over his mouth to shush Manny, but that just made our son more excitable.

I looked from one of them to the other. "¿Qué están jugando?" Neither would confess to what they had planned. Manny escorted me to the patio table. There were five places set. "¿Tenemos visita?"

Manny giggled but didn't tell me who was coming for dinner. *I hope it's not Marjory. Robert wouldn't do that to me. Right. Right?*

Robert poured me a glass of water from a pitcher on the table. It had lemon slices and mint leaves floating in it.

"Fancy," I said.

"Your son insisted. He's going to grow up to be a chef like you." Robert sat.

"I'm not a chef."

"Says the woman with a cooking show." Robert leaned across the corner of the table and kissed my cheek.

"I hope I still have the show after I tell them about . . ." I patted my abdomen. "You said you wanted to tell me something about your golf game."

"Yeah, babe. Pimpkin Development won the contract for the hotel. Paul told me today. We were on the tenth hole, and he was all like, 'Can you see it? Bubba Watson on that balcony and Tiger on the other.'"

"Bubba who?" I looked at my husband for a clue.

"He's won two Masters."

I shrugged and shook my head.

"The green jacket. Anyway, the point is the project is a go, and Paul is hiring me to do the environmental survey. I was a little worried after Paul and Samford's argument the other day that the whole thing would blow up, but thank God it didn't. This is my chance to show how a golf course can be green. The hotel will be LEED-certified, and I have an idea for recycling the gray water and capturing runoff so fertilizer doesn't get into the canal and out to the bay."

Robert was alit with the joy of a bright and better future. He always saw the positive and potential solutions to any problem. And golf was a significant environmental problem. I smiled as he rambled on about microenvirons and plants that filtered pollutants. When he finally stopped for a breath, I asked him about the Pimpkin father-son argument. I couldn't understand how Robert could work for a Pimpkin after everything that had gone down with Juliet. She, Paul's daughter and Samford's granddaughter, was a drug dealer. She'd tried to hook Sunny Weatherman on cocaine again, and it had killed her. What was that American saying? *The apple doesn't fall far from the tree.* But Robert swore Paul was a decent man who tried his best to distance himself from his father's Machiavellian ways.

"I don't know if Paul apologized to Samford or vice versa, but the whole thing seems to have calmed down."

"Isn't Juliet Samford's protégée? She's in jail for smuggling! If she is second in command at Pimpkin Global, don't you think Samford was in on the c-o-k-e?" I spelled it out since Manny was within earshot, and I didn't want him asking for a soda. That was a new thing for him.

"From what I've heard, Samford's hired a million-dollar legal team to prove that Juliet was under the spell of the herb doctor."

"Fuentes? He's a get-rich-quick scam artist. He is not the mastermind of a multinational smuggling operation. He's slimy but not that smart or ambitious. Juliet, on the other hand, is a conniving—" I let the unsaid hang in the air.

"I know. I know. I know. She's definitely not the Juliet I grew up with, but maybe she got caught up in something she couldn't get out of."

"*Roberto.*" I rolled my *r*'s and gave him a *You can't be serious* look.

"Fine. She's a criminal, but that doesn't mean her father and grandfather are. Samford's ruthless in business, and I don't like him, to be honest, but trust me, Paul and Samford's businesses are completely separate."

"Wait. Then why were you worried their argument was going to mess up the construction bid?"

"Because Samford is on the club's board."

My head was a whirlpool. Samford Pimpkin was on the Coral Shores Country Club's board of directors, and his son's company had been awarded a multimillion-dollar contract. *Nepotism much?* How was Robert not seeing the connection?

The doorbell rang, and an image popped up on my phone. It was Omarosa and Gordon carrying a pizza. Manny couldn't contain himself. I grabbed my phone, shot a quick video of his happy dance, and sent it to my parents.

"Hola," Gordon said. "Special delivery from Hialeah."

I saw the cartoon king logo on the boxes. "Rey's!" I kissed Omarosa. She looked different out of work clothes. She had on a red jersey dress and strappy espadrille heels. "I haven't had a Cuban pizza in years. Yum!"

We sat outside and divvied up the slices. One pizza had jamón y maduros and the other had picadillo. The Gouda-mozzarella cheese blend was golden and crispy at the edges. Manny sat next to Gordon and mimicked his every move. When his favorite relative took a bite, so did he. It was very cute. After Gordon and Omarosa told us about their bike ride through Shark Valley, Manny asked if he could go next time.

"Are there sharks?" Manny asked.

"No hay tiburones, pero si hay cocodrilos," Omarosa answered. She proceeded to tell us about the alligators they'd seen on the fifteen-mile trail through the Everglades. "There was one blocking the road that was longer than this table and big and fat, like he'd just chomp, chomp, chomped a kid." She made jaws from her hands and chomped at Manny. His pupils were black buttons, and I worried he might have nightmares. But his fear became laughter pretty quickly when the conversation turned to birds with spoons. Omarosa and Gordon had seen several roseate spoonbills feeding in the shallow waters along the edges. Omarosa took two spoons and made a bill from them.

I leaned over to Gordon. "She is so good with him."

"I know, she's great." Gordon beamed.

I began to collect the plates, and Gordon immediately stood to help me.

"I can get that, babe," said Roberto.

"No, mi amor. Gordon's helping, and I need to stretch my legs anyway."

A knowing look passed between my husband and his cousin. As if they actually knew anything about a pregnant lady's swollen ankles. "Omarosa, did you see any butterflies?" I asked to steer the conversation to Robert's pet project.

Gordon held the door for me. Tom, who'd been in the house during dinner, waited for permission to exit. "Go on, boy." The dog barked a thank-you, then went out to join the people.

"How's he doing? Does he get along with Camo?" Gordon asked.

I pointed to his dog bed. Camo was curled up, asleep in the middle of it like a little island in the big ocean. "They get along great. I had no idea dogs and cats could be friends." Gordon put the plates in the dishwasher, and I got down five bowls for ice cream. "Weird how quickly he's become part of the family, but I know he misses Nelson. He whines whenever he sees his house. How is Nelson doing?"

"He's still in the hospital, I guess," Gordon replied.

"You don't know? I thought you were working the case with Pullman."

"Yeah, but today was my day off."

I opened the freezer and got out the Valentini brand mamey ice cream. "What about Lois Pimpkin? Has she recovered?"

"She went home yesterday."

"Really?" I found the ice cream scoop and warmed it under hot water to make serving easier.

"Pullman didn't notify you?" Gordon held a bowl for me.

"No, I haven't heard a peep from anyone." I plopped two balls of reddish-orange ice cream into the green bowl.

"Yep, she's been discharged. She doesn't remember much about the incident. But you and Bobby have been cleared."

"Wait, what? Robert and I were *suspects*?" I used the rubber-handled utensil in my hand like a finger pointing from him to me and back again. A drop of ice cream flew off and landed on the floor. Camo, who was stretching herself awake, noticed and galloped over to clean it up.

"For like a second, Miriam. The injured lady had Robert's DNA on her." Gordon answered my confused look. "The Frankenstein bolt in her pocket."

"Oh, right. But why me?"

Gordon cleared his throat. "Well, you do have a tendency to be at the scene of crimes, *Veronica*."

"Ha, ha, ha. Don't you start too." *Great.* Pullman's nickname game was spreading to the rest of the force. "So what was it that caused Lois's coma? Did the drone hit her that hard?"

"No. It was cyanogenic glycol somethings. That's also what caused her confusion and weird behavior."

I added a sprig of mint to each bowl and a Marie cookie. "Do they know from what? I mean, that's like not a common thing." I knew that cyanogenic glycosides was a form of cyanide found in plants—apple seeds, bamboo, eucalyptus, flaxseed, peach pits, and yuca.

"Yeah. The tox report said it was from cassava. That's why you were a suspect."

"Huh?"

"You had a pot of it on your stove. Yuca is another word for cassava, right?"

I thought back to the day. I had had a pot of the root vegetable soaking, and Pullman had seen me dump the water. *Ay mi madre. Gracias a La Caridad that he didn't arrest me.*

"Yeah, they are the same. So wait, the doctors are saying she was poisoned over a few weeks. Like those old black-and-white movies where the nice old ladies poison the tea with arsenic until the houseguest is so frail they die, and then they bury the body in the backyard."

Gordon carried the tray of dessert, and we went to the patio. I looked at my backyard, and the green grass lawn morphed. I imagined rectangular mounds of dirt everywhere. I shook off the disturbing day-mare.

How and why did Lois Pimpkin get poisoned?

Did she do it herself, not knowing the root vegetable has to be soaked to leach the poison from it before cooking?

Lois doesn't seem the yuca con mojo type.

I doubt she watches Cocina Caribeña!

But maybe she should. I laughed to myself, but with every spoonful of ice cream, I began to wonder. *Are Lois and Nelson connected? Maybe it wasn't a seafood allergy after all.*

Chapter
Twenty-Four

I watched the closing segment of *La Tacita* from a makeup chair at the UnMundo studios. *Thank goodness I don't have to cook live.* Ileana Ruiz was such a pro. She made it look so natural, no one would guess she was reading off a teleprompter. Viviana, the makeup artist, brushed a rosy-brown tint onto my lips and shooed me out of the chair. I moved to the seen-better-days sofa to wait for Delvis to get me for our taping. The mustard-colored couch was a discarded set piece from a short-lived telenovela about a doctor and an alien called *Mi Amor de Dos Corazones.* The Spanish-speaking world was not ready for a sci-fi/soap opera mash-up. I laughed to myself, remembering Mami's reaction to it. She was okay with the alien having two hearts, but the "sangre azul y cuatro ojos. No gracias." The actor playing the alien was handsome, but when he was in character and removed his wig to reveal another set of eyes, he went from cute to freaky. And the blue blood bath during the open-heart surgery scene was more Quentin Tarantino than *Grey's Anatomy.*

Viviana kneed the leg of the sleeping late-show comedian. He was in his usual chair, and his legendary status—or possibly his advanced age—got him special treatment. That was *his* barber's chair, and no one else was allowed in it. When not on-screen, he was snoring in it in the makeup room. *I actually think he might live at the studio.* Viviana ran the cup of coffee under his nose, and he snorted to life. He opened one eye, drank the coffee in a single gulp, then leaned his head back on the rest. She patted his arm and said something to him, which got a roguish but closed-eyed grin in reply. Their relationship was intriguing. She was twenty-five or thirty years his junior. They were *not* an item, but there did seem to be some serious flirty energy around them. It was weird and captivating. It was like she was devoted to him.

I was so distracted by the real life May-December telenovela in front of me that I almost missed the news report on the screen above the mirrors. The sensational headline *Dentista Muerto en su Sillón de Examen* danced across the bottom of the screen. A still shoot of Fuentes's teeth whitening office was over the reporter's shoulder. I jumped from my seat, grabbed the remote, and turned the volume up. The anchor went to a live report from the scene. The young reporter in front of the camera looked a little like Amara La Negra but without the crown of natural hair. I was glad to see an Afro-Latina getting her chance. Reporters and talk show hosts tended to be on the lighter side of the skin tone spectrum because hundreds of years of European colonization had made pale skin and light eyes the beauty standard.

The reporter kept repeating that it was a developing story. When the dental assistants arrived to work, they'd found Dr. Mario Fuentes in an exam chair. He had on the dark glasses worn when operating the ultraviolet light wand, and a mouth guard filled with enamel bleach. It looked like he was giving himself a treatment, but when he didn't stir, they realized he was dead. The news camera moved and zoomed in on a pair of women crying. The station's anchor came back on-screen and told us the story would be updated at the next break.

"Y yo tenía una cita con él esta semana," Viviana said with a sigh.

It amazed me that people couldn't see through his sham. I couldn't believe Viviana had fallen for Fuentes's false promises and had made an appointment with him. There was no way his whitening process was natural or safe. *Just like his herbal teas.* Sure, the actual teas had been natural, but he'd been negligent in how he administered them. *And lest we forget he helped Juliet Pimpkin smuggle in tons of cocaine . . .* The man was a criminal.

"Ay, no. *No.*" *If Fuentes is dead, then who's going to testify against Juliet?*

"No, you're not ready for set?" Delvis asked.

"Huh?" I hadn't noticed her standing beside me.

"I asked, 'Are you ready to shoot?' and you said no. I can give you five minutes, but we need to stay on schedule." Delvis scratched the star tattoo on her elbow.

"That no wasn't for you. It was for—never mind. Let's go." I handed the remote to Viviana and followed Delvis to the *Cocina Caribeña* set. As we walked through the cavernous studio, all I could think about was that the queen-bee mean girl was going to get off scot-free. There was already the fear that her grandfather's money would buy her a very reduced sentence, but now with the main witness dead, the likelihood that her fancy lawyers would win the case was extremely high.

It was hard to ignore the gnawing in my stomach. Juliet was going to go unpunished. There would be no justice for Sunny Weatherman. Nor would Fuentes pay for his negligence in Elliot's or Miz Fiyah's deaths.

"Earth to Miriam." Delvis snapped her fingers.

I came down from the clouds and blinked myself into the moment. The food and other prep for the segment were on the kitchen set's counter. I'd been on autopilot and pulled everything out from the hidden, cold drawers and shelves. Now I had to focus on my job, not on Fuentes and Juliet.

"Sorry, I was thinking about something," I said.

"I could tell. Do you need five, or are you ready to start?" Delvis asked. I couldn't see her well in the inky shadows behind the camera and sound crew, but I could hear her tapping a pen. When I didn't answer immediately, she said, "Okay, It's time for a cafecito." She told her assistant to go on a coffee run. "What's going on, Miriam? You seem very distracted."

There were a number of legitimate reasons. The pregnancy. *Which I'm not telling them about yet.* Fuentes's death and all that that meant. *I can't believe that comemierda is dead.* Bodies were dropping all around me. *Lois and Nelson, to be specific.* And then there was the gala. *The gala is five days away!*

"I think it's the gala," I said.

"The hurricane relief thing? You never got back to me about that," Delvis said.

"I know. I know. There's just been a lot going on, and the gala is this weekend."

"Café." The assistant had returned with a small metal pitcher and a stack of plastic espresso cups that looked like thimbles for giants.

"¿Hay café?" Ileana Ruiz said from the darkness. The smell of Cuban coffee was powerful. *La Tacita's* host walked over to us.

The assistant poured a shot for the big boss and set one on the counter for me. I inhaled the aroma and let the sweet jet fuel touch my lips, but I only pretended to drink it. I stealthily threw it away in the hidden garbage can as if I'd finished it.

"¿Qué estás cocinando hoy?" she asked.

"Caldo Gallego," I replied. Now was my chance to talk to her about her charity and the gala. "Ileana, are you still on the board of Karib Kids?"

"Sí. ¿Por qué?"

"Well, I'm helping with the Coral Shores Women's Club annual gala, and your organization is the charity."

"I know. The board bought a table a few months ago. The tickets arrived yesterday."

Gracias a La Caridad that Sally was on the ball and the previous committee had kept good records.

"Pero wait. How are you involved?" Ileana asked.

"My suegra asked me to organize the food. The original person had to step down suddenly," I said. And then to myself, I added, *Because she is a drug-smuggling murderer and is sitting in jail.*

"Our *Cocina Caribeña* star is cooking for an event that benefits Caribbean children. Why am I just hearing about this now? Delvis!"

Oh, shoot. I didn't mean for Delvis to get in trouble. Delvis gave me a hard glare. "It's the first I'm hearing about it too. Miriam!"

Great. I had two sets of angry eyes staring at me. My underarms became waterfalls.

I fumbled through an apology, told them about the food trucks and calypso band, and mentioned that most of the planning had already been done before it was handed over to me to set the menu.

"Bueno, it's settled. Delvis, have her record a teaser for the event. Schedule your crew to be there. They can shoot the whole thing, and I'll make it a segment on the show. What celebrities are on the guest list?" Ileana put her hands on her hips.

"Um . . . um . . . I don't know. My sister-in-law is in charge of the tickets," I said.

"I can kick the Suarezes out of my table and replace them with Freddy and Lola." Ileana pointed her finger at Delvis, who was taking notes on her phone.

"Actually, there aren't table tables like at a normal fund raiser. We want people to go from truck to truck and to dance, of course. The event is outside."

"Perfecto. Get Wichie and Tatiana." They were the pro dancers from UnMundo's version of *Dancing With the Stars*. "Y tambien Dom y Estrella." They were judges from the wildly successful kids' talent show that was similar to *The Voice*. "Y check if Jorge Ramos is in town. He and Chiquinquirá can be my guests. No te preocupes, I'll call him myself." She pulled her phone from her pocket, and within two seconds she was talking to the Emmy award–winning news anchor. She stepped away but returned a moment later, disappointed. "He's interviewing Argentina's new president." She looked to the rafters. "Is Marc in town? He owes me a favor. Si no, then I'll call Enrique."

I looked at Delvis, and she mouthed, "Marc Anthony and Enrique Iglesias." My knees buckled at the thought of either of the two singers showing up to the gala. This was snowballing out of my control. *Will I need to get security? A-listers have their own bodyguards. Right?*

"Bueno." Ileana clapped her hands and smiled. "Save me some caldo. It's one of my favorites." She waved and left.

The filming went well. I spoke a little about the Galician origins of the stew. I explained that either canned or soaked white beans were fine but that a good-quality Spanish chorizo was important. And then I proceeded to nearly slice my fingers as I peeled the casing from the cured sausage. Ten minutes into the taping, the studio smelled of bacon. I added the paprika-colored chorizo, onions, garlic, bell pepper, bay leaf, parsley, water, and potatoes. I covered the pot and talked to the viewer about Spain's colonization of the Caribbean and how that had influenced many of our cooking flavors. When it came time to add the greens, I told them not to be too strict. Kale, Swiss chard, spinach, collard greens, and callaloo all worked well in the stew. The original recipe from Spain called for turnip greens because turnips were also in the original Gallaecian version. The cold-weather root veg didn't grow in the Caribbean, so it was left out of the Cuban version. I'd seen malanga substituted for the turnip, but that wasn't how I had learned it.

As I removed my stage makeup after the taping, I watched the news update on Fuentes. There was no sign of a break-in, and no cause of death had been released. The report was live from the scene. In the background, I saw a familiar face, Detective Frank Pullman. He stood outside the yellow-taped perimeter but conversed with a Hialeah police officer on the other side of the tape. Pullman looked toward the camera and squinted. *Freaky! It's like he knows I'm watching.* The police officer lifted the tape, and Pullman swooped under it and into the building.

Before leaving, I made sure a serving of the stew was delivered to la jefa, Ileana. Keeping the big boss happy was important.

"Be here Wednesday at one so we can shoot a teaser for the gala," Delvis said.

"No problem," I replied as I left her and UnMundo.

I'd planned to go by Yoli's café and tell her the baby news, but instead, I took a detour. The scene around Fuentes's office was bustling. UnMundo had apparently been first to the scene and gotten the prime inside-the-chain-link-fence spot. The other local stations, WSVN and WPLG, were on the sidewalk. I parked two blocks away and walked over.

Miriam, what do you think you are doing? This is none of your business.

I couldn't answer my own question other than to acknowledge that the scales of justice were teetering the wrong way, which made me mad. Snaking through the crowd of onlookers and television people, I found an open spot from which to watch the scene. A ten-by-ten canopy had been erected, and the doctor's staff were under it. The two women that had found him were still in shock. They sat in folding chairs and stared into the distance, twisting their empty water bottles like they were wringing dirty laundry.

I wished I could read lips. Pullman and a man in a suit came out of the white building. When one spoke, the other nodded, and vice versa. The man Frank was talking to had to be his Hialeah equivalent, another detective. I knew Detective Pullman didn't have jurisdiction outside Coral Shores. So why was he here? The same reason I was—there was something fishy about Fuentes's sudden death.

"Electrocution. Maybe Taser," said a voice from the news crew.

I moved a few steps closer to hear better.

"Is that official?" the WSVN report asked.

"Nope. Off the record from a junior officer. He's my girlfriend's little brother." The speaker, a beefy guy with a beard, got behind the camera and adjusted it.

I moved to avoid being in the WSVN shot and found myself beside the UnMundo van. The station's—my station's—reporter had just lowered her handheld mic. Her three-person crew quickly dismantled their setup, and all of them began walking my way.

"Miriam, right?" the reporter asked. "*Abuela Approved*. My daughter loves your show. She's nine and wants to be on *Top Chef*. Ella es candela," the proud mom said. "Did Ileana send you?" Her mood changed from friendly to territorial.

I wasn't quick enough to lie, so I went with the truth. Plus I didn't want to tick her off. I wanted information from her. "No, no, no. I just left the studio, and de verdad, I was curious." A white lie and an avenue to get her talking flowered in my brain. "I was here last week. Viviana mentioned my teeth looked yellow on camera, and she recommended this place."

"Viviana," she said with a smile and a roll of her eyes.

"But it doesn't look like my appointment is going to happen." I pointed to the scene.

"No, mi'ja, The doctor is out of business."

"Do you know what happened?"

"No, pero entre nosotros, I think he was killed. This was no accident."

I gasped. "What makes you say that?"

"One of the assistants told me he had been very jumpy lately. He'd told them not to take any patients with Russian accents." She raised an eyebrow. "¿Me permites un selfie?" She took out her cell phone, cocked her head to mine, and held the phone at arm's length.

"Claro," I said, and smiled.

"Mi hija is going to love and hate me. She's been begging me to introduce her to you."

"We have to make that happen. Maybe the two of you could be guests. We could cook her favorite dish or something."

We ended the conversation by exchanging phone numbers. I learned her name was Silvia and she was Dominican. She showed me a picture of her daughter with a mixing bowl. As

I walked away, I patted myself on the back. Delvis would be proud of me. Another opportunity to cross-promote our show. I'd made the offer sincerely. It wasn't just a quid pro quo, but I was thankful for the information I'd gotten. Mario Fuentes was worried about Russians. *Why?* What had he gotten himself into this time? Juliet and he had been importing from China, not Russia. *New business partner?* Every Cold War KGB stereotype came to mind. I envisioned torture—Fuentes tied to the dentist's chair and a man with a scarred face holding jumper cables. That's why I jolted out of my skin when I heard my name being called.

"Ms. Quiñones, stop right there."

I obeyed the detective's order.

"What are you doing here?"

This time a lie was on my tongue instantly. "I was on UnMundo business."

"Hmmm," Pullman said with disbelief.

"It's the truth. Silvia will confirm it." I crossed my fingers behind my back and hoped he wouldn't ask the reporter.

"Don't go sticking your nose in this. This has nothing to do with Juliet Pimpkin."

Why would he say that unless there was a connection?

"Ms. Quiñones." He narrowed his eyes at me.

"Detective Pullman."

"*Miriam.*"

"*Frank.*"

"Miriam Quiñones, I mean it. Stay out of this. I don't want to hear you've been arrested for breaking and entering. You aren't very good at it anyway."

"I don't know what you mean." A nervous laugh escaped. I'd have gotten away with breaking into Fuentes's herbal shop if my cell phone hadn't rung and if the rat hadn't scared me out of my hiding place, and if Alma, my getaway driver, hadn't been spotted. *Actually, Detective Pullman should be thanking me for leading him to the drugs and exposing Juliet and Fuentes's smuggling ring.* I was about to say something along those lines when my sirena announced *baby hungry.* Excusing my growling stomach, I promised he would not see me again.

Next time I'll be more careful and put my phone on silent.

Chapter Twenty-Five

I'd texted Yoli and had asked her to keep Tía Elba from leaving until I got there. The jingle-jangle peal of the café's door hitting the overhanging bell sent a wave of nostalgia through me. I'd loved my summer job at Tres Sillas back when it was Tía Elba y Tío José's. I loved the family homeyness of the chipped linoleum tiles by the threshold. Bette waved and pointed to Tía at the counter. Her short legs were dangling from the stool. There was a plate of ensalada de aguacate in front of her.

"Permiso," a voice behind me said.

I was blocking the entrance during the lunch rush. I was stalling. I had to get it over with. *Just rip off the Band-Aid, Miriam.* Stepping out of the way, I apologized and moved toward Tía.

"Hola, Tía." I kissed her.

She smiled, then pushed her plate toward me. "Eat. The aguacate is good for the baby."

My eyebrows moved to my hairline. "How did you know?"

"I know things." She tapped the plate with her short red fingernail.

I speared a piece of avocado. "Did Mami tell you?" The yellowish-green fruit was perfectly seasoned with olive oil, lime, salt, and a sprinkle of garlic powder. I took another forkful.

"Tuve un sueño. And then your mother called me."

As I'd suspected. Tía had a direct line to the woo-woo. I wondered what her dream had told her. Was I having a girl, a boy, or a mermaid? And, of course, Mami could not keep a secret.

"¿Cuándo ibas a decirme?" Tía asked.

"Today. That's why I'm here. I came to tell you the news."

She accepted my plea for forgiveness, jumped down from her seat, and began a litany of advice. I had to drink plenty of milk for strong bones. And I needed to wear a sweater. "Ponte un suéter." It didn't matter that it was still eighty-five degrees outside.

Plates were piling up in the pass-through window. Yoli poked her head out of the kitchen, looking for the restaurant's waitress. One of the customers had the woman in an earlock. Yoli took two ropa viejas and handed them to her mom. Tía delivered them to the appropriate tables and got the waitress's attention. Soon everyone in the café had their meals, which gave Yoli a moment to chat.

"So I hear we have a new addition to the family," Yoli said. "Que Dios te bendiga." Her blessing came with a kiss. Bette joined her in wishing me well. The three of us talked a little about dates. They didn't want to be on their honeymoon and miss the birth.

"I'm having another May baby, which, as long as she isn't late, means I might fit into a nonmaternity dress for your June wedding," I said as I bit into the spinach empanada Bette had served me.

"Mayo no. Abril." Tía refilled my water glass. "It's going to be a girl, and she will come early. Esa beba tiene prisa." She pursed her lips and nodded.

Tía's uncanny predictions were usually correct. So there was no arguing with her insistence that we go next door to the botánica for protective supplies. Tía was friendly with the santero that offered divination services at the store and arranged a quick consulta. The man said a few words in Yoruba, then requested my question to the orishas in Spanish. *I don't know. This is Tía's thing.* I decided to ask what every expectant parent wanted to know. Will my child be healthy? The santero threw the cowrie shells onto the grass mat. Some of them landed mouth-up and others mouth-down. There were something like 250 possible combinations from the sixteen shells. Diviners study for years to be able to interpret them.

"Sí y no," said the santero.

My heart pounded. His dark-brown finger pointed to a three-mouth-up-and-one-mouth-down combo. He explained that it meant mostly yes, but one had turned against the others. It was best to throw again.

The man spoke to the orishas in Yoruba and dropped the shells onto the mat again. It was the same combination. Neither Tía nor the santero was at ease. They exchanged looks.

"Dígame. Tell me. Is the baby okay?"

"Sí, por ahora. Pero debes tener cuidado." He gathered his tools and returned them to their vessels.

His words had me catastrophizing. *Safe for now, but I need to be careful. Careful of what?*

He and Tía agreed that I needed to come back for a longer, more thorough consult, possibly with the babalawo. In the meantime, I could help strengthen my ashé to Yemayá, the protector of mothers and children, by lighting a white candle and giving her ebbós—an offering of black-eyed peas, homemade mariquitas, or molasses. He advised me to pay attention to the preparation of the foods—to make the dish for the orisha and only for her. I left the botánica with an arsenal of protection—candles, oils, an abalone shell, and incense to burn in it.

The trip to the botánica had not been in my plan. Not only had it made me nervous about the baby's health, but it had also made me late. Pepper always did me the favor of taking Manny to her house on Mondays and Wednesdays to give me extra time on recording days, but I didn't want to abuse her kindness. And I had Patricia Campbell coming over to show me how to prepare ackee and salt fish. I zoomed back to Coral Shores, got my son, and got home with enough time to set up my altar.

I raised the wooden blinds in our bedroom to keep an eye on Tom and Manny in the backyard while I repurposed the floating shelf above the night table. I took down the framed photographs. The one of my maternal grandparents was faded. It had been taken on the patio of their house in Cuba last time I saw them in person. I was a teen. Mami sent them money every month. Last year Mami had gotten them a smartphone. We could video call them thanks to the loosening of some government restrictions. The photo of my paternal grandparents had been taken more recently, and Papi was in the picture. I dusted the shelf with a T-shirt from the laundry hamper and moved the saint Tía had given me a few months ago from the nightstand to the shelf.

Camo had been watching me with much interest. She pounced on the plastic bag after I'd emptied it and let it float onto the bed. I put the seven-day candle, the abalone shell, and a fresh glass of water on the wide shelf. After trimming the wick, I lit the candle and an incense cone. Tom barked, and Camo abandoned the bag to leap onto the windowsill. She pawed the window, wanting to join her person and our canine guest.

"Come along, Camo. I'll give you a few flakes of codfish. That dog won't be here forever. You'll get your person back soon." I scooped the calico into my arms, grabbed the plastic bag to recycle it, and closed the bedroom door behind me.

"Here you go." I put a piece of the rehydrated dried fish into her food bowl, then called Manny. "Lávate las manos, por favor."

My son skipped to the hall bathroom to wash his hands. Tom slurped half a bowl of water and then settled on his bed, where he graciously let Camo play with his tail.

"¿Qué quieres de merienda?" I asked my son as he climbed onto the kitchen stool. At four years five months, he was a little smaller than his peers. I had to remind myself he didn't need help.

"Cereal con coco, pasas, y dulce de leche," he said.

I laughed. There was no way I would give him oatmeal Os with dulce de leche drizzled over it, but I gave him points for his creativity. Coconuts and raisins were a maybe. He'd been eyeing the two cocos on the counter ever since I'd bought them from the fruit truck that visited UnMundo's parking lot on Wednesdays. I sat the coconut in the drain, then made a hole in one of the monkey face eyes with an ice pick and a hammer. I drained the liquid into a glass and gave it the smell-and-taste test. The flavor of coconut water was always hit or miss. The salinity of the soil could make the water taste gross, almost putrid. But this coconut was sweet. I drank half of it, then put a cube of ice in it and gave it to Manny. The high potassium would be good for the baby. I cracked the fuzzy brown shell into pieces, revealing the white meat inside. I gave Manny several chips of it along with a box of raisins.

The bell chimed just as I'd swept the stray shell pieces into the trash. Patricia Campbell was at the door with her bag of provisions.

"Welcome. Come inside," I said.

"Did you soak the salt fish like you said you would?" Patricia asked. She gave Tom a wide berth as we passed him on the way to the kitchen.

"Yes, overnight. I changed the water three times." Patricia set her oilcloth bag on the stool next to Manny. "You've met my son, right?"

"Hello, Mami's friend," Manny said with a wave.

"Hello, young man. What is your proper name?" she asked in a serious tone.

The image of her as a schoolteacher was easy to formulate. Manny looked at me with a question on his face. His English was very good, but he was stumbling over *proper*. I told him in Spanish that Sra. Campbell had been a teacher in Jamaica and she wanted to know his full name.

"¿Los cuatro?" Manny asked dubiously.

I nodded yes, all four of his names. Learning his full name and his parents' full names was the only homework he'd gotten from his Montessori school to date.

"Manuel Isidro Douglas Smith," my son replied with pride.

"Mr. Smith, are you going to cook with us today?" Patricia asked, tilting her head.

Manny looked at me for the answer. I'd expected him to have his quiet time while Patricia taught me her recipe, but I loved that he was so interested in cooking. I told him he could stay.

Patricia unloaded her parcel, one white onion, two bell peppers, a few Scottish bonnets, a large tomato, garlic, two sprigs of thyme, and the ackee. I got the salt fish from the refrigerator and placed it on the counter. She took a pinch of it, tasted it, and approved my contribution to the meal.

"Mr. Smith, I give you an important job." Patricia ripped a paper towel from the roll and put it before Manny. Then she gave him the thyme sprigs and told him to pull the tiny leaves from the stem. My son was thrilled to help and took his job seriously. I smiled at Patricia in appreciation for including him. The task was a made-up one. She told me what else she needed, and once I got her the cutting board, knife, oil, pot, and pan, she ordered me to sit and watch.

"It's very easy and quick." First, she filled a pot with water and set it to boil. "That's for the ackee." She explained that the fresh fruit had to be boiled but the canned version didn't need to be. Then she showed us how to separate the ackee flesh from the seed. "Listen to me, Mr. Smith, you never eat this." She held up the shiny black seed for him to see. "It will kill you dead. You understand?"

I didn't know if he fully understood what dead was, and I didn't remember at what age I'd understood it either. Maybe when I was eight. One of my friend's pet parakeets died. We'd had a shoebox burial. But Manny's eyes were wide, and she had his full attention. There was something about the seed that niggled at me. She proceeded to pull the yellow, almost waxy meat from around the seed. It was added to the baggie of ackee she'd already cleaned.

"Where's your garbage can?" Patricia asked.

I pointed to the under-counter cabinet. She took the cutting board with the fruit skin and seeds and dumped them into the trash.

"Now you let this boil for ten to fifteen minutes, but not any longer. The ackee is delicate." She added a generous pinch of salt to the water before putting the pulp from the baggie into the water. Patricia then chopped the onion and julienned the red and green bell peppers. "You aren't Jamaican, so maybe I only add one pepper." She chuckled, then sliced the Scotch bonnet into threads. With the stove set to medium heat, she poured vegetable oil into the pan and added the minced garlic—three cloves. A moment later, she added the vegetables to soften. "I like to add the tomato at the end. I don't like soft tomato, but when me sista make it, she cook the tomato down good."

The buzzer signaled it was time to drain the ackee. I came around to Patricia's side of the counter and got a strainer for her. The steam from the hot water made a cloud above the sink. She patted her face with a paper towel, then dumped the cooked ackee into the pan. "Where's me herb, Mr. Smith?" Manny carefully gave her his contribution. She sprinkled the thyme into the mixture and flaked the fish into the pan. Before adding the tomato, she gave the pepper grinder a couple of twists. Patricia mixed the ingredients gently with a few turns. "It's ready to eat. Give me the plates."

Patricia stored half of the meal in a Country Crock margarine container to take home with her, and the rest she divided onto three plates. I poured us drinks, a guava-peach-orange juice. We sat at the table. Manny, an adventurous eater, dug in.

"Pica. Pica," he said, fanning his mouth.

I told him to eat only the fish and the egg-looking bits. The Scotch bonnet peppers were the perfect heat for me, but if Patricia had added the second one, I too would have been crying about the spicy burn. While the ackee looked like scrambled eggs, it tasted nothing like them. It tasted a little nutty.

"This is delicious. I like the fresh tomato and the cracked pepper," I said.

"Some people use paprika. Every family has their own way. Some put scallions," Patricia said.

I told her I liked green onions and might try it that way. Manny asked to be excused, and after saying thank-you to our guest, he scurried off to his room with the dog and cat at his heels.

"When you having another one?" Patricia asked.

I'd never liked that question. It was a lot of pressure and, to be honest, very nosy. Strangers and family had asked it way too many times to count. But instead of reacting with *none of your business*, I wanted to clap and shout, *May!*

"We are definitely thinking about it," I said. I took a forkful of Jamaica's national dish and chased it with some juice. "How is Gillian? I thought she might've come with you."

Patricia tutted. "She's cooking for Mr. Pimpkin. Acting like a lovestruck teenager."

The Pimpkin name needed to come with a trigger warning. The mention of it sent a sensation down my spine like a spider had been dropped in my shirt.

"Really? Paul or Samford?" I asked.

"Paul. The man have a wife." She tutted again. Patricia proceeded to tell me that Lois was home but still weak. Gillian had insisted on making chicken soup for her. But it wasn't Lois Gillian wanted to help. It was Paul. She'd been carrying a torch for him for years. "Foolish woman. He not leaving his missus for her."

"Pobrecita. Did they date or something?"

"No! It all in her head. He build the library extension for the school twenty years ago. They shared a few cups of tea, and he spilled his heart to her. I don't understand that woman." She closed her eyes and shook her head. "Tell me. Did the police catch your vandals?"

It took me a beat to figure out what she was asking. "Oh, the garbage can thing. No, they haven't said anything. But it was probably Lois that wrote it, not the teens."

"The woman was trying to tell you who killed her, like in the movies." Patricia picked her plate up and headed to the kitchen.

I wish she'd left a letter or a name. I had so many questions and no clues.

Why was Lois in my yard?

Why did the drone attack her?

Who gave her the cassava cyanide and why?

Did it have anything to do with Tim Nelson's or Chef Sebi's accident?

And Fuentes! Very convenient for some people that he died.

I was so caught up in my thoughts that Patricia had to say good-bye twice and snap her fingers. I thanked her for the recipe and promised to acknowledge her on the show when I demonstrated it. After checking on Manny, who was telling a story to his menagerie of real and plushie animals, I cleaned the pots and pans. Scraping the gunk from the pan into the trash, I had déjà vu.

"That's the same thing that was in Nelson's trash can. It wasn't a mussel. It was a seed. Or is it a pit?" I dug the shiny black ackee seed from the garbage, rinsed and dried it, then put it into a snack-sized plastic bag. I closed my eyes and tried to remember Nelson's dinner party food. "The ceviche! Could it have been ackee?"

Something swam up from the memory of my graduate school days. It was a paper on contraband tropical fruit seized by airport security. Seedlings with their roots wrapped in a wet paper towel and tinfoil. Passion fruit vines. Whole fruits like mangoes and avocados. Everyone thinks the tree in their abuelos' backyard produces the best-tasting fruit, and they want to have that in their home away from home.

In the study, I dug out a three-ring binder that held some of the research from my dissertation. "I hope it's here." Flipping through the pages rapidly, I found the photocopied article on tropical fruit trees. One of the grainy pictures was of a bread-fruit. I'd always thought the fruit's skin looked reptilian and that it would make a good dragon egg prop. Scanning the two-page report, I found the information I needed.

Blighia sapida came to the Americas in the eighteenth century from West Africa, where it is known as akye fufo. The importation of fresh ackee is banned in the United States. The fruit, if prepared improperly, can cause symptoms as mild as vomiting and as severe as coma.

Nelson hadn't had a shellfish reaction. He'd been poisoned.

Chapter
Twenty-Six

I woke up Tuesday morning as gray as the cloudy sky. Grumpy was the correct adjective. My dreams had been riddled with anxiety. Was the ackee I'd eaten safe for the baby? Was the santero's caution a premonition? Thunder clapped, and the windows shook. Tom whined and came galloping into the bedroom. He put his head on my thigh and looked at me with his golden eyes. I patted his flat head and reassured him that we were safe inside. Another clap of thunder sounded, followed by a flare of lightning that lit up the room.

"Wow, that felt like it hit in the backyard." Robert got up and opened the blinds fully.

Another display of light and sound got Manny and Camo up. Pretty soon, our bed was full. The dog burrowed under the foot blanket on Robert's side. I sat up with a pillow behind me. Manny was in the middle, and Camo was tucked into the crook of Robert's arm. Rain splattered the glass, and we sat in silence watching nature's show like it was a sold-out movie.

The hairs on my arm stood up with the charged air of another close flash. A morbid thought entered my head. *This is how Fuentes died.* Not by lightning but by electrocution. I shifted my position, and Manny adjusted accordingly. He then put his head on my belly.

"Mami, estas gorda," Manny said.

"That's not fat. That's a baby," Robert said.

I gave him the *Did you really say what you said? Because this wasn't how we were going to do it* glare. He made a lipless grimace.

"¿Bebé?" Manny eyed me with doubt. He poked my baby bump that hadn't been there yesterday.

"Sí, mi príncipe, vas a tener un hermanito," I replied.

Manny looked from me to his father, trying to compute the new data. "A brother?"

"Or a sister," Robert said.

Manny snuggled next to me and began talking gibberish to my belly. I asked him what language he was speaking, and he told me "baby." Robert and I laughed heartily. Despite the raging storm outside and my restless sleep, my mood was improved. *It's all going to be okay.*

The rain stopped, and a beam of sunshine broke through the gray. That was our cue to get moving. Four of us got out of bed. Camo stayed curled on Robert's pillow.

I guessed I'd have to start telling people or wearing a tent dress—which I didn't own. I pulled on a pair of leggings and an oversized retro T-shirt that I'd bought for a back-to-the-eighties faculty costume party. The shirt said *Wake me up before you go-go* in large pink-and-lavender font. I remembered doing a search and finding out it was from a song by a band called Wham! and not the girl band The Go-Go's, which is what I had thought when I found it at the thrift store.

After breakfast and good-bye kisses from Robert, Manny and I took Tom for a walk. The sky had cleared, but rain puddles spotted the sidewalk. Manny splashed from one puddle to the next. I tried to remember the house where I'd met Patricia stealing the ackee fruit. After a backtrack, I found it. The two-story stucco house was in the Spanish Revival style. It had a carport with arches but no car parked under it. The house numbers were tiles on the top riser of the front steps: 4521 Hammerhead Road.

Manny pretended to be a frog and leaped into a large puddle. I whipped out my phone and recorded the moment. He was in get-messy heaven and would probably require a bath when we got home. I didn't care; I loved his joyful play. Mami had never let me splash in puddles because I might *coger frío*, which would lead to *un catarro*. I wondered if that was just a Cuban thing or if others believed getting wet outdoors led to an *instant* cold. Manny kept hopping and ribbiting. Tom wanted to join in the fun, but wet dog was different than wet kid, so I held his leash close to me. While I was filming my amphibious child, I made sure to get the ackee house in the background. I panned to the steps and got a clear image of the house number. Alma could look it up for me and tell me the owner.

When we got home, we entered through the side door where we'd found the *Help Murder* message. What had Lois Pimpkin meant by it? Was she referring to the drone that had chased and sliced her forehead? Or was it something more sinister? I got a chill. Maybe there was something to my mom's superstition about wet weather. I had Manny strip out of his soaked clothes and put them directly into the washing machine. Then I made myself a cup of tilo tea in the microwave.

As I monitored Manny's bath, I texted Alma that I needed to drop by. We settled on ten at her office, which gave me enough time to bake a tray of pastelitos to take with us. I told my son we were going to bake, and he hurriedly dried off and got dressed to help.

"Corta la pasta así, papi," I said, instructing him how to cut the guava paste into strips with the butter knife. I unboxed the puff-pastry dough. Next, I lined the cookie sheet with parchment paper and unrolled one dough package onto it.

"Yo quiero hacer el huevo," Manny said.

I gave him a bowl and the egg. He cracked it on the side the way he'd seen me do it a thousand times. His little fingers helped slit the shell. A few chips fell into the bowl. I used a large piece of the shell to remove them quickly. It was a trick I'd learned from our Dominican neighbor in NYC. She made the best sugar-syrup-soaked cakes. I was sure there was some science to it because the shell trick worked like a magnet. Manny then broke the yolk and tried his best to whisk the egg.

"¿Y el queso?" he asked.

I hadn't planned on making guava and cheese pastries. I checked that we had a block of cream cheese and compromised with him: half would be guayaba and the other half guayaba y queso.

The oven dinged that it had reached four hundred degrees. Manny arranged the paste on the dough, and I neatened his efforts before putting strips of cream cheese over half the squares. The second packet of dough went on top. I cut the fruit-only pockets into squares and the combo ones into triangles. Manny painted them with the egg wash. I slid them into the oven and turned the oven light on. He loved to watch them transform from flat white sandwiches to golden pillows.

I made myself a decaf café con leche. *This feels like sacrilege.* Manny and I enjoyed a sample of our efforts before I packaged up a few of each kind to take to Alma. Throwing a coloring book, crayons, and a few toys into my carryall, I left the house with Manny. Ana greeted us at the real estate office and got Manny set up at a table. She gave him a colorful packet of highlighters too.

"Hmm, yum! Did you make these?" Alma asked, biting into a triangle. Flakes of pastry cascaded from her mouth like a landslide.

We were in the glass-walled contract signing room. Ana joined us, bringing napkins.

"Mi'ja, are those your pajamas?"

"No," I replied to my BFF. "These are my baby-bump-is-showing-and-I have-no-maternity-clothes clothes."

"Okay, well, then I'll forgive you. But chica, you need to go shopping, like, today." She took another pastelito. "What are you going to wear to the gala?"

I hadn't thought about it, and I didn't want to. I waved her query away and got down to business—sleuthing business.

"Can you look up an address on the MLS?" I asked.

"Are you unhappy with your house? Oooooh, you need more room for the baby." Alma said.

"No. We have plenty of room, loca. I want you to look up an address and tell me who lives there," I said.

"Ana, can you bring the laptop to me?" Alma cleaned her sticky fingers. "The MLS won't tell me that unless the house is for sale. Is it?"

I shook my head no. "The house is 4521 Hammerhead Road."

"I can find it on the property tax roll." Ana typed in the information. "That's weird."

"What?" Alma and I said in unison, followed by a joint "Jinx," and then we did the break-the-curse thing like we were back in middle school.

"A company owns the house. That's not unusual." Ana's Russian accent came out on the last word, making the *u*'s into *oo*s. She was fixated on the screen and clicked the wireless mouse several times. "I see this in Aventura and Sunny Isles but not Coral Shores. Very *oonoosooal*."

"Can't you Google the company?" I asked.

"I did. Nothing came up. I'll find it, but it might take a little time. We have a busy day—so many showings from yesterday's open houses." Anastasia picked up the laptop and left the signing room. Alma had told me Mondays were open-house days for Realtors to visit listings. I was glad my BFF's business was rebounding. Ana stepped back into the room and stole a pastellito.

"By the way, what's the company's name?" I asked.

"C&C International," Ana replied with her mouth full. She wiggled her fingers at us and exited.

"So when are you going maternity shopping? Today, right?" Alma said.

"You know I'm terrible at fashion stuff, and I don't have time to go shopping. There is so much to do for the gala."

"Chica, you have to look perfect. Your suegra is going to be watching every move you make, trying to find fault in something."

Alma wasn't wrong, but I was more concerned about the actual event being a hit. "I promise I'll get something decent to wear to the gala. Tell me how the silent auction is going."

Alma rattled off a list of items and donors. She explained that Ana was designing the bid sheets and labels. Pointing to a box in the corner, she showed me she had plenty of clipboards. She was repurposing the tabletop displays they used at open houses—the kind that held an eight-by-ten sheet between two pieces of Plexiglas. Each clipboard would have a number, and the number would coincide with the Plexiglas display, describing and showing the auction item in more detail.

"Good. I can check auction off my list. Gracias, chica." I squeezed her hand in thanks.

"Okay, so now we go shopping!"

"No. I still have to see Marie about the food trucks and touch base with Sally about the tickets, and I'm forgetting something." *Find out who gave Tim Nelson the toxic ackee.* It took a beat, but I remembered. "Pepper. I need to make sure Pepper hasn't gone overboard with the music."

"What about decorations? We never talked about decorations."

"It's all outside. Do we need decorations?" I countered.

"Well, you at least need a color scheme for the napkins and table linens. And if the bar is the in-case-of-rain place, it should be decorated."

She had a point. "Okay. I'll stop by the club and see what they have." I'd ask Valerie and maybe find a way to mention that I had seen her at the Dia de Los Muertos service. *Why did she put the chef's photo on the altar? Were they friends? Friends with benefits?* "Okay, my day just got super crazy. Besitos. I've got to go." I kissed her.

"Gracias for the merienda," Alma said, crumpling the tinfoil into a ball. "Remember when you complained that you weren't a chef and that you weren't right for the show? Boba."

I had been a fool. Once I'd gotten used to the camera and studio, I'd fallen in love with the career shift. And I had my BFF to thank for it, as she reminded me often. "You were right, like always."

"Uh-huh. You are like a size fourteen normally, right?" Alma was looking at her phone.

"What are you doing?" I tried to see the screen, but she hid it from me.

"Nothing."

Chapter
Twenty-Seven

S omeone honked. "This is a residential area. Slow your roll, bro," I said.

In the back seat playing with a toy, Manny giggled. Then he repeated, "Slow your roll, bro." The honking continued as the car passed us and diagonally blocked our car. I slammed on my brakes. "¡Coño!" I let a curse word slip. I turned around to make sure my son was okay after the near collision.

Short, lacquered fingernails tapped on the glass. I twisted back around, ready to give the dangerous driver a piece of my mind.

"Marjory!" I lowered the window.

"Miriam! I've been calling you. Why have you not answered me?" My mother-in-law had her head in my car and was inches from my face. She was like that ostrich at Lion Country Safari that had scared our van that one class trip. All twelve of us had screamed, but the bird was undeterred from its quest to get milady's Chifles.

I unbuckled my belt and shooed her away so I could get out of the car and speak to her on equal footing.

"Answer me. Why haven't you picked up my calls? Are you in your pajamas?" she asked. She gave me a hard stare as I stood.

"No, these aren't my pajamas," I said through a clamped jaw.

"Mami's pregnant." The high-pitched voice of my darling son came from the car.

"Did I hear correctly? You're pregnant. When was *I* going to be told? Is there a reason you are keeping it a secret? Does Robert know? Are you keeping it from him too?" Marjory crossed her arms. Under her breath, she mumbled something that sounded like *Just like Meghan Markle.*

What the hell does that mean? I was sure it was another one of her passive-aggressive insults, but I couldn't deal with digging into it just then. I had a mad ostrich in the middle of the street to contend with. For a woman who constantly chided me about the volume of my loud Cuban voice, she was the one making a scene and drawing the attention. If I didn't calm her down, we'd be the trending news on Around Town. Also, Manny was watching and hearing all of it. Not a good example of adult behavior.

"Marjory, we were planning a special way to announce it. We wanted to have you and Senior over for dinner after the gala." That was a complete lie. I never wanted that woman in my house if I could avoid it.

A car honked. The driver gave us a dirty look as they drove around the butt of Marjory's car. We were taking up most of the lane.

In my periphery, I saw another vehicle approaching. Marjory continued to huff and puff. *Miriam, don't apologize for something that is not on you. You don't owe her anything.*

"Marjory, I'd hoped you'd be happy for us. It is happy news, no matter how you found out. Right?"

"*Happy?* I'm not happy. I'm wounded. It's an arrow to my heart." Marjory slapped her hand onto her chest.

Melodramatic was a new adjective to add to the word list I used to describe my mother-in-law. *Wounded.* Our baby news was our business. Robert and I didn't owe her first notification.

"Is there a problem?" Detective Pullman asked.

I looked toward the voice and realized it was his car I'd seen. I was sandwiched in with my MIL in front and Pullman in back. My Prius was in between like a sad, wilted piece of lettuce.

"This is none of your business," Marjory said.

Pullman flashed his credentials. It didn't change Marjory's dismissive attitude. "Mrs. Smith, you are blocking the flow of traffic. Please move your vehicle."

Anger vibrated off my MIL. She did not like to be told what to do, especially by someone her tax dollars funded. She took the *servant* in *civil servant* literally. The fact that Pullman was Black only fueled her sanctimoniousness. If her ostrich feathers had been ruffled before, we were now at the peck-and-claw stage. Part of me wanted to diffuse the situation for Manny's sake, but another part of me wanted to watch her say something and get arrested.

"I will move when I'm good and ready," she said.

"Mrs. Smith, that time is now. Please move along." Pullman's body language was calm and controlled. He was not going to contribute to Marjory's theatrics.

"I'll leave as soon as I've collected my grandson," she said.

"Is that all right with you, Ms. Quiñones?" Pullman asked.

"Did we have plans?" I had been forgetful lately.

"I've been calling you! Come along, Douglas. Get in Grandmother's car. We are going to story time at the library." Marjory tried the door handle. Manny shied away from the door, straining the seat belt to its max.

Kids are smart. They know. Marjory had defrocked. She'd exposed her nastiness, and he'd registered it. I doubted he'd ever be as happy and willing to spend time with her as he had been. She's done it to herself, but I was sure I'd get the blame.

"Maybe another time. Today isn't good," I said.

Marjory went to try the handle again. Pullman blocked her. "Mrs. Smith, you do not have a child restraint seat in your car. I'm afraid I can't allow you to drive with your grandson at this time. And his mother hasn't agreed."

"The mayor will hear about this, Detective." Marjory stomped off, her platinum bob swinging with every vexed step.

"Thank you. I hope this doesn't cause you problems with the mayor," I said.

"The mayor and I have an understanding," Pullman said, and then lowered his voice to a whisper. "And I have pictures he doesn't want released to the *Miami Herald.*"

My mind was hopscotching to all the possibilities. *What dirt does Frank have on Mayor Jones?* I didn't have to guess for long. Pullman scrolled through his phone and showed me.

"These were taken at the Booty Trap."

"Ironic," I laughed.

"The dancer is my cousin's stepdaughter. She tells me he comes in every week, pays for his drinks in cash, and calls himself Jimmy Talls."

"Ay Dios."

"I don't think his Sons of the Confederacy pals would like seeing their brother with a *sista.*" Pullman chuckled and put his phone away. "But that's not why I stopped. I need your expertise."

A Maserati slowed and crept around us.

"Come again?"

"You're the food know-it-all, and I have a question." Pullman leaned against my car.

"Go on. I'm always happy to help the police." My saccharine tone got a *pfft* from the detective.

"Don't get ahead of yourself. You ain't getting deputized. Tell me what you know about ackee fruit. Where would someone buy it?"

A pang of guilt gnawed at me to confess what I'd discovered. We were both on the same path. *Tell him, Miriam. Stop pretending to be Jessica Fletcher.*

"So you figured out the ceviche had unripened ackee in it and that probably caused Nelson's reaction."

Pullman nodded.

"Did all the servings have it? Has Nelson said anything? Why would he use ackee? *Maybe* for a vegan substitution."

"Veronica, I'm asking the questions. Where can a person buy fresh ackee? It's not imported to the USA," Pullman said.

"No. But the tree grows in South Florida. I saw one the other day. Most people don't know what it is, so they let it grow."

"Where?"

For a half second, I thought about lying, but then I remembered the santero's warning. *Stop playing amateur sleuth, Miriam.* "It's around the corner. I don't know who owns the house. I asked Alma to look it up, but that was a dead end. It's owned by a company."

"When were you planning on sharing this information with me?" Pullman gave me the squinty-eyed glare. It felt like the one time I had skipped class and Papi caught me buying candy at the tiendita.

"I just found out like two minutes ago. I literally just left her office." My voice pitched upward.

"Uh-huh. What else have you uncovered, Veronica Mars?"

"Give me a second." I got in the car and put on the Radio Disney for my son. He instantly began singing. I turned the AC up a notch and closed the door. "Okay, so I did a little research on ackee. When it's ripe, it's harmless, but I guess he didn't know that. Whoever gave him the recipe should have warned him. Or did the caterer make it? Was someone trying to poison the whole dinner party?"

"Miriam, this is not how it works. I ask. You answer. Where is the tree? What else do you know?"

I showed Pullman the photos I'd taken of the tree and house, then sent them to him per his request. "I know that Fuentes was murdered."

"You do, do you?"

"Yeah, well, it makes sense, doesn't it? No one accidentally electrocutes themselves while whitening their teeth. But what I can't figure out is who did it. Did you know he was worried about some Russian? Did he have a new business partner?"

"Stop asking questions. Seriously. Stay out of this." Pullman lifted himself from his resting lean and began walking away.

"Fine, but at least tell me about Nelson. When is he getting out of the hospital? Can I take his dog to visit him?"

Pullman beeped his car unlocked. "Tim Nelson is in an induced coma. It's not looking good." He got behind the wheel and left.

As I drove to Marie's food truck, Pullman's words repeated in my head. Nelson was in a coma. I could not believe it. I hadn't thought a single serving of ackee could have that effect. I made a mental note to ask Patricia if she'd ever heard of anything like that.

The service windows of Fritay All Day were closed, but voices were coming from the metal box on wheels. As we got closer, I heard a few cuss words in Kreyòl. The back door opened, and Marie clomped down the metal grate steps. She raised her fists and shook them at the sky before taking a deep breath to calm herself.

"What's wrong? Can I help?" I asked. Manny pulled my arm, wanting to run to the playground. I told him un momento.

Marie turned to my voice. "Oh, hey, Q. The fryer is acting up. *Again.* You can't have a fry shop without a fryer. Jamal has called the repair guy, but there is no way it will get fixed before the lunch rush in an hour. And I hope it gets fixed by Saturday, or else no bannann peze for the gala." She let out a frustrated sigh.

"Oh, not good."

"Yeah, no bueno! At least the freezer is working. I can still sell popsicles and sodas to the after-school kids, but lunch is off the menu today. I need that fryer fixed, or else I'll have to change the truck's name. And I'm a little worried about it for the gala."

"Me too. That's why I stopped by."

"Give me a second to grab my notes, and I'll meet you by the bench." Marie pointed to the playground area.

Manny wiggled from my hand and made a dart for the sandpit. A few minutes later, Marie joined me on the bench by the swings. We reviewed the menu and the confirmed trucks.

"Do you know anything about preparing ackee?" I asked.

"The Pepper Pot isn't making ackee and salt fish. He's a Rasta. So everything is vegan. I have him down for corn soup, which is more like a stew, really. It's delicious. It's made with coconut milk, yellow split pea, pumpkin, corn, potato, ginger. Q, it is so good. And he'll also have patties with curried jackfruit filling. You want me to ask him to make something with ackee? I'm sure he can. It's very versatile."

"No, forget about the ackee. It's for something else," I said.

"Okay, so the mixologist has like five cocktails, each representing a different island, and three mocktails."

"What's a mocktail?"

"No alcohol."

"That's good, because I'm pregnant, and I was hating missing the—"

"Hold up, Q. You're pregnant?"

I nodded.

"Congrats!" Marie gave me a big hug. "I'm so happy for you!"

"Thanks."

"Maric, I've got some bad news," Jamal said as he crossed a patch of green to us. "The repair guy says he's ordered a new thermostat, but it won't be in until Friday. He can give us a loaner, but I measured, and it won't fit."

Marie's mood plummeted back to subterranean. "That's cutting it close for the gala. Q, I might have to use the club's kitchen for the bannann peze. Can we run over there and see? We need a contingency plan in case the part doesn't fix the fryer's problem."

"Of course. I was on my way there anyway to check the decorations."

Manny dusted the sand from his hands and skipped to the car ahead of us. Jamal told Marie he'd drain the oil from the fryer while she was gone with me.

I got all the usual baby questions on our way to the club. When? May. What? We don't know yet. Names?

"I have no idea, but for now, I'm calling the baby a mermaid," I said, getting out of the car.

"Have you been craving fish?" Marie asked.

"Huh? A little bit, I guess. Why?"

"'Cause you asked about the ackee and salt fish."

"No." I leaned in and lowered my voice so that Manny wouldn't hear. "The club's GM is in a coma from eating the fruit."

"What! How did that happen?"

"Chica, that's what I want to know."

"Very weird and random."

"I know, right?"

We divided in the lobby. Marie went to the kitchen to find the Haitian line cook, and I went up the grand staircase to find Valerie. I held Manny's hand tightly as we ascended, reminding myself it was high enough to kill the chef.

At the top, a man dressed in a loud Baroque shirt brushed by us. His cologne was an assault on my olfactory system, and I fought back a sneeze. The receptionist desk was vacant, but Valerie's office door was open. Walking in, I smelled the man's cologne lingering in the space. Valerie, on the phone, had her back to us.

"Dasvidaniya," Valerie said. She swiveled her chair and set her phone on the desk. "Oh, hello. I didn't know you were there." Valerie removed a glass jar with an orange bow from her desk and stored it in a drawer.

"Sorry to have startled you. Do you have a moment to discuss the gala?" I asked.

"Of course." Her phone lit up. A *K* in a circle filled the screen. She quickly hit the red decline button and turned the phone on its face. "Have a seat. Is this your son?"

"Yes. This is Manny." He waved.

"Would you like a candy while the grown-ups talk? If that's okay with you, mom." I nodded. She got an orange gift bag from under her desk. "Pick a few."

Manny looked at me, and I made a V with my fingers for only two. He smiled and took his treats to the armchair in the corner by the door. I heard the rustling of a candy wrapper and then an *mmmm*.

"How can I help you?" Valerie asked.

We spoke for about ten minutes and looked at a few pictures from past events. Before long, we had the decor ironed out. I told her that UnMundo might bring a film crew, as a few of their stars were attending. She said that wouldn't be a problem. She could reserve one of the tall tables for them with stanchions around it.

"Oh, that's a good idea. But maybe make it two tables, because they're small, right? They will have plus-ones, so it might be a party of five or six people."

"Done. Anything else?"

"No, I think that's it. Did I mention we're having signature cocktails? Should I talk to the bartender about that?" I asked.

"Yes, you did, but it wouldn't hurt to talk to him. We still have time to order any special mixers. Let's go down there now." Valerie came around her desk.

I wiped Manny's mouth with the underside of my long T-shirt. It looked like he had badly applied light-brown lipstick.

The phone on the desk vibrated. Valerie looked at the caller's name.

"I have to get this. I'll meet you in the bar." She pointed and motioned us out. "Ask for Kyle." Valerie took the call.

As I crossed the threshold, I heard her say something like *dras-tree* to her caller. *Is she speaking Russian?* I cocked my head, wanting to confirm what I thought I'd heard. Manny did a wiggle-dance that meant he needed the bathroom, and I abandoned my eavesdropping. Waiting for him to do his business in the ladies' room, I remembered I'd wanted to ask Valerie if she'd been at the CSUUC service. *Oh well, maybe I'll get another chance.*

I found Kyle, the bar manager. He gave me a worried once-over as if I was in the wrong place. *Miriam, you really do look like you are in your pj's.*

"I'm here about Saturday's gala. Valerie sent me to speak to you," I said. "But we should probably get my friend. She has the details about the drink menu."

Kyle set down the glass he was polishing, and we went to the kitchen to find Marie.

Marie and the Haitian line cook were in the walk-in storage unit. The insulated metal door was open. The pair were conversing in rapid Kreyòl. I couldn't understand the words, but I sensed that they were gossiping. When Manny pointed to and asked about a three-foot-long vacuum-packed smoked salmon, the two noticed us.

"Q. Sorry. Pierre was just telling me—never mind, I'll tell you later." Marie and the line cook shared an allies-to-the-end look before they laughed. "I'm ready if you are. We've got it sorted if I need to use the kitchen's fryer."

"Cool, and I've got the decorations squared too, but we need to get Kyle here up to speed on the special cocktails," I said.

"Of course," Marie said, extending her hand to the bar manager as she exited the cooler.

Before Pierre closed the door, I stuck my head in and took a look. It was clean and orderly. There were no health inspector red flags like the smell of spoiled food. One side had produce and the opposite side meat. White buckets, two deep, were on the floor at the narrow side of the cool storage. One was labeled PICKLES, another PEPPERONCINO. The rest of the bucket labels were obscured.

As our group moved through the kitchen, I heard Beverly on the phone in her cubbyhole office.

"Stop yelling at me. I did what I did," the head chef said. She pulled a strand of blonde hair from her pinned twist and wrapped it around a finger. Beverly was propped on the edge of a cluttered desk with her foot on a lidded bucket.

I waved at her as we passed her open door. She made a fake-friendly smile before kicking the door shut with her clog.

Marie and Kyle went through the drinks menu while Manny ate his weight in maraschino cherries. The donated rum Marie had procured would be delivered Friday. Kyle convinced us paper umbrellas and neon-colored palm tree swizzles were essential camp and not tacky. With everything settled and golf-ers entering the bar for lunch, we left the club.

I guess Valerie got held up on her call. Maybe the club's silent partner wasn't being so silent. She did tell me he was Russian.

Dras-tree.

I'll ask Ana what it means.

Chapter
Twenty-Eight

As we stepped away from the club's valet area and headed to my Prius, a silver car zipped by us and into a staff-only parking space. I pulled my son into a protective embrace. Drew's angry rant about the reckless Fast & Furious driver Halloween night wasn't unwarranted. If Manny had run ahead of us, he'd have been in the driver's path and too short to have been seen.

I bet it's the same driver!

"Marie, can you take Manny to the car? I'll be there in a second." I handed her the fob and told my son to listen to Tía Marie.

"Q, are you making me an honorary auntie? I love it."

With Manny safe, I marched toward the car to give the speed demon a piece of my mind. The driver closed the car door with their hip and hurried to a back entrance with two bags.

"Hey, you. You almost ran over my son," I called, but the person didn't turn around.

I followed them through the door. They were walking deceptively fast. *What are you, an Olympic race walker?* I stopped to catch my breath and watched as they entered the kitchen. Peering through the porthole, I saw the driver unpack his parcel of bananas, pudding, and vanilla wafers onto the steel prep table before disappearing into the bowels of the kitchen. Pushing the hinged door, I opened my mouth to call *Stop* but then shut it quickly. Valerie was in Beverly's office.

"Here's the caviar I told you about," Valerie said. In her hand was the same orange bowed jar I'd seen on her desk. "This is a sample from the vendor to try. If you like the quality, we can get it at a *very* good price."

"It doesn't fit our menu," Beverly said.

"Certain clients *would* order it if it was an option." Valerie smiled like a prizewinning top seller.

"Give me a break. Not our regulars. They're traditional. Hell, today we got a request for banana pudding. Banana pudding! Not a special and elaborate pastry. Pudding! With the mushy wafers on the bottom." The chef made a face.

"Well, I know my wedding clients would love to have it as an hors d'oeuvre option. Take it home and give it a try with some champagne or ava." Valerie pushed the jar into the chef's hand. She then noticed me at the swing doors. "Ms. Quiñones, did you find Kyle?"

"Yes, thank you," I replied.

Beverly took the car keys from the prep table and pocketed them. She then went back to her closet office.

"Can I help you with anything else? The gala is going to be great. Don't you worry."

"Oh. Yes. Um, I was just looking for my friend Marie. I guess she's already outside. Thank you. We'll see you Saturday," I said, and left.

The car belongs to Beverly! She catered Nelson's dinner party. Ay Dios, I need to tell Pullman.

Marie was giving Manny a Kreyòl lesson when I returned to them. On the ride to drop her off, I tuned them out. My brain was like that meme that had all the numbers and geometry like a cloud above someone's head. How was Beverly connected to Nelson? Was it an accident? Or was it deliberate? Why would she have a beef with him? Did it have anything to do with the country club? He was technically her boss. Did she hate him for some reason? Did she hate him because Chef Sebi had gotten promoted? Had she pushed Sebi Malkov?

"The chef killed the chef."

"Q, you're mumbling," Marie said.

"Sorry. I was thinking out loud."

"That's nothing new." Marie laughed and said good-bye. "I'll keep my fingers crossed for the fryer repair."

We arrived home to find two surprises. Roberto was home, and he was accepting a delivery.

"Papi!" Manny scrambled out of the car to his father.

"Hey, there, little man, high five." Robert bent to let his son slap his hand.

"Hola, mi amor. What are you doing home?" I asked.

"I've got a meeting at the club at two, so I thought I'd come home and have lunch with my family." Robert held up a bag with a receipt stapled to it. "Deli sandwiches from the gourmet shop on the boulevard. I got you the caprese with heirloom tomatoes."

"What did I get?" Manny asked as he followed Robert into the house.

"For you, I got a ham and Swiss. No mustard. Extra pickles."

"What's in these bags?" I asked about the large brown paper bags with handles by the hall table.

"I don't know—it was here when I got home. It has your name on." Robert let the dog out. "It's nice out. Should we eat on the patio?"

"Sure. I'll be there in a second." I opened the stapled top of one of the bags and read the invoice inside. Maternity clothes from Miami Mami, a chic boutique on Coral Way. *Alma*. I took the bags to the bedroom and unwrapped the outfits from their lavender tissue paper. "Wow. One hundred and seventeen dollars for a shirt." I shook my head but still tried it on. The fabric was extra soft, and it made my leggings look less pajama and more yoga. Unpacking the rest, I discovered she'd also ordered an evening gown. It had a green-and-black palm frond pattern with a V-cut neck and a sash belt. Strategically placed black crystal beading gave it a little pizazz and bling. Admiring myself in the mirror, I had to give my BFF props. She was the fashion queen and always knew what looked right on me. I hung up my new wardrobe and left the empty bags for Camo to play in.

"New shirt?" Robert asked as I sat and joined them.

"Alma. You like?"

"I do. That color looks nice on you."

I smoothed the teal fabric over my belly and shot off a thank-you text to my BFF before biting into my sandwich. The mozzarella, tomatoes, and spinach were perfectly seasoned with balsamic vinegar. And the bread had a nice chew. Manny ate half of his adult-sized meal and then went to play fetch with Tom, who'd been waiting patiently at his feet.

"Do you know anything about Beverly, the country club's chef?" I asked Robert.

He dabbed horseradish mayo off his chin. "Samford's girlfriend?"

"¿Que qué? Beverly, the chef at the club, is Samford Pimpkin's girlfriend?"

Robert nodded and took a bite of his roast beef on rye.

"When were you planning on telling me this?" I jutted my splayed hand in his direction.

"I thought you knew. It's not like it's a secret anymore."

"Roberto, *querido*, you are doing that thing again! That thing where you think I know all the things about Coral Shores and all the founding family history and all about your childhood friends and yeah, that thing." I exhaled, and my nostrils flared. I imagined I looked like un toro about to charge the red cape.

"Calm down, babe. I hear you, okay?"

"Don't *Calm down, babe* me. This is like when you assumed I knew about the trust fund and the stocks and all that old-money stuff. Tell me everything, no matter how trivial. Tell me now!"

"¿Mami, porqué estás brava?" Manny asked from the lawn with concern.

"Mami is mad at Papi because I forgot to tell her something. But I'm going to tell her now, little man. Don't worry." Robert stroked my forearm. "Deep breath. You'll upset the baby. I'm sorry. You're right. I just assume you know what I know, but you didn't grow up here."

My husband proceeded to tell me that Beverly had been Samford's mistress during his last marriage. Since the divorce, he'd not exactly hidden their relationship but also hadn't put a diamond ring on it to make it legit.

"You're telling me everyone knew he had a side chick," I said.

"Yep. He even bought her a house, I think."

"She's like thirty years younger than him."

Robert shrugged. "Yeah, well, that's par for the course."

I wanted to slug him on the bicep for that shrug, but I let it go. Samford was on the club's board. His girlfriend was in line for the head chef position, but he'd given it to Sebi Malkov. The executive chef position had been part of a deal with the silent partner. Samford had burned his girlfriend for the sake of profit.

I didn't particularly like Beverly, but I was beginning to feel un poquito sorry for her. *Yeah, but Miriam, she might have pushed Sebi over the railing.*

"Okay, family, I'm off to my meeting."

"Thanks for lunch, mi amor. Please be careful at the club," I said.

"Okay." Robert drew me to him. "Careful of what? What are you worried about?"

"If I told you, you'd think I was loca." My cheek was on his chest, and I could hear his heart beating.

"*Babe.*" Roberto tucked a snake of hair behind my ear. "Tell me."

"I think Beverly pushed the Russian chef to his death and that maybe she might have something to do with our neighbor's poisoning."

"What? Nah. You really think so?"

"Yeah, maybe. Just stay away from her and don't eat anything. And don't take the stairs."

Roberto promised to be on high alert if he encountered Beverly but assured me he'd mostly be outside inspecting the build site with the permitting officials. As he pulled out of the driveway, I called Detective Pullman. The santero's words were haunting me. And Pullman was right; I was not the stealthiest sleuth. I had no business investigating any crime, no matter how close to home it got. Frank didn't pick up, so I left a voice mail. "I think Chef Beverly poisoned Tim Nelson, and she probably pushed Sebi Malkov too."

It was only two in the afternoon, but I was tired. I needed a nap, or maybe my mermaid needed one. Either way, I convinced Manny we should build a blanket fort in his room. While he and Camo played, I dozed on his bed. A notification from my phone woke me an hour later. It was Alma. Ana had something to tell me. They were on their way over.

I got up and began making coffee. A cafecito at 3:05 pm was a very Miami thing. I decided to make mine a mostly milk café con leche. Tom alerted me that someone was at the door before the bell rang.

"When did you get a dog?" Ana asked.

"He's not ours. We're just dog sitting until his owner gets out of the hospital. Come on through; I have coffee," I said. I put a blue tin of butter cookies on the tray, and we—dog and kid included—went onto the patio. Alma opened the container, and we each selected our favorites. The fluted one for me, the square sugar-crusted one for Ana, and the pretzel-shaped one for Alma.

"So, what did you need to tell me?" I asked.

"Go on, tell her," Alma encouraged her assistant.

"The house—you know, the one you had me look up? I know who lives there," Ana said.

"¿Quién?" I leaned in.

"Emily Martin," Ana replied.

"Is she the owner? I thought a company owned it." I dunked a cookie into my warm latte.

"The company, C&C International LLC, is a tax shelter. The owner's name is well hidden. But Emily is Emilia B. Martinez. She's—"

Alma interrupted with, "Aka Beverly Hills! El chefie from the club! Sigue, tell her how you know."

Ana gave her boss a pained look and blew a blonde hair from her forehead. "I saw her in her backyard. You know"—she flirted her hand in front of her chest—"nude by the pool."

"You've been to the house?" I asked.

Alma cocked her head and jutted her lips out. Ana threw her head back and held it a moment before confessing. "I saw her with a drone."

"You have a drone?"

"It belongs to a *friend*. That's what the police questioned me about." Ana thumbed toward Nelson's house. "I have a drone license."

"Why?" I let my jaw hang open.

"Because Kostas Borisova!" Alma slapped the table.

"The Russian Mafia guy?" I glanced from one to the other.

"Tell her," Alma said.

"I—" Ana began.

"She owed him a favor!" Alma *pfft*ed.

"It's not what you think." Ana took a deep breath, exhaled, and told her story.

When she'd first arrived in Miami, she'd thought she was going to be Instagram famous. Everyone she met was an influencer. *So*, she thought, *why not me too?* "It looked easy." She and her boyfriend got drone licenses to shoot yacht parties. Russian yacht parties. She got a few sponsors. The money started to come in. But then one day, while filming some bathing beauties on a giant flamingo floaty off Golden Beach, she filmed something she shouldn't have. The bikini babes were having sun and fun on the waves in their pink raft, but in the background, something criminal had transpired. Kostas Borisova took the footage, spared her life, and told her she owed him a favor. "I had dated his nephew. That is the only thing that saved me from being shark chum."

"What did you see?" I asked.

Anastasia turned an imaginary lock on her lips.

"Okay, fine, but what was the favor?"

"He sent one of his bodyguards to visit me a few weeks ago." Ana shook like an icy Siberian gust had hit her. "The favor I owed was due. He gave me a suitcase with a drone in it and told me to film the backyard of 4521 Hammerhead Road."

"But why?" I asked.

"I didn't ask questions. I did what I was told and hoped my debt was cleared."

"When was this?"

The pain of embarrassment crossed Ana's usually stoic face. "The weekend before that lady in your yard. But I didn't have anything to do with that. Different drone. Not me. I swear."

Maybe the helicopter Manny and Sophia saw was Anastasia's? Do I believe her that she wasn't the pilot of the drone that attacked Lois Pimpkin? I don't know. I hope she's telling the truth.

"I still can't believe that you didn't say anything to me. Coño, Ana, I'm not a boss-boss. I'm your friend too." Alma crossed her arms in an X on the table.

"I know that, but you don't know how serious the Bratva are. I didn't want to get you involved in my mess." Ana's stoicism returned.

Is that why a lawyer materialized by Anastasia's side so quickly? What was the favor? To film a topless sunbather. That makes no sense. Or was it to injure Lois? That makes less sense. Or was it to film whipped-creamed Sebi? That makes even less less sense. Sebi is—was—Kostas Borisova's nephew.

My head was still swirling with questions as boss and assistant hugged, then left.

Maybe Ana was set up. Maybe she was meant to take the blame. But for what?

That evening I took Tom for a long walk. I passed by 4521 Hammerhead at least five times, trying to understand how all the pieces fit. I didn't know what I'd do if Beverly caught me. *Compliment her ackee tree.* No matter how hard I stared at her silver car or the tree, I couldn't put the puzzle together.

How were all the victims connected?

Ana is told to film Beverly in her backyard. Lois is attacked. Nelson is poisoned. Wait, Lois was poisoned too.

And then the Francophile Russian chef is photographed like he's a cream pie. A few days later he's dead. Either he slipped and cracked his head open or someone pushed him.

And don't forget Fuentes's odd death.

There are too many pieces to this puzzle.

Miriam, is it even the same puzzle?

Chapter
Twenty-Nine

D elvis had messaged me a reminder at five AM. The promo for the gala was today, and it was live. I got to the studio, changed into a freshly ironed logo shirt, and sat in the makeup chair. Viviana did her magic, and I tried to hide my quickly inflating beach ball stomach under a salon cape.

"Comiste bastante candy," Viviana said, pointing to my belly with the end of her makeup brush.

Rude. I wanted to clap back at her, but I also had to thank her for the perfectly plausible excuse. I could avoid telling them the truth for another week or two by complaining that I'd gained a few pounds taste-testing. I mean, I wasn't a rail to begin with; I've always had a little padding. *It might work.*

The palms of my hand were sweating. I didn't like live TV. I liked that I recorded my show and mistakes could be fixed. Delvis hadn't noticed my belly, or if she had, she was polite enough not to say anything about it. But I did register that the prop mistress put a large pot in front of my abdomen.

I counted down the seconds for my cue and hoped my armpits weren't betraying me. Ileana gave a tease and went to commercial break. She joined me behind the counter, and before I could overthink it, the director pointed at us. We were live.

252

Ileana led the short conversation with a sound bite about Karib Kids and the assistance they provided. Then she volleyed to me for the gala details. I rattled off the names of the food trucks and the islands they'd be representing. I even mentioned the Coral Shores Women's Club's philanthropic history. Then a duo with steel drums strapped around their necks appeared out of nowhere. Ileana started dancing, which meant I was supposed to dance too. Above the *plink-plink*, the morning show host mentioned the celebrities that would be attending, then she said, "El teléfono para reservaciones está en pantalla." I managed to make my jaw drop look like a smile—a creepy-clown smile, but better than a surprised *My sister-in-law is going to kill me* look. I couldn't believe the host had just given Sally's cell number to millions of viewers.

The show went to a prerecorded thirty-second spot to give the host time to return to her couch. The crew moved with her, and my cooking stage went dark with me still standing there. I let my eyes adjust to the sudden change in lighting and made my way to the makeup room without bumping into anything. As I removed Viviana's artistry from my face, I watched Ileana interview her guest, the assistant who had found Fuentes. The graphics and music intro were sensational and made me feel icky, but I was glued to the screen.

"¿Hija?" I shouted. The sleeping comedian shushed me.

I could not believe what I'd heard. The assistant was Fuentes's *daughter*. He'd never known about her until a paternity test a few months ago. Her mother had never told him she was pregnant, but when by fate she'd started working as his assistant, the mother had confessed. The assistant was determined to continue the business in memory of the father she'd tragically lost. She was his *only* heir.

"If there was one, I bet there are more." My outburst got another shush.

I hoarded the makeup remover wipes and waited. A PA escorted the woman from the set and back to the makeup room as I'd hoped. I listened as the PA thanked her for her bravery in telling her story, then I pounced, offering her the wipes. Viviana gave me a quizzical *You are acting weird* glance but continued with her brush cleaning.

"Mi más sentido pésame," I said.

"Thanks, but I didn't really know him. He was kind of a jerk," the woman replied.

"Miriam," I said, extending my hand.

"Fabiana."

"But still, it had to be a shock to find him like that."

"I guess." Fabiana was about twenty-five, with pouty lips that had to have been enhanced. Her flat-ironed hair had the lightened streaks that seemed to be in style. And her nails must have cost a hundred dollars and two hours in the chair. They had gems in them. "I thought he was watching porn, which would have been *awkward*."

I stifled a gasp and played it cool. "Yeah."

"He was that kind of creeper. He hit on me like day one. And like that's how I found out he was my dad. And like I mentioned it to my mom, and she freaked out, like went to see him and like got in his face. He didn't even remember her, but she had like a photo of them together. She met him in Brazil or something. Anyway, so like after that he changed. I mean, he was still suss but like not to me. And like he was teaching me the business so like I wouldn't have to worry about money because the tooth whitening stuff is *lucrative*." Fabiana overarticulated the word while fanning her fingers.

"Didn't he like have some legal trouble, though?" I crossed my fingers that she'd keep rambling on and not think too hard about my question.

"Naw, he'd straightened that out. He was like testifying for the feds against like the boss, some old white dude, and like he only had to pay a fine or something and like never import anything again. He was kind of bummed cause like he was into that herbal remedy stuff, pero like the teeth whitening is *so* much better." She rubbed her fingers together to symbolize money, then cleaned a lipstick smudge from her pearly whites.

"Oh wow, that sounds heavy. The feds."

"He wasn't worried about the legal stuff, actually. Like the feds, you know, were gonna protect him or something, but damn they didn't protect him from the Russian. Mario was super paranoid the last week. Like *Black Mirror* stuff. He told us to only take appointments for women. No men. No one with a Russian-sounding name. He was like checking the locks and the security cameras all the time."

"So you think the Russians killed him?"

"For sure."

"Have you told the cops? Are they doing anything?"

"Cops? Hell no. I'm not a fool. One, I don't trust cops. Trayvon. And two, I don't want any problems with whoever did it. I'm not going to ruin a good thing. I'm set for life. I got a business." Fabiana's face was clean. She lifted her hefty purse onto the counter and pulled out her personal makeup bag.

I watched as she put on her regular makeup, which, to be honest, didn't look that different from what she'd just taken off. I wanted to know more about the Russian killer, but Fabiana was as mute on the subject as Anastasia.

So who killed Mario Fuentes? The old white dude, which has to be Samford Pimpkin? I mean, he'd have been pissed that Fuentes was turning state's evidence against Juliet. Wait, what did Fabiana say?

Oh.

OH.

He was pointing the finger at the big boss, at Samford. Does Samford Pimpkin have the connections to order a hit? Did he kill Fuentes for snitching? How is Samford Pimpkin connected to the Russians? No, THE Russian. Is it Kostas Borisova? Is he THE Russian?

There was a piece of the puzzle just out of my reach. If I could see it, I'd figure out how all the incidents connected. I was in a fog—half in my mind, half watching the comedian and Viviana do their flirty banter.

"Earth to Miriam." Delvis snapped her fingers.

"Huh?"

"You were on Mars. Meet me upstairs in the recording booth in five. Okay?"

"Sí, voy," I replied.

I couldn't shake the whirl of questions in my head as I changed shirts. *What am I missing?* I waved good-bye to Viviana and the comedian, who were having an animated conversation. They replied "Ciao" in unison, never breaking eye contact with each other. Viviana was enamored with him. She'd do anything for him.

The dubbing went smoothly. Delvis asked me if I had anything I needed to tell her. *So she's noticed my belly.* I deflected by saying I'd been stress eating because of the gala prep. *I don't think she believes me. I'm going to have to tell her next week for sure.*

I stopped off at Tres Sillas for lunch. Tía had made chicken noodle soup. I ordered a bowl and asked Bette for extra lime and soda crackers. As I squeezed the citrus wedges into the steaming soup, I went through my mental list of corpses and near-corpses. It had all started with Lois Pimpkin. She was struck and injured in our backyard. The image of my tossed-out noodles stuck to her head sent a shiver down me. How was she connected to Nelson? Both were poisoned but not with the same thing. *I need to talk to Lois.*

"Bette, dame una sopa de pollo para llevar, porfa," I said.

Yoli brought the to-go soup out to me about five minutes later. She asked about the baby and if I was craving anything yet. I joked about the baby being a mermaid since, yes, I was craving seafood more than usual.

"Espérate," Yoli said.

She returned with a tinfoiled brick.

"What's in here?" I asked.

"Croquetas de bacalao. Mami made them a few days ago, but I forgot to defrost them for today's frying. Mejor que tú las uses."

"Gracias, pero I have to make a few stops before I get home."

"No problem, I'll pack some ice around it."

I thanked them for my hot and cold takeout and left. As I crossed the Coral Shores village limit, it dawned on me I didn't have Lois Pimpkin's address. I pulled over and shot a text to Robert explaining I was doing what *we* should have done days ago: visit the person carted off our lawn in a stretcher. It was the proper thing to do. And I could hear my MIL and Mami on my shoulders like a devil and an angel. They'd both agree it was the right thing to do, but not for the same reasons. Mami's visit would have been out of kindness and concern. Marjory's would have been about not looking bad to the social circle.

So what is your reason, Miriam?

I hated when my conscience called me out. My visit was contrived, but the soup was heartfelt. Tía Elba's soup could bring a person back from death.

Robert didn't have the house number, but he said it was hard to miss. Paul and Lois Pimpkin had the corner house on Pompano and Bay, a few streets down from Pepper's house. I could zoom over there and hopefully pick Manny up on time for once.

A woman in a pastel maid's uniform, complete with lace-edged apron, answered the door. I took the hazard and guessed she spoke Spanish, since the name embroidered in script on her uniform was Ouilda, a very old-school name.

"Buenos días. Con tu permiso ¿puedo ver a la Señora Pimpkin? Tengo una sopa que darle."

"Un momento, por favor," Ouilda replied, letting me in the foyer.

It was in the same style as the country club's lobby. The stairs were on a smaller scale, but they had a similar white wrought iron banister. There was an oil painting dated 1896 above a hall table. The couple in the portrait were seated at a table set for tea with an Everglades-like swamp behind them. An egret, an alligator, and a panther were at the edge of the wilderness.

"Pase," Ouilda said. She took the soup and motioned for me to follow her.

She led me to a ground-floor room in the back of the house. Lois Pimpkin was in a wicker chaise with a blanket over her legs. Her side table was full of medicine bottles. The gash on her forehead still had sutures and shone with ointment.

"Good afternoon, Mrs. Pimpkin. We haven't been introduced properly, but I'm the person that called the ambulance for you. I'm Miriam Quiñones-Smith." I hoped I'd hit the right notes of concern and respect.

"So you're Robert's wife." Her voice was weak but full of judgment.

This is not going to be easy.

I sweetened my voice and lowered myself onto a chair near her. "Yes, ma'am. I've been so worried about you. It was such a relief when Gillian Brown told me you'd been released from the hospital."

"Gillian Brown. That woman is a vulture." Lois adjusted the pillow under her elbow.

"I beg your pardon."

"She's just waiting for me to die so she can snatch up my husband."

I tried to keep the surprise off my face.

"Can you believe she came here to make me soup? Paul *let her in*. I told the maid to throw it all out. She'd probably poisoned it."

"Oh my, well, I'm so glad you're out of the hospital," I said, not wanting to get her too far along that path. Patricia had mentioned that Gillian carried a torch for Paul. But I just couldn't imagine Robert's sweet British librarian as a killer. Although didn't most of the sweet old ladies in Agatha Christie novels have cupboards of poison in their kitchen? So maybe, but I was certain Gillian was not the type to have a drone. "Have the police caught whoever attacked you?"

"*No.* Worthless man. I'm going to see that that detective is fired. The mayor is a good friend of mine."

I remembered her threatening something similar at the Fall Festival. It was time to play the mother card. Even bitter and mean women softened around small, innocent children.

"I'm sure they will catch the culprit soon. Do you remember anything about the drone? You know, we have a small child. He's only four. I worry about him playing in the backyard. What if he's attacked? I just don't understand why a drone was even in our backyard to begin with."

"That was the peculiar thing. I swear the thing was spying. It was looking into your neighbor's window. I swung the garden hose at it. And then it turned on me. It dove at me like a hornet. I swung again and hit it. Then a dog started barking. I remember that that's when I tried to escape, but your garbage can was blocking the gate handle. I must have fallen over it. I don't remember much after that." Lois closed her eyes, sighed with a practiced whimper, and leaned her head back onto a silk pillow.

"Why were you in our yard anyway?"

"I don't remember."

I got the feeling she was lying. "Do you remember writing a message on the wall?" I asked. "What did you mean by it?"

"Message?"

"You wrote *Help Murder*," I said, and reached into my purse to show her the picture on my phone.

"I was being attacked, I suppose. Why are you asking me so many questions? Oh-ill-da," Lois called.

Ouilda appeared quickly.

"Show this woman out. I'm tired. I need my rest."

Ouilda gestured with her head for me to follow her. We took a detour to the kitchen, where she turned off the faucet she'd left running. There was a tub of soapy bubbles in the basin and an array of dirty crystal glasses on the counter. Since we were out of earshot, I asked her not to mention the chicken soup to Mrs. Pimpkin. I didn't want Lois claiming I was trying to poison her too.

"Llévesela a su casa. Está hecha por mi tía y es deliciosa," I said.

She thanked me for the soup and promised to enjoy it at home. I asked how long she'd been working for the Pimpkins. Five years. The woman was demanding, but the pay was very good, with eight AM to four PM set hours. And she got weekends and holidays off. And she didn't have to do any cooking, only cleaning.

"¿Pues quién cocina? ¿Ella?"

Ouilda laughed at the idea of her employer cooking and informed me that she'd never seen Lois near a stove. The Pimpkin household had had a scheduled delivery of lunch meals from the country club the entire five years she'd been working there. Monday was a large container of chicken salad. Tuesday's meal was pimento cheese spread. Wednesday they got a cream of potato or a pureed soup. Thursday was chicken and dumplings, and Friday it was carved roast beef. Ouilda had no idea what they did for breakfast or dinner, as there were rarely any dirty pots and pans for her to clean in the morning. Toast and orange juice? Leftovers? Ouilda made a disapproving face. I had to agree. Boring and predictable. But it provided the perfect opportunity for someone to slip something into her food.

As I repositioned the car a few blocks north in front of Pepper's house, I convinced myself it wasn't Ouilda who had poisoned Lois with cyanide. It had to be someone from the club. Yuca could easily be camouflaged into a creamy potato soup or a puree.

But why?

Chapter Thirty

Thursday morning, I got a visit from Sally. She'd turned her phone off because of the constant calls about tickets to the "Enrique Iglesias event" and changed her voice mail message to *Sold out. Please donate to Karib Kids on their website.*

"I'm so sorry. I swear I had no idea she was going to give out your personal number. It was all unrehearsed," I said.

"I'm not mad. It will all quiet down. I just wish I'd had a heads-up." Sally sat in one of the blue chairs. Camo immediately jumped into her lap, shedding white and orange hairs onto her black skirt. "And we are actually sold out. If we let more people buy tickets, we will have complaints that there wasn't enough food."

"Camo adores you," I chuckled. The cat was purring loudly and rubbing her head against my sister-in-law's hand. "I think you're going to need the lint roller."

"It's probably the lox I had for breakfast."

"Changing subjects. Can I ask you about some Coral Shores gossip?" I tucked my feet under an orange pillow and threw a lap blanket over me. Miami had gotten a cold snap, and I'd opened the French doors to let in the free sixty-three-degree air conditioning. And to keep an ear out for Manny and Tom playing in the cottage.

"Shoot."

"What's the story with Beverly from the country club and Samford Pimpkin? They seem like an odd couple."

"Why, because of the age difference?"

"Thirty years is a big gap, but—"

"Try forty," Sally interrupted.

"Okay, yeah, wow. But how did they meet? What do they have in common? It's been going on a while, right? And he *bought* her a house. So it's serious, right?"

"I don't know how they met. But money is attractive to a certain kind of woman. So that's what they have in common. She likes money, and he has it."

"But it's not like she's sitting in a silk robe eating bonbons. She works. Being a chef is long, sweaty hours."

"So, if I remember correctly, he paid for her to go to culinary school. That was when Samford was still married to his last wife. And I think he set her up with a restaurant."

"Really?" Restaurants weren't cheap, and they often failed before the financial investment was recuperated. "What was it called?"

"I don't know, something like sugar or tobacco. It had a cigar lounge when that was the big trend. I think it served Latin-Asian fusion. Probably why it bombed; that's a weird combination."

The food anthropologist in me wanted to educate her on the fact that the Caribbean and Latin America had strong ties to Asia. Just like in California and the Pacific Northwest, there had been waves of labor force immigration, mainly from China but other Asian countries too.

"That's a big investment in a person—school, a restaurant, and a house," I said.

"Yeah, but I don't think any of it was in her name, though. But whatever it is, those two are definitely as thick as thieves." Camo jumped off her lap and moseyed over to Tom's bed. "I think I need that lint roller after all."

I got up, found it, and handed it to her.

"Thanks. I've got an appointment at the courthouse today." Sally ran the sticky tape over her skirt. "I just wanted you to know why I wasn't answering my phone if you called."

"Thanks, and again, I'm sorry about that. One last thing: do you remember where the restaurant was located? And how many years back are we talking?"

Sally thought for a second. "It was in Coconut Grove, I'm pretty sure, and like five years ago."

As soon as Sally drove off, I grabbed my laptop and set up on the patio. It took several searches before I found an article in the *Miami New Times* about Beverly's restaurant, Cassava y Caña. Yes, it was a Latin-Asian fusion theme restaurant with a humidor and collection of aged rums. The logo, a backward C and a forward C interlocked, was unremarkable, but the food described in the article was interesting. Tapioca pearls, a cassava product, were prominent, as were other Filipino dishes using the starchy root. The article was accompanied by photographs of Beverly in the kitchen's vegetable and herb garden. A further search produced a few lackluster reviews and one *very* intriguing one-paragraph mention in a crime column.

Customs officials raided a local restaurant and cigar lounge. Four thousand illegal Cohiba cigars were found in the humidor rooms of Cassava y Caña. The operation called Up in Smoke placed tracking devices on suspicious cargo imported into the Port of Miami. The cigars were fraudulently labeled as Dominican on the shipping manifest. Once cleared, they were repackaged with the iconic black and yellow paper band of the embargoed cigar so many aficionados crave.

"Everything Pimpkin touches is illegal," I mumbled. He wasn't named as the importer, but it served to reason it was him. He'd set his sweetie up in business as a front for his illegal cigar smuggling. "I wonder if she knew. *Is she a partner or a fool?* Ella no me parece boba."

"Mami, tengo hambre," Manny whined.

"Y yo tengo frío." I exaggerated a shiver and a *brrr*. "¿Vamos pa' dentro y nos tomamos un chocolate caliente?"

"Sí. Sí."

A group text arrived from Pepper during our hot chocolate and sweet corn bread repose. It was a playdate invitation to Sophia and Manny's class. I let Manny know we'd be seeing his best friend after our weekly grocery shopping trip. He loved going to the store with me. And had already won the hearts of several of the staff with his culinary curiosity. Maybe Roberto was right. Perhaps our son was going to be a chef.

In the bright and colorful produce section, I asked Manny to put a bag of limes into the cart. I added six grapefruits for the marmalade I needed to recipe-test for next week's show. At the root vegetable bins, I stopped. There was cassava, malanga, boniato, and some very large ñame tubers. White ñame root was used in many Dominican recipes. Its taste was similar to a mild yam or sweet potato. But it wasn't an idea for a recipe that had my mind zapping. It was that the roots all looked similar enough that an untrained cook might not know the difference. And that the two varieties of cassava, the sweet yuca and the bitter one, were not visually distinguishable. The bitter yuca had more cyanide. *Could Lois Pimpkin's poisoning have been a mistake?*

"¿Mami, cuantos plátanos?"

I signaled for him to get three green and three brown plantains. *Wait, isn't that one of the ways farmers tell the difference? The bitter yuca has a brownish-purple stem, and the sweet is green or white.* I'd read an article about the cultivation of the plant in water-stressed areas of Ghana.

But Ouilda said Lois never cooks. So the poisoning was not a mistake. It had to have come from the country club's kitchen, which means Beverly. 'Cause come on, she had a restaurant named Cassava. But why? Lois is a Pimpkin, and Beverly is practically one. And then there's Nelson. Why poison him? Maybe she's just a psychopath, or perhaps just an inept chef.

"Mami. Mami." Manny was trying to lift a large bag of rice into the cart. He'd climbed out while I'd been playing Jessica Fletcher in my head, and I hadn't noticed. Returning the bag to the mound, I told him he was smart and strong but we had plenty of rice at home. *I really need to talk to Pullman before Beverly poisons someone else. Gracias a La Caridad that the gala's food will not be made in her kitchen.*

My time management was a bit off, and we had to rush to Pepper's after unloading the groceries. Most of the parking spaces were taken. We ended up parking closer to Lois Pimpkin's house than to Pepper's. As we approached, I swore I heard a steel drum. In the outdoor living space, several mothers were gathered, each with a tumbler of what I suspected was Pepper's famous and potent San Tropez sangria. The kids were giggling and playing on her state-of-the-art jungle gym. Manny ran to join his classmates. I said my hellos and was handed a glass that I quickly exchanged for nonalcoholic.

Ting-tinka-plink-pa-di-da-din-don.

"That is definitely a steel drum," I said.

I looked toward the direction of the sound. Beside the water feature, a clinging cascade of crystal-blue water from the rooftop pool, a door slid open. Pepper stepped out surrounded by costumed dancers and musicians.

"Hey, everyone, please welcome the Calypso Crew and Carnival Dancers. This is a preview of what we will have at Saturday's gala!" Pepper began swaying to the music. There was a round of applause, and the kids stopped their play to join the scene. Two festooned stilt walkers limbo-ed out of the tall opening. All the kids squealed. The walkers beckoned them over to the cement patch to dance with them. One of them had the bouncy kind and was pogoing about, blowing a purple whistle. The other walkers had the rigid type of stilts that were about three feet tall. The musicians started a new song without stopping for a breath. It was one I recognized, and I caught myself singing the song I'd learned from the *Beetlejuice* movie.

"My mother loved Harry Belafonte," Stormy said.

"Oh, hello. I didn't know you were here. How are you?"

Stormy grinned and sang along to the rest of "Jump in the Line." After it was over, the musicians took a moment to show the kids and a few of the moms their steel pan instruments. The *plink, plonk, plink*s were discordant as the novices tried to hit the notes.

"The question is, how are *you*?" Stormy eyed my abdomen.

"Fine. Manny let it slip to Marjory, and that was a scene, but overall good," I replied.

"That woman. I can tell you I'm so much happier not having to see her regularly. Her and her clique. Why I put up with it all those years, I'll never know." Stormy rolled her eyes. "I will never go to another Women's Club meeting again. And because Sunny died at one, no one has *dared* asked me to. After the memorial service, I haven't heard from a single one of them."

"I'm sorry your friends have abandoned you," I said, imagining the pain of losing a child.

"*Friends.* No, my dear. *You* are a friend. They are sheep, and your mother-in-law is the sheepdog herding them. I don't give one feck about losing them."

I could not help but laugh full-throated at the idea of Marjory nipping at legs and barking. A few heads swirled at what they thought was an f-bomb. Stormy joined me in laughter. She explained that *feck* was an Irish word she'd picked up from the virtual coven she'd joined. Everyone in it was Irish or of Irish heritage. She was planning a trip to the Emerald Isle soon.

I like her so much. Why can't she be my MIL?

"Well, since you have no effs to give, can I ask you about some Coral Shores dirt?"

"By all means."

"What do you know about Beverly, the chef from the club?"

"Not much. Juliet introduced them, if I remember correctly. I think Beverly catered one of Juliet's parties. She was always throwing parties. Lois pitched a fight when Samford started dating her. I remember she said it didn't look good. The age difference. There is no love lost between those two anyway."

"Lois and Beverly?"

"Samford and Lois. He can barely stand her. He offered Paul a million dollars to divorce her."

I blinked. "Wait. What? Are you serious?"

"That's what Paul told me. Paul is a decent man. He reminds me a little of Prince Harry. You know, more like his mother and deeply affected by her death."

"That's what Robert says too. But then how did Juliet turn out so awful?"

"I don't know. But Lois and Samford have always had a tug-of-war over Juliet. Lois would send the girl off to camp or lessons. Juliet would hate it and call her grandfather to come save her. Samford gave that girl anything and everything she asked for. Really spoiled her."

The band started up again, this time with a rendition of "Don't Worry Be Happy." Stormy bopped toward the dancers and joined the line for the limbo.

I wanted to ask her more about Lois and Samford, but the chance had passed.

Was Beverly poisoning people at Samford's behest? But why? And why Nelson? And why the drone attack?

Around five, the entertainment was over, and many pitchers of sangria had been consumed. I was worried about buzzed driving, but thankfully most of the moms lived within walking distance. The cars on Pepper's street turned out to belong to the performers. I thanked Pepper for the preview, and we both agreed the band would add a fun vibe to the gala.

As Manny and I walked to our car, I saw Gillian leaving Lois Pimpkin's house. I waved to her, but she didn't see me. Speeding up our pace, I got within earshot.

"Gillian. Gillian. Hi."

The woman looked like a possum caught in a spotlight. Her hair was frizzy, and she was frozen. Eventually, she blinked and animated. "Oh, sorry, pet. I've just had the strangest encounter."

"At Lois Pimpkin's?"

"Hello there, young man." Gillian smiled down at Manny, then brought her gaze up. "Yes. I came over to cook for her and Paul, like I'd promised." She held up a cloth bag with can-shaped lumps and a frill of green leaves poking out from it. "But the daft maid wouldn't let me in."

269

"What do you mean? She didn't answer the door?" I asked.

"She came to the door. I saw the peephole darken. I expected the door to then open, but it didn't. I knocked again. The hole went black again. I told her I was a friend of the family, but I got no reply."

"Maybe Lois was napping and Ouilda didn't want to wake her," I offered.

"Well, she could have opened the door and told me that. I've walked all this way for bugger all." Gillian gave an exhausted huff.

"I'll give you a ride home."

"Oh, that would be grand!"

Chapter
Thirty-One

F riday morning, after doing my rotation as drop-off-lane monitor at Manny's school, I went home and reviewed my gala checklist. My first call was to Marie. She told me the fryer had been repaired and that she'd be checking in with all the food trucks in the afternoon. Marie informed me the trucks should have access to the club's parking lot by three PM to set up and cook, except for the caja china man, who needed to be there earlier to start roasting the pig. Then she sent me an image of the parking lot with labeling. Each food truck had a designated spot. Next, I called Valerie and asked her if the rum had been delivered.

"Yes. Don't worry. Everything is on track," Valerie assured me over the phone.

"Okay. I need to send you a map of where each food truck will be parked. Can we mark them off with a sign or something? I hadn't planned on being at the club that early."

"Absolutely. We can handle that too. Just send it to my email."

"Can I text it to you?" I asked.

"If that's easier for you." Valerie gave me her cell number, and I held the line until she confirmed she'd gotten it. "Perfect.

I'll print it out and make sure everyone has a copy. Chef Beverly has the kitchen preparing your desserts today. The first floor smells like coconut and vanilla. It is all going to be perfect. Don't worry."

I hadn't been worried until Valerie said Beverly's name. If Beverly was poisoning people, I certainly didn't want her baking the desserts for the gala.

"Is she baking them?"

"No, no. The pastry chef is, but she's on top of it. Don't worry."

Valerie's *Don't worry* had me worried.

What if the flan kills everyone?

After we hung up, I opened my laptop and found Beverly's restaurant article. The photo of the garden was what I wanted to reexamine. Hitting the plus sign a few times enlarged the image enough for me to confirm that there had been cassava plants in that garden. The color image showed both the bitter and sweet kinds.

But Miriam, that was five years ago.

"Five," I said aloud.

Woof.

Meow.

"Exactly. Ay, ay, ay. Now not only am I talking to myself, but I'm having conversations with the pets. Miriam, get a grip, girl."

I closed the computer. I needed to confirm my suspicion before calling Pullman with my panic about poisoned flan. And yes, I was *definitely* going to call him. Stuffing my swollen feet into my shoes, I threw Tom a dog treat before I left the house.

Alma was at her desk when I walked into the real estate office.

"Hola, chica. Everything okay?" Alma asked.

"Sí y no. I need a pair of shoes that fit. This baby is making my feet swell." I sat on the chair across from her and rubbed the top of my right foot.

"Do you have any low heels to wear with your evening gown?"

"Ugh. I haven't even thought about what I'm putting on my feet tomorrow."

"Mira, there is a shoe repair place just off the boulevard. They can stretch your heels a half size. But chica, you need to take them there like now. *Okay.*" Alma wagged her finger at me.

"Okay. I'll do it. But first I need to see Ana. Is she here?"

Alma pointed to the copy room.

Ana was at the copier with earbuds in. When I tapped her on the back, she jumped.

"Sorry, I was listening to a podcast," Ana said. "How can I help you?" She stopped the podcast and pocketed her earbuds.

"You told me you took pictures of Beverly's backyard. Right?"

"Yes."

"Do you still have the drone photos?" I asked.

Ana busied herself with tapping the copied flyers into crisp and even stacks.

"Do you still have them?" I repeated.

"The police have everything. I don't want anything to do with it."

"Okay. But do you remember if there was a garden in the backyard?"

Ana looked at me, then she looked at the ceiling and screwed her jaw to the side before letting out a deep sigh. "Promise me you will not say anything. Like, don't even mention my name. Promise."

I crossed my heart and held my hand up in oath. I followed Ana to her work space and watched as she turned on a personal iPad. She showed me a bird's-eye video of the backyard. At first, Beverly was on her stomach, sunbathing by the pool. Then she turned and looked at the drone. She flipped a finger at the flying machine but didn't bother covering her exposed chest.

"Play it again," I said.

That time I focused on the surroundings and not Beverly. There were four raised garden beds near the hedged perimeter. I asked Ana to rewind and pause the video. "That's what I'm looking for. I need to call Detective Pullman."

"You promised," Ana hissed.

"No, no. Not about you. I won't mention you at all."

She glared at me, and I held up my hand in an oath again.

"Tell me again why you were filming Beverly's backyard," I said.

"I don't know. Honestly, I don't. When you owe the head Bratva a favor, you just do it and don't ask questions. But I got the feeling it wasn't about the lady. It was just Russian mind games."

"What do you mean, mind games?"

"You know, like just to mess with someone's mind. Like *I'm watching you. I can get to you whenever and wherever.*" Ana tapped a manicured nail to her temple.

"Ay mi madre, Miriam!" Alma shouted.

"What? ¿Qué pasó?" I returned to her office with Ana close behind me.

"Lois Pimpkin was found dead last night." Ana pointed at her computer.

Ana and I gathered around her and looked at the screen. A news clip was playing. Emergency lights bounced off the house, and Gordon stood guard at the Pimpkins' front door. The camera panned to Paul Pimpkin, his tie loose and his white shirt untucked. He was talking to Detective Pullman. The anchor reported over the silent footage:

Paul Pimpkin arrived home at seven pm to find his wife, Lois Pimpkin, dead. She had recently been attacked and sustained a head injury. The police are investigating if her death is related to the attack.

"Oh my God, I've got to go," I said.

"Where?" Alma asked.

"I have to find Pullman," I replied.

"Don't forget about your shoes," Alma called after me.

I called Pullman from my parked car. No answer. So I texted him that I had information for him and waited several minutes for a reply that didn't come. Next, I called Robert and put it on speaker so that I could drive.

"Hey, babe. Everything okay?"

"Did you hear that Lois is dead?"

"What? Where did you hear that?"

"It was on the news last night. I just saw it. You haven't seen Paul today, have you?"

"No. We don't have another meeting until next week. I was with him yesterday until six. When did it happen? I thought she was recovering. I didn't think it was that serious."

"I know. I mean, I don't know. I'm trying to find out exactly what happened. Can you call your cousin and ask him?"

"*Babe.*"

"Por favor."

"Okay. I'll text you if I find out anything. You could always ask Mom."

There was a weighty pause.

"Okay. I'll call Mom if I don't hear from Gordon."

"Gracias, mi amor," I said, and disconnected.

I drove by Lois and Paul Pimpkins' house. There was no police presence. I wanted to stop and ask Ouilda what had happened, but if Paul was home, I didn't want to disturb him. Ouilda was probably the last person to see Lois alive.

Oh my God, did she kill Lois? No. She liked the pay and the schedule. Eight to four, weekends and holidays off. Eight to four! It's not Ouilda. I saw Gillian at five something. Someone was in the Pimpkins' house, and they wouldn't let her in. That was when it probably happened.

"Espérate un segundo. I didn't go to the door. I didn't see the person in the peephole. What if Gillian did it? What if her surprised look was me *catching her*? Oh my God." A cold sweat dampened the nape of my neck. "Gillian Brown killed Lois, and I gave her a ride home."

My phone trilled. Pullman's name marched across the screen. I tapped and answered.

"Gillian Brown did it."

"Slow down, Veronica. Did what?"

"She killed Lois Pimpkin."

"What makes you say that?"

"Have you interviewed her yet?" I asked. "I saw her yesterday at five coming out of the Pimpkin house. I even gave her a ride home. Ay Caridad, I had a murderer in my car with my child."

"Slow down, Jessica. You are jumping to conclusions. But the timing is interesting. Where are you right now?"

"I just got home."

"Put some coffee on. I'll be there in a few minutes."

After prying off my tight shoes and letting Tom out, I packed the espresso grounds into the filter basket. The bell rang, and Pullman's face appeared on my phone's notification. He sat at the counter after I let him in, and Camo jumped onto the stool next to him.

"So take it from the top. Who is Gillian, and why were you giving her a ride?"

I told him all I knew about the ex-librarian as I served the coffee. "And according to her friend Patricia Campbell, Gillian has been carrying a torch for Paul Pimpkin."

Frank Pullman drank his espresso slowly, keeping his wary eyes on me the whole time. When he set the demitasse down, he inhaled before speaking. "You think this British lady killed Mrs. Pimpkin to steal the woman's husband?"

"Okay, when you say it like that, it sounds weird. But she was coming out of the house at five, and the maid, Ouilda, leaves at four. And Gillian had been over there a few days ago making meals for Lois. She was probably casing the place."

"Hmm."

"Hmm? What does that mean? I'm right, right?"

"We've interviewed the housekeeper. She's in the clear. She has a gas receipt for 4:10 PM, and Lois Pimpkin made an outgoing call at 4:12 PM that lasted six minutes. We know the victim was alive during that window of time."

Pullman rarely shared information. I hoped he'd keep talking, but he didn't. He scratched under Camo's chin before standing to leave.

"Do you have an address for this Gillian Brown?"

I described the house and told him the street. He thanked me for the coffee and reminded me not to do my own investigating.

"I called you! I'm reformed. Good girl here." I pointed to myself.

Pullman guffawed. "Let's keep it that way."

I locked the door after him, grabbed a cookbook, and went to the patio to get some fresh air. Tom, tired from chasing a squirrel around the mango tree, laid down by my chair. Fridays were my test and prep day for the following week's recipe, but I was having a hard time focusing on work. What if I'd exposed Manny to a killer? I was staring at Manny's cottage, where Lois had probably hidden, when the phone beeped, causing me to jump and Tom to bark. It was a text from Robert.

She was suffocated with a pillow.

"Let's go inside, boy. It's all of a sudden chilly."

To keep the awful images of Gillian Brown holding a pillow to Lois Pimpkin's face out of my head, I made a draft proposal to double up on filming *Abuela Approved*. And selected the sixteen dishes I'd be demonstrating over the next two months.

After school, Sophia came home with us. She and Manny begged to help me cook. After the potatoes had boiled, I set the kids to mashing them. When one got tired, the other took a turn. It was a bit of a mess but a lot of fun. Seeing the kids in the kitchen reminded me about the reporter's daughter that loved my show. Having her and her mother on would make a great episode. I needed to speak with Delvis about it. I also wondered if there were any new details on the Fuentes story. *If THE Russian killed him, what was the motive? And was the Russian Borisova? South Florida has a lot of Russians.*

I encased a spoonful of picadillo in the fluffy mash, then passed it to the kids to roll into a smooth ball. With a light spray of olive oil on their hands, the potato didn't stick to them or the counter. When we'd finished, our production line had made a pyramid of snowballs. I had them wash up and sent them out of the kitchen for the frying part.

Pepper came to collect her daughter at five thirty.

"Mmm, it smells good in here," Pepper said.

"Come try one. I've got some for you to take home. Sophia was a great helper." I put one of the golden balls on a paper towel and gave it to my friend.

"What is it?"

"They're called papas rellenas. It's mashed potatoes stuffed with a ground beef center."

She took a bite. Steam whiffled out once she'd cracked the toasty exterior. She fanned her mouth but kept chewing. "Yum. It's like a shepherd's pie but racquetball size."

I nodded and smiled.

"So, are you ready for tomorrow?" Pepper rubbed her hands together in excitement.

"I think so. Keep your fingers crossed it goes well and people like the food and bid high."

And no one gets poisoned.

Chapter
Thirty-Two

Saturday morning, Robert made pancakes and bacon before slinking off to his tee time. He'd been invited to take Paul Pimpkin's place in a foursome that held the coveted early slot. Paul was in shock over the death of his wife, as one might've imagined. I could have hated Robert for leaving me alone on gala day, but nah. We'd had a sexy snuggle earlier, and I knew he'd be back in time for me to put my feet up so I could stuff them into a pair of heels.

"Olvidé mis tacones. Coño." I cussed about forgetting to take my heels to the shoe shop. "Manny, ayúdame con algo."

My son skipped over to the kitchen from his room. He had his father's bathrobe belt tied around his waist like a tail, and Camo was chasing after him trying to swat it. I took a short video and sent it to Mami. There was no way she could visit us in our new home until the summer. November through May, the holiday rentals she and Papi managed were booked solid.

I asked Manny to get my heels from the closet and a pair of his father's athletic socks. The project I needed help with required an extra set of hands. I held the sock necks open and asked him to scoop rice into each. Once we had them to about the size of a plump pear, I used a rubber band to tie them off.

Then I microwaved the rice socks for a minute and stuffed them
into the toe of my shoes. I hoped the heat would soften and
stretch the leather just enough to give me some comfort tonight.
Manny thought the whole thing was great fun and very silly. He
rolled on the floor laughing about making arroz con zapatos.
Tom added barks and bounces to the mania.

To calm them down, I took them both on a walk. As we
passed Beverly's house, I tried to see over the garden wall, but it
was too high. Was she poisoning people on purpose, or was she
just a lousy chef? Maybe hiring Sebi Malkov hadn't been nepotism
but a safety move. Maybe the club knew Beverly wasn't executive
chef material. Maybe her boyfriend on the board knew it too.

Honk.

"Mami, cuidado, es Grandma," Manny said, spreading his
little arms in a protective barrier between me and the car rolling
its window down.

"Why aren't you at the hair salon?" Marjory asked from the
driver's seat.

Grrrr.

I patted Tom's head and whispered that I had it *bajo control*.

"Good morning, Marjory." I smiled but didn't step onto the
swale.

"Do you need me to call my girl? I know they're booked
solid. It's the day of the gala, but she will fit you in for me."

"Thank you for the offer, but I think I'm fine." I ran my
hand through my hair and pulled the ends up to check if they
were split or frayed.

"What do you plan to do with it? Don't embarrass me with
a head of hair that is messy. I hate that morning-after look that's
so popular. Don't do that. Do you hear me?" Marjory huffed
and drove off.

"Mami, a mí no me gusta Grandma. She's not nice."

I was about to remind my son to speak to me in Spanish, but I let it go. He was right, Marjory Smith was not nice, and it was fine that he no longer liked her. Despite not wanting to bow to Marjory's insinuations that I was a fashion disaster and would embarrass the Smith family name, I texted Jorge. *Can you come over at four and help me with my hair and makeup?* I wanted to look my best for my own sake and the TV cameras. Ileana was sure to have a crew there to document her UnMundo stars. Plus I *was* terrible at hair and makeup.

Bark.

Bark. Bark. Bark. Waggy tail.

"What do you see, buddy?" I asked. Tom's whole back half was happy. He was practically dancing. As we got closer, I saw that there was a car in front of Nelson's house. Tom was straining to be let loose, but I feared his joyous reunion would knock Tim Nelson down. The man looked frail and unsteady.

"Welcome home."

He turned toward my voice. Instead of replying, he held his hand to his throat and made a pained expression.

"Can't talk? Throat sore?" I asked.

He nodded. A smile took the place of his grimace as he gazed at his dog. I helped him to the front steps, and he sat. While Nelson and his canine best friend had their reunion, I took the keys from him and opened the door to his house. It was eerie being in there. And it hadn't been cleaned since that night. There was black fingerprint powder on the counters and fridge.

"Um, if I'd known, I would have cleaned up for you. I'm afraid it's a bit of a mess in there," I said, returning to the stoop.

Nelson waved it off like it was no big deal.

"I can come by tomorrow and help."

"I can help too," Manny said.

Nelson gave a thumbs-up to me and a high five to my good-hearted son.

"Do you want me to bring Tom's bed and things over?"

Nelson shook his head no and made a going-to-sleep pillow with his hands.

"Okay. I can keep him until you're stronger. Maybe he can come for a long visit tomorrow. He has really missed you. You know, I think he saved your life. His barking and whining were why we came in."

Nelson scratched Tom on his neck and mouthed *thank you* to me.

"I know you can't talk right now, and you need to rest, but can I ask you this? Just nod yes or no. Was your dinner party catered by the country club?"

He affirmed it had been.

"Was Beverly the person that cooked the food?"

His shrug came with a mouthed *I guess.*

"But she was the one that delivered and plated it, right?"

He nodded yes and stood up with a wobble.

I helped him into the house and promised to check on him in a few hours. "I'll bring you some soup. It will help your throat." I guessed it was sore from the intubation tube being removed. I watched him go down the hall to his bedroom before closing the front door.

I made a large pot of garbanzo soup from canned chickpeas, bell pepper, onion, and Caribbean pumpkin for lunch. I debated putting in the extra garlic that I loved because part of the pot was going to Nelson, but garlic was excellent at fighting germs, so I threw in all six cloves. Robert wasn't home by lunch, so Manny and I ate the stew without him. It was thick, hearty, and delicious. I realized it might be hard for Nelson to swallow. Using a wand blender from a new sponsor Delvis had given me to try, I pureed the remaining stew and portioned it into three glass containers. The bowls with lids were the perfect meal size and microwavable.

"Sorry I'm late," Roberto said as he entered the house.

"You'll have to figure out lunch for yourself. I'm taking what's left of the stew to Nelson."

"He's back? That's good. Don't worry about me. I had a burger at the club." Robert kissed me. "They've got the parking lot roped off with cones, and I think your pig roaster guy is already there. I smelled charcoal."

"That's good to hear. How was golf? Did you make a hole in one?"

"I wish. No. But I did get to meet the club's silent partner. It was a bit like meeting Thanos."

"Who?" I stretched my legs out on the dining room table's bench.

"The bad guy that has all the gemstones in the Marvel movie. Never mind. My point is he was big and intimidating, but then after I got to know him, I liked him. He's throwing a lot, and I mean *a lot*, of money at this project. I told him my idea for greening the course with a mangrove, and he was all for it. He's a serious golf fan and wants to make Coral Shores the star in the PGA tour. And since he has a vote on the board, he should be able to counter Samford's objections and push the plan to approval."

"Why is Samford objecting? I thought he'd be all for the project."

"I don't know, but I get the feeling that the two have had dealings with each other that didn't go smoothly, and now Kostas is the big dog, and Samford hates that, especially on his home turf, if you know what I mean."

"Kostas? Is he Greek?" I asked. *Why does that name ring a bell? I swear, pregnancy brain fog is hell.*

"I think he said his mother was from Bulgaria. She was a gymnast. But he's Russian. I'll introduce you at the gala. He said he'd be there. He's got the accent and everything. And the vodka too. The bartender keeps a special brand in the freezer just for him. I'm going to grab a shower. You need me to do anything for you?"

"Can you wait and keep an eye on Manny while I run this over to Nelson?"

"No problem, babe."

I used the spare key Nelson had pressed into my hand a few hours earlier. Tom ran straight to his owner, who was in the back sunroom with a blanket over his lap.

"I've brought you a puree. There's enough for two more meals. And I can make chicken soup for you on Sunday. Or something else if you don't want that."

Nelson mouthed a thank-you. I put the extras in the fridge and served the still-warm stew with a spoon from his kitchen. The TV tray that held his water glass was the kind that was cantilever. I put the bowl on it and moved it closer to him. Tom was at his feet with a paw on his owner's slippers.

"I promise to come by tomorrow and clean the kitchen. I'm so sorry this happened to you. Thank goodness you will recover and no one else in your party was poisoned." I remembered the ackee pit I'd seen that night. "Is one of your friends vegetarian?"

Nelson nodded and held up two fingers.

"But it looked like a seafood menu had been planned."

"Pescatarian," Nelson said in a gravelly and low whisper, "and one vegan."

Maybe Beverly substituted the ackee for fish in the ceviche for the vegan and just didn't know better. Perhaps it was just an unlucky accident. Vegan is a whole other skill set. I mean, she hasn't been arrested.

"I'll leave Tom with you for a bit and have my husband come get him in an hour or so. Okay," I said.

"Thank you. Delicious." The warm puree seemed to have soothed his throat some.

I locked his front door and went back to my house. My worries about the gala guests eating poisoned flan were quieted. Beverly had no motive, and she hadn't been arrested. Pullman loved to arrest people. Gillian was probably responsible for Lois. And Nelson was an accident. But what about Chef Sebi?

I bet he slipped. Vinaigrette on marble terrazzo steps would be very slippery.

Stop worrying, Miriam. It's all going to be okay.

Chapter
Thirty-Three

At four, Jorge arrived with his wheeled case and a zipped garment bag.

"I have an outfit, just so you know," I said.

"Mi'ja, not everything is for you. That's my traje. I'm going to meet Prince *Char*-ming, and he's going to fall in love with me," Jorge said.

"Who is this prince?"

"Enrique. Y si el no, I'll take a telenovela hottie." Jorge opened his mobile makeup studio and began pulling out his tools. "Go wash your face. Does your dress zip, or is it over de head?"

"It zips up the back," I replied. "Y tú sabes que Enrique is married with kids."

"Cállate." Jorge shushed me. "A girl can dream."

Jorge put my hair into a high ponytail with a wide black crystal holder that made me want to wear harem pants and grant wishes. He gave me winged eyes using a liquid liner. Then with a long thin brush, he accented the wing with a thin line of emerald-green to match the color of the palm fronds on my dress.

"Bella," Roberto said.

"He speaks Spanish?" Jorge asked me.

"I try." Robert moved to kiss me.

"No!" Jorge put a hand between my husband and me. "No kissing until after the party. Do not ruin my makeup."

Robert winked at me, and later we stole a peck in the hallway. I left the men with instructions to check on Nelson and retrieve Tom before they left. Robert knew to drop Manny off at Pepper's, where Gabriela was babysitting a few kids for a fee. I'd been getting update texts from my squad all afternoon. Marie was on-site, and all the food trucks had set up. Alma and Ana had staged the silent auction area at three and then gone home to get ready. They planned to arrive at the club at six thirty. Jorge was Alma's date. He left my house and headed to hers to do her makeup and dress there. Sally planned to be there at six to set up the guest check-in. I put my heels in a bag and left for the club at five.

"How's the fryer working?" I asked through the open door of Fritay All Day.

"Q! You look amazing," Marie said.

"Thanks."

"The fryer is on, and I have the main kitchen's on too. Just in case. I've par-fried everything in the kitchen, and then I'll finish them off in the truck so that each serving is hot."

"Smart. Can you take a break and introduce me to the other trucks? I'd like to thank them all personally."

Marie took me to Quban's Caja China first. The man tending the coals had a big belly and a friendly face. I knew a whole pig was in the wooden box even if I couldn't see it, because I smelled the garlic and fat. The cooking method was very popular in Miami. The name came from the Chinese import crates that had been repurposed in Cuba as cooking vessels. Hot coals were placed on the metal tray that sealed the wet-rubbed pig into the box. The passive heat slow-roasted the pig over many hours. Cubans in Miami had made a cottage industry of selling the wheelbarrow-type cooking boxes.

The sun was setting over the golf course, and it made for a fiery backdrop. With all the food smells, the parking lot felt like the Dade County Youth Fair minus the funnel cakes. The twinkle lights twined into the potted palms that encircled the high-top cocktail tables switched on. It instantly made the carnival feel morph into a magical wonderland feel. Valerie had insisted that we needed little pockets where people could gather and converse. She'd been right. I noted all her decorative choices as Marie introduced me to the rest of the food truck owners.

The band arrived a few minutes after Pepper. She showed them to the Flamingo Room, where they could warm up. She and I agreed it would be nice to have the band welcoming the guests as they pulled up to the valet.

"It will put everyone in the party mood," Pepper said. She was dressed in a flowy red silk jumper with a plunging neckline.

"How are you"—I motioned—"not falling out?" I asked.

"Tape."

"Ouch."

I left Pepper and headed to the silent auction area. Each item had a clipboard illuminated by a hurricane lamp. Looking at the starting bids, I did the math. Karib Kids was going to get a nice check.

"Mrs. Smith," a voice called.

I looked for a place to hide. I didn't want to be grilled by my MIL. Nor did I want to hear her comments about my hair.

"Mrs. Smith," the same voice called. "Miriam Smith, they need you at the reception desk."

"Oh." I stepped into the passageway. "No one ever calls me Mrs. Smith. I thought you meant my mother-in-law. Please call me Ms. Quiñones or just Miriam."

The staff person—a server, I guessed, judging by the guayabera-style polyester shirt—didn't care. He just wanted me to follow him. Which I did, and then I saw the issue. Sally was alone at the guest check-in, and there was a mob of UnMundo people on the other side, all speaking Spanish at high volumes. I stepped in and put order to the chaos. Ileana wanted to stage some photographs with her celebs, Wichie and Tatiana, Dom and Estrella, and two twentysomething telenovela heartthrobs with their dates. They also had to record a video for the Sunday morning talk show. I directed Delvis to the cordoned-off VIP area we had for them and left her to organize the crew. Then I came back for Ileana and her eight guests. Enrique Iglesias wasn't there yet, but he'd promised to make a brief appearance later in the evening.

We had to enlarge the UnMundo VIP area to accommodate Ileana's party. The two telenovela hotties helped move a table. *Wow. They're handsome and sweet. Jorge is going to have two princes to chase.* The princes each had a female plus-one that I didn't recognize. One of them might have been a Miss Puerto Rico, but neither of the females seemed interested in her date. The young women were following the digital SLR camera lens that was documenting their red-carpet moment. I got one of the steel pan players and one of the dancers for more photos with the beautiful entourage.

By the time I'd had a few photos taken, per my boss's insistence, it was a quarter to seven. I switched my flats for my heels. My rice socks trick had helped some. I stowed my purse and bag under the reception desk.

"I'll take your stuff upstairs with mine and put it in Valerie's office," Sally said.

"Thanks. Mind if I look at the guest list?" I took the sheets from her. I recognized the founding family surnames and several parents from the Agape school. The UnMundo folks had checks by their name. Running my finger down the list, I stopped at Kosta's name. *Why is that name bugging me? Mermaid, stop hogging all the brain juice.*

"Susan and Fred Clark," said a woman in a sequined top and black skirt.

Our first guest had arrived five minutes early. *Americans.* I texted Pepper to send the band to the valet area. Before long, the *plink, plink, plonk* of steel drums filled the place. Alma and Jorge arrived. Alma's dress was a bold and busy print that looked like thousand-dollar resort wear. Jorge wore a trim-cut suit with an open shirt that showed the top of his sculpted abs. It could have gone papi chulo, but it didn't.

"Guapísimo," I complimented him.

"Armani. I took it from an ex as alimony." Jorge grinned.

"Where's Miriam? Why is there a line? This is a disaster." It was my MIL's voice. I could hear her calling me but couldn't see her in the arrival line. Robert had promised me he would stay close to his parents and keep Marjory away from me. I saw Robert's head above the din and knew I needed to make an exit before I was caught.

"Come on, let's go check the auction," I said, leading Alma and Jorge away.

While Alma waited for Ana to arrive and staff the auction, I introduced Jorge to the UnMundo princes. My gaydar wasn't perfect, but I got the feeling one of them might be interested when there was an added twinkle to his hazel eyes. My hunch was confirmed later when I saw them by the Pepper Pot feeding curried jackfruit patties to each other.

When the band and dancers paraded from reception to the main area, I knew that meant most guests had arrived. I made a circuit and taste-tested all the food. The chicken pinchos from Isla del Encanto hit the spot, and my sirena did a flip. The dress Alma had gotten for me hid my pregnancy well. With a spiced coconut mocktail in my hand, I stayed two steps in front of my MIL. Everyone was having a good time. There were even some people dancing—badly and off the beat. But they were clearly uninhibited and having fun. I suspected the heavy pour of rum I'd witnessed at the drinks station might have something to do with it.

Squawk.

I turned around to see a pair of macaws on the shoulders of a man and a woman wearing Jungle Island uniforms. Pepper hurried by me and went to welcome them.

Squawk.

Once she'd greeted them and sent them into the party, I approached her. "I thought we agreed no animals."

"Just a few parrots," Pepper said. "And *maybe* a monkey."

"A monkey!"

"But not at the same time. The monkey is in the van. His name is Chico, and he is very friendly. And other than *that one time*, he doesn't bite."

I rolled my eyes. "Pepper, if this goes wrong, I will throw you under the bus." Visions of my MIL being bitten by a capuchin flashed in my head. *To be honest, if it happens, I want to be there to see it.*

"Don't worry. Nothing's going to go wrong," Pepper said.

Gasps.

I turned toward the sounds and hoped it wasn't a parrot breaking a septuagenarian finger.

Applause.

Wichi and Tatiana were doing twirls and dips. The professional ballroom dancers were grace and power. Delvis and her crew filmed it all.

A trumpet pealed the chorus of "Guantanamera." All heads turned toward the call. It was time to witness the lechon being lifted from the crate. The big-bellied man I'd met earlier and a guy who looked like he could be his son placed the pan with the steaming pig onto a table. The aroma took me back to Nochebuena feasts from my Hialeah childhood. I got closer to the action and hoped I could snag the coveted crispy ear. The man had two cleavers in his hand, about to crack the toasted skin. Before I could protest, Delvis grabbed me, put me beside the butcher, and yelled action. The man chopped off the ear and handed it to me. I turned toward the camera and took the bite. *So good.* Mami would probably call tomorrow when she saw it on *Domingos con Daisita.*

The butcher's assistant led me away from the show with the offer of a wet wipe. While the pig was plated, the calypso band took a break. I decided to take a break too. My toes hurt. I went inside to find a chair. A few guests were milling by the auction tables in the main bar. I waved at Ana, who looked striking in a pink gown that was gathered at the shoulders with brocaded roses. At the far side of the curved wood and brass bar, I saw Omarosa.

"Hola. I didn't know you were coming." We kissed, and I took the stool next to hers.

"I didn't know until a few hours ago." Omarosa laughed. "Gracias a Dios, I still had the dress I bought for my sobrina's quince cruise."

The sunset-orange cocktail dress had a high-necked front with an open back. Her coily hair was off her face and held with golden combs. She looked stunning.

"Where's Gordon?"

"I don't know. I think he's kind of working. We were supposed to be at a movie, but then he calls to say his boss wanted him to go to his cocktail party."

"What do you mean, working?"

"You know, like keeping an eye on someone. Or algo así." Omarosa took a sip of her umbrellaed drink. "He feels so bad about it, but like it's not his fault. We had some food from the Flying Fish before he had to leave me." She smiled.

"Chica, come with me. I'm going to introduce you to some people from my work." I took her to the UnMundo VIP area and told them to take good care of her. "She's my prima." When Yoli married Bette, Omarosa would be family by marriage, so it wasn't a lie. And if she and Gordon got married, we'd be in-laws on both sides.

What is Gordon doing here? Who is Pullman having him watch?

I scanned the crowd but didn't see Gordon or Pullman, so I returned to the bar, hoping to rest my feet finally.

"Ana? What's wrong?" I asked. She looked shaken.

"Um, I just saw someone I never want to see." Ana steadied herself with the wall.

"Who? Are you okay?"

"Bratva," she whispered. "Can you watch the auction for me?"

Ana walked toward the lady's room with a hand over her mouth.

Who has made her so scared? Did she say Bratva?

294

I looked at the last name on each of the silent auction clip-boards. Kosta Borisova had bid eleven thousand dollars on golf clubs autographed by Tiger Woods. He was the country club partner Robert wanted me to meet. And he was the guy that Alma had said owned half the properties in Aventura and Sunny Isles. He was Bratva, Russian Mafia. He was who Ana had seen.

"Omarosa."

I recognized the voice calling for her.

"Hey, did you see where the beautiful girl that was sitting there went?" Gordon asked the bartender.

The bartender shook his head, and Gordon exited as quickly as he'd entered. I followed him and saw him go up the staff stairs. No way I could make it up the stairs quickly with my swollen feet. I grabbed the elevator and hoped I'd catch him on the second floor.

Bing.

The elevator doors opened, and I saw Gordon on the terrace. He was using a pair of binoculars to look at the party below.

"Gordon." I opened the glass door to the empty rooftop dining area.

He folded the small binoculars and put them in the inner pocket of his jacket. "Oh, hey, Miriam. I was just looking for my date."

Gordon put his hand on my sleeve, kissed me on the temple, and slipped out the door before I could ask him a question. I followed him and watched him scramble down the grand staircase like a mountain goat.

"I give up." I wanted to sit down and take off my heels. "No, I want to change my shoes, and I'm going to." I went to Valerie's office and found my things right where Sally had said they'd be. Sitting in the armchair, I exchanged my heels for flats. My phone slipped from my lap. When I bent to get it from the floor, I noticed a candy wrapper. Feeling responsible for the trash, since it was probably Manny's from the other day, I reached for it under the chair. The crinkly wrapper was definitely from the same candy Valerie had given my son. I studied the milkmaid graphic and Cyrillic writing. It was a Russian candy.

My phone lit up with a message.

Did you try the caviar yet? The vendor is here and wants to seal the deal.

A second later, I got another text.

Oops, wrong person.

Chapter
Thirty-Four

"Are you near the kitchen?" Marie asked.

"No, but I can be. Why?" I asked with the phone on speaker.

"I'm out of bannann peze. Your guests keep coming back for thirds. I need you to get a bag of sweet potato fries from Pierre. Or something. Anything. I'll make it work."

"Okay. I'll be there in two minutes." I hit end.

I went downstairs to the kitchen but found it empty. Pierre was not there, and I didn't immediately see a bag of fries. But I did notice that all the mini desserts were on trays, ready for service. Maybe Pierre was a smoker like so many kitchen workers and was taking a cigarette break. I called Marie.

"Where are the fries?"

"In the walk-in."

"Duh. Sorry, I should have thought of that." I ended the call and set the phone on the side counter to open the walk-in's door. There were potatoes in a black bin on one of the metal shelves but no bag of cut spuds. I kept looking. There were vacuum-sealed racks of ribs, heads of broccoli, and several bags of dinosaur-shaped chicken nuggets. *The kids' menu. Gracias a La Caridad Manny doesn't know about them.* In a last-ditch effort to find a presliced item Marie could use, I looked in the white bucket on the floor. *Bingo.* Halved and quartered cassava tubers were floating in the milky water. I guessed someone on the staff must be Latinx or Caribbean and had this stash for kitchen crew meals. *That must be why it says don't use.*

I turned to exit and find a slotted ladle.

"Beverly, please try the caviar. The owner is here and wants to meet the executive chef," Valerie said.

I pulled the walk-in's door almost closed and left a small crack so I could eavesdrop. *Miriam, como te gusta el chisme.* I ignored my inner voice's chiding. Yes, I was not above "accidentally" overhearing something.

"I told you I don't like fish eggs," the chef replied. "And neither do our members. They are vanilla pudding people."

"Well, we have a lot of *new* members asking for it. Chef Sebi had caviar on his menu."

Beverly *pfff*ed at the mention of her predecessor. "I guess I could use it as garnish for the deviled eggs. Fine. I'll try it."

I heard one of them walk away and return to set something on the metal prep table. It sounded like a box of crackers was being opened and then a jar lid teeter-tottered to a stop.

"I hate that fishy smell," Beverly said.

I could see a sliver of the scene from my position. Beverly held a toast point to her mouth and ate it.

"I guess it's fine."

"Do the eggs pop like champagne bubbles?" Valerie asked. "Try some more."

Beverly dipped another toast point into the jar. She opened her mouth wide for the miniature mountain of glossy black eggs.

"It has a nice tooth. They pop—" The chef gasped for air. She tried to speak but was having trouble breathing.

Valerie didn't rush to help and, in a mocking tone, asked, "Are you all right?"

Several minutes passed with me paralyzed in fear. The santero's words echoed in my head. *Debes tener cuidado.* Valerie stood there and watched Beverly struggle. It was at that moment that my phone rang. The one that was not on my body but on the side counter. Valerie turned toward the sound. I pushed the door open. *I need to get out of the kitchen.* I had to call for help. Chef Beverly was fighting for air. She was clutching the edge of the large prep table.

"Don't you dare!" Valerie's voice was not the jolly wedding planner one. It was threatening, and so was the knife in her hand. "Don't move."

I stood at the mouth of the cooler. Warm air hit the front half of me, but that wasn't why I was sweating. Valerie looked maniacal. She kept the long knife pointed at me while she took a food prep glove from a dispenser box. Using it like a tissue, she picked up my phone and dropped it into the warm oil of the double fryer.

"Oops." She tucked the glove into her bra. "Now get in there."

"What?"

"You heard me. Get in there." She put the tip of the steel blade to my shoulder.

Gasp.

Gasp.

Bang.

Beverly's body had hit the table. Her eyes were rolling white.

"Oh no. Is that caviar bad? I wonder how that happened. Hazards of the trade. I bet Sebi would have known better. Oh, but somebody took his toque and pushed him over a balcony!" Valerie's voice spiked to an opera singer's octave.

Gasp.

Bang.

Beverly's head hit the table when her body spasmed. Her legs moved like she was playing *Dance Dance Revolution* on hyperspeed. Then it all stopped, and her body slid to the floor.

"Get in there now."

Valerie poked the knife at my chest. My heart was racing, and my sirena was feeling the adrenaline. I got in the cooler. I watched Valerie damage the safety release before closing the insulated door.

The cold that I hadn't noticed before was now like an arctic winter. The interior thermometer read thirty-eight degrees.

Six degrees above freezing. I'm going to die in here if someone doesn't find me.

I counted to sixty, hoping that was enough time for Valerie to leave. Then I picked up the smoked salmon, which had been vacuum sealed on an oak plank. I clobbered the door with it. The staff would be coming to collect the dessert trays soon. Someone would hear me, I prayed.

My arms grew weak, and I sat on the five-gallon bucket with the DO NOT USE lettering on the lid.

Marie. Marie will come looking for yuca fries.

"Yuca, cassava, malanga, batata," I sang. I was losing it. I was making up crazy songs. My breath no longer made vapor clouds. My fingers were purple, and I wanted to sleep.

"Come on, Miriam. Stay awake." I kicked the door, but my foot barely made a sound. "Come on, Miriam. Keep making noise."

I got up and beat the door a few more times with the plank.

"Help. Help. Valerie poisoned the chef!" I yelled. It was futile. The beating on the door was my best bet, but I could barely lift the smoked fish anymore.

I tried to warm myself up by hopping from one foot to the other.

"Why?"

Hop.

"Why?"

Hop.

"Why did Valerie poison Beverly?"

I kept up my one-person conversation and tried to piece it all together, but my thinking was getting fuzzy.

"Valerie killed Beverly because Beverly killed Sebi. But why?"

I tried to swing the oak plank at the door again. It was hard to lift it.

"Because a nosy woman saw a baby helicopter being a peeping tom."

"Tom, Tom, Tom, Tim."

I sat on the floor and put the bigger, heavier end on the ground to tap the handle part against the door.

"No, that's not right."

"Baby, baby, baby. My baby."

I kept tapping the wood against the door.

"Morse code. SOS. What is it? Like on the cartoons. Short, short, long. Long, long, short. I don't remember."

I beat the door in a rhythm.

"That sounds like clave. I'm Johnny Pacheco. No, no, no, I'm Rubén Blades. *La vida te da sorpresa.*"

Ticky. Ticky. Ticky.

"I'm cold. I should dance."

Stand up, Miriam.

"I can't feel my feet. At least my feet aren't swollen anymore. That's not good. No, not good. Muy malo. Muy, muy, muy malo."

301

I don't know how long I was in the cooler before they found me. I was on a stretcher with a silver blanket over me when I came to. I could hear people talking, but none of the voices were clear. It was all noise, no words. Then Robert's face was directly over my face.

"Roberto. Mi Roberto. Where's Manny?"

"Shh, babe. Everything is going to be okay," Robert said.

"But what about the party? I need to stay, and Marie needs her boniatos," I said.

"Babe, don't worry about the party. We need to get you to the hospital."

The ride in the ambulance was a blur. I vaguely remembered the trip as bouncy and annoying. The following morning, Robert told me I'd kept falling asleep on the way to the hospital and that the EMT had to keep waking me up. I hadn't liked it, and I'd cussed him out in Spanish. I'd repeatedly called the EMT rude/maleducado, then I'd asked him for café y flan.

"Roberto, what's that machine monitoring?" I asked.

We were in a hospital room, and I had an elastic belt around my middle.

"Um, the doctors are monitoring the baby," Robert said.

I pushed myself up in bed, and a different machine began beeping.

"Calm down, babe. It's all okay. They just want to be extra sure everything is okay."

A nurse came in and stopped the machine's alert. She punched a few buttons, read and recorded some numbers, then asked me how I was feeling.

"I'm not worried about me. I'm worried about the baby. How is my baby?"

"The doctor will be in to see you soon. Would you like another heated blanket for your feet?" The nurse smiled as she checked several of the round foam stickers and electrodes on my chest.

I looked at my husband. He gave me a neutral smile and patted my hand. My heart rate spiked and made the machine alarm again.

"Ms. Quiñones, you are going to be fine. Breakfast will be here soon. Try and eat something. The doctor will be here soon," the nurse said as she left us.

"Roberto, what are you not telling me!"

"Babe, it's probably nothing. They just want to be extra careful."

"What does that mean?" I took a deep breath to lower my heart rate. I didn't want the machine to squawk anymore.

"The doctors are just being cautious. You were pretty bad last night. Moderate to severe hypothermia. Your temperature fell to eighty degrees. If Marie had been five minutes later—but she wasn't, and so let's not go there."

"Tell me what happened. Tell me everything you know. I remember Marie was out of plantain fries, and so I went to the kitchen to get a substitute," I said.

"Yeah, and then when you didn't show up at her food truck, she went looking for you. She opened the cooler, and you fell out. You had been leaning against the door holding a cutting board."

"Not a cutting board. An oak plank for smoking fish."

"Good, so you remember that part," Robert said.

"Do you remember anything else?" Pullman asked as he walked farther into the room. "I'm glad to see you awake and talking in full sentences. You had me worried, Veronica."

"What happened?" I asked him.

"That's what I want to know from you. What can you tell me about Chef Beverly?" Pullman was at the foot of my bed.

Hearing her name brought a flood of memories back. "Valerie made her try the caviar. Like she was very insistent about it. There was something in it. Because a few moments after she tried it, she began gasping for air."

"Did Valerie make you try any of it?" Pullman asked.

"No. She didn't even know I was there until my phone rang. She threw my phone into the fryer. Do you think it survived?"

"I doubt it. But I'm glad you did. Beverly wasn't so lucky. She's dead. Strychnine."

"Rat poisoning?" Robert asked.

Frank Pullman nodded. "I need to clarify how you came to be trapped in the cooler."

"Valerie threatened me with a knife," I said. "She made me get in the cooler. I mean, I was in there to begin with, listening and watching, but then my phone rang. I thought I could run out and get help, but she was closer to me than I thought. I could feel the knife tip through the fabric of my dress." I rubbed my chest, remembering it. "And then she broke the safety release. You've caught her. Right? Tell me you've got her in custody."

"Detective?" Robert asked when Pullman remained quiet.

"We'll find her. Don't worry," Frank said. "You concentrate on making sure your wife gets better. Okay?"

"Yes." Robert kissed my hand.

"Coral Shores needs their Jessica Fletcher back." Pullman chuckled as he exited.

Chapter
Thirty-Five

O nce they were satisfied that the fetus was undamaged, I'd
been released from the hospital. There was still a slight
chance that our sirena might have some developmental issues
due to the hypothermia. But the human body was an amazing
machine. The doctors explained that when my temperature had
started dropping, my body had diverted the blood flow to the
fetus to keep it safe.

After a week, I'd been able to resume shooting *Abuela
Approved*. My pregnancy was no longer a secret. Ileana and
Delvis knew. They'd visited me in the hospital. Everyone loved
my idea of doubling up on recording episodes. UnMundo didn't
want to lose me—or my young followers.

"Mi'ja, siéntate," Tía Elba said.

It was Thanksgiving Thursday, and my house was full. Tía and
Yoli were handling the cooking. I was not allowed to lift a finger
or stir a pot. Both the outdoor and indoor kitchens were in use.

"Siéntate, por favor," she repeated.

"Okay, Tía. I'm sitting. See," I said. Camo jumped in my lap
and used my pregnant belly as a pillow for her head.

We weren't seeing Marjory for Thanksgiving. Robert had
promised to go over there for pie later, but I'd put my foot down

that Manny and I were not going. The gala had been a success. It had earned over one hundred thousand dollars for Karib Kids. But all my mother-in-law had been able to talk about was the Latinos who had hijacked her event. Marc Anthony and Enrique Iglesias had made an appearance. I'd missed it and was still mad about it. I joked with Roberto that my being strapped to a gurney had not been a good enough excuse. He *could've* wheeled me over there. They'd sung an impromptu duo with the calypso band. The gala patrons had applauded wildly. Talent was talent. And even though most of Coral Shores' elite didn't speak Spanish, they'd recognized star power when they'd seen it. Delvis had sent me the video, and I'd watched it from my hospital bed. Marjory was in one of the crowd shots. She was the only one not swaying to the song. Her face looked like she'd smelled sewage.

Ding-dong.

"Tía, can I at least answer the door?" I asked.

"No. Bette, abre la puerta."

Bette stopped slicing plátanos and went to open the door. It was her sister Omarosa and Gordon. Everyone had arrived.

While Yoli and Bette fried the maduros outside, Tía had Alma help her bring the food to the table. There was a turkey stuffed with picadillo, congrí, sweet plantains, and a watercress salad. We were dining alfresco. The teak table was decorated with the gourds we'd bought at the Fall Festival. At each place setting was a construction paper turkey courtesy of Manny.

I looked around the table. I loved all the people here—my husband and our son, Tía and Tío, Yoli and Bette, Gordon and Omarosa, and my best friend, Alma. They all made my life better. I did not miss Marjory or her dry turkey and boxed stuffing.

"Más pavo, por favor," Gordon said.

"Your accent is very good," I said as I served him a slice of turkey.

"I've been getting a lot of practice lately." Gordon winked at Omarosa, who blushed. "Miriam, thank you for inviting me today."

"Of course. I'm glad Pullman gave you the day off. He's been working you pretty hard. Any news you can share?" I asked.

"Yeah. Like have you caught the woman that hurt my best friend?" Alma asked.

I put a finger to my mouth and gave my bestie a stern look. "Later." I motioned with my head to Manny.

"It can wait until after dessert," I said.

"Did I hear someone say dessert?" Nelson asked from his side of the fence.

Bark.

"Tom! ¿Mami, puedo jugar con Tom?" Manny asked.

"Nelson, we have plenty. Please join us." I went down the side of the house, past the place where Lois had scrawled *Help Murder.* As Tom bounded through the gate, I thought about all the recent deaths and near deaths. Lois, Sebi, Fuentes, and Beverly were dead. And Nelson and I could have been.

Manny asked to be excused from the table to play with Tom. Robert cleared our son's plates and set the place fresh for Nelson.

"I didn't mean to crash your family gathering," Nelson said.

"*Stop.* I'm sorry for not asking if you had a place to go today," I said, then introduced him to the people he didn't know.

"Okay, little ears are gone." Alma glared at me. "So tell me, Gordon. Have you found Valerie?"

"Yes and no. She's in Moscow."

"Moscow!" I said too loudly. "How and why?"

"That's all I can tell you," Gordon said.

"Maybe I can fill in some details. Valerie was in love with Sebi Malkov. They had an on-and-off thing. She took it way more seriously than him," Nelson said.

"So let me get this straight." I waved a clean utensil in the air. "Beverly *for sure* killed Sebi. Right?"

Gordon and Nelson nodded.

"And so Valerie murdered Beverly in retaliation?" I asked.

Tía gasped. "Ay, ay, ay. That could have been you, mi'ja. The santero was right." Tía Elba started clearing dishes. "José, ayúdame con el café. Yo no quiero escuchar más."

Respecting her wish not to hear anymore, I waited to ask my next question until she and Tío had gone into the house to prepare the coffee.

"Okay, so Beverly pushed Sebi because he got the executive chef position that had been promised to her," I said.

"Yeah, we think Beverly grabbed his chef's hat and either pushed him or he slipped. Either way, her action caused him to fall over the railing." Gordon took a sip of lager.

"Oh wow. So that's what we heard." I turned to Alma. "The voice we heard before the thud. *Give me that.* That was Beverly taking the chef's hat that should have been hers."

"We found it in her office. It has his DNA on it," Gordon said.

"So Valerie killed Beverly with the caviar as payback for Sebi's death. That's awful, but it kinda makes sense. What doesn't make sense is what happened to you and Lois." I pointed to Nelson. "Did Beverly poison you two on purpose or by accident? Or was that actually Valerie all along?" I asked.

"In my case," Nelson started to say, then finished chewing. "In my case, I know it was on purpose. Beverly brought the food and made sure I tried it. I thought it was odd that she was dressed up to look like you." Nelson pointed at me.

"But why?" Robert joined in the conversation.

"Maybe Samford told her too." Nelson took a forkful of congri.

"Samford Pimpkin?" Robert and I said in unison.

"Do you mind if I take some notes?" Gordon took out his phone.

"This is so good. What exactly is it?" Nelson asked.

"Black beans and rice seasoned with bacon and drippings. I'm glad you are enjoying it, but please go back to Samford. How is he involved in all of this?" I asked.

Everyone at the table was leaning in and glued to Nelson's every word.

Nelson took a sip of water, looked from me to Gordon and back again, then it all came out. After Juliet's and Fuentes's arrests, Samford Pimpkin needed a new drug smuggling cover. He found it in a wealthy Russian expat with a food import business: Kostas Borisova.

"I knew Kostas from a resort that I helped turn around in Colombia. He's a smart businessman. And seventy-five percent of his business is legit—the real estate and the Russian foodstuff—and you just don't ask about that other twenty-five. Know what I mean? The man has serious connections. I warned Samford not to cross him, but he didn't listen to me," Nelson continued. "After Fuentes agreed to help the prosecution by giving evidence against Juliet, Samford asked Kostas if he knew any hitmen. Kostas said maybe, but he wanted to be a partner in the country club expansion. Kostas loves golf."

I looked at my husband. His face had lost all color.

"That's the guy I played golf with?" Robert asked.

"Sí, mi amor." I squeezed his hand.

"So this is what I think happened," Nelson said. "I think Kostas agreed to get rid of that doctor guy in exchange for a silent partnership in the club but knowing all along that he wasn't going to be silent. First, he asked for his nephew, Sebi Malkov, to be made head chef. Then Kostas said he'd never agreed to the Fuentes hit. That's how I got involved. I didn't want to be, but Samford blackmailed me." Nelson rubbed his nose and sniffled.

Does Nelson have a coke habit? Oh, I hope not. I hope it's in the past and he just doesn't want it to ruin his career.

"I won't go into details because we have an officer of the law at the table, but I'll just say I really wanted to get the club on the PGA circuit, and I let Samford twist my arm. He asked me to stage an embarrassing scene with Sebi. Kostas is a big T guy." Nelson laughed.

"What do you mean?" I asked.

"Testosterone. Have you seen those memes of Putin with his shirt off doing *manly* thing—hunting, fishing, horseback riding? Kostas sometimes teased his nephew for being soft. Samford knew it. That's why he had me stage the whipped-cream thing and leave the curtain open so his drone could take photos."

"The drone that attacked Lois?" I asked.

"Yep," Nelson said.

"So there are two drones?" Alma asked.

I would have kicked her under the table if she had been closer to me. Alma was going to get Ana in trouble if she wasn't careful. I knew the police had questioned Ana about her drone license. She'd sworn she hadn't been the one piloting the drone that attacked Lois. Her drone belonged to Kostas Borisova, and it was becoming very clear that she hadn't lied about him being dangerous.

"Why was Lois attacked?" I asked, hoping to steer the conversation back.

"Lois was in the wrong place at the wrong time. Samford hated his daughter-in-law for many reasons but especially because she was interfering in his plans to get Juliet exonerated. I think she knew about his plan to have Fuentes knocked off." Nelson took another forkful of rice.

"Gordon, maybe that was what the message on the wall was about."

"Maybe," Gordon replied with a shrug.

"I think Samford saw Lois on the screen, he got angry and dive-bombed her. The drone was his play toy. He knew how to fly it. And if Lois opened her mouth about what we were doing in my house, then his scheme to pressure Kostas with embarrassing photos of his nephew was ruined. It was ruined a few days later anyway. When his girlfriend lost her mind and pushed Sebi."

"But why was Lois in our yard?" I asked.

"I can answer that. Remember the scene at the Fall Festival? She was still ranting about Cuban cartels when she woke up in the hospital. Her thinking was scrambled by the low-dose cyanide Beverly was giving her. She was stalking you but was too dazed and confused to act on it. She spent the night in Manny's cottage," Gordon said.

"Wow. I think we need to get rid of that playhouse." I squeezed Roberto's hand. "Poor Lois. She was being slow poisoned by Beverly."

"You know, Miriam, you distracted us for a day when you put us off the scent with the British lady," Gordon said.

"Gillian Brown? My old librarian?" Robert asked.

"Sorry about that. I really thought it was her. She was leaving Lois's house at the right time," I said. I mouthed another sorry to Robert.

"Yeah, the timing was right, but it wasn't the Brit. We were pretty sure it was Beverly. I think you left Pullman a voice mail about suspecting Beverly too. Pullman was pushing for evidence. We just needed a few of the forensics tests to come back from the lab to confirm it. That's why I was at the gala that night." Gordon reached for Omarosa's hand. "We had Beverly under surveillance."

"If you were *supposed* to be watching Beverly, then how come you weren't in the kitchen when it all happened?" I asked.

"Because I was also keeping tabs on Kostas Borisova. Pullman was looking for evidence to link him to the Fuentes murder."

"Kostas murdered Fuentes?" Nelson asked. "That doesn't make any sense."

"You're right, but I can't say anything else about the Fuentes case," Gordon said.

There was a long silence. The wheels in my head were spinning, and apparently, so were Nelson's, because we reached the same conclusion at the same time.

"Samford did it."

Gordon didn't confirm our statement, but he didn't tell us we were wrong either.

"That makes sense," Robert said. "According to the courthouse gossip Drew and Sally have been hearing, the state had a lot of evidence against Pimpkin Global thanks to Fuentes. With Fuentes out of the picture, Samford might have a chance of buying his and his granddaughter's freedom."

I bit my tongue. I wanted to pound the table and say *Told you so* to my husband. Samford Pimpkin and Juliet Pimpkin were criminals. "Okay, so back to Lois. Why was she poisoned to begin with?"

"We think Beverly and Samford were trying to make it look like Lois had dementia. Samford wanted to get rid of his daughter-in-law meddling in his plan to free Juliet. We linked some potato soup from Lois Pimpkin's refrigerator to a bucket of cassava at the club. Beverly had been poisoning her slowly over many months," Gordon said.

"I saw that bucket," I said. "She grew the stuff in her backyard. And there was an ackee tree in her front yard. That's what you ate, Nelson. I was hoping it was all an innocent mistake, an accident. You know, uninformed about the proper preparation of the fruit and vegetable. But no, it was all very much on purpose. What makes a person do something like that?" I was flabbergasted. "Do you think Samford turned her into a bad person? Or was that what drew them together in the first place?"

"Dysfunctional love makes people do all kinds of horrible things. Just look at Valerie. She killed someone in the name of love." Gordon crossed his arms and leaned back in his chair.

"Did she put the strychnine in the caviar?" I asked. "Or did *someone else* mastermind it?" Kostas Borisova owned a Russian food import business, and I was pretty sure that was who Valerie had been talking to on the phone that day in her office.

"We won't know until she's apprehended. Moscow winters can be brutal. I think she'll show up in sunny South Florida again. And when she does, Pullman and I will be here to arrest her." Gordon had a determined look.

Yoli, Bette, and Omarosa had kept their mouths shut as the twisted story was laid out. Once the table was quiet and it didn't look like there was going to be an epilogue, Yoli had a comment.

"Prima, you need to call your boss at the network. This would make a great telenovela."

The whole table burst into laughter.

Recipes

Caldo Gallego, Miami-Cuban Style

This stew originated in Galicia. It was a simple farmer's meal that used lard but had little to no meat. Made mainly in the winter months, it was eaten for breakfast (bread soaked in the broth), lunch, and dinner. When Spain colonized Cuba, many of the ships' crew were Galician. They brought their recipes with them and adapted them to what was available on the island. Boniato and other root vegetables could be substituted for the unavailable cold-weather turnip. The newfound wealth of the Spanish settlers allowed the addition of cured meats like chorizo and smoked bacon.

Servings: 6

Ingredients:

5 strips bacon or 1 thick strip smoked pork belly, cubed
4 links cured Spanish chorizo
1 white onion, diced
1 green bell pepper, diced

3 cloves garlic, diced
2 medium-to-large yellow potatoes, peeled and cubed
2 cups chicken stock
3 cups water
2–3 bay leaves
1½ teaspoon parsley (dry is fine)
2 cans cannellini beans, rinsed
2–3 handfuls dark leafy greens (collards, spinach, callaloo,
     kale) in bite-size strips
Salt to taste

Instructions:

This is cooked in one pot. I recommend a Dutch oven, but a wide stockpot will work.

Fry the bacon or pork belly. Drizzle a little olive oil if needed so the bacon doesn't burn before it renders its fat. Once cooked thoroughly, remove and set aside for later. Leave the rendered fat in the pot.

Peel the skin from the chorizo and slice. Add the sausage and the diced onion to the pot. Sautee until onion is translucent, then add the green pepper and garlic.

Once the pepper is tender, add the cubed potatoes. Cover with chicken stock and water. Add bay leaves and parsley. Add beans.

Cover and simmer on low to medium until potatoes are fork-tender (20 to 40 minutes).

Add greens and bacon.

Taste and add salt if needed (it will probably have enough salt already due to the meats and stock).

Serve with a piece of crunchy-crusted bread.

Miriam's Ensalada de Pulpo

This is based on the octopus salads I loved to eat when I lived in Puerto Rico. Many online recipes call for green olives. I don't remember that being a common ingredient, but you are welcome to add it if you like. Sometimes I add avocado.

Servings: 2 for a meal or 4 for a ramekin-sized salad.

Ingredients:

2 4-ounce cans jumbo calamari (octopus)
2 tablespoons white wine vinegar
2 tablespoons olive oil
1 teaspoon oregano
¼ teaspoon sea salt
2 cloves garlic, pressed
1 tomato
½ bell pepper (orange or yellow)
¼ red onion
Wedge of lime

Instructions:

Open the tins and let them strain in a colander while making your vinaigrette.

Combine vinegar, oil, oregano, salt, and garlic in a small jar. Secure the lid and give it a good shake.

Dice tomato, pepper, and onion into similarly sized pieces.

Squeeze a wedge of lime over the octopus, but don't let it sit. The lime juice is just a little extra help to remove the safflower oil the octopus is packed in.

In a bowl, combine the meat and vegetables. Shake the vinaigrette before pouring. Toss the salad.

Serve with saltines.

Pastelitos de Guayaba y Queso / Guava and Cheese Pastries

This Cuban pastry is greatly influenced by French pastry techniques that came to the island in the late eighteenth century. Uprisings by enslaved Africans in Haiti caused an exodus of farmers and plantation owners. Many of them, along with their house servants, settled in the eastern part of Cuba, from which the pastelito heralds.

Servings: 6

Ingredients:

1 puff pastry sheet (in your frozen food aisle)
Guava paste
Cream cheese (soft or block)
1 egg, beaten
Sugar

Instructions:

Defrost your boxed puff pastry sheet in the refrigerator overnight.

Preheat oven to 365 degrees.

Roll pastry sheet to ⅛-inch thickness. You may need a little flour, but I've found the flour it is packaged and folded with is usually enough.

Cut into 6 equal-sized squares.

Place equal amounts of guava paste and cream cheese in the middle of each square. Use your finger to coat the edge of the square with egg. Fold into a triangle and gently seal the edges with your fingers. *Do not use a fork.* Transfer the triangle to a parchment-lined cookie sheet; a plain metal one works best.

Slice or poke a few air vents in the top. Wash with the egg and sprinkle granulated sugar on top.

Bake 20–25 minutes or until golden. *Do not let them go brown.*

Enjoy with a cup of coffee.

Marie's Fritay All Day's Pikliz

Pikliz is a fermented slaw that is a staple in most Haitian households. The name is most likely derived from the Dutch word pekel, meaning to brine or to pickle, and the French word piquer, meaning to prick, sting, or bite. And yes, this slaw has a bite. Marie, owner of the food truck Fritay All Day, makes two varieties, a hot one for Haitian palates and a milder one for American palates. This version is the mild one. You can raise the heat level by adding more Scotch bonnet peppers.

Servings: Plenty

Ingredients:

½ sweet onion
¾ of a small head of white cabbage (or ½ of a large head)
¾ large yellow bell pepper (red will do as well)
2 large carrots
2 Scotch bonnet peppers
1 cube Maggi seasoning (chicken or vegetable flavor)
1 teaspoon black peppercorns
1 teaspoon thyme
10–14 ounces white wine vinegar
½ teaspoon salt
2 limes

Instructions:

You will need a 6-cup/64-ounce widemouthed canning jar or something similar.

Finely slice your onion, cabbage, and bell pepper. Shred or grate the carrots. Deseed and finely slice one Scotch bonnet pepper. *If you are not used to working with hot peppers, consider wearing a glove to protect yourself from the oils.* Place all into a bowl or colander and use your fingers to combine equally.

Crumble the Maggi cube into the glass storage container. Add peppercorns, thyme, and some vinegar. Shake. Once the cube seasoning is dissolved, place a whole Scotch bonnet pepper in the bottom of the jar. Pack the jar with the slaw mixture. Sprinkle the salt on top, add the juice of the limes, and pour the remaining vinegar on top. The vinegar should be about a finger or two from covering the slaw. Tighten the lid and turn upside down a few times to incorporate the ingredients. Place in the refrigerator.

Let the slaw mature for four to five days. You can give it a gentle shake or turn daily.

Serve the relish with tostones, fried fish, breakfast eggs, or any other dish that calls for a spicy relish.

Raquel's Cala-flan-za

This is a hybrid of a traditional flan with a flan de calabaza. I don't love the texture of flan de calabaza/pumpkin flan, so I've modified my recipe to have a hint of the flavor while keeping true to the silky texture of a Cuban-style flan.

Servings: 8 slices

Ingredients:

1 stick cinnamon
1 12-ounce can evaporated milk
½ cup sugar
1 14-ounce can sweetened condensed milk
3 eggs (use the best and freshest eggs you can, preferably with a dark yolk)
¼ cup pumpkin puree (from a can, but homemade is fine as long it is smooth)
1 teaspoon vanilla

Instructions:

I use a stainless-steel 1-quart flan mold/flanera with a locking lid. It is available online from big-box stores if you do not have a Latino grocery store near you. You can use any flat-bottomed baking mold, but it should be deeper than the average pie pan, and it needs to fit into a bain-marie pan.

Place the cinnamon stick in the can of evaporated milk 8 to 24 hours before baking and store it in the refrigerator until time to prepare the flan.

Preheat oven to 350 degrees.

Pour the sugar into a small, clean, dry pot and heat over a medium temperature. Stir with a wooden spoon, making sure it does not burn. The sugar will liquify and turn a golden brown. Remove and immediately pour into your mold.

Remove and discard the cinnamon stick from the evaporated milk before combining the remaining ingredients in a blender for 30 seconds.

Place the mold in a pan, then pour the milk-and-egg mixture into the mold. Secure mold lid. Open your oven, place the pan on the grate, and pour water into the pan until it comes to the middle of the mold's sides.

Bake 50 minutes.

Raise temperature to 365 and bake an additional 20 minutes.

Remove from bain-marie and place in refrigerator for 2 hours or more.

To release the flan from the mold, briefly place the mold's bottom in hot water to warm the caramel. Use a sharp knife to free the flan from its sides, place the serving dish over the mold, and flip. Slice and serve with a dollop of whipped cream.

Acknowledgments

Thank you to:

All the readers that found the first book in the series, Mango, Mambo, and Murder.

All the bloggers, podcasters, reviewers, and booksellers who have championed this "new flavor of cozy" by recommending it.

Gustavo for never shaming me about my grammatically incorrect Spanish. Your nonjudgmental red pen corrections are little love letters.